CHRI

THE SPINS

"Wow! This book! Couldn't stop reading. I had so many ideas in my head about how it would play out. So many twists. Don't want to say more. Just read it."

Goodreads

"Genius! A very cleverly written book that I couldn't put down. A well-crafted modern gothic novel."

Amazon Canada

THE GODFORSAKEN DAUGHTER

"Best read of the year. Poignant, romantic, thriller, relationships, love and so many more. How could a book carry so much emotion, and yet flow so fluidly? A compelling read. If there is only one book you have time to read in a year, better make it this one."

Amazon UK

"*The Godforsaken Daughter* is an enthralling, well-drawn and incredibly evocative story of love, grief, redemption and faith. I couldn't read a passage or two without picturing the rolling Irish countryside, and the idea of life on a small pastoral farm was intoxicating."

Write Meg!

THE DISENCHANTED WIDOW

"I've been racking my brain to pounce on at least one minor flaw in ... Christina McKenna's riveting account of a new widow and her nine-year-old son fleeing the IRA in 1980s Belfast, and all in vain. So I have no recourse but to succumb to the pleasures of her prose."

Free Lance-Star

"There are at least two ways to read this story. One is an Irish prose version of an Italian opera buff—a tragicomic tale with emphasis on the bumbling comic. The other is a satire, along the lines of ... Henry Fielding's classic novel *Tom Jones*."

Washington Independent

THE MISREMEMBERED MAN

"Her portrait of rural life is amusing and affectionate, wittingly and winningly detailed."

Kirkus Reviews

"Known chiefly as a painter ... McKenna proves in this, her first novel, to be equally adept at creating word portraits."

Washington Times

Mrs Purboy
Takes a Chance

Also by
CHRISTINA McKENNA

My Mother Wore a Yellow Dress (memoir)
The Dark Sacrament (non-fiction)
Ireland's Haunted Women (non-fiction)

The Misremembered Man (fiction)
The Disenchanted Widow (fiction)
The Godforsaken Daughter (fiction)
The Spinster Wife (fiction)

Mrs Purboy Takes a Chance

Christina McKenna

PARSIFAL PRESS

Published by the Parsifal Press, UK, 2023

A CIP record for this title is available from The British Library

ISBN: 978-1-7395937-9-7

Cover design by David M. Kiely

Set in 11 on 16 Minion

For

Maryanne and Marcus

A house is never still in darkness to those who listen intently; there is a whispering in distant chambers, an unearthly hand presses the snib of the window, the latch rises. Ghosts were created when the first man awoke in the night.

The Little Minister, 1891
James M. Barrie, (1860-1937)

PROLOGUE

The world spins. The days pass, falling behind you like yesterday's news. You power along, but where you're going is anybody's guess. There isn't a map, only the crazy thoughts inside your head to guide you. And who gave you those? You don't know that either. But you follow them anyway because they're the only compass you've got.

So you're roaming all over the place, looking for something. Something to feed this hunger inside, because you know that, all too soon, darkness will fall upon you like a guillotine blade, and you'll be gone.

I was like you for the longest time. Steering the same path. Living out my unblemished days. Doing the right thing. Hoping things would change. But they never did. Nobody took much notice of me, no matter how good or how noble I tried to be. That caused me such vexation. Ah, the fires that burned inside me! The beasts that feasted on my poor, tired soul.

That yearning to make my mark upon the world never let up.

To be validated.

To be *known.*

To be worthy of the name I carried and the crosses I'd been forced to bear.

Life is not about suffering, you see.

Life's about conquering.

So, for a man such as I, there came a time when something had to give.

Circumstances forced a radical rethink.

Pushed me in an altogether more interesting direction, without all those piffling rules and edicts.

Now I do what *I* want. I act the part that situations demand.
Entice them in.
The fact that you don't really see me is a gift.
I'm the ghost that moves amongst you.
Invisible.
Free.
Your ignorance is *your* tragedy.
Your blindness my sweet *v-i-c-t-o-r-y.*

NORTHERN IRELAND
SUMMER, 1985

ONE

Mrs Ellen Purboy trekked towards town, her thoughts in turmoil, her nerves on edge. It was a beautiful morning: the day breaking warm, the landscape glancing bright in the early sunlight. But Ellen didn't notice. To the troubled widow the sky was grey, pressing down upon her with a damp presage, the trees waving anxious, hedgerows chattering fretfully to the beat of her clacking feet.

The walk into town was a good twenty minutes. She'd worn a pair of toe-pinching stilettos on purpose. "If you want to stop worrying, wear a pair of too-tight shoes," her dear father used to say. Or, in her present case, bronze courts with three-inch heels *and* pointy toes. They belonged in the cocktail lounge, not out here, braving the often-gritty roads. Torture of a kind that no man—least of all her long-dead father—could even imagine. But these days Mrs Purboy had an ocean of regrets to outswim, whole skeins of agonizing futures to unvision.

The casual onlooker, however, would never have guessed at her disquiet. She was good at showing the world only the bloom on the rose, keeping the thorny stem that hurt so much buried deep. Her mother had always made an effort and Ellen did likewise: wore colourful clothes, pink lipstick and matching blusher to lift the face. Kept her blonde hair nicely set and the needle on the bathroom scales hovering at just under nine stone: an acceptable weight for her five-foot-seven-inch frame.

She was heading towards the town of Castlebrook and the practice of her GP, Dr Flynn. The trusted doctor would surely have a solution. He and her solicitor, Fintan Kavanagh, were the only two men she could really depend on now. They were blessed with integrity and good common sense, and had been solid fixtures in her life for a long time.

Another night of lucid dreaming had pulled her awake in the early hours. Something needed to be done about them: those dreams. It was getting to the stage where she dreaded going to bed. But at the same time it was oddly gratifying to behold *him*—George, her husband—dearly departed just over four months. Mercifully released from the gnawing cancer that had cut him down at fifty-three. She was still not over the horror of having watched him fade: a strong man morphing in the end into skin and bone, a mere shadow of his former self.

But in these dreams he was his old self again, sitting buoyant in an armchair at the foot of the bed, delivering messages of an enigmatic nature in a poet's voice. She'd jotted down snatches of them on waking, because the soft burr of his words still echoed in her head—measured, quiet, calm—as if he were dictating them to a secretary or into a Dictaphone.

By rights she should have been joyful at such an unexpected development. She'd prayed long and hard for a sign that George was happy and free, beaming light and love from the celestial realm she imagined paradise to be. Now her prayers were being answered. But George was not in heaven; he was back in this drab old world again.

Last night had left little doubt.

She stopped abruptly at the thought, her heart thumping painfully.

"Oh, God, let it not be there! Let this be my imagination or a bad dream. Please let it just be that and nothing else!"

Carefully she drew her left hand from her pocket and pulled up her cuff.

Tears pricked her eyes at the sight of it: the red welt just above the wrist *was* there. And the mark had been put there by the clasp of an unseen hand. That unseen hand surely must belong to George, because he was sitting at the foot of the bed when she woke up.

But, alas, when she realized it was actually George she was seeing, he'd promptly disappeared.

Poor Ellen, so frail, precarious, fragmented and broken in this third act of her life, dabbed away her tears, quickened her step.

Did it mean he wasn't at rest? He'd been an unbeliever all his life; was he now being punished for that?

She tried to push away the memory, wipe it clean.

Honk! Honk! Honk!

Sudden in her ears: the notes of a car horn.

She stumbled.

My goodness me! What am I doing in the middle of the road?!

An open-topped white sports car was drawing up alongside her as she hastened towards the grass verge, her flimsy skirt flattening against her knees in the sudden turbulence.

"Are you all right?" the driver called out. A young man with aviator sunglasses and floppy fair hair was regarding her with interest.

"Er ... erm ... yes, thank you. I-I'm fine ... I think."

"You need to be careful you know. Had I been coming any faster I might have run into you."

Even in her state of shock she registered the singularity of the voice. Polished and mellifluous; the voice of someone well educated. From the moneyed classes certainly.

"Er ... I'm sorry ... I'm terribly sorry. It's ... it's just I-I thought I'd dropped something ... that's all."

She could tell by his puzzled expression that he didn't quite believe her. His foppish air was a little unsettling. She'd never seen his like before in these parts. Well dressed from what she could see: white shirt, linen jacket, gold-coloured tie expertly knotted. Sebastian Flyte from *Brideshead Revisited* came to mind.

Men didn't dress like that here. Men like that didn't visit Castlebrook. He had to be a passing tourist.

"If you're going to Castlebrook I can give you a lift," he said.

So he isn't just passing through. But she'd never get into a car with a stranger, no matter how well meaning he might appear—even though her feet were aching and a lift would be most welcome.

"Er ... erm, it's very kind of you. But I-I need the fresh air and it's not far now ... the town I mean."

"Right! Did you find it?"

"Sorry, what?"

"You said you dropped something?"

"Um ... no. I-I was mistaken."

"Not to worry," he said, his face splitting in a schoolboyish grin. "Mind how you go then."

"Yes ... thank you. Bye now."

He put the car in gear and it roared off.

She waited until it disappeared, exhilarated by her strange encounter—but, more importantly, baffled as to why she'd ended up in the middle of the road.

Perhaps I'm finally going mad. I'm coming fifty so it wouldn't be so surprising. The grief of losing George and the loneliness has done something to my head.

She thought about the note in her handbag. Maybe Dr Flynn would be able to make sense of it all. Her sister Nettie had been of little comfort, showing no sympathy whatsoever.

"You need to get yourself stronger sedatives, Ellen, and get out of the house more during the day. It's all that moping about, gazing at his things that does that. Not good for you. Mother was the same after Father passed on, and you wouldn't like to end up like *her*."

Ellen didn't want to think about how her poor mother had ended up: bedridden, clutching a cuddle-toy monkey, her mind splintering to the point where she believed her two daughters were spies sent by the Ministry of Defence to poison her by way of the water supply.

Oh, what tricks the mind could play! Stealing into old age and wreaking havoc until you finally became demented or longed for death. In a way George was lucky. He knew his time was finite and the morphine carried him through the worst of his torment. He was resigned but rational right to the end.

She pressed on painfully in her puny high heels, really regretting having put them on.

What was I thinking? Perhaps I should have accepted the lift from that young man. He looked very respectable. What must he have thought . . . me wandering into his path like that? I simply wasn't thinking straight. Oh, dear. . . .

A lorry thundered past, buffeting her into the hedge. The jolt of it made her drop her handbag; some of the contents spilled out.

Dismayed, she bent down and gathered up her purse and diary. Checked in the side-pocket for the note: the note that contained George's ethereal words—the words she'd written down for Dr Flynn to read—but it was nowhere to be seen.

Something fluttered upwards and she saw the unfolded notelet drifting like a giant butterfly to the top of the hedge. She made to catch it, but it was swiftly borne away—as if a ghostly hand had snatched it from her.

The widow stood by the roadside, dejected and saddened at the loss of the note. But the words . . . those beautiful words George had spoken from the spectral realms, did not need to be written down or memorized.

She welled up again as his soothing voice echoed all around her, carried to her from another realm and time:

> *"The world needs all its flowers, my darling Ellen.*
> *"It's time for you to bloom, dearest love.*
> *"Time for you to bloom."*

TWO

It was a slow morning in Castlebrook. Manny Bryn, pushing 38, overweight and over-anxious, raked fingers of frustration through his curly fair hair—badly cut by the half-blind barber in town—and wondered what in God's name he was going to write.

He'd been sitting at the kitchen table for a good ten minutes, pen poised over a blank jotter, working himself up to a letter of introduction to recently widowed Cousin Ted, a man of some means who lived in Galveston, Texas.

Some means? No, that didn't *begin* to describe Ted's vast fortune—if Manny could take his mother at her word.

"Married a hotelman's daughter, don't yeh know. Pearl her name was. God, the world was his oyster when he married Pearl! Not much to look at ... no Merlin Monroe, as they say ... a wee sharp fox's face on her ... but she had the money. The Daisy Motel Chain I believe the bissness was called, if I mind right. So there'll be money."

His ma had paused, looking skyward, as if focusing on a heavenly fall of manna.

"Shares and vestments and the like, son. Nobody to leave it to ... couldn't have no children 'cos Pearl was barn. And yeh wouldn't want it going to some tomcat's home or a church fund, God forbid ... not that Ted had any religion at the best of times, but yeh never know. When some of these heathens get within sight of the wooden overcoat they think it's a way of slipping into heaven by the back door, sins forgiven, penance paid. Last I heard he was poorly with the chest; a touch of assmer I believe."

Manny, half-listening, had pricked up his ears at the word

"assmer". What if the oul' fella did indeed die and bequeath it all to the Church or whatever, and him and his ma—in dire need of money all of a sudden—missing out completely? Now *that* would be a crying shame. Manny knew he had to get something down on paper sharpish before his ma reappeared. 'Cos if he didn't he wouldn't hear the end of it.

A couple-a months previous he'd lost his job at JM Cooney's Baked-4-You bread shop. Too many grog-induced late starts and too many run-ins with the short-tempered chef had led to Mr Cooney finally losing it.

The dreaded unemployment slip had dropped through the letterbox the very next day, leaving Manny free to lie in his disordered bed for as long as he wanted and dwell on his transgressions.

A career in baking had not been inevitable however. An interest in cars had driven him towards the mechanic's trade for a time. But the cruel winters—open-fronted garages a given—had nearly frozen the digits clean off him, turning hands from nimble to fumble within minutes, and it couldn't last.

By comparison, the warmth of Cooney's kitchen was a godsend. But a price had to be paid for his good fortune at the bakery. All that temptation was just too hard to fight. Whatever cakes JM couldn't sell found their way into Manny's car boot, thence to Hillside Cottage and into the bellies of mother and son. The pounds piled on—waistbands expanded, spirits drooped as the needle on the weighing scales climbed high.

He looked down at his unsightly paunch, despondent. Maybe he could lose that, now he was out of seduction's way. And if he could lose a pound or two he wouldn't feel so worn out and depressed.

He'd been the main provider, his ma's extra bit of pension putting treats in the cupboard and beer in the fridge. No such luxuries in the foreseeable future for sure. Now he was reduced to claiming welfare, standing in a queue of crotch-scratching losers every fortnight, shame and guilt churning in his head like gravel-mix.

He put pen to paper with renewed incentive.

Upstairs, Ma Bryn was having a nap.

"You'd need-a get that letter writ!" she'd gasped, climbing the stairs. "Time's goin' on and there's no guarantee you'll be gettin' another job anytime soon, son."

"Aye, Ma," Manny said again, shooting a glance at the ceiling, wondering what his life would indeed be like if his ma were to suddenly pop her proverbial clogs. The thought had him tensing up and clenching down hard on the end of the biro.

Ma Bryn, overweight also, seemed to attract ailments to her like gawpers to a car crash. She'd raised him single-handedly after the husband had taken off and Manny barely out of nappies. Andy Bryn—no great loss, a shiftless alcoholic, drinking and passing out in the Dog 'n' Duck most nights—had disappeared one morning in his beat-up truck, and neither he nor the truck were ever heard tell of again.

"The fairies must-a tookin him," his mother used to say when the boy was old enough to understand. When he reached his teens, however, all questions on the subject of Andy Bryn were met with what his ma called "the bald facts".

"Yer da was a useless blackguard, truth be tolt. We're better off without him. He made his fists do the talkin' and snored like the Divil when the dhrink was in him, which was every friggin' night and then some. So all I got from yer da was insomnier and a pair-a black eyes when the bull was up in him. But you're not gonna turn out like him, son, 'cos you take after *me*."

He was putting pen back to paper when the phone rang.

"Hello ... "

"Is Mrs Bryn at home, please?" A female voice, crisp and businesslike.

"Well, she is and she isn't, but she can't come to the phone right now. Can I take a message?"

"Empire Stores' accounts department here. She's in arrears

again. She must pay £10 before the end of the month or we'll be forced to take action."

"Uh, eh ... aye, I mean yes, I-I'll tell her that."

"Thank you. Good day." The line went dead.

Manny, deflated again, shuffled to the foot of the stairs and gazed up. There was no movement from above. His mother had three catalogues on the go—Empire, Grattan and Littlewoods—and paid a bit off each month. Since he'd lost his job she hadn't been able to keep the payments regular.

Things were bad and it was all his fault. Had he not eaten so many leftovers from the bakery he wouldn't have put on so much weight. Had he not put on the weight he wouldn't have felt so tired and wouldn't have overslept. And if he hadn't overslept he'd still be in his job and none of this would-a happened.

He went back to the table and sat down again, feeling sad and dejected. The letter to Cousin Ted really needed to be finished before his ma rose.

The phone rang a second time.

A woman from another of them catalogues, he decided, going to answer it.

"Hullo ... "

Silence.

"Hullo ... Er, anybody there?"

He heard a deep sigh at the other end.

Then:

"At a loose end these days, Manny, me oul' son? Lost yer job I hear."

He didn't recognize the voice with the thick Belfast accent. Didn't know anyone from that dangerous city.

"Dunno ... dunno what yeh mean," he said, trepidation rising.

"Could be useful tae *us*, in that case. The boys need all the help they can get these days tae fight the cause."

Manny felt his legs go weak.

"L-L-look, who—"

"Be seein' yeh."

Promptly, the caller hung up.

With a trembling hand, Manny put the phone down.

Was that an IRA commander? "*The boys need all the help they can get . . . tae fight the cause.*" That was the lingo of the terrorist group and no mistake.

He'd never been in that kind of trouble before. But now, due to his joblessness, was he on their radar?

In a state of shock, he went back to the table and sat down.

Oh, my God! Ma can't hear of this. Never, ever, ever!

Maybe it was a crank call. He tried consoling himself. Maybe somebody from the bakery having a laugh.

He picked up the pen again but, to his horror, his hand was still shaking.

Nobody from the bakery came from Belfast.

Nobody he knew had an accent that sounded anything *like that*.

VIVIENNE

In the city of Belfast, Vivienne Dundas sat at a desk in her studio, gazing intently at her subject for the afternoon: a single white lily.

She needed to know the flower intimately before tackling it. It was the way she always worked. It was the way she'd always been: eyes thirsting for the detail, angling the lens of her forensic gaze to focus and refocus.

Such scrutiny showed itself in the stunning images ranged around the walls: myriad prints of flowers, their hidden nectaries exposed; wedges of fruit weeping seeds and stones; a close-up of a vibrant shelduck, its feathers shimmering in the early-morning sunlight.

Those studies served as templates for her textile designs: repeat motifs, which would be printed onto fabrics and costumes, bed-covers, linens and drapes. She'd always loved the idea of taking her passion for nature into the bedrooms and closets of other women. To have her creations worn, slept in—inhabited if you like—gave her a power few other art forms could embrace.

The natural world had always interested Vivienne. People, not so much. When she looked at human faces she was deconstructing them, seeing patterns instead of features.

In childhood she deserted her dolls and stuffed animals for the garden. Her mother's flowers and plants were the embodiment of beauty, and therefore much more interesting. She'd pluck them, carry them into the house and study them for hours, then weep when they bowed their pretty heads and died.

"You could draw them before they die, sweetheart," her mother would soothe. "That way, they'd always be alive. Come, I'll show you."

So she'd cupped her daughter's tiny fist in hers. And little Vivienne, pencil poised, learned another language—an altogether more magical one—of steady lines and curves.

One more artist in the maternal line was born.

Now she'd realized her ambition: had just completed her first year in Fashion and Textiles at the Belfast College of Art. Halfway through the summer holidays, she regarded it as unthinkable to leave her passion behind. It consumed her.

Her father, with reluctance, found her the studio near the city centre. It had taken a lot of persuading, but she knew he'd relent. Her doting parent could not deprive her of her dearest wish. How could she be creative in the stuffy, book-lined home that was so redolent of his courtroom?

She needed a space of her own; to create her own art, carefree and untrammelled.

"Belfast is a dangerous place, Vivienne," he'd warned. "You need to be careful. My job makes you a target in this godforsaken city. You know that."

"Yes, Your Honour."

"Now don't be churlish! You know very well what I mean. Your mother and I have only your best interests at heart."

"Oh, Daddy dear, I know that, but I can't be a prisoner of your choices for ever. I'm nineteen now. I need my own space to work . . . my freedom. I can take care of myself; believe me."

Finally Judge Dundas had given way. He paid a retainer on the disused office space. But with a caveat.

"Only on one condition . . . that you use it *for your work only*. No staying over. I want you home every night in your own bed, where your mother and I know you're safe. It's just too dangerous."

She'd fallen in love with the place the moment she set eyes on it: the glossy, lacquered floor and wide, plate-glass windows stretching from floor to ceiling. It had been on the market for some time, so the estate agent was only too pleased to let it to the eminent judge at a knockdown rate.

Her furniture consisted of an adjustable easel desk and chair, a trestle table for her screen-printing and to hold her myriad paints and dyes, an ancestral chaise-longue her mother had gifted her—"For resting, sweetheart. Sitting bent over an easel for most of the day is not good for you." And that was all.

The antique couch of sea-foam green struck a note of nostalgia in the modern space.

Vivienne was of slight build, and as slender and delicate as the lily she was drawing: pale oval face, almond eyes, wrists and ankles frail and bony, like some frangible creature from a fairy tale.

Modigliani could have painted her into life.

In her early teens she suffered from anorexia, brought on by the trauma of seeing her father ambushed. The family had just left the Central Library when the would-be assassin struck. He appeared out of nowhere at the foot of the steps, gun raised. Miraculously, the weapon jammed and he fled the scene. The memory of the incident still haunted her. If only she could go back in time and edit out those few seconds of footage.

Vivienne understood at age thirteen the impermanent nature of life. How things could change in an instant because of evil men. Not eating was her way of disappearing, of becoming invisible, so as not to draw such evil to her.

She tucked a tress of her long dark hair behind her ear and blinked, conscious of the noise radiating up from the street, the clicking of doors and heels from the office below. She was on the top floor of the three-storey building, which was all but deserted. A solicitor—an old colleague of her father's—occupied the ground space. The first floor housed his files. Sometimes she met his secretary on the stairs: an exacting, cautious lady in tweeds and high heels.

"Fuck off, yeh bastard!"

Out on the street a man was shouting. She sighed. Got up to close the window. Saw the drunk stagger away from the pub: the Kevin Barry Arms. A security man stood watching him go, fists clenched. They looked comical in their foreshortened way, like a pair of naughty schoolboys.

An army vehicle trundled past.

From off in the distance she heard the wail of sirens, the choppy spinning of helicopter blades—Belfast's mood music. She'd never known it any other way. Bomb scares were a frequent occurrence, but she had an unwavering trust in the beneficence of the world.

The gun jammed because my father is a good man.
My parents are good people.
I believe in God.
I believe in love.
I'm a loving daughter.
Bad things do not happen to good people.

The Kevin Barry Arms across from her was the only blemish on an otherwise peaceful street. Bankers, lawyers and accountants plied their quiet trades in the majority of premises that flanked the avenue. Shoppers tended not to venture this far, so there were few cafés or restaurants to draw them in. But the pub opened at eleven and the alcoholics and homeless congregated to void their pain.

The security man went back inside. The drunk disappeared, wisps of a rousing rebel song fading as he pursued chaos elsewhere.

A degree of quiet returned.

Her eyes travelled up to the top floor of the building that housed the pub. It had been vacant since her arrival a few weeks earlier, a set of beige roller blinds pulled down on each of its two high windows.

Now she saw, to her consternation, that one of the blinds was raised three quarters of the way. There was a potted plant on the sill with an Irish tricolour stuck in it.

When did *that* happen?

A gust of fear assailed her. Something tightened in her gut. The dim interior of the dwelling opposite was mocking her. She couldn't discern whether anyone was in there. It bothered her because if there *was* someone in there, they'd have an unimpeded view of her at work.

Unsettled, she returned to her beautiful lily.

Lifted the pencil.

Her hand trembled as she traced the first of the flower's five stamens. She persevered, becoming increasingly aware that she had no protection against the unseen presence across the way—her window had no blinds to block his view. And she felt certain it was a *he*.

The more she tried to concentrate, the more exposed she felt. Her head began to ache. Her attention was not on her work and she resented that fact.

How long has that blind been raised? How long has he been watching me? I wouldn't have noticed had I not heard the drunk out on the street.

Her pale fingers gripped the pencil more tightly, sweat beading in her palm.

An oft-repeated maxim of her father's came to her: "The more knowledge you have, the less you indulge fear, Vivienne. Knowledge is power. Never forget that."

He would repeat the mantra every morning he checked under his car for a booby-trap bomb. Like all representatives of the security forces in Northern Ireland, members of the judiciary were "legitimate targets" for Republican and Loyalist terrorists alike.

Vivienne decided, against her better judgement, to call it a day.

She flung down the pencil, annoyed with herself for being so cowardly. Crossed the room and shut the window.

Panic raked her insides as she dared to look across.

There *was* a man in the room, his face in shadow. He was wearing jeans, one forearm exposed. There was something on his arm. A tattoo? Perhaps.

He was standing watching *her.*

Her father's words rang in her ears:

"*The more knowledge you have, the less you indulge fear.*"

She was being invited to put that maxim to the test.

Would she have the courage to follow through?

FOUR

When Mrs Purboy entered Dr Flynn's practice she was happy to see she was the first patient of the day. Save for the receptionist the waiting-room was empty. She had barely sat down and was selecting a magazine when the doctor put his head around the door.

"Morning, Ellen! Good to see you. Come in, won't you."

The GP—a plump, smooth man in his early fifties with a shiny face and paintbrush moustache—wasn't surprised to see her. She'd been visiting every few weeks since her husband's death, to obtain tranquillizers and share tearful reminiscences of George. Prior to the tragedy she'd been in excellent health.

"How are we today?" he enquired, seating himself. "You look a little tired."

Ellen settled herself and drew a hankie from her pocket.

"Well, my sleep isn't the best, doctor, and ..." She dabbed at her eyes, not knowing how to phrase the next bit.

"Mmm ... and ... ?"

"I ... I really don't know how to put this, doctor. You're going to think me awfully foolish I'm afraid."

"Try me, Ellen. I hear many things in this consulting room and 'foolish' is not the word I'd use. It's normal to see things in a different light when we're going through the grieving process."

"Th-thank you, doctor. You're so ... understanding." But how was she going to say the next bit without sounding crazy? "It's just that ... well, it's just that ... "

"I can give you a stronger sedative if you like. That isn't a—"

"I saw George last night. Sitting ... sitting at the end of my bed."

There. She'd said it.

She heard the silence mocking her.

"Hmm... I see. But sitting at the end of your bed *in your dream*, Ellen."

She'd guessed he'd dismiss it all as a dream, and in that very tone. The implication was clear: You're being delusional.

"But that's just it, doctor. I was *awake* when it happened. It's . . . it's not a dream, you see. How could it be a dream if I'm awake? And then... and then this morning I noticed *this*."

She pulled back her cuff and raised her bruised wrist. He got up to examine it.

"Hmm... well, there's nothing broken. Did you have a fall?"

"No . . . that's just it. In the dream I felt someone touch my arm. That's what woke me up. It was only... it was only this morning, when I saw the bruise, that I remembered."

Dr Flynn went back behind his desk. Removed his spectacles. Pinched the bridge of his nose.

"Is it painful?"

Ellen shook her head, feeling chastened. Her GP was discounting everything she'd just said by ignoring it completely.

"That's good. I'll give you a gel to rub on it. It'll take down the bruising and a tonic as well. Bruising easily is a sign that you're probably low in iron. You need to keep your strength up. As to the cause: you perhaps slept on it or knocked against something yesterday and were not even aware you'd done so. It often happens. There's always a logical explanation."

Ellen, close to tears, put the hankie to her nose. "Oh dear, doctor... perhaps I'm going the way of my poor mother."

"Now, Ellen, that's foolish talk. The mind can play tricks; that's all. You mark my words. You miss George a lot and you want to see him again... to just know that he's all right on the Other Side. That's a natural response when suffering a loss. Your subconscious is a very obedient servant. Whatever you dwell on most will show up in your life sooner or later."

He sat back in his chair, twined his fingers over his paunch.

"Now, what's happening is you're having *a dream within a dream*. It's a rare thing, but it happens from time to time."

"A dream within a dream?"

"Yes... or a false awakening. You dreamt that George was sitting at the end of your bed, but you also *dreamt* that you awoke to find him sitting there."

"I-I see," Ellen said hesitantly, not knowing what to think. "When you put it like that I suppose it's possible. It's just that it was so *real*."

"Yes, lucid dreams can be very convincing."

"I wrote down what he said, but I remember the words. H-he said something about the world needing all its flowers and that... that it... it was time... for me to bloom."

"How very poetic! George was always good with words and he knew how much you loved gardening."

"Yes, yes... he was... But, doctor, what can I do about them... the dreams?"

"Well, there's nothing much you *can* do about them. Dreams are simply dreams. There's nothing paranormal about them. Look at it this way, Ellen: you're still grieving for George and he wants to reassure you that he's all right. So, maybe if you could see your way to getting on with your life the dreams would cease. Those lovely words he used—time for you to bloom—that's what he's trying to tell you. Go your own way. He wants you to let go and be happy."

She never expected to hear that the dreams were somehow brought about by her holding onto George.

Her tears welled up again.

"But I just can't let George go, doctor. How could I do that?"

Dr Flynn sat forward in his chair once more, adopting his best professional, authoritative pose.

"I think, Ellen, you need to stop dwelling on what might have been, and take a chance on something new... become absorbed in something different... say, a new project. Something to take your mind off things."

"Erm... I don't understand. Like... like what, doctor?"

"Well," he said carefully, an idea coming to him, "that office of his. I remember visiting your mother there when it was a little bedsit."

Ellen looked at him dubiously. "Yes, it was converted for her when we realized she couldn't be on her own. Then George made it his office after she . . . "

"But it's no longer his office."

"Yes... I-I know... but I just can't bring myself to go in there since he... " She twisted the rings on her wedding finger. "It's just too painful, and it was his private space. He never wanted me going in there... even to clean. I'd be trespassing in some way. Letting him down in some way."

"Now look, Ellen, the sooner you face up to reality the better. You only *think* you can't go in there. It's *your* house now... *your* space, and the sooner you truly make it your own the better. Stop putting limits on yourself. George would want you to be in control now. When you stop fearing things you free yourself from a lot of unnecessary suffering."

George would want you to be in control now.

She dwelt on those words. How alien-sounding they were to her. George had always been in control of her world; she was continually fitting in with his plans. He made all the decisions and she gladly let him do so.

"Now, what I'm suggesting would not only improve your social life," Dr Flynn was saying, "but would earn you a bit of income too. Freshen up that little office space and convert it back to a bedsit—a studio, as some people call them now—then get a lodger in. There's a need for it in the town you know. My temporary covers have to rent in Killoran—ten miles away—which is a bit of an inconvenience."

"Oh, I don't know, doctor. I... I just don't know if I'd be... er... comfortable with that. Letting strangers in I mean."

"You could vet them first. You can always tell when people are on the level or not. And you could rent to women if you didn't feel comfortable with men."

"I... erm, I..."

"Promise me you'll think about it. It's just an idea, and you never know what interesting people you might meet."

The GP smiled and Ellen sensed that the consultation was at an end. She lifted her handbag off the floor and placed it on her knee.

"Well, I'll think about it," she said, knowing that she'd have to follow through on the doctor's advice. He was right about most things and she didn't want to disappoint him.

"That's good," he said, getting up. "A mind that is stretched by a new experience can never go back to its old dimensions."

"Sorry, doctor?"

"Oliver Wendell Holmes; not me, alas. No wiser words were ever spoken. Set about redecorating for starters and take it from there."

He patted her shoulder.

"Now, just rest that arm of yours for a little. You'll be right as rain in no time, Ellen. Trust me... and call anytime. You know where to find me. Bye now. Mind how you go."

Mrs Purboy took her leave, feeling a little better. Maybe she *had* hit her arm without being conscious of it. Maybe George's apparition *was* simply a dream within a dream and she was making too much of it all.

She made her way across the street to Heron's pharmacy. On the threshold, her attention was drawn to a car parked not far from the solicitor's office. She immediately recognized the white sports car that had nearly collided with her earlier.

Intrigued, she pushed open the door to the shop, and as she did so, got the strangest feeling that it wouldn't be the last she'd be seeing of that flashy car or its handsome, debonair young driver.

FIVE

Manny's mother Tilda—affectionately referred to by the locals as Ma Bryn—was 58 years young, hair a lacquered orb of bubble curls; her best feature. Every couple of months she'd visit the Shearlock Combs salon and have Elish, the stylist, slap on a Sunshine rinse to bedaub the greys. Her figure was as full and formless as a sack of flour but what the heck; her height could take it. She enjoyed her food. Could eat in her sleep: "If God didn't want us to eat in the dark, He wouldn't-a put a light in the fridge."

Tilda's sunny disposition and kind heart carried her over the rapids, brought the weak and wounded to her door. A cuppa tea and a bitta chat eased and healed a multitude. In another life she could have been a therapist, working out of a shiny office amongst the suits, dealing out her homespun tropes, and charging big. But she'd found that her calling in fortune telling was the shinier side of the psychology coin, and delivered just as good.

Hillside Cottage might be falling about her ears but Tilda, never house-proud, didn't care. Saucepans in the attic caught the pitter-pattering rain. Warped cardboard, jammed in windows, kept the draughts at bay. Never enough money for house repairs but God was good: a roof over your head, food on the table, wild flowers in the garden where the birds touched down to feed; what more did a body need?

Coming on for eleven she roused herself, blinking back to consciousness in her pink-themed bedroom—frilled and flounced with the vigour and bounce of a pre-schooler. In a woman who retained a childish sense of wonder despite life's cruel blows it was kind of appropriate.

Tilda recalled the shopping expedition to Barney's supermarket and the palpitations that had driven her under the covers.

"Dearie, dearie me!" she yawned, before fighting her way into a voluminous kaftan and throwing on a silver necklace the size of a tow-truck chain.

Thus attired, she billowed over to the dressing-table mirror and applied a generous slash of Cherry Bomb lipstick.

"There, that's better," she said, releasing a gusty sigh of approval at her reflection. Ma Bryn was never seen in public without her make-up. The face might have sagged, but oh what marvels could be wrought with a touch of powder and paint!

Feeling ready to face the world again, she exited the bedroom and trundled downstairs.

On the threshold of the kitchen Tilda perked up. For there was her beloved son, Manny, seated at the table, addressing an envelope. Her finely tuned senses were registering an air of disquiet too, but she'd ignore them for the time being.

"God, have yeh got it writ, son?!" she puffed, beating her chest to get the voice back in gear after the lie-down. Tilda's larynx only ever got time off in sleep mode. There was a running joke in the locale: "Haven't spoken to Ma Bryn in a couple of days. Didn't wanna interrupt her."

"Aye, Ma," he said, looking up from the task. "Have it writ. Are you sure that's the right address? 'Fofanny Heights, Scutch End.' Sounds a bit funny."

"Well, if it's what he writ on his last Christmas card it must be right," she said, sailing towards the stove as if on autopilot, ostrich plumes waving on her two-tone satin pumps.

She pushed the kettle back on the heat. Found a couple of side plates. Fetched a cake tin from the treats cupboard. There was enough sugar in Tilda's diet to make her digits twitch in diabetic song, but what the heck?

"His writin' isn't the best: Uncle Ted's, I'll give yeh that. But none of me father's side was good at the writin', as I tolt you afore. Me mammy now was the opposite. Lord, she had the greatest handwriting! Like the Queen does on all the banknotes, only curlier." She studied a patch of floor. "You'd think her hand would get sore doin' all that writin'—the Queen's I mean. But yer granny was great with her hands, as I say. Could knit a jumper, pluck a chicken and tell yer fortune, all at the same time. You take after her, Manny, 'cos your handwriting is right and good too. Cousin Ted'll be impressed when he gets that letter, so he will."

"Hope he'll be able to read it. *His* letter looks like a wain writ it."

"Aye, maybe a touch of arthur-ritis in the hands, now that yeh say it." She cut slices of a marble cake with the grandma's old knife, dulled from years of wear. Arranged them on a plate. "Old age robs a body of the best bits of hisself. God, he was such a handsome man in his day," she continued dreamily. "All the girls in Derry were after Ted."

She brought the teapot to the table spread with green oilcloth. Set down the cups and plate of cake. If Manny didn't want any, sure she'd have them all herself....

"Go on: have one," she said brightly, pulling out a chair. "I feel things is gonna work out for us, yeh know."

"Aye ... why's that?"

"Redwing Maeve came through in me ritual last night. And not only that; this mornin' if I didn't see two magpies on the lawn, a robin on the sill, and when I mention me mother, if I didn't dream about her there when I was lyin' down. Saw her in Dan Buck's barley field, singing 'Donald Where's Yer Trewsers' and dancin' round her crystal ball like a young wan. Got me tae thinkin' it was a sign I should start up me readings again."

Tilda had grown up avoiding ladders, waving at lone magpies and surrounded by all things mystical: horoscopes and lunar projections spread out on a rickety table when the moon was full. Mrs

Bryn divined that her wee Tilly would delight in the pleasures of the world, would spread warmth and joy wherever she roamed. Meet a rich man who'd give her the best. Live in a large, lavish home; have a patio full of flowers and a garden full of gnomes.

The rich man hadn't materialized, but there was still time. Tilda clung to the promise that one day her handsome prince would come. The crystal ball and cards had said so. There was no reason to doubt them.

Back in the day, the mammy—Madame Silver-Crown—had made a tidy living, spinning such yarns out of a Hemley Dormouse caravan at seaside resorts around Northern Ireland. Little Tilda acting as bait to reel the ladies in. Standing on the Portaluce promenade in her knee-socks and Shirley Temple curls, she'd held a sign that read:

MADAME CROWN, THE BEST IN TOWN.
SHE'LL READ YOUR PALM FOR JUST A POUND.

Women hunkered down to stroke her pretty pink cheeks; pat the silken locks as soft as a Persian kitten's fur. "Och, look at the wee darling," they'd coo. "Aren't you just the prettiest wee thing!"

And Tilda would toddle off in the direction of the caravan, the women streaming behind like ducks, hopes rising, purses opening in expectation of futures only a fraud could see.

"Och, Ma, that's a stupid idea... readin' fortunes," Manny spoke up, voice edged with alarm. He was recalling the bullying he'd endured at school: "*Yer ma's a gypsy. Yer granny's a witch.*" He'd never told his mother what he'd suffered, the memories a canker sore inside him still. "People'll think we're gypsies, and what would Father Mulcahy say?"

He couldn't give a flying monkey's about the parish priest's opinion, but thought he'd throw it in, to try and dissuade her.

Tilda wasn't listening, however. She had a deaf ear for anything that conflicted with her plans. Manny was simply afraid, but he'd get over that when the money started coming in.

"God, son, there's a leaf floatin' in me tea... a sign that a letter's coming with word of money."

Manny didn't have the heart to say, That'll be a bill from Empire catalogue. They rang about an overdue payment when you were in bed.

"Father Mulcahy, me eye!" Tilda on fire now; another slice of cake disappearing, crumbs falling like snow. "Didn't I do a bitta palm-readin' when you wuz a nipper, to make ends meet when yer da took off and left us in the lurch? Brought us in a good bit too. Dunno what I'd-a done without it, son."

She gathered up crumbs with a moistened finger, carmine-painted nails a-gleam. Took a sip of the tea, leaving an imprint of Cherry Bomb lipstick on the rim.

"And there's nothing wrong with being a gypsy. There's a bitta Romany in me blood and I'm proud of it—and so should *you* be. Heaven's above, you maybe have the gift too, if you'd only let it rise."

Manny was sullen. "Och, Ma, men don't do that stuff. And anyway, it's only wimmen that can't get men that bother with fortune tellers."

He stuffed the letter into the envelope. Wished his mother had stayed in bed. Life was easier when he was working. Out of the house most of the day. By the time he got home and got his supper the TV filled the evening and stifled all such talk.

"And there's plenty of *them* about, son," Tilda continued, painting a picture now that only she could see, adding brushstroke after brushstroke, warming to the theme. "Plain wimmen that need-a be tolt there's a man waitin' for them round the corner... give them a bitta hope. That's the way it works, son. You tell people what they wanna hear and they bring it on themselves by believing it. I'm just the con-dewit—or whatever that word is."

There was a lot of truth in his ma's philosophy. Admen and hucksters had been dining out on the strategy for yonks, but…

"God, son, afore I forget, I saw that grand widda-wommin in the town the other day!"

"What widow woman?"

"Och, Mrs Purboy… y'know her that lives in that haunted house that belonged till that oul' boy Sir Willie-what's-his-name…. Fell a clatter down the stairs back in the day and kilt hisself, so he did. Not that nobody believes that tale. They say he was into black magic and god-knows-what and that's why he got so wealthy and—"

"Aye, right, so what's that gotta do with anything?"

"Could do a reading for Mrs Purboy… a séance, like, since she's going through the grieving process. That's what they call it these days: the 'grieving process'. I think it's Amerkin."

A strained silence ensued. Manny knew he wasn't making much headway.

"Oh, and another thing, son, afore I forget . . . was talking to Minnie Bain in Barney's and she tolt me Fred broke the leg and is lookin' a taxi-driver to fill in till he's back on his feet again. She wondered would you be interested. I said I'd run it past you first."

"Taxi-drivin'? Me?" Manny was incredulous.

"Well, why not, son? Yeh can drive already, and there isn't much till sittin' on yer arse all-day-long behind the wheel-of-a car, havin' a bitt-a craic with the locals. Sure a monkey with no eyes could do it…. And it'll bring us in a bob or two 'til you get something more steady."

"Aye, maybe… I'll think about it."

"Well, don't leave it too long. Minnie said Fred'll give yeh first refusal."

"Aye… maybe," he repeated. "But… "

"Now, no aye-maybe-buts, son. Between the pair of us we'll make a go of things. Yer ma knows what she's talking about. God, you know what I think I'll do… put an ad in the post-office windee.

See what happens. That Mrs Purboy might see it. Yer ma's not one to sit on her morals—"

"Laurels."

"Aye, whatever. Now, gimme over that jotter. God, this could be the start of a new life for the pair of us! Me mammy always said there were three types of people in this world: them that make things happen, them that watch things happen, and them that wonder what happened. Us Bryns is in the first cattiegory."

There's no deterring her now, thought Manny with a sigh.

He got up.

"I'll go and post this letter."

"Aye, you do that, son."

He left the house to get away from his ma for a while. But the gruff voice down the telephone line he couldn't ditch so easily.

Those words, "*need all the help we can get tae fight the cause*," were clanging in his head like a death knell.

SIX

Castlebrook, one of a clutch of towns straddling the border of counties Derry and Antrim, lay ten miles to the north of Killoran, the main borough of the locale.

The sleepy town, with its impressive stone keep and idyllic tinkling stream, had an interesting history.

Founded in 1845 by a wealthy merchant, one Sir Wilfred Theodore Blackbourne, it was once the site of a thriving linen business. Evidence of those bygone days can be glimpsed in the neat rows of terraced houses Blackbourne built for his millworkers. These two-up, two-down little dwellings, with their granite façades and neat gardens, border the main square in the town.

The staunch churchgoer had his principles when it came to Castlebrook. His ethics were based on the Three P's—there should be no Pubs, no Pawnshops, and therefore no need for Police.

But times change. Mr Blackbourne would be appalled to see that in 1985 his once-bustling mill was now home to a police station; that there was not only one pub but two—The Mucky Mallard and The Castle Inn—and if that wasn't bad enough, a betting shop *as well*, to provide the townsfolk with the merriment he so steadfastly opposed.

Cedarwood Manor, now the Purboy residence on the leafy outskirts of Castlebrook, was the former home of the town's founder. Built in 1846, the grand Edwardian residence, standing three storeys tall, lay at the end of a winding, cedar-lined avenue in thirty acres of landscaped garden and parkland.

Ellen Purboy was proud of her home. It had been in her husband's family since the early 1930s, acquired by George's grandfather, a barrister of some note in his day, who could afford the best that money could buy.

When she married George she married the house too—and gladly so. Having been brought up in a modest terraced affair with barely room for herself and her sister Nettie, Ellen regarded Cedarwood as the proverbial palace in a story-book. The high-ceilinged spacious rooms with their maple floors—and furnished with the best of Queen Anne and Chippendale, complete with fabric coverings of the finest brocades and silks—spoke of an opulence that few could aspire to.

Her parents were so proud of the match their elder daughter had made. She'd "married up" in the local parlance, whereas Nettie—not as good-looking as Ellen and resentful of her, even to the present day—had only managed to nab humble postal-worker John, a kindly little man, whose hopes of a quiet life had vanished at the altar with those fateful words, "I do".

Ellen turned the key in the door in ruminative mood. Dr Flynn had planted an idea, which she would now have to nurture. She wasn't one to let people down, most especially the doctor. He was full of wisdom and a good sense she relied on completely.

She paused for a moment in the cavernous hallway, feeling forlorn and vulnerable in the shadowy house. Would she ever get used to the loneliness, that desperate sense of abandonment that seemed poised to ambush her every time she stepped over the threshold?

Standing now in contemplation, as the door's complaining cries died on the air, she became aware of music playing somewhere. It was very faint but seemed to be coming from upstairs.

I must have left the radio on.

Warily, she climbed the stairs, up past the gloomy portraits of the Blackbourne clan, her footfalls quietly protesting her every step. Since George's death it seemed the house with its many mysteries and secrets was pushing her out somehow, causing her to feel like an interloper in what always had been *his* domain.

When she gained the landing, she grew concerned at the sight of the door to the master bedroom standing slightly ajar.

I always shut doors.

Oranges and lemons say the bells of St Clement's.
When will you pay me? say the bells of Old Bailey.

She recognized the tune immediately, and it was not the radio.

Perturbed, she sped down the corridor and pushed open the door. Her jewellery box lay open on the dressing-table, its satin ballerina pirouetting to the familiar little melody.

Ellen's heart did a somersault. Had she been robbed? With trembling hands she checked the contents. But all items were present.

How come I forgot to shut it? She tried to think.

I was in a hurry to see the doctor. That was it. Yes, because I was walking I needed to give myself extra time and I rushed off, forgetting to shut both the box and the door.

But as she left the room and descended the stairs she was aware of another more troubling thought pushing in: one she did not want to hold onto, due to its alarming connotations.

Had you forgotten to shut the jewellery box, the tune would have alerted you to that fact and you'd have turned back to close the lid.

In the living-room she sat down, trying not to weep, and levered off the high heels, mightily relieved to be finally free of them.

"I'll not be wearing *you* for a while," she admonished the shoes, trying to calm herself. The high heels were for special occasions. When George was alive there had been many such occasions: weekends away, dinners at fine restaurants, a concert or two. Now all that was gone.

She grew tearful at the memories. How blessed her life had been! How lonely and pointless the future seemed now, spooling out before her like the most desolate highway stretching into nothingness. The grief of her great loss flowed into every crevice of her being. It filled her up and pulled her down, keeping her weighted in an alien landscape she felt powerless to navigate, much less escape.

Dr Flynn was correct. She really did need to be "stretched by a new experience." And with George telling her that it was "time to bloom", it seemed she was being pointed in a direction she felt compelled to take.

Perhaps all these strange things will cease when I absorb myself in something new, like the doctor said. I really can't go on like this. My grief is driving me to distraction. It could even drive me mad.

She thought of the office and steeled herself. There was no point in delaying the inevitable. It had to be faced, and the sooner the better.

The room was on the ground floor. She went out into the hallway and stood staring down at the door, took a deep breath and slowly moved towards it.

A pong of stale air hit her immediately as she entered. She halted momentarily and caught her breath, feeling as tense and charged as a diver at the cliff edge.

When George was bed-ridden and the office no longer part of his life she still hadn't felt it proper that she go in there. It was his domain and he was very fussy when it came to his papers not being disturbed. He had a chaotic filing system only he could understand. Even peeping in during his confinement would have been a betrayal of sorts, signifying that she'd lost all hope of his pulling through. And there was always hope as long as he was breathing, no matter how tiny and wavering that flame of hope might seem.

Saddened by the ineffable memories, she made her way to the windows, drew back the curtains and pushed them wide, admitting some much-needed air. Then turned to confront a wealth of clutter surfacing out of the gloom.

There were files and papers all over the place. This open-plan area with kitchenette didn't contain much furniture—a dusty leather sofa, a chair, a commodious desk and a couple of filing cabinets.

At the opposite end, screened off from view by a series of stained-glass panels, was the en-suite bedroom.

The whole place, once so occupied and alive, looked forlorn, as if all the work done there had come to nothing.

She drew back the stained-glass door and tried not to think of her dear mother breathing her last in the big bed. Tears threatened again, but she had to be strong. There was a chance now to actually do something constructive, as Dr Flynn suggested.

Then: "Ellen! Are you down there? It's only me." A woman's voice, sudden in the hallway.

Nettie. How, Ellen asked herself, did *she* get in? The last person she wanted to see was her nosy sister.

She exited the office, quickly pulling the door behind her.

"Er . . . Nettie. There you are. I-I didn't hear you come in."

"Obviously not," the sister blustered, unbuttoning her coat.

Nettie Buckley was a prim, cantankerous little woman, who thrived on catastrophe and gossip. Plain-faced with sagging eyes and blunt-cut hair, she eschewed make-up and jewellery—such adornment was "for floozies and doxies"—dressed like a nun and acted like one too. Wore sensible shoes, hand-knitted cardigans and practical, knee-length skirts. She held down two jobs: as secretary to the parish priest, Father Mulcahy, and at weekends behind the counter of the local pharmacy, to help tighten the slack of her husband's meagre pay. Proud of her standing in the community and conscious that between the priest's house, the pharmacist's counter and her husband's dispatches from the post office, she knew pretty well all that went on in the private lives of the townsfolk. Such knowledge was pure gold to a gossip like Nettie. She knew what she knew, and the community feared her because of it.

"You forgot to lock the front door," she said accusingly, removing her beret. "Any Tom, Dick or Harry could have wandered in. You need to watch that you know."

"Really! I thought I *did* lock it," Ellen lied. The melody from above had drawn her upstairs without thinking, but her sister didn't need to know anything about that.

Nettie marched through to the living-room as if she owned the place, and planted herself on the sofa. Since George's death she'd become something of a fixture in Ellen's life, and while Ellen appreciated her support she couldn't help thinking she was being monitored in some way: that Nettie was looking for signs that she might be going the way of their mother.

"What on earth are you doing in your bare feet? You'll get your death."

"Oh, don't fuss, Nettie, please! I walked into town to see the doctor, if you must know . . . to get the air, and my feet are a bit sore—that's all." She wondered why every time she met her sister she felt compelled to explain herself. "Can I get you anything?"

"No, thanks. I can't stay long." She looked askance at the discarded high heels. "My goodness, is it any wonder your feet are sore. You didn't walk into town in *those*, did you?"

Ellen didn't respond, aware that a pregnant pause was often the best weapon against a jibe. She heard a bluebottle zigzagging in through the open window. Saw a rose petal fall on the sill. How quickly beauty dies, she thought, wanting to weep, but knowing that in that moment there'd be no soft landing for her sorrow.

"Well, what *did* Dr Flynn have to say then?"

"What?"

"Dr Flynn. What did he say?"

"Erm . . . h-he said there was nothing to worry about. I'm not seeing George's ghost; simply having a dream within a dream. That's all."

Ellen quickly pulled the cuff of her sweater over her wrist. There was no way she was telling her sister about that peculiar injury.

"Part of the grieving process he says."

"Hmm ... well, you know my feelings on that score."

"They'll go away, when I stop brooding and start a new project ... to lift my mind. And that's what I intend to do."

Nettie shook her head. "I told Father Mulcahy about your experiences and he said he'd come and bless the house, just to be on the safe side."

"What?! I don't understand you, Nettie. I told you in confidence and trusted that you'd keep it to yourself. They're only dreams, nothing more. You shouldn't go making mountains out of molehills."

"Well, Father Mulcahy is hardly going to announce it from the pulpit. He's very dependable and knows about these things. And he said, 'just to be on the safe side' he'd come and do a blessing, and the sooner the better. I paid him to say another Mass for the repose of George's soul. I think he's having difficulty on the Other Side."

"That was thoughtful of you, Nettie. But George wasn't a believer and—"

"And that's just *it.* He didn't repent before he passed away ... didn't die in a state of grace. Now he's coming back to get prayers, because he knows how wrong he was."

She plucked at some imaginary lint on her sleeve, unable to meet Ellen's eye.

"There. I've said my piece. Is it any wonder statues of the Blessed Virgin are moving down in Cork? It's a warning that the people of Ireland must return to the faith. Smutty TV programmes and drink have put them all on the road to hell."

Ellen had heard about the strange phenomena of the moving statues in southern Ireland but hadn't paid them much heed.

"But if I were you," continued Nettie, digging in her spurs and going full pelt, "I wouldn't turn down the priest's offer of a blessing. It can't do any harm. And it's long overdue. That Blackbourne lot who owned this place ... how do you know what they got up to? They didn't believe in the clergy, you know. A pack of pagans if you ask *me*." She jerked a thumb in the direction of the hallway, where hung a portrait of the patriarch, Sir Wilfred. "And that boyo out there wasn't a good'un. Into the Black Arts if I'm any judge... brazen about it too.... That hidden hand of his says it all."

"What on earth are you talking about? The man's long dead. You know nothing about him."

"I know enough. It may interest you to know that posing like that with his hand concealed lets others know he's part of their cult .... It's a signal. That portrait should go. The Devil's disciples, the lot of them."

"It's only a *picture,* Nettie!"

"It's not godly... that's all I'm saying."

Ellen, not much of a churchgoer, bit down on her annoyance. In George's book organized religion did more harm than good. Nothing would persuade him to the contrary. Even in the face of death he wouldn't relent. Now Nettie was suggesting she bring a priest in. What would he have thought?

"Look, Nettie, I don't know about that. I know George wouldn't approve of that at all."

"But that's neither here nor there. It doesn't matter what George thinks, now does it? You must protect yourself... that's all I'm saying."

"Protect myself from *what* exactly?"

"Well, look at you, Ellen. You're a nervous wreck. You can't sleep. You're not eating, and when your defences are down, these things can get a foothold, Father Mulcahy says. You have to come back to the faith. George was bad for you on that score."

It was time to change the subject. "I'm going to do up his office and let it out as a bedsit. Dr Flynn advised it."

Nettie made tut-tutting noises, scanning the palatial, high-ceilinged room with its shimmering cream walls and bespoke fixtures in marble and glass. "Oh, I don't know about that. Not as if you need the money. Besides, you don't know what kind of lunatic or serial killer might show up."

"Don't be preposterous! And stop exaggerating. I'm trying to be constructive, to do something to stop me brooding. And all you can do is find fault."

Nettie sprang to her feet and pulled on her beret.

"Well, if *that's* your attitude then there's nothing more to be said! I came here to tell you I'd arranged for the blessing. This house always gives me the creeps, if you must know. Always has. Always will."

"Nettie, really, don't be like that. I'm sorry. I—"

But before she could finish, Nettie had left the room. "I'll see myself out, thank you very much!"

"Oh, dear. . . . " Ellen sighed as the door banged shut, sending shudders through the house. She turned back to the hallway. "Some things never change, do they? Well, Nettie's not going to put me off. I'll do what *I* want now."

She retraced her steps to the office, more determined than ever to follow through on her plan.

But just as she reached the door, it creaked open, *all by itself.*

SEVEN

At the local job centre Manny Bryn shifted from one foot to the other, wanting desperately to run away from his least favourite spot on the planet: the dole queue. He stood behind a bald man who was reeking of booze. There was a tattoo of a spider's web fanning out on each of his elbows.

He'd left his mother off at the post office, so that she could place her fortune-telling ad. There was no deterring her, alas. Psychic readings had saved their bacon in the past when times were tough. Desperate times demanded "a bitta creative thinking," she claimed, "and you won't be moaning when the money starts rolling in."

Aye, well, maybe she was right.

He was still feeling uneasy about that threatening phone call, but they hadn't rung since, so maybe it was nothing more than some crazy with too much time on his hands, trying to wind him up.

A man at the front finished his signing and the queue moved forward. Manny had always been in paid employment, so it was a bit of a shock to the system to suddenly be one of society's spongers.

It was his fourth claim in two months, and while he was glad of the lie-ins and not having Mr Cooney roaring down his neck every day, he knew he couldn't go on taking "the Queen's shilling". It was too embarrassing and made him feel like a waster. He'd always regarded himself as a bit of failure, but it took the Castlebrook dole queue to really drive the message home.

The long rectangular room had two desks positioned at the far end—at one desk you signed and at the other collected your Bank Giro cheque. A young woman, overweight like himself, with mousy hair, was dealing with the claimants. Manny hadn't seen her before. IRIS RAINEY was printed on a card in front of her. She looked a bit lost, as if it was her first day on the job.

At the adjacent desk sat skinny paper-shuffler David O'Ryan, in suit and tie, hair swept back in an Elvis quiff. He was always there, doling out the money.

The queue comprised men around Manny's own age with a scattering of school-leavers. Most of them stood uneasily, eager to get it over with.

In the background Dire Straits were belting out "Money for Nothing", the music punctuated by the frantic chatter of a D.J.

The queue inched forward once more.

Spider Elbows shifted up another wee bit. Turned to him, hands dug deep in his boiler-suit pockets.

"They're fuckin' slow the day. Too fuckin' slow for my likin'."

"Aye," Manny agreed, staring into blood-shot eyes flashing menace like a pair of hazard lights. "That's the way of it. They're always a bit slow."

"Aye, if yeh ask me they do it on purpose, the Prod bastards . . . tae make us fuckin' feel it, like."

Manny didn't know what to say. This baldy was in combative mood. He didn't want to get on the wrong side of him. "Have you been signin' on for long?" he asked, trying to mollify.

"Too friggin' long, if yeh must know. But the way I look at it, if the Brits can't give us jobs I've no problem takin' their bloody hand-outs."

The conversation was turning political. He hoped the young woman would call him soon. Save him from a harangue about "the Bother". He kept away from politics. These were dangerous times. The present conflict between Protestants and Catholics had been raging for well over a decade. Castlebrook—a predominantly

Catholic town—hadn't seen much of it, thankfully.

"... shouldn't be in our bloody country," Spider Elbows was saying. "The sooner our boys run them out the better."

Our boys sent a shiver through Manny. That strange phone call coming quick in his mind.

"Next, please," the female clerk spoke up.

"About bloody time too! See yeh about, then."

Manny nodded and sighed as his new acquaintance stomped off to sign his claim.

"Tuck yer time!" he barked at the woman. "D'yeh think I've nothin' better tae do but stand around here waitin' on *you?*"

"Uhh ... you're ... you're down for 12 o'clock in my file," Miss Rainey said nervously. "You're too early."

"I'm fuckin' here *now* and I'm signin' *now,* 'cos it suits *me.*"

"Er ... hmm ... I'd ask you ... I'd ask you, sir, to mind your language, please," the clerk said, face reddening.

She rubber-stamped the paper and slid it across for him to sign.

He scribbled on it. Threw down the pen, got up, splayed his big hands on the desk and glared down at her.

Iris Rainey shrank back, alarmed.

"Aye, and what are you gonna fuckin' *do* about *my* language, *miss?*"

Manny, taken aback, looked about the room, hoping someone would intervene. But nobody moved, not even her colleague, Mr O'Ryan. He kept his head down, pretending not to hear.

Well, Manny Bryn would not be a coward.

"Now, there's no need for that," he said, approaching Spider Elbows.

The bully swung round.

"Well, look who it is! Fatso to the rescue."

"Sh-she's only doing her j-job," Manny stammered.

But before he knew it, a fist shot out and hit him square in the jaw. He stumbled back, landing on his rear end, as the bystanders scattered like mice.

"*Leave here now, Mr Magee, before I get the police!*" he heard O'Ryan call out.

But Spider Elbows seemed totally unfazed by the threat. He leaned over Manny, who was scrabbling to right himself.

"You're gonna regret crossin' *me*, boyo," he snarled, jaw muscles flexing. "Nobody crosses Bumper Magee."

He pushed Manny back onto the floor with his boot. Stepped over him and left.

A stunned silence swamped the room.

The two clerks rushed over to help Manny to his feet. They guided him to the chair at Iris's desk.

The sheepish claimants shuffled back into line, mumbling to one another.

"Are you okay?" Iris asked, handing him a hankie. "We can call an ambulance. You're bleeding."

Manny shook his head, dazed. He wasn't even aware he was bleeding until he looked at the hankie. "Nah . . . it's nothin'. Only me nose."

O'Ryan gave him a glass of water.

"We'll report this incident to the police . . . that's if you want us to of course," he added.

Manny noted the hesitation and the hint of reluctance in his tone.

"It would be better if yeh just let it be, Manny," a voice at the back was heard to say.

They turned to see a man on crutches hobbling towards them. It was Fred Bain, the local taxi-driver.

"That Magee fella's in the IRA," he muttered, leaning in, "and if you involved the RUC yeh just might make things worse for yerself."

The two clerks nodded, fearful. There were murmurs of assent from the others. Hearing "IRA" and "RUC" in the one breath was enough to frighten the bravest of men.

Manny understood the implications.

"Aye, I suppose you're right," he said to Fred.

"Sure I'll see you later about that wee bitta business. Did yer ma mention it?"

Manny nodded.

"Sure call me later." He gestured at his injured leg. "I'm not goin' nowhere with this."

"Aye, Fred … thanks now."

Fred hobbled back to his place in the queue.

The atmosphere returned to normal.

David O'Ryan went again to his post. Iris sat down and found Manny's card in the index box. She stamped it and passed it over. Her hands were shaking.

"Thank you for doing that," she said timidly.

Up close, Manny saw that she had bad acne scars on her cheeks, but her hazel eyes were kind and she had a nice smile.

"That's all right," he said sheepishly. "I don't like bullies … that's all."

He found that his own hand was trembling as he signed his name.

"Thank you, Manus," she said. "See you the next time then."

"Maybe … aye, maybe." He was embarrassed, but delighted that she'd used his first name. He couldn't meet her gaze.

"You should go to the doctor. Just to check there's nothing broken, like."

"Aye … maybe. Maybe I'll do that."

She smiled weakly as he got up.

"Right, then."

He collected his cheque and made for the door, feeling unsteady. What had he let himself in for? Would Spider Elbows be waiting for him outside? The only positive was that he'd defended Iris. Proved himself to be a man when all the rest were cowards. Hopefully his gallantry wouldn't come at a price.

But when he exited the building, he saw to his dismay that his fears were indeed justified. Across the road, in the entrance to The Mucky Mallard pub, stood his attacker. As Manny watched, Magee raised two fingers to his temple in the manner of a pointed gun.

And with that, Manny knew, with a sinking feeling, that life would never be the same again.

VIVIENNE

Back in her studio, Vivienne Dundas checked her watch. It was approaching 3 p.m. She'd been working on the lily since ten. Several studies were pinned to a corkboard by the window; the day had not been a complete waste. Now she had to leave her project because of some idler across the way spying on her.

She pushed to her feet, resentful, conscious that her every move was being tracked.

He'll know I've seen him. He'll be predicting my next move. Know I'm likely to leave because I can't stand the scrutiny.

But why should I give him the satisfaction?

Well, I'm not leaving. I'm going to find out exactly who you are and why you're spying on me.

Emboldened by the decision, she threw down the pencil, pulled on her cardigan, grabbed her backpack and marched out the door.

The Kevin Barry Arms occupied a tall Georgian house of red brick, wedged between a bank and a jeweller's shop. It struck a discordant note in the row of bland office façades, causing one to question how it had survived—thus far—the restructuring reach of the city's planners.

Vivienne had never set foot in the pub. At college, she socialized among her own kind in the student's union. Not that she'd ever want to frequent such a place as the Kevin Barry Arms. The name itself was reason enough to stay away.

Barry was a young IRA volunteer, who was hanged by the Crown forces in 1920 for being involved in the ambushing and killing of three British soldiers. He was eighteen and studying medicine at the time. After attending Sunday Mass and before sitting a medical exam in the afternoon of September 20, he and his comrades carried out the shootings.

The hostelry was consequently a stomping ground for IRA sympathizers and their ilk: the kind of people who'd tried to murder her father. The kind who believed they had a right to shoot or blow apart those who didn't support their cause for a United Ireland, free of British rule.

Politics had never interested Vivienne. Following on from the attack on her father, she could have become a diehard supporter of all things Unionist. But it was simply not in her nature to bear ill will towards anyone. That just wasn't the way she'd been raised.

There were few on the street when she stepped out. At that time, in the afternoon with lunch hour finished, workers were back behind their desks.

An empty beer can, propelled by a sudden gust, skittered across her path. No prizes for guessing where it came from. She tut-tutted, deposited it in the nearest bin and waited for a car to pass.

Outside the pub door she stood for a moment, readying herself.

"Don't do this," a small voice in her head warned. "You don't know where it might lead." But it was drowned out by her need to take control of things. She'd fought hard to get her studio. She would not be intimidated.

Bravely she straightened, took a deep breath, and pushed open the door.

When she stepped inside, the stench of booze and peat smoke was overpowering, and she imagined the pong clinging to her hair and clothes for a good while afterwards. She paused to get her bearings, eyes adjusting to the gloom. After the sunny street it was unsettling to be in such a dark, enclosed space all of a sudden. She saw to her relief that the place was deserted, save for an elderly man seated at the bar counter, his back to the door.

He hadn't heard her come in.

The area was divided into two sections: one, a glorified hallway housing the bar counter, with ten or so tall stools bolted to the floor. Tables and club chairs were set about the larger part, which was given over to the main lounge. A turf fire smouldered weakly in a large grate.

She felt her bravado wobble as she took in the plethora of Republican memorabilia adorning the walls.

Everywhere there were pictures of a young man she supposed was Kevin Barry, alongside other faces that were likely those of Republican martyrs also. The ceiling was hung about with folksy Irish kitsch: items of junk rescued from kitchens of yore, and ancient artefacts. A tricolour the size of a tablecloth was stretched across the rear wall.

It was the kind of place she didn't want to delay in for long, and not only because of its patriotic leanings.

Best to get this over with quickly.

She steeled herself and approached the sole customer, seated in the murk of his own pipe smoke.

"Excuse me, is anyone serving?"

He flinched a little. Turned his old, bald head in her direction—a turtle craning from its carapace.

"Eh … wha-what's that yer sayin'?"

"Is anyone serving … I mean: where's the barman?"

She said it a bit more loudly, because he appeared not only tipsy but deaf too.

"Went upstairs there … aye, went upstairs there, tae get a crate, so."

"Upstairs?"

"Aye. He'll be down in a wee minute."

"R-right."

She paused. "Does he … I mean, the barman … does he live up there?"

"Who, Declan? Nah, nobody lives up there … not that I know of anyway."

She heard footsteps coming down the stairs. Her nemesis was on his way….

Looking back, Vivienne knew she should have left at that point. The old codger didn't have a clue who she was and this Declan character wouldn't even know she'd been in his pub.

But she didn't leave. Hubris and a misplaced sense of entitlement held her there.

"Aye, there's him now … Declan."

Presently, a man entered carrying a crate of bottles. He crashed it down on the counter, affecting not to see her standing there.

Tall, mid-thirties, unshaven, dark hair cropped to the skull, cleft chin. He was wearing a T-shirt—which barely fitted his bulky frame—showing a raised fist entwined in barbed wire. The whole look seemed designed to intimidate. Not the type of man you'd want to meet on a dark night—or any night for that matter.

He proceeded to stack bottles from the crate onto a shelf, ignoring her completely.

Vivienne waited. It was obvious he'd seen her.

He's snubbing me on purpose to unnerve me further.

Well, she'd no intention of playing his silly game.

"Excuse me!"

He turned, a beer bottle in his hand, blinked several times and staggered back, as if seeing an apparition.

"Well, look who it is! What can I do for you, m'lady?"

"I'm not here to drink. You were spying on me from up there, weren't you?"

He didn't answer. Placed the bottle carefully on the counter and slid a cigarette from a pack. He lit up, his eyes never leaving her face. They were cruel eyes, hooded, the eyes of some swamp-dwelling creature.

Vivienne stood rigid, fear passing through her like a riptide.

Her better instincts were urging her to run, to get far away from this offensive character with his deadly eyes and gaudy T-shirt—and fast. But part of her refused to back down, not to be cowardly. She had to finish what she'd started.

"I *said* why were you spying on me?"

"Who wants to know?" He took a deep drag of the cigarette, grinning.

"You don't need to know who I am."

He chuckled to himself. Ran a hand over his chin. Shook his head. "Jaysis, the cheek of it!"

"I saw you spying on me. If you don't stop it I'll report you to the authorities."

He guffawed loudly, holding his stomach in a mock display of amusement.

"For fuck's sake, d'yeh hear that, Séamie? She'll report me to the RUC for lookin' out me own windee. That's the trouble with these bloody Prods ... think they own the place ... domineerin' bastards."

How does he know I'm Protestant?

"You don't frighten me!" Vivienne turned to go.

"Don't I? Shouldn't say things like that. I might put you to the test."

"You *don't* frighten me. Just grow up!"

But before she banged the door shut she heard something that very surely *did* frighten her.

"*Vi-vi-en-n-n-n-e*," he called after her in a creepy, singsong voice. "Be seeing you."

He knows my name. And the sound of it coming from his ugly mouth was an outrage.

On the pavement she gasped for air, near to tears. She looked up at the window of her studio and could not bring herself to return there.

The day was tainted. Nothing could be salvaged now. She'd catch a bus and go home. Let Declan the voyeur win this one.

She quickened her step in the direction of the bus-stop. Dared to glance back at the Kevin Barry Arms as she rounded the corner into Royal Avenue.

As she was dreading, he was standing there in front of the pub, watching her go.

NINE

Ellen Purboy needed not one but two sleeping pills to get herself over. She couldn't banish the image of the jewellery box from her thoughts, even though she'd hidden it in a drawer of the dressing-table. Out of sight it might be, but it was certainly not out of mind.

Now, sitting at the breakfast table, she was being tormented afresh by the sinister occurrence, which was making her question things all over again. Had someone been in? But nothing was stolen. Is the house cursed, as Nettie suggests? Well, it does have a questionable history. Still, I can't hold with the idea of it being haunted. I don't believe in such things. Never have. So if it wasn't a thief and it wasn't a ghost it has to be me and my own forgetfulness. Maybe it's a side-effect of those sleeping pills. Maybe—

Bang! Bang! Bang!

A robust rapping on the front door made her jump.

It was 7.45.

Who on earth can be calling at this hour?

Her hands were shaking as she released the locks and bolts. Tentatively she eased open the door, its security chain still in place.

A man wearing a clerical collar stood on the doorstep.

She hastily uncoupled the chain and pulled the door wide.

"Eh ... um, Father!"

"Good morning, Mrs Purboy. Father Hill. I'm pleased to make your acquaintance." He proffered a hand.

"Good ... good morning, Father," she said, a little unnerved by the tall, disquieting figure that stood before her, dark hair oiled back like some Ealing-comedy villain.

"I'm the new curate," he said, seeing her bemusement. "You were maybe expecting Father Mulcahy, but he sent me instead.... "

"Yes... but I... "

He held up a briefcase. "To do the blessing, Mrs Purboy."

"Oh, the blessing... yes, of course... of the bedroom you mean?"

"Of the *house*, yes. I hope it's not too early for you. I can come back another time if it's more convenient."

Nettie having her way. She had a good mind to send him packing at that hour, but knew she'd be considered the Devil's disciple if she spurned a priest.

"Uh... well, it's... oh, no, no, it's fine, Father. I just wasn't expecting you so early; that's all."

"I left a message on your answering machine last night. You maybe didn't hear it. Have the confessions at ten, you see, so thought I'd leave myself plenty of time, so."

"Yes, well that explains it. Sorry about that."

She stood back to admit him and got a mildewy whiff off his person. Damp closets in the parochial bedrooms obviously.

"Best not to leave these things too long, Mrs Purboy. In my estimation the sooner we get things under control the better." He was scanning the vestibule, clearly impressed. "What a grand place indeed!"

"Thank you, Father. Will you take a cup of tea before you start?"

She noted a dusting of dandruff on his black-clad shoulders and felt a stab of pity for him. Men need women to point out such things. What a lonely life he must lead!

"No, I'll save that lovely treat for after. A slice of dry toast with it, if you wouldn't mind. I like to fast before carrying out the sacred ritual. One is more alert to the unseen, you understand."

"Er... "

She suddenly felt frightened—but indignant at the same time. The blessing of her home could hardly be considered a full-scale exorcism.

What on earth has Nettie told him? That Satan himself is loose in Cedarwood?

He plonked his bag down on the sofa. "If it's not too much trouble, that is?"

"What?"

"The toast."

"No-no. No trouble at all, Father."

"That's grand, so."

He drew a purple stole from the bag and draped it about his neck.

"Your sister said your bedroom was the focus of the haunting. So we'll do in there first, so."

Now she really had to speak up.

"Oh, don't mind my sister, Father. She tends to exaggerate things. This house isn't haunted."

"No?" He seemed disappointed.

"No. I'm just having strange dreams about my deceased husband; that's all. There was really no need for Nettie to bother you. She fusses far too much I'm afraid."

"Aye … well, there's no harm in doing the blessing anyway, Mrs Purboy. First the rooms and then of you?"

"Me?!"

"You're having odd dreams, aren't you?"

"Yes, I know."

He looked at her keenly.

"But they're only dreams. The doctor said so."

"Even so. Just to be on the safe side. That's if… that's if you have no objection. The afflicted need to be willing to surrender, you see."

She smiled nervously, but could see he was deadly serious. "Yes, well, I suppose if you think it'll help … I'll-I'll show you up then, shall I?"

She climbed the stairs ahead of him, wondering what George

would make of it all, and led him down the corridor to the master bedroom.

"Another grand room, Mrs Purboy!" he exclaimed, following her in.

"Thank you, Father."

The spacious room of dusty rose and muted teals was indeed impressive: the sateen wallpaper, the four-poster bed, and a shag-pile carpet offset with chunky brass accents and lacquered effects exhibited a grandeur of near-regal status. Ellen, so used to her surroundings, rarely gave them a second thought. She imagined Father Hill was simply being gracious.

He opened the briefcase and extracted a bottle of Fairy washing-up liquid.

"We'll give it a good drenching with this, so we will."

Ellen stared at the bottle, mystified.

"I-I didn't realize we had to … er … to wash down the walls first."

"Oh, heavens, no! There's holy water in here, you see. I don't bother with the aspergillum in these situations. You can squirt it up good and high with the squeezy bottle, especially into those high corners, this being an old house. It's just my way."

"R-right. Have you … have you done many blessings, Father?"

"Oh, yes! But they're mostly for people who move into a new place. They'll have the priest round, just in case the owners before them left bad energies behind them. I prefer tackling the real hauntings, but there's not many of them about, thank God."

"I'm glad to hear it," she said, looking lovingly at her vintage floral walls, hoping the holy water wouldn't leave a stain.

"Still, negative energies can enter a house at any time … after the death of a loved one too. Especially if they didn't die in a state of grace. The blessing is a protection against all of that."

He was hinting at George's atheism as well as the history of Cedarwood, but she would not be drawn on either.

"I see."

He moved into the wide bay-window and gazed down on the courtyard, to the driveway unspooling itself amongst the cedars, dense and dark. "Aye, a grand place indeed ... a lot of history to be sure."

A beat. Then: "Is it always cold in here?"

"Cold? Yes. Well, the windows are quite tall and draughty. It *is* an old house after all."

"Ah, so.... Not to worry. Logical explanations are the first line of defence in these cases."

She could have challenged him, but didn't want to push on that door, lest a bundle of his lurid experiences fighting the unseen should tumble forth. There was enough to worry about without the priest adding to her burdens.

"Well, I'll leave you to it, Father. You don't need me at present, do you?"

"No-no, you're grand. I'll say a prayer of protection over you to wrap things up at the end, so."

"That's fine." She made to go.

"I'll bless the other rooms up here too, if that's all right?"

"Is it necessary? I really only use *this* room."

He cast her a grim glance. "Just to be on the safe side, Mrs Purboy. Don't worry. I'll find my own way around."

"If you're sure?"

She went back down the stairs, feeling unsettled. After all, he was a complete stranger and she'd just given him access to her private space.

She went through to the kitchen to prepare the tea.

Can Nettie be right after all? Perhaps this place has always been haunted. I simply didn't notice because I never had to be on my own. Looking at it that way, perhaps getting a lodger in would be a good thing.

She studied her bruised wrist as she filled the kettle. Well, I won't be showing Father Hill *that*. Heaven knows what ungodly explanation he'd put forward. The conundrum of the jewellery box she'd also be keeping to herself.

That prayer of protection he promised will hopefully be enough to protect me.

But from *what* she wasn't quite sure.

TEN

August 1985, and in Ireland statues of the Virgin Mary were on the move. Not just moving. They were spinning, speaking, bleeding, weeping and even levitating in several parts of the country.

Ma Bryn, sitting in the Shearlock Combs salon, a cap of twenty-five Velcro rollers pinned to her scalp—Sunshine rinse aglow—was leafing through the *Mid-Ulster Vindicator* when her eye fell on an article reporting one such phenomenon.

> *A mile to the south of the Cistercian Monastery of Mount Melleray stands the grotto of the Virgin Mary. It is set in one of the finest areas of natural beauty in County Waterford, on a hillside amid trees and brambles with a lovely little stream emanating from a spring on the grotto floor.*
>
> *A group of young lads were there one day, on their way back from hurling practice. One of them, Tom, heard the voice of Our Lord speaking to him and soon after that, the voice of the Virgin herself. She moved her hands and said to the boys: "Pray for the people of Ireland afore they lose their souls."*

Tilda looked up from the page at her amazed reflection.

Heavens above!

The whirr of hairdryers and babbling voices were giving way to some strangely recognizable signs—a ringing in her right ear, a tingling sensation on the top of her head. And out of the corner of her eye the familiar blue flash that would suddenly become an orb, and bob about under her very nose.

Tilda was elated.

Redwing Maeve, her Celtic spirit guide, midwife to the fairies and guardian angels, was about to come through.

She glanced about quickly, hoping no one would interrupt. To her surprise, saw the terribly grand Mrs Purboy coming through the door. There was a sadness clinging to her like the funeral shroud itself. Only to be expected with the husband took so sudden. But no time for that now, for here was Maeve whispering to her—

"Good fortune shines. Time is now. Many souls need your guidance."

Tilda heard the words clearly in her right ear.

Granted, similar platitudes had been channelled through her mother from time to time, especially when the day's takings were down and the gin bottle empty, but Tilda understood that the words had a definite import on this occasion. Otherwise why would Redwing Maeve come through in such a humdrum place as the Shearlock Combs, and not wait till her candlelit meditation ritual before nightfall, when her auric field was at its most receptive and the work of the day was done?

All at once the bouncing orb slowed, rose above her head, spun three times then promptly disappeared.

The tingling in her forehead ceased.

Goodness gracious me!

Tilda blinked at her reflection. She was back in the real world once more. The newspaper was still in her lap and she looked again at the picture of the Ballinspittle Virgin—a circle of electric light bulbs crowning her head.

That's it! That's why Redwing Maeve came through and made that halo over me. She wants me to connect with the Blessed Mother herself.

Imagine that! Here she is talking to complete strangers down in Cork, of all places; people with no psychic ability at all. And here's me with a direct line to the Other World. Me spirit guide's pointing me in that direction. I need to get to the nearest shrine and plug meself into the energy source as soon as possible.

"I'll go to St Timmy's right away!" she exclaimed a little too loudly to the mirror, patting her rollers. "Get Manny to run me—"

"Are you all right, Tilda?" a voice cut in. Elish the stylist was looking at her queerly.

The newspaper slipped from her grasp. Elish caught it.

"Oh, goodness gracious, Elish! I was miles away there. Here, did yeh know the Virgin Mary was moving down south, did yeh?"

"The north not good enough for her then? I'd move meself if I had the dough."

"Och, away with yeh, Elish!"

Elish peered at the page. "Ah, *that*. I wouldn't believe a word of it. Attention-seekers the lot of them. When the one says they saw something they all pile in."

"All the same, they wouldn't be reportin' it in the paper if there was nothing to it." Tilda—given her background in all things spiritual—felt she had the edge in this conversation.

"Aye, I s'ppose yer right." Elish pulled a trolley close and unpinned one of the rollers. "These are about ready too. Doing anything nice this evening then?"

"Just thought I'd treat meself, Elish... wanna be nice for me customers, like, 'cos I've decided to start up me reading again."

"Get away!"

"Aye, had a dream about me mother dancing round her crystal ball and knew it was a sign. Then at me breakfast this mornin' if three crows didn't land on me cherry bush right outside me windee."

"What have three crows got to do with anything?"

"Well, three crows means that big changes is coming... a rebirth if yeh like. Lost the way of meself when Manny came along. When he was a nipper at school they'd tease him, saying his granny was a witch and that sort of thing. You know what youngsters is like... so didn't wanna upset him. But sure that's all by the by now and he's big enough to understand the gift God give me and wants me to use. That's why when I saw that bit about the movin' statue I thought to meself: Me time's come, so it has."

"You'd clean up in here," Elish said, throwing a glance over her shoulder. "My lot are always talking about this and that fortune teller. Steady running to them to hear about boys. How is Manny anyway? Has he got a nice girl himself yet?"

"Not yet, Elish. But I see a nice girl for him. I spread the cards and look in the ball for him but he doesn't know… there's a bright future ahead for my Manny. You mark my words. Sure he'd be a gift for any woman."

Elish thought of the overweight, mollycoddled—now jobless—Manny and wondered how he could possibly be an attractive prospect in the marriage stakes. But she reckoned that Ma Bryn, and her ma before her, had spent so much of their lives imaging bright futures for their clients that they'd come to actually believe in one themselves.

She envied Tilda in many ways. There she was: living in a run-down cottage with few creature comforts and not much money, but she brimmed with optimism and good cheer wherever she went. There was always something better on the horizon. Tilda Bryn was without doubt the cheeriest customer to come through her door.

"Now, how's that?" she asked, holding up a hand-mirror so Tilda could see the back of her head.

"God, it's lovely, Elish! You've got such good hands on yeh. And the colour's just right, so it is."

In the mirror Tilda caught sight of Mrs Purboy now having her hair trimmed. She had the distinct feeling the grand widow was an important link in the cosmic chain that had fired off only moments ago.

"Isn't that Mrs Purboy?" she whispered. "Didn't think she came in here."

"Aye, that's her… She doesn't come in often, mind you. I think

Mane Obsession in Killoran is her regular salon."

Elish helped Tilda out of her gown. "Why d'you ask?"

"Och, just wundered, like."

"That's £5.50 all told, when you're ready."

Tilda rummaged in her handbag, leaned in as she passed over the money. "She's still grievin' something terrible 'cos I see her ora's a wee bit muddy."

"Her what—"

A hairdryer had shut off suddenly, plunging the room into silence.

"Right-ye-be," Tilda chirped, feeling a little embarrassed.

On her way to the door she beamed and nodded at Mrs Purboy, paving the way for a possible reading further down the line.

The stranger acknowledged her kindness with a wan smile.

God help the cretur, but she's not in the best place right now. I'll remember her in me meditation tonight. I wouldn't like to say anything to her about a readin' now. Would be a bit forward, but I have the feeling the chance will come very soon.

With that, Ma Bryn left the salon, marvelling at how a simple trip to the Shearlock Combs salon could yield such unexpected bounty from the spirit world.

ELEVEN

His first day as caretaker taxi-driver and Manny Bryn was nervous. Venturing into a world where he'd have to communicate with strangers would not be easy. He worried about what he was going to say, or not say, what people might think of him. And latterly—perhaps most importantly—whether he could avoid damage to Fred Bain's 1979 Austin Maxi, with its walnut-veneer dashboard and single rear fog-light housed in copper plating, a feature Fred was particularly proud of.

"Watch when you're reversing her," Fred had stressed the previous evening, leaning on crutches, cigarette smouldering at the corner of his gob as he delivered a meandering monologue, and the motor into Manny's care. "I wouldn't want her smashed, 'cos it'd be expensive to replace her. But if yeh did smash her yeh'd have to replace her yerself. I'd be taking it outta yer tab, so. Aye, any damage a-tall to me motor would be coming outta yer tab."

Fred was a straight talker. With him there was no skulking around corners of civility.

"R-right," Manny said, unsettled, never having considered the possibility of crashing. But now that the seed had been sown he'd be sure to water it every time he got behind the wheel.

Fred pulled open a rear door and pointed with one of the crutches.

"See that back seat? That's where everybody sits. Nobody in the front, even if they wanna. Drunk boys have a habit of grabbin' a holt of the wheel when they're out of it. Don't know where they are, bejaysus, and think they're in their own bloody car. Could put a body off the road, so don't say I didn't warn yeh, like."

"Nah, Fred, I won't let that happen," Manny assured him, heart thumping, palms sweating. Not only had he to be careful of the fog-light and drunks but he knew by Fred's frowning and deep sighing there was more coming.

"Aye, good ... now, another wee thing about that back seat ... "

He threw down the fag-end and crushed it with his plaster-cast foot, at which point his mangy mutt slunk over to nose it.

"Away-a-that, Andy-Joe," he growled and, to the relief of Manny —a cynophobe all his life—the dog slouched off again.

"Now see that cover? It's the latest 'Marle' fabric. Me last Maxi had that bloody basketweave leatherette rubbish, which was the divil tae clean, even if it was plastic. So I keep plastic sheetin' in the boot. You'd needa be puttin' that down of a Friday and Sa'rday night, just to be on the safe side. For the Doody sisters too, but it only happened the once with them, but better to be on the safe side, like."

"Uh, eh ... I-I don't get you, Fred?"

"Well, when them boys get a skinful then you run the risk of them throwin' up or pissin' theirselves. That bitta plastic saves my seat. Aisier to clean, if you get me drift, Manny."

He slammed the door with the crutch. "Watch that Johnny McFaul 'specially. He's drinkin' his way through a farm-a land left him by his oul' Uncle Mick-Paddy-Joe last month, and pissin' it down the Mallard toilet of a weekend. He threw up over me, begod, when he was leaning over paying me last Friday night. But that's the way o' taxi-driving, Manny. Yeh meet all sorts."

Fred had then furnished him with a list of regulars who had fixed timetables. In between times, he was to sit in the village square and be available. Mornings would be the busiest period, with a slackening off in the afternoon before things picked up again between six and nine. He could knock off then, but was warned that at weekends he'd be driving through the early hours of Friday and Saturday, when the punters let their hair down in the two hostelries in town.

Now Manny, on his way to collect his first fare—pensioner sisters Nan and Brigid Doody, who lived out in the sticks—was running a loop of all Fred's dire pronouncements, until finally he spotted the tiny byroad that would lead him to their home.

It took him a while to navigate the bumpy lane, remembering another of Fred's warnings: "Take it aisey on that Doody lane. Don't want me suspension wrecked."

Finally the whitewashed cottage hove into view, its bright red roof stark against a cloudless blue sky.

Red for danger.

Manny swallowed down a lump of panic as he drove slowly into the yard. He proceeded to make an orderly three-point turn, carefully avoiding a rooster poised on an old tractor tyre, one foot raised in warning. Well, the rooster could hardly do much damage. Not unless he jumped onto the bonnet and scratched the paintwork.

Another thing to worry about.

He sighed, cut the engine and sounded the horn.

Nothing stirred.

He scanned the front of the house and waited. And waited; gave the horn another quick poke.

Still nothing.

A couple of cats eyed him suspiciously from atop a woodpile, heads tilted in steady scrutiny. He didn't mind cats; his ma used to have one. Dogs were another matter—a Jack Russell terrier had taken a lump out of his thigh when he was six, and since then all dogs, never mind how small, scared the hell out of him. He hoped and prayed there weren't any about, if indeed he did have to exit the car. And it was looking like he might have to.

Maybe he was at the wrong house. He checked Fred's list again. Alongside Nan and Brigid's names was a note:

Hard of hearing. Don't sound horn.

Well, that explained things.

He saw that the rooster was now at a safe distance, heaved himself out of the car, picked his way over some poultry poo and knocked loudly on the door.

"Hello there! It's yer taxi."

After a short wait the door was pulled open a fraction and a stern-faced old lady peered at him.

"You're not Fred," she accused. "Gettaway tae blazes or I'll call the polis!"

She banged the door shut.

Manny hadn't expected that.

"It's all right!" he shouted through the letterbox. "I'm Manny. I'm filling in for Fred for he's broke the leg. Covering for him till he's back on his feet, so I am."

The door was inched open again.

"Who's that, Nan?" another voice called out.

Presently a second withered face appeared, the mirror image of the first one.

They must be twins. He'd never seen twins that old. They looked like a pair of wizened dolls. Maybe most twins died before they got to eighty and these two were a rarity, like the ones he'd sometimes see in the *Guinness Book of Records*, with unpronounceable names, from places like Okinawa or Kathmandu.

"Sez he's the taxi, Brigid. Fred's broke the leg."

"God savus! Are you gonna take us then? What leg did Fred break?"

Manny thought it an odd question.

"The right one… I think. Aye, I'll wait in the car. Are yins ready, are yins?"

"And what's *your* name?"

"Manny Bryn. You can ring Fred if yeh wanna check."

"Don't have no phone!" Nan snapped, seemingly the sharper of the two.

Manny returned to the car and opened the rear doors.

A good five minutes passed.

Finally the pair emerged, dressed in matching blue coats and pull-down hats. Each carried a black handbag and a walking stick.

"Can I help yins in?" Manny asked, because he thought that might be the protocol with elderly folk.

Nan rounded on him, getting in first. "We're not invalids!"

"Och, don't mind her," Brigid whispered. "She's always a bit crabbit in the mornings."

With the pair finally installed, he shut the doors and got behind the wheel. Adjusted the rear-view mirror.

"It's the post office first then, is it?"

"Aye, for the pension," Brigid said, giving him an encouraging little smile. "And then—"

"Then Barney's for the groceries," Nan cut in. "After that we needa call on Mrs Barkley for our knittin' patterns and buttons."

"Righty-o."

He sighed inwardly. No doubt Nan Doody would be telling Fred exactly what she thought of him, and it would be far from positive.

He threw the car in gear and eased out of the yard.

"And don't drive fast. I've got the rumortism. Fred never drives fast. Forty miles an hour is what he does."

"No bother."

As Manny turned onto the main road he suddenly remembered something: what Fred had said about a roll of plastic sheeting and the Doody sisters. He'd been afraid to query him further, but kind of knew what Fred was getting at.

He eyed them in the mirror once more, anxious now. They had their heads turned, each looking out of a window, lost in her own little world. No way was he going to stop the car and ask them to move. But he had an idea. He'd broach the subject casually.

"Forgot tae say. D'yins need the toilet? 'Cos I can turn back, so I can."

"What sort-a durty question's that tae ask us, laddie?"

"Now, Nan, the lad's only being polite."

"Polite, indeed! You call that polite, do yeh?"

"Well, I just thought I'd ask, 'cos it's a bit of a journey to the town, like." At which point Manny had a brainwave. "Aye, Fred said to make sure and ask yins."

"Fred never ast us a durty thing like that. The cheek of you! We'll be havin' a word with him about you when he comes back."

"We're all right, Manny," Brigid assured him. "Just you drive on and don't worry about us."

"Right… right yeh be."

He was thankful the pair couldn't see his flushed face.

He shifted up a gear and continued on, thinking of the red-for-danger roof and hoping his future passengers wouldn't be as abrasive and demanding as Nan bloody Doody.

TWELVE

"*Ellll-en!*"

In her dream she heard his voice but did not awaken.

The clock, ticking quietly beside her, read 11.45. The rain, which had been relentless, was tapping faintly against the windowpanes, gradually losing its strength.

It was almost pitch-black in the bedroom. Drapes pulled resolutely against the night. The way she liked it.

Ellen, never a good sleeper, needed all the help she could muster to "get over".

She'd retired earlier than usual. The rain-sodden day had depressed her, swathing her in a mantle of misery she felt powerless to shift. Better to delete her depression with a couple of sleeping pills and hope for better in the morning.

So far, Father Hill's blessing seemed to be working, so she felt more assured. No disturbing dreams for three whole nights. No frantic awakenings in the early hours. Perhaps she was getting her sanity back at last.

Perhaps?

"*Ellll-en.*" The voice, again.

Concern begins to stir, stretch, raise her slowly out of the dark depths of slumber.

"George," she mumbled, reaching out to what had always been his side of the bed, her hand questing into the soulless emptiness of cold linen.

"*Ellll-en! Ellll-en!*"

Her eyes snapped open.

She sprang up and fumbled for the light switch. Gazed wildly about the room.

"G-George . . . is-is . . . that you?"

Was this another "dream within a dream"?

But . . . she *was* wide awake.

The room was cold. Colder than usual.

She recalled Father Hill's query: "Is it always cold in here?"

Maybe he'd sensed something. Something . . . *sinister* after all.

She thought she heard a downstairs door bang shut. She raised herself on the pillows, listening hard. She *had* locked all the doors. The windows were locked as well.

Don't be silly! There's no one in the house. You have to stop this!

Bracing herself, she slipped quietly out of bed, tiptoed to the door to make sure she'd secured it, then moved to the window and peeped through the drapes.

All was darkness, save for the amber glow of a lamp out on the drive, revealing the faintly falling rain.

Oh dear, why did nothing like this happen when George was alive? I always felt safe. Things like this never happened. Not once.

Is he giving me a warning from the Spirit World? Is that why I woke up?

Oh, dear God!

She was beginning to unravel again: thoughts spiralling unchecked. An intruder! Is he warning me of an intruder?

Would-be burglars know I'm on my own now. Think I'm fair game. A woman on her own is easy prey. They see a grand house and know there must be valuables in it.

BANG! THUMP! BANG!

What was that?

The office! It was coming from the office.

Someone was in the office.

The heart-stopping realization left her no choice.

She reached for the phone and dialled 999.

. . .

Before long the police arrived. There were two of them. Only one got out of the car. She remained at the bedroom window to make sure, then flew downstairs at the sound of the bell.

When she pulled open the door and saw an RUC officer standing there she felt foolish. The police had enough to do hunting down terrorists without *her* bothering them.

"Er, thank you... thank you for coming," she said.

The officer nodded. "Mrs Purboy. I'm Constable Jones."

He gave her the once-over. "You think you might have an intruder then?"

Conscious of her rumpled appearance, she shifted uneasily and gathered the nightgown more tightly about her.

"Er... yes, yes, down there in the office," she said, pointing. "I-I heard a loud noise when... when I was asleep, you see. It woke me up."

"Right, but a burglar would hardly make loud noises."

He was dismissing her as just another silly woman frightened of the dark. His eyes, shaded by his peaked cap, were disconcerting.

He stepped inside, bringing the odour of the damp night with him.

Meekly, she followed him down the corridor, feeling like a chastened schoolgirl, conscious of his holstered gun and the rasping heft of his heavy uniform.

"Nothing here, Mrs Purboy," he said, after entering the office. He crossed to the outer door. "You forgot to lock this one. My guess is it banged in the wind."

"But it's *always* locked! I've no need to enter from outside, having this inner door."

He scanned the untidy room, eyebrows raised.

"Yes, I know. It's a bit of a mess at the moment. I... I'm trying to reorganize things."

"Well, did you have anyone in? A cleaner maybe, who forgot to lock it?"

"No … I'm clearing the place up myself."

He shrugged. "Human error then. We're all forgetful at times, Mrs Purboy."

She could see he was anxious to get going.

"Yes … yes. Maybe so."

"You could always have a security light fitted," he said on the doorstep, "or get yourself a guard dog."

She'd never thought of that.

"Yes … I'll-I'll think about that, Constable."

"You live on your own I take it?"

"Yes … my husband … he passed away recently."

"Sorry to hear that." He looked up at the house. "Well, I'd strongly advise one or the other. It's quite a place you've got here … for your peace of mind. Just to be on the safe side."

Just to be on the safe side.

It was the second time she'd heard the phrase. Father Hill had said the same thing, even if it was in an altogether stranger context.

After the constable left she returned to the office to check the door. Turned the key to make sure.

She didn't quite trust the "wind blew it open" theory offered by the cop. And she wasn't losing her mind. No one had been in there apart from her.

As she was trying the door-handle something caught her eye: on the floor, close by the jamb. She bent down and retrieved an empty bottle of washing-up liquid. How on earth did *that* get there?

Then she remembered.

Father Hill!

Of course! He'd blessed the office. It was the last place he'd treated. He'd neglected to lock the door.

But why would he have opened it?

By mistake?

Maybe he thought it led into another room.

Reconciled, she climbed the stairs, beaten back by fear—but trying desperately to remain in control.

In the morning I'll act on what the constable suggested and see about getting a security light fitted.

Just to be on the safe side.

THIRTEEN

"Come on, son, get up! It's nearly eight and you promised tae drop me off at the church this morning."

Manny roused himself from slumber, to see his ma standing over him, in a gaudy dress and matching bandana.

He rubbed the sleep out of his eyes. Levered himself up on his elbows. Had she said *church?* And could it be rising time already?

"Uhh . . . but yeh hardly ever go to the church, Ma."

"D'yeh not mind what I tolt yeh last night, son?"

He threw back the bedcovers and sat up, yawning.

"Nah. What was that?" He'd had a few beers after his ma went to bed so his recall was hazy.

"Och, Manny, about the moving statues down in Cork! I'm goin' to the shrine at St Timmy's for tae see if I can connect. Do you not mind what I tolt yeh about Redwing Maeve in the hairdressers? And then last night in me trance if she didn't come again! So now I know I'm being guided."

Manny didn't like the sound of that. The last time his ma talked about her spirit guide Dr Flynn put her on nerve tablets.

The time before that he was fourteen, and was parcelled off to live with his Aunt Joyce for a couple of months until she recovered. The aunt made him do so many prayer-filled genuflections in front of a picture of Archangel Michael "for tae make the Divil leave yer sick ma's head" that he ended up with a sore knee, which carried some stiffness still.

Tilda moved towards the door, excitement rising, bracelets jangling in joyful song.

"Come on, quick! I've got your breakfast all ready, son. Wanna get there afore them priests come to say Mass."

So St Timothy's church in Castlebrook would be his first fare of the day. Not that he'd be charging his ma. Fred Bain understood that he needed to run his ma places, so long as the places weren't too far outside the perimeters of Castlebrook.

Half an hour later, having dropped her off, Manny cruised back into town and parked on the square. He'd pick her up in an hour's time and, since there were no bookings scheduled, he maybe could take a wee nap while the going was good.

He eyed the two-way radio on the dashboard—the one Fred managed from his home—and hoped it wouldn't squawk into life anytime soon.

There was not much activity in the town at that hour: a couple of delivery vans off-loading stuff and a truck with beer kegs idling outside the Mucky Mallard.

He shut his eyes and settled down, trying not to think too much about his ma and what she was getting up to. Hopefully nothing would happen at the shrine and she'd forget all about the moving-statue business. He couldn't dissuade her from taking up her readings again though, but as long as she did them from home and didn't drag him out to Portaluce to catch the tourists, he could maybe live with it.

The Hemley Dormouse caravan that once belonged to his grandma was still there on the promenade in Portaluce, rusting quietly in the salt-sea air. Sometimes he'd spend the odd night or two in it when the weather was good with old schoolfriend Mickey Mullan. Mickey was a plasterer, who picked up casual trade wherever he found it. Often he was down south, skimming the walls of social-housing projects, but occasionally he'd show up in the Mallard and they'd head to the caravan for a booze-up, and reminisce there into the wee small hours.

VROOM! VROOM!

Manny stirred himself at the sound of the beer lorry roaring off.

Through the window of his former workplace, Baked-4-You, he could just make out the big red face of JM Cooney. He was swivelling about, barking orders and insults. Manny was glad he was no longer on the receiving end.

Barney drew up in his van and proceeded to unlock the security shutters of the supermarket.

And then ...

Manny crouched further down in the seat at the sight of Nettie Buckley; a nosy parker who spent her time buzzing about like a bee, stinging everyone she got the chance to light on.

Hopefully she wouldn't notice him.

But nothing evaded her attention, and next thing, her annoying face and probing little eyes were peering down upon him.

"Manny Bryn!" she called out, rapping the glass. "I *thought* it was you."

With a heavy heart, he rolled down the window.

"Aye. Mornin', Mrs Buckley."

"How's your mother?"

"All right ... keepin' the best, so she is."

"Thought I saw her kneeling at the shrine when I was coming past in me car there now. A strange sight indeed, 'cos she's not much of a churchgoer, as far as I can see."

Manny didn't know how to respond to that.

"Um ... well, she goes ... goes sometimes, aye." Then a thought struck him. "She's ... she's doin' a novena, so she is. Started it today."

"And what novena would that be now?"

Manny, caught on the hop, wavered.

"One tae ... one tae Padre Pio I think."

She peered at him more closely. "There's no such novena in the ecumenical calendar in July. And *I* should know."

He could feel his face reddening to match JM Cooney's.

"I dunno… must be another one then."

Mrs Buckley tut-tutted and checked her watch.

"It's half-past eight in the morning!" She clasped the window edge in earnest. "I hope she's all right?"

"Aye, no worries."

Because she worked in the pharmacy the oul' biddy pretty much knew everything about his ma's medical history. He just wished she'd go away and mind her own business, but he could hardly tell her that.

"Nah, nothin' wrong with Ma, Mrs Buckley. Don't you be worrying about her. Leave that to me."

"So long as she's not taking bad with her nerves." She eyed him suspiciously and straightened herself. "That's all right then. How's the taxi-driving going anyway? Fred'll be out a while with the leg."

As though at the mention of his name, and much to Manny's relief, Fred's two-way radio squawked into life on the dashboard.

"Right yeh be, Mrs Buckley. That'll be him now."

He made a grab for the receiver, grateful, as the oul' buzzard took off in search of another poor soul to annoy.

FOURTEEN

Within a few days of the police visit, Ellen Purboy had the security light fitted and the office space cleared. The constable's words had spurred her on to take action and get some order back into her situation.

After all, the office wouldn't tidy itself. So she threw herself fully into the task, discovering that the distraction was indeed good for her.

Each night before retiring, she made sure all doors were firmly locked and, thus assured, would collapse into bed and drift off, thinking about what she needed to buy to make the bedsit as appealing as possible.

The brooding about George, the mystery of the jewellery box, and the dread of that eerie voice calling her name were temporarily subsumed by more important demands: deliverymen and decorators to be scheduled, furniture ordered, the kitchen updated with fresh utensils and crockery.

She'd invested in a new bed—believing the one her mother died in hardly appropriate for her prospective tenant. There was also a new sofa with matching armchairs and a nest of occasional tables, to add a modern touch.

She sat in the living-room as the removal men dismantled the old divan. They would get rid of it before installing the new one. That was another godsend—one thing less to worry about.

The only problem left facing her was the disposal of George's papers.

With the clearing of the office, the boxes containing them had simply migrated to the living-room. She didn't have the heart to dispose of them. Like his closet upstairs, they were her only tangible, physical link to him. How could she dispose of a whole way of life—and so excise his very existence—so soon?

Tears filled Ellen's eyes as she gazed across at the stack of boxes. He'd worked so hard to give her a good life. She'd wanted for nothing materially, and the evidence of his long days of toil preserved in those boxes was a testament to that.

Where was he now? Was he alive in spirit? If the dreams had any substance then surely he was.

Oh dear, perhaps if I'd stuck up more for my Christian beliefs I wouldn't even need to ask such questions now. Wouldn't feel such guilt.

George had been raised an Anglican. His father's dearest wish: that his only son follow him into the ministry and become a vicar.

But his son had other plans. He wanted to be a man of the world and lead his own life, unencumbered. His childhood had never been his, he claimed—waifs and strays drifting in and out of the house at all hours, demanding his father's attention. "How could that be fair, Ellen? He played father to the whole parish and forgot about *me*. Then he expected me to follow in *his* footsteps." And she'd see his face tighten at the unfairness of it all.

No, God and religiosity were not for him. Therefore he chose a totally different path. He studied economics at university and became a banker, securing the position of manager at a relatively young age.

She had the feeling that marrying a Catholic was another victory over his unceasingly single-minded father: taunting him in a way. But the Reverend Purboy, tactful and kind to a fault, never wavered. He accepted Ellen without reservation, his sole stipulation being that he conduct the marriage ceremony. George could hardly deny him that?

With her husband's resistance to all things religious she soon fell into step with his ways, attending Mass only occasionally, to keep the priest and her own family happy.

But her greatest regret during those twenty-three years of marriage was surely that they were barren years. A son or a daughter would be so comforting now: a bulwark against the horrendous tide of despair and isolation engulfing her.

George had never wanted children. He'd overruled her on that too and Ellen never felt courageous enough to take a stand.

"I'm not cut out for fatherhood," he'd said early on in their relationship. "Just so you know, Ellen." And she'd gone along with it, hoping he'd have a change of heart once they'd married. But every time she tried to raise the subject he simply did not want to know.

"With my workload it would be unfair. I have no time to be a father. Truly."

"But I have all the time in the world to be a mother."

"Well, if you feel that strongly about it, Ellen, why did you marry me in the first place? I told you from the outset my feelings on the subject."

The years passed, and with their passing her dreams of motherhood faded. There would be no children.

There was some consolation in Nettie's two boys. At least little Jack and Peter—all grown up and flown the coop now—filled the yawning gap to some small degree. She doted on the pair, and Nettie was only too happy to hand over the mothering while she went out to work.

Oh, how she would have loved a little boy of her own! They were more independent and fearless than girls: little warriors who knew their own minds and could take their places in the world, undaunted.

She smiled now at the memory of her nephews and got up. Went over to the row of boxes and opened one. It was full of correspondence: business letters. She dug down and lifted out a handful.

They glided to the floor like so many leaves.

A few were from their solicitor: Fintan Kavanagh.

The spectre of the will raised itself again. Fintan had sent her a letter to call and arrange an appointment, but she simply could not bring herself to do it. Hearing George's last will and testament read out would conclusively mean he was gone.

She couldn't face that. Not yet.

Everything was hers anyway. George had assured her of that. So what difference would it make?

There was one of the solicitor's letters that hadn't been opened. It piqued her interest because it was dated November 25th of the previous year. Not so many weeks after he'd received the devastating news about his illness.

She was about to open it when one of the removal men put his head around the door.

"All done," he said. "This was in one of the drawers of the old divan." He was holding out an ornate little casket, the size of a jewellery box.

She'd never seen it before.

"Erm … th-thank you," she said, taking it from him with a mix of surprise and apprehension.

"Might be a fortune in there," the man joked.

She smiled.

"Well, we'll be off then." He doffed his cap.

"Thank you," she said again, following him to the front door and shutting it behind him.

She bore the box into the drawing-room to take a better look.

It was quite pretty, the glossy wood held together with brass trim and secured with a sturdy little padlock.

There was something inside: or, rather, several things. When she turned it over there was the distinct clink-clank of objects hitting together.

Her mother never owned such a thing because Ellen would

definitely have come across it before now.

She sat down on the sofa and placed the box carefully on the coffee table alongside the letter.

It had to be George's. He was the only one who used the office. Why had he concealed it? Could it be a Pandora's box?

The very thought set her nerves on edge, causing a wobble on the tightrope of her resolve.

What might I unleash if I open it?

Best not to. Not now. I can't afford to be thrown off course when I've come so far.

With that, she picked up both the casket and the letter and set them on the sideboard, out of sight.

There were more pressing things to attend to.

I'll call the newspaper right now and place the advertisement for the bedsit. All is ready so there's no excuse.

This is *my* life now, and I must take risks, take chances for the sake of my sanity.

She went into the hallway.

Clack-clack-thump!

She spun round sharply, gripping the receiver like a weapon.

One of the framed photos from the far wall was lying face down on the floor.

Unnerved, she turned it over.

It was her *wedding photo.*

To her dismay, she saw that the glass had cracked—all the way across the faces of the happy couple they once had been.

FIFTEEN

Ma Bryn had visited the shrine at St Timothy's three times, but the Virgin hadn't stirred; the Holy Mother's placid smile and dreamy blue gaze remained steadfastly fixed in their plaster mien, no matter how much imploring or pleading on Tilda's part.

It was hardly fair. Here she was: getting up at seven to avoid the parish priest, and having Manny run her to the shrine on his way to work, so she could snatch this private time to make her psychic connection. And nothing was happening; not so much as a nod or a wink.

There had to be another way.

Following on from the third fruitless attempt, she decided to be more earnest during that evening's ritual with Redwing Maeve.

She conducted this observance in the confines of her bedroom before retiring. That was the best time of day. Chores done. Ablutions over. Manny asleep. Prayers said.

Tilda made a point of praying for everyone she knew at the close of each day, even for those who hadn't been so nice to her on account of her psychic gifts. They included Nettie Buckley, who thought she was the Devil incarnate. Miss Curl, the librarian, who considered her a heathen. Barney the grocer, who thought she simply needed a husband "tae take yer mind off all that tomfoolery." And Father Mulcahy, who felt she was one slice short of a loaf.

But Ma Bryn's simple motto was "Judge not, lest ye be judged," and this blessed attitude, cultivated at her mother's knee, enabled her to forgive her detractors, and sail through the rough times as buoyant and bouncy as a brace of cluster balloons, no matter what.

As would befit a soothsayer, the bedroom was a repository of all things mystical and other-worldly: a place where religious iconography clashed with New Age paraphernalia, sprawling and spilling out in a gaudy mishmash, which somehow worked.

Ma Bryn took up position on her mother's "inspiration cushion"—a large velvet affair appliqued with starbursts—and settled herself in front of her altar: a collapsible card table draped with a silver cloth set with two candles, an incense burner, a smoky quartz crystal and a snow globe.

She joined her hands and began the ritual.

First: the globe needed a good shake to get things going.

She gazed, entranced, as the snowflakes swirled and twirled in their little glass prison before setting it back between the lighted candles. When the snow fragments settled, her mind would clear and images from the etheric realms would flow into her crown chakra.

Tilda shut her eyes, slowed her breathing and waited.

By and by three images revealed themselves, one after the other: a shelf of books, a tiny lamb and a circle of glowing light bulbs.

She waited some more and, when nothing came, picked up the snow globe and went through the ritual a second time.

Again the same three objects floated into view, going round and round in her mind's eye like toy animals on a kid's carousel.

But wait! There was an image of Manny too. Looking sad, a great black cloud hovering above him.

Oh, dear, what can *that* mean? I hope he isn't in trouble and not letting on. I'll have to have a word with him.

She said a rapid prayer to dispel the vision, and with that it disappeared. Regarding the other revelations, she'd just have to work with what she'd been given: the shelf of books, the little lamb and the circle of light bulbs.

They were connected in some way.

Well, the books could mean a library, and the bulbs were

definitely the halo around Our Lady's head. The wee lamb she couldn't figure out, but it would come.

She wrote down the messages and studied them. Trying to find the links. Then it occurred to her: she needed to read up more on the stories coming out of County Cork and the like, where the phenomena were occurring. Maybe there were special prayers a body had to recite to get the Virgin moving.

The library would be the place. That's why she'd been shown the shelf of books. There would be newspapers with stories that might give her some more clues.

Content with the results of the meditation, she gave thanks to Redwing Maeve for the fascinating vision, extinguished the candles, said another prayer, expressed gratitude for a productive day, called on the angels for protection, and fell into bed with a clear conscience and a happy heart.

The following morning she had a word with Manny, but he assured her over his Ulster fry that all was fine.

"Well, you just be careful, son! You don't know what type of eejit might get in that taxi with yeh. They could pull a gun on yeh, given the times that's in it, and ask to be dhriv god-knows-where. It's not for nothing Redwing Maeve shows me a pitcher of you with a cloud over yer head and a face on yeh like McCrudden's sow pig."

"Ma, them things is all in yer head. I don't like it when you start talkin' like that." But even as he said it, he knew she was right. He'd walked into a mess of his own making, but she wouldn't be hearing anything about that if he could help it.

"Well, you just be careful, mind. That's all yer ma's sayin'."

He couldn't argue with that, as the face of the lunatic Magee flashed in his mind's eye, making him quiver.

VIVIENNE

Several sleepless nights followed the run-in with Declan from the Kevin Barry Arms. When Vivienne did fall asleep, troubling dreams would jerk her awake again.

At 6 a.m. she gave up. Infused with adrenaline and useless fury, she skipped breakfast and caught the bus into town, leaving a note for her mother:

Decided on an early start.
The light is better. See you at 4.
Love you. V x

At least she'd get a few hours in the studio before her "nemesis" opened the pub at eleven.

He is doing this to me; ripping into my life like a hurricane, upending everything. *He* is now having me alter my routine, throwing *my* life out of rhythm. A man I never knew existed until recently.

She really thought she was strong enough by then; that was the disappointing part. Thought all the terror was behind her. Truly believed that she'd conquered the demons let loose in her life on the Central Library steps at the end of a gun all those years ago.

But here they were again, rising up to meet her. No longer locked in the ship's hold of her mind, where she'd managed to keep them for so long. In the night they'd broken free, clambered up on deck, grabbed the wheel from her grasp, steering her way off course.

She was sitting near the back of the bus, staring out grimly at the awakening day; a gauzy sun held out the promise of a rainless morning. That was something at least. The summer of 1985 had been dreadful thus far, with weathermen predicting that it just might turn out to be "the wettest one since records began."

The bus roared down Donegall Street, braking abruptly for a red light. The backpack in her lap slipped to the floor and she bent down to retrieve it. Inside were her purse, a bottle of mineral water and a lunchbox—sandwiches her mother had prepared the night before. She knew they'd go straight in the bin the minute she entered the studio. Food was the last thing she wanted when stressed, and she *was* stressed. But her parents must never know. She was old enough to deal with these things now. Were she to mention anything about the spy, her father would have her out of the studio immediately. Could she allow this complete stranger to curtail her hard-won freedom?

Never.

Whatever lay in the future was hers to deal with.

The bus was empty save for an elderly lady in a brown hat seated at the front. Where might she be heading at this hour? Maybe she's just like me: a raging insomniac facing into the day because the night was beyond endurance. Or maybe she has a hospital appointment. At her age hospitals must figure a lot.

She let her thoughts roam through thickets of possibility—anything to keep her mind free of the little monsters sitting on both shoulders jabbering in her ear. Paying them any attention would only magnify her fears to the point where she might just scream. She couldn't afford to do that—not on public transport with the nice old lady and the unassuming driver going about their business.

The bus pulled in at a stop and a young man wearing a bright green sports top got on. She inspected his profile. Gaunt face, cheekbone jutting painfully, dark hair in a crew cut. Not pleasant she decided. She averted her gaze and fiddled with her backpack as he lurched down the aisle, aware that his eyes were upon her.

She wished she didn't draw attention to herself, but it was always there, the minute she stepped out; from men and women alike, but mostly men. Their probing eyes annoyed her.

He climbed into the seat right behind her. She tensed, hearing him shift over to the window so that he was, quite literally, breathing down her neck.

Of all the vacant seats why did he choose that one?

She was immediately on edge. Irritated.

Should she move?

Should she simply leave the bus and walk the rest of the way?

The bus stopped to let a young woman on. Vivienne was about to get up but saw that the woman had a buggy.

The driver went to her assistance and there was much manoeuvring of the stroller in the doorway. No way could she add more stress to the already harassed mother by trying to get past her. The child was already bawling like some feral creature at the sight of the driver, so she'd just have to sit it out.

Then...

A tap on her right shoulder had her whole body stiffening. She turned to face *him*.

"Is this yours?" he asked, holding up her purse.

At close quarters his eyes were pinpoints of darkness, disconcerting in their intensity. Grey, uneven teeth, a front one chipped.

She was totally thrown off guard. Didn't know what to say. Looked away.

"Saw it on the floor under your seat," he continued. "You must-a dropped it, like."

"Erm... er... "

A beat.

When the bag slid off my lap, it must have...

"Y-es, yes. It is mine," she said, taking it from him. "Thank you ... thanks very much!"

"No problem," he said.

The bus stopped again and she saw, to her dismay, the elderly lady and the young mother and baby leave. There were no other passengers waiting to board.

She was alone with *him*.

The old lady smiled up at her from the kerbside as the bus moved off. Nervous, Vivienne returned the smile.

Another tap on her shoulder.

"Wanna fag?" He was waving a pack of ten Embassy Regal.

She shook her head. "No, no thanks … I-I don't smoke."

"Didn't think you would … nice girl like you. Mind if I do?"

She shook her head again, turned back to the window, hearing the click of a lighter. Of course she minded, but could hardly object in the circumstances.

"Are you an artist?"

The question hit her like a punch. *Who the hell is this?*

Boldly she turned to face him, again.

"Yes, I am," she said evenly. "How did you know that?"

"Dunno … yeh just have that arty look about yeh."

I need to get out of here, but I can't let him see I'm afraid. There are fifty pounds in my purse and he could have stolen the lot. Perhaps he has, but he'd see me checking and that would upset him. Even though he looks shifty, he was honest. If I get off now he'll think I'm doing it on purpose. And who's to say he won't get off and follow me?

The smoke from his cigarette was wreathing her like some amorphous creature of the deep.

She felt faint. *Oh, dear God, let me out of here!*

The shops on Royal Avenue scrolled past the window as the bus headed towards the Cathedral Quarter.

Nearly there, she told herself, clutching the backpack more tightly. Two more stops and I'm free.

A shuffling behind her and unexpectedly he was getting up.

"This is me now," he said, grinning down at her, cigarette dangling from the corner of his mouth.

"R-right," she said, faking a smile to humour him.

"Maybe see yeh about."

She shuddered at the very thought.

Mercifully the driver braked abruptly, throwing him off balance and catapulting him down the aisle away from her.

"Fuck *you!*" she heard him shout at the man as he dashed uncontrollably towards the exit.

On the pavement he stood looking up at her. She ignored him. Busied herself with the bag till the bus moved off again.

Only then did she feel free to check the purse.

Amazingly, the two twenty-pound notes and the tenner were still there, as was her credit card. She always carried five business cards. Something told her to count them.

Four!

She sat back in the seat, a terrible reality dawning.

He'd taken off with one of them.

SEVENTEEN

Tilda bustled through the library doors like Miss Marple on the scent of a new case. She felt a bit guilty because she had an overdue book—*The Horoscope Addict*—which she couldn't find anywhere. She hoped that Flo Curl, the librarian, wouldn't remember her borrowing it: because if she did she'd be demanding another ten pence of a fine. In Tilda's present circumstances, with money so tight, even parting with such a small sum would be painful, when it could be better spent on the like of a pint of milk or a bag of sugar.

Miss Curl, as stiff as a doll, was seated behind her desk as usual, grey hair lacquered into a stiff mesh above a pinched face, wire spectacles perched on a beaky nose. She was garbed in her customary attire: grey pinafore, white blouse, filigree brooch pinned at her throat.

Her eyes were trained on a group of schoolchildren.

"Now, get on with your *reading*," she scolded, in a school-assembly voice. "I said *no whispering*. I hope I don't have to tell you again."

Oh, dear, she's not in good form. An underactive base chakra, if I'm any judge. Well, she sits on it most of the day anyway.

The librarian gave the children one final, scathing look and slowly brought her attention back to the new visitor.

"Ah, Mrs Bryn!" she exclaimed, blinking at the coruscating vision that was Tilda—an emergency flare of reds and yellows topped off with a headband the colour of a traffic cone. "Haven't seen you for a while."

"Oh no, Miss Curl, yeh haven't 'cos I've had a lot on me plate of late. Now I—"

"Have you found that book yet?"

"What book would that be?" Tilda shifted from foot to foot, trying to stall the inevitable.

"*The Horoscope Addict*."

"Oh, that one. Well ... er, n-no I h-haven't, but that's not to say it isn't about, and I just haven't had the time to look proper. But Miss Curl, I wonder—"

The librarian tut-tutted. "I'm going to have to ask you for another ten pence I'm afraid."

Tilda reddened and hoked in her handbag. "Yes, indeed. Hope I have me purse out with me, so I do."

"It would be cheaper if you just gave me the price of the book and I'll write it off as lost."

"Er ... well, money's tight these days, Miss Curl. Yes, I have me purse, now that I see it."

With reluctance she handed over a ten-pence piece.

The librarian dropped the coin into a box marked OVERDUE FINES ST MARTIN DE PORRES ORPHANS and recorded the penalty payment in her ledger.

Tilda could have been one of the admonished children who were now sitting like mice, observing her very public chastisement.

"Now, I was wondering if you had anything on the moving statues down south," she said, addressing the top of Miss Curl's grey head as she snapped the ledger shut.

The librarian removed her spectacles and gave her a puzzled look.

"Oh, it's much too early for a book to be written about *that* nonsense."

"You don't believe it then."

"Certainly not! It's the Devil's work if you ask me." She shook her head briskly as if to dislodge the odious idea. "Father Mulcahy had some very stern words about it in last Sunday's sermon."

"Oh, did he now?" Tilda regretted the words as soon as they left her lips, for they implied that she hadn't attended Mass. It was too late to rectify the situation, but …

"God, that's a lovely brooch yer wearin', Miss Curl!"

"Thank you," she said briskly, adjusting her glasses, looking at Tilda more intently, like a cop weighing up a suspect. "Why are *you* interested in it anyway?"

"What? The brooch—"

"*No!* The moving-statue nonsense, Mrs Bryn."

"Er . . . well, I like to keep an open mind about these things. There's more things in heaven and earth than's dreamed of in yer fancies, as me mother used to say."

"Philosophy."

"Eh … what?"

"There are more things in heaven and earth than are dreamt of in your *philosophy.* Not fancies, *philosophy* … and your mother didn't say that; Shakespeare did."

"Oh, did he now?" Tilda reddened. "Me mother was very well read, God rest her soul."

"Indeed. Well, if it's a book you're looking for on that disagreeable subject, there aren't any, since it's far too soon, obviously. The first sighting was only a few weeks back. That's not to say that any number of fools will be writing books about the whole sorry business soon."

"Yes, but I was thinking more of stories in the papers and the like."

"Mmm … as it happens … "

She reached under the desk and produced a scrapbook. "One of the pupils from the secondary school is doing a project on it. You're free to have a look at it."

She slid the scrapbook across the desk.

Tilda squinted down at the cover—unable to believe her eyes. It showed a crudely drawn picture of the Blessed Mother with a circle of garish light bulbs around her head. Underneath, in big blue lettering, were the following words:

MARYS MOVING STATUES BY AINE LAMB CLASS 3A

Tilda clasped her cheeks in astonishment. Redwing Maeve had scored again: the circle of lights, the wee lamb, the library. It was all there in her ritual the night before.

"God, Miss Curl, that's great altogether ... just what I was lookin' for. I'll sit over here and take a wee look."

"You're not allowed to take it home with you. You know that, don't you?"

"Understand that completely, Miss Curl. Thank you very much!"

As Tilda made her way to a table by the window her attention was drawn to a car pulling up outside; a white sports car no less. Strange sight to see in Castlebrook, she thought, intrigued to discover who owned it.

Presently out of it stepped a young gentleman. Very well dressed, she could see. Maybe a tourist or one of them managers from the library board, come to check up on Miss Curl.

She settled herself and opened the scrapbook, eager to learn more about the miraculous moving statues. Moments later, however, her attention was distracted once more.

"How lovely to see you, James!" she heard Miss Curl say in a fawning tone.

Tilda wondered who could induce such grovelling politeness in the normally stern librarian.

She turned to see the owner of the sports car approaching the desk.

"Miss Curl, how delightful to see *you* again!" the man said. "I was wondering about—"

"—the book you ordered," the librarian interrupted smoothly. "Why, of course." She reached under the desk. "How very timely that you call in today! *The Antique Collector's Guide.* It arrived in only yesterday."

At which point James threw Tilda a curious look. Embarrassed, she went back to her reading.

Well, if he's borrowing library books it can only mean he's putting down roots for a while. I wonder what brought him to Castlebrook, of all places—a well-to-do gentleman like himself.

There's a story behind him if I'm any judge. Aye, and an interesting one at that, I'd say.

EIGHTEEN

Manny drove into town, a jumbo bag of Maltesers opened on his lap, hand alternating mechanically between it and his gob. Taxi-driving wasn't the most active trade and he found he was eating more than he had in the Baked-4-You, alas. It was the boring waits. The boring drives along the same boring roads: a boredom that could only be relieved by chocolate—and lots of it.

He slowed as he approached the security gates to Castlebrook.

From the start of the conflict, every urban area across the province had such barriers put in place to prevent terrorists driving car bombs into town centres.

These security gates were manned by the British Army, backed up by members of the local police force: the RUC—Royal Ulster Constabulary.

Manny, being a known face, was normally waved through. On this occasion, however, as he approached the barrier two soldiers stepped out—one tall and lanky, the other older and more heavily set. They were wearing the tartan berets of a Scottish regiment.

The tall one raised a hand.

Manny slowed to a halt.

"What the hell's this about?" he muttered to himself as Mr Lanky sidled up to the car window, cradling his rifle.

"Afternoon, sir. This vehicle yours, is it?"

Scrawny face. Hard eyes, the right one slightly shut, as if focusing through crosshairs was its prime function.

"Uh ... um, no, it belongs to Fred Bain ... a taxi-driver.... I'm fillin' in for him 'cos he's broke the leg."

"Licence."

"Aye." Manny smiled—to keep on his good side—and handed over his driving licence.

The soldier studied it for a few seconds, shot him an unreadable look, walked over to his comrade, who was standing at the front of the car, muttering into a walkie-talkie.

It doesn't look too promising, thought Manny, drumming his fingers on the steering wheel, hoping he wouldn't be detained for too long. He was dying for the toilet and a quick cup of tea before his next fare.

There was something about the pair though that made him uneasy. He'd never been in trouble with the law, so why would they be checking him out so thoroughly? He'd been seen often enough coming and going. But maybe these two were new to the job. Garbed up in their fatigues, one Brit looked very like another, so he never paid much attention. Either that or they were simply pulling rank to show him who was boss.

Moments later Mr Lanky was back, his smug expression hardening into a scowl.

"Pull over there, please, mate. Cut the engine and step out of the vehicle. We need to do a search."

He'd sensed that that was coming. Did as he was ordered and got out of the car.

At which point, an RUC officer appeared out of nowhere and escorted him into a mobile cabin placed behind the lookout post.

"Wait here," he said gruffly. "We won't be long."

The cabin was sparsely furnished: a desk, a couple of filing cabinets and two bench seats.

Manny was about to sit down when, to his relief, he spotted a door at the rear marked TOILET and headed towards it.

When he emerged from the lavatory he was glad to see he was still alone. He crossed immediately to the window and peered through the grill. They were still going over the car. The boot cover had been removed and the bonnet lifted.

Manny sat down quickly, but at the sound of approaching feet got up again.

The door was opened and the gruff policeman entered.

"Did you know that spare of yours is as baldy as a baby's butt?"

"Er . . . ah, no, 'cos Fred—that's Fred Bain the taxi-driver that owns the car—said everything with the car was all right, like."

"Well, it's not and he's wrong."

"Aye—I-I mean yes—sorry. I'll get it seen to right away."

"You'd better. Should be booking you, by rights, but I'll let it go this time since you're not the owner of the vehicle."

Manny returned to the car under the sly gaze of the two soldiers. He settled into the driver's seat—only to discover that the seat was wet.

What the blazes... his eyes took in the mess they'd left behind: his bag of Maltesers upended on the passenger seat, contents of the glove compartment on the floor, his lunchbox overturned.

Where was his bottle of Fanta Orange? He spotted it down behind the passenger seat, lying empty. Only then did it dawn on him the reason his seat was wet.

"Feckin' bastards!"

"Problem, mate?"

Mr Lanky was at the window again, rifle pointed menacingly.

"What?"

"I *said* is there a problem?"

He was goading him, a twitch of disdain at the corner of his mouth, daring Manny to kick off.

But Manny knew the game. Reined himself in. Any retort would give the bastards reason to detain him even longer.

"No bother," he said, putting the car into gear.

As he drove off he caught sight of the psycho in the rear-view mirror, tracking him.

Bad enough having the IRA to watch out for.

Now the bloody Brits were hovering as well.

NINETEEN

A still afternoon. The sky, a grey sulk of low cloud, and Ellen Purboy was in her living-room, checking herself in the mirror yet again, and hoping the rain would hold off.

It was important that she looked well when meeting someone for the first time. You never get a second chance to make a good first impression, as her mother used to say.

"Oh, dear!"

She sighed at the memory of her once-vibrant mother reduced to illness and dementia in her latter days, and switched her attention immediately to the brooding sky beyond the window.

One might have dominion over one's looks but hardly over the weather. The forecast promised "sunny intervals in the afternoon" and the bedsit would look so much more appealing in sunlight.

A couple of days previously her ad had appeared in the *Mid-Ulster Vindicator* and only yesterday, quite unexpectedly, she'd received her first enquiry. Not from a female, as she'd been expecting, but from a man by the name of Lavelle.

The viewing at 2 o'clock was an hour away.

She stood back from the mirror and turned to get a side view. Yes, the cashmere sweater and matching skirt in honey beige struck the right note: not too serious but at the same time formal enough to let the client know she would be a practical and dependable landlady.

It was strange to think that the appellation "landlady" could now be ascribed to her. Her previous job title, "secretary", had given way to "housewife" when she married.

It was a title she'd embraced with brio after the tedium of office life. She'd never been one to seek independence, so in that respect things had worked out extremely well.

But with George's passing all had changed.

Independence was suddenly hers, whether she wanted it or not. Nothing had prepared her for it.

"Oh, why did he have to leave so soon?!" she appealed to the glass. "It just isn't fair." He'd worked so hard and deserved his retirement. They'd planned on touring the Continent as free as birds, the years of hard work but a memory.

It was not to be. Instead he was lying beneath the soil in a cold cemetery and she was starting a new chapter without him. How cruel!

She thought of the smashed wedding picture. Was it an ill omen? A warning of sorts.

The notion brought a tear, blurring her reflection.

But there was no time for tears. Not now, when she had to keep it together for her visitor.

She blinked rapidly to spare her make-up. Eyed the string of pearls. Perhaps ... perhaps they're too much. They might give the impression of trying too hard. She touched them briefly and her rings flashed, as if to say, "They're too much as well!"

Should she be wearing them now at all? The triple-stone diamond engagement ring and gold wedding band seemed at odds with widowhood. They celebrated a union that was no more.

On a whim, she twisted them free and slipped both into her pocket.

"Yes: landlady," she said, squaring her shoulders. "That is my role now and I must play it well."

Mr Lavelle had sounded very cultured on the phone. Something she hadn't expected. During their brief exchange he'd refrained from divulging many details, aside from the fact that he was a businessman who travelled a lot. She liked the sound of that. He seemed respectable and of a mature age. Another plus. She didn't want some young chap who might bring girlfriends back and cause all manner of upset.

In fact she'd never considered that possibility until now.

She turned back to the room and sank down on the sofa, the thought making her anxious. Of course a young woman could be just as problematic, bringing boyfriends back.

Well, I'll simply have to tell them that no one is allowed to stay overnight. But would that not limit my prospects of getting a tenant and having all my hard work on the place going to waste? Perhaps I'm too old-fashioned in my views.

I should have drawn up a contract with a set of rules. Why didn't I think of that before? I went headlong into all of this without thinking. God knows where this venture might lead. It might be the worst idea in the world.

She scanned the room, feeling deflated, and her eyes locked on the little casket the removal man had found. It sat on the sideboard—where she wouldn't have to look at it—along with the unopened letter from the solicitor.

Perhaps now was the time to open both?

The distraction would take her mind off all those niggling questions she'd no answers to at present.

It was going on for 1.30 p.m., still a good half-hour before Mr Lavelle's arrival. She got up. Went through to the kitchen and brought back a letter-opener and a small hammer.

The little casket was the more intriguing.

A couple of precise whacks on the padlock and it gave way.

She carried it over to the coffee table, feeling intrigued but anxious, and sat down.

What on earth could be in here that George didn't want me to see?

The hinges creaked balefully as she raised the lid.

She peered inside and was confronted by a strange sight: several pieces of gold jewellery.

Carefully she lifted each one out and set it down. The first piece was most unusual: a small scimitar, suspended from which was a half-moon encasing a five-pointed star. At the apex of the half-moon was a sphinx. It was beautifully made. The other three pieces were rather mundane by comparison: an eye with a diamond tear-drop, an owl with diamante plumage, and a tiny slipper. What to make of such a surreal collection? They were too big to belong on a charm bracelet. They did not have the necessary appendages to make them brooches, earrings or indeed pendants. Most odd. Perhaps they were a job lot he got in some thrift store. He was always collecting curios of one sort or another. She turned the box over, looking for a sticker: some kind of clue that might indicate its provenance. But there was nothing.

She examined the gold objects once more, mystified as to their significance. Possibilities surged. They'd obviously had some sort of sentimental value for George. Were they linked in some way? And why the secrecy? Were collector's items so expensive he didn't trust me to handle them?

So many questions! Well, age must have made him more fastidious. She returned all the items to the box.

Might as well open the letter from Fintan, the solicitor. It seems like a day for unexpected discoveries.

The single page didn't say much.

Dear George,

As per our conversation of 2/11/84, I have arranged for the sum of £100,000 to be brokered with your client MH Ltd. The monthly sum of £200 will cease to be paid in lieu of this lump sum as and of the 2/1/85.

When agreement has been signed I will retain copies for your records.

Please let me know if there is anything further I can assist you with.

Sincerely,

F. Kavanagh LLB

She looked up from the page. One hundred thousand pounds was a lot of money; some kind of investment or life-insurance policy most likely.

She'd rarely concerned herself with George's finances and he rarely discussed such things with her. A personal allowance of £300 was credited to her bank account each month, which was quite sufficient for her needs. All other bills were met by George.

Now she'd have to acquaint herself with the money side of matters. She really needed to visit Fintan Kavanagh and sort things out with regard to the will.

Perhaps the sooner I do that the better. Maybe he'll be able to shed some light on this odd box of trinkets too. Tell me if the items are of any value. Maybe that's why George concealed them. Didn't want them to come to any harm.

The sound of a car startled her.

The clock in the hall struck the hour.

My word, my visitor is very punctual!

A good sign.

She went to the window and peered out.

Could not believe her eyes.

A white, open-topped sports car was drawing up at the front.

TWENTY

Ellen Purboy went to greet her prospective tenant, feeling vaguely apprehensive.

This was the young fellow who'd nearly run her over not so long ago; now he wished to rent her bedsit. She knew it had been an accident of course—her thoughts being in such turmoil that day, she'd absentmindedly wandered into the middle of the road.

But all the same, what a curious coincidence that their paths should cross for a second time!

On opening the door she found him, back turned, one hand shading his eyes, gazing out across the gardens.

The clipped lawns of Cedarwood were indeed something to behold, and especially in summertime. Borders bursting with snowy chrysanthemums, deep blue delphiniums, trumpet lilies nodding their waxy heads amongst the hybrid-tea roses in every hue from the deepest velvety reds to the lightest silky pinks.

Even at this distance Ellen could smell their enchanting fragrances on the air.

"Hello ... umm, Mr Lavelle?" she said nervously.

He didn't move.

Perhaps he hadn't heard her. Could the garden be so captivating?

She gave a little cough.

Slowly he disengaged himself from his contemplation and turned.

"My goodness me! I was miles away there."

She saw him do a double-take. Swiftly remove his sunglasses.

"My word! Is it … is it *you* … the lady—"

"—on the road, yes."

Back then he'd reminded her of a character from *Brideshead Revisited.* Now, at close quarters in his off-white suit and silk cravat, it was Jay Gatsby who came to mind. His tone was as smooth and mellifluous as she'd remembered, even if his phone-voice had sounded much deeper.

"So *you're* Mrs Purboy? What a coincidence!"

"Yes … what a coincidence indeed! You've come about the bedsit?"

"Yes, that's me. James Lavelle." He held out a hand. "But you must call me Jay…. "

Jay. She thought again of Jay Gatsby.

" . . . all my friends do. What a small world we inhabit! And what an absolute pleasure it is to meet you in … " He gazed over the lawns again. Looked up at the house, drawing a majestic arc with his sunglasses. " … in … in, how shall I say … more conducive circumstances, and in such a beautiful setting. This place of yours is simply splendid!"

Ellen smiled, her reserve thawing. He was certainly very well spoken and so very charming. The sports car, the suit, the smartly coiffured hair and handsome features spoke of someone at ease with the finer things in life. The word "privileged" came to mind. Perhaps her humble bedsit might not appeal at all. If he was expecting the old-world charm of Cedarwood he might be sorely disappointed.

"Thank you … kind of you to say so." She stood back to admit him.

"And it only gets better," he enthused, stepping onto the glossy, chequerboard tiling, taking in the imposing walnut staircase and chandeliers of Tiffany glass. "How very grand! Such richness of decor! Is it all your own doing?"

"Yes … well, the more modern aspects of course. Cedarwood has been in my husband's family for quite some time."

"So these must be the ancestors?" He was viewing the row of oil paintings marching up the staircase.

"Well, no . . . that's the Blackbourne family, who built this place. Sir Wilfred there was the founder of Castlebrook. He started the linen-mill, you see. Most of the paintings—and indeed the furniture—came with the house."

"Ah . . . how very interesting!"

She saw him check himself in the hallstand mirror, discreetly smooth the cravat.

"Beautiful fretwork!"

"Sorry?"

"Your hallstand. Early Chippendale I'd say."

"Oh, you're interested in antiques. You're a collector?"

He shook his head. "Heavens, no. I used to work for a dealer; that's all. Had to learn the trade from scratch . . . so I know quality when I see it."

"I see . . . and now?"

"I'm in insurance . . . been sent by my company to cover this region . . . mid-Ulster, that is. I normally work out of our head office in Dublin, but we're expanding our reach. This town would be a perfect base from which to operate . . . hence my interest in your rental, which—if your splendid home is anything to go by—would be simply perfect. I'm just dying to see it!"

"Oh, it's kind of you to say so, Mr Lavelle—"

"Jay, please."

"Erm . . . Jay, yes. I hope you won't be disappointed. Please, come this way."

She preceded him down the hallway in a state of uncertainty. All this was happening far too quickly. A female tenant was her preference. But, by the way this Jay was acting, he'd already made his mind up.

"Of course this inner door will be locked at all times," she said, easing it open.

He moved to the middle of the studio and did a little pirouette. Spread his arms wide.

"And," she continued, "that outer door over there is—"

"—perfect!" he said cutting across her. "Absolutely perfect."

Ellen pulled back the sliding doors to the sleeping quarters. "The bedroom and en-suite. There's plenty of space, as you can see."

He came forward and scanned the room briefly before moving away again. "Indeed! You have excellent taste, Mrs Purboy."

"Erm … I'd glad you think so, but—"

"Oh, how presumptuous of me. … "

She closed the sliding doors and turned back to him.

"Presumptuous?"

He inclined his head and approached her, hands pressed together like a penitent altar-boy's.

"You have other clients who are interested? Please say you haven't."

"Yes … well, I mean the ad has just appeared so I expect there'll be—"

"You mean I'm the *first* view?"

He looked so hopeful and Ellen couldn't bring herself to tell even the whitest of lies.

"Well … yes."

"You simply *must* let me have it then. You won't regret it. It'll only be for three months initially and I'll pay the total amount up front in advance right now. How's that?"

"But you … you don't know the rental fee."

He bit his lip. Made an apologetic face.

"Oh, dear, silly of me! How much then?"

"Seventy pounds per month, and there's a deposit of seventy also."

He immediately produced his wallet.

"Erm ... I need to draw up the contract first.... "

But he was already counting out the notes on the table. She could see quite a lot of cash in the wallet.

"There we are, Mrs Purboy ... two hundred and eighty pounds exactly." He was studying her. "You remind me of my Aunt Edith in her younger day. A real lady just like you, before she ... "

He glanced away, eyes misting over.

"I'm sorry ... is she, erm ... ?"

He shook his head sadly. Gazed at the floor.

"Alas, in a nursing home now ... Getting on for eighty-five and not in the best of health."

"I *am* sorry to hear that."

"Well, such is life." He waved a dismissive hand. Looked back at her, face quickly morphing again into one of cheerful expectation.

"I'll be as quiet as a mouse. I promise. You won't even know I'm here. Well ... I'll be out on business most of the time anyway. Just need somewhere to berth my boat."

How could she refuse him? He seemed so eager and she did sense that he wouldn't give her any trouble. Besides which, it might be good to have a man about the place: especially in the night-time, when she felt at her most vulnerable.

She smiled. "Indeed. I'll need to write you a receipt then."

"No need." He returned the wallet to his pocket. "I can tell you're a woman of the utmost integrity. Now to more pressing matters: may I move in tomorrow? Say, around six?"

Ellen was taken by surprise, *again*. "So soon?"

She saw the smile fade and instantly regretted having disappointed him.

"Let me think," she said. "I-I think ... I think I have an appointment in the afternoon. I'll just need to check my diary."

"No need," he said, placing the money in her hand. "You can give me the keys now and I can let myself in. That way, I won't disrupt your plans and we'll both be happy."

Ellen could hardly argue now. Having accepted his money she was obliged to give him the keys.

"Yes... yes, of course."

"Splendid! That's settled then." He pocketed the keys. "See you tomorrow then."

He skipped back down the hallway like a delighted child.

She had to admit there was something very endearing about Jay Lavelle. Sophisticated, but somehow innocent at the same time.

On the doorstep she waved him goodbye and turned back inside, wondering how everything could have moved so quickly.

The door to the studio stood open and she went back down the hall to lock it, thinking: *This is the last time I'll have to do this for three months anyway*. It's the property of Mr Lavelle now.

Only then did it dawn on her.

He'd taken off with *both* keys—the one for the outside door *and* the inner one.

Never mind. I'll get it back tomorrow.

On returning to the drawing-room she studied once more the box of strange objects and the letter from Kavanagh Solicitors she'd left on the coffee table.

Mr Lavelle's visit had somehow managed to make her forget all about them.

I need to act now, she decided. The studio is rented.

The next hurdle is dealing with George's will and the reason for that large sum of money being paid out to whoever MH Ltd might be.

Fintan Kavanagh has certainly some explaining to do.

TWENTY-ONE

Ma Bryn had to take a break in Meg's Café for a reviving cuppa tea and a bun before returning to the library. There was so much to read in wee Aine Lamb's project about "Ireland's Moving Statues" that she was going cross-eyed betimes and needed to give the eyes a rest.

Late afternoon and she was back at her post again.

Miss Curl, the librarian, was still at her desk, but the schoolchildren had gone. The only other visitor was an old man, looking the worse for wear, slouched in a club chair in the corner, coughing sporadically and riffling his way through a copy of the *Daily Mirror*.

Ma Bryn was glad of the peace and quiet as she continued her perusals.

> *Kitty Walls was passing the Marian shrine in Ballinspittle late one evening with her sixteen-year-old daughter when she decided to stop and say a few prayers.*
>
> *"I said to wee Mary we'll say a mouthful at the grotto . . . offer up our intentions for the holy souls in Purgatory and no sooner had we knelt down when the statue started moving. Her chest was heaving up and down like she was breathing and her hands started going in and out like she was playing an accordion. We kept praying because we were frightened. My wee Mary said she saw the eyes growing bigger and bigger till they nearly fell out of her head, but I didn't see that. She couldn't sleep and was off her food for days, the poor creature."*

"God save us!" Ma Bryn murmured under her breath, conscious that Miss Curl was within earshot. She studied a photograph of Kitty Walls and wee Mary in front of said shrine, the words AVE MARIA traced in light bulbs over their heads.

Turned the page, eager for more.

Lizzie Magee from Glenbragh had her own story to tell about the happenings at a roadside shrine not far from her house.

"Well, I'd prayed at the shrine on many occasions. I thought all talk of moving statues was just a load of oul' hooey. Somebody said they'd seen the face of Mary with a beard on it and thought it might be the Lord himself or St Joseph. I didn't know what to think, so I thought I'd go and see for meself.

"It was getting dark when I got over to the shrine. There were about twenty people there already and we all started to pray the rosary. The Virgin's hands were joined like they always were but of a sudden they flew into the air, rising up to heaven. I could tell the others saw it too because we all stopped at the same time to draw breath in our prayers. It was a wonderful sight. She stayed like that until we'd finished the rosary, then folded her hands together again and smiled at us. There was a great feeling of calm and peace after and none of us wanted to leave because we all knew something wonderful had happened."

Not all experiences are so positive, however. Two young boys from Monagar, John and Peter Ryan, had this to say:

"We saw Mary's face change to the Pope's, then it turned into Mary's again and she had a long white beard. After that the beard went away and she was bald. We ran away because we were so scared."

John and Peter are not the only ones to be running scared of the moving statue phenomenon. Pensioner Patrick Lynch had an altogether more alarming experience at a shrine outside his hometown of Killycarrick.

"Me and the wife went in the car because it's a fair bit from the house and we wanted to see what all the fuss was about. It was dark when we got there and the wife was afraid of falling so we stayed in the car and shone the headlights on it to see for ourselves. There was nothing for a good wee while, then begod before our very eyes the pair of us saw the face change to Our Lord's face and from that to a dark brown face which we think might of been Padre Pio. But it was the face after that that had us driving away like the Divil because it was the Divil. It was all twisted with fiery red eyes and horns where the ears should be. We nearly died the pair of us and we're nivver going back and we'll nivver forget it."

"What do you think it means?"

"Phyllis says it's a warning that the people of Ireland need to pray more. I wasn't much of a believer meself but when I saw that, it rattled me so I've started going back to Mass and mending me ways."

"Dearie, dearie me!"

Miss Curl gave one of her "keep quiet" coughs and Tilda took the hint. She read on, transfixed.

In Boxtown, Deirdre O'Kane explained her experience of praying at Our Lady of the Wayside shrine on the evening of July 24th.

"On the third decade of the rosary, Our Lady turned into an old woman. God, the light nearly left me eyes! We could see her getting wrinkled like it was a photo developing. Then she was young again, skin as smooth as a baby's, but she was crying. You could see the big teardrops shining like diamonds falling down on her cloak. I think she was telling us that we're all

gonna die so we need to amend for our sins before it's too late. It put the heart across me, I can tell you. I wouldn't of believed it had I not seen it with me own eyes."

Not everyone is convinced of the supernatural phenomenon, however. The Catholic Church is keeping an open mind. Canon McCracken of Stralucan had this to say:

"The Church is all too aware that experiences, especially emotional ones, can affect people who are not of sound mind. It's early days yet, and we do not know exactly what is happening at those shrines. However, I might point out that those sightings of moving statues take place at night, so it's either an illusion or a trick of the light."

Ma Bryn mentally clapped her hands when she read that last sentence. So *that's* what I'm doing wrong. The statues move at night when it's dark. *And there was me going every morning. Is it any wonder she didn't move for me?*

"Thank you very much," she said to Miss Curl, handing back the scrapbook. "I've learnt a lot from wee Aine Lamb's project."

"Glad to hear it, Mrs Bryn. So long as you don't believe in it."

"Oh, I keep an open mind, like I say. Cheerio now."

Ma Bryn flounced towards the exit, exotic plumage billowing.

"And don't forget to bring back *The Horoscope Addict*," the librarian called after her, but she feigned not to hear and continued on her way, eager for her next visit to St Timothy's grotto.

In the dark. In Tilda's experience, the most wonderful and unearthly occurrences she ever encountered happened *in the dark.*

VIVIENNE

Vivienne realized that she now had *another* stalker to deal with: aside from Declan in the pub there was the weirdo on the bus who'd nicked one of her business cards.

Why the hell did he steal it? Not unless...

She'd no wish to pursue that line of thought and rushed along Royal Avenue, sizzling with hatred for this sudden pair of gate-crashers in her life.

Her backpack was securely fastened, her thumbs tucked firmly into its straps. Even in haste she moved with a coltish grace, her diaphanous skirt floating out behind her like a vapour trail: the insubstantial waif weaving her way through the war zone that was Belfast.

So far, over 2,000 civilians had perished in the conflict, the majority losing their lives in this hapless city—Vivienne gleaned those stats and figures from her father's work; she never watched the news—and the grim tally would keep rising; she was in no doubt about that.

It was important that she aimed her gaze into the middle distance. In an arena of conflict everyone was your enemy. You moved fast. You kept your wits about you.

A woman was approaching, handbag over her right arm—middle-aged, unassuming. A bomb could be primed in that bag. She could walk into a crowded café or shop and simply leave it there. It wouldn't be the first time.

On this blossoming new day who would die? What evil would rise to cloud the sun breaking over the rooftops?

The morning was properly awake now: shops opening, security grills being lifted clear of windows, RUC personnel already patrolling.

Always two officers on the beat: a male to frisk the men, a female for the women. They were coming towards Vivienne. She hoped they wouldn't stop her. They were walking in tandem, hands behind their backs, like a pair of toy soldiers.

She avoided their gaze as they drew closer.

Saw the woman raise her hand.

Pretended not to notice.

"Stop, please!" They blocked her path.

Vivienne halted, breathless.

"You seem to be in an awful hurry this mornin', madam. Where are we headin' at this hour?"

"To work," Vivienne said, taking in the small chunky woman with a broad, plain face and determined little mouth. CONSTABLE printed on a name tag.

"And where might that be?"

"My studio ... on Cathedral Street."

She could see that the word "studio" threw the constable a bit. Her colleague, a sergeant, looked on, but said nothing.

"I'll have a look in that bag," the woman said. "And I'll need some form of ID. What's your name?"

Vivienne unstrapped her backpack. "Vivienne Dundas."

She sensed them trading looks as she rooted for the purse. Held the bag out to be searched. Took out a business card and gave it to the man.

"Anything to the judge ... Robert Dundas?" he asked, glancing briefly at the card.

"He's my father."

This information was met with ingratiating nods.

"Sorry to have detained you, Miss Dundas," the sergeant said, as the woman hurriedly zipped up the bag and returned it, giving her a fawning smile.

"Mind how you go now, Miss Dundas," she said.

"Thanks." Vivienne rushed off, grateful that she didn't have to endure a frisking. Her father's good name had got her off that one.

On the second flight of steps to the studio she met the solicitor's secretary, Miss Mills, carefully descending with a tea-tray, the morning newspaper tucked under one arm.

They greeted one another.

"May I give you a hand?" Vivienne offered, fearful she might fall. The tray looked quite weighty, with its heavy-duty load of silver and crockery.

"Thank you so much. If you could get the door that would be splendid."

Vivienne retraced her steps and opened the door.

But on her way back up she saw that Miss Mills had dropped the newspaper.

She picked it up and glanced at the front-page heading.

ESCAPED IRA PRISONER MARTIN CONNOR STILL AT LARGE

There was a grainy photo of the miscreant and a quote in bold lettering, with her father's name attached.

"Connor is a man capable of some of the most wicked and barbarous acts."

Another evildoer my redoubtable father had to put away.

She had no desire to read it. Her father was a public figure. That was the downside of his job. From time to time he was quoted in the papers. From time to time his photograph appeared.

The door behind her opened. Miss Mills put her head out.

"Yes, you dropped it on the stairs." Vivienne handed the paper over.

She tut-tutted. "Thought so. That's what I get for taking the lazy man's burden. Thank you so much, Miss Dundas."

"You're welcome." Vivienne continued up the stairs.

She heard the door shut, then open again.

"Oh, Miss Dundas . . . "

"Yes?"

"Mind how you go, won't you?" She gave her a look of motherly concern.

"Of course," Vivienne smiled. "And you too—"

But already the door was closing quietly as she reverted to secretary-mode.

Odd thing to say. Like she was echoing that female constable. But she saw my father's quote, obviously. Well, it's kind of her to be worried on my behalf. But I'm a big girl now, Miss Mills; I can take care of myself.

She unlocked the studio door, anxious to get started. It was going on for 8 a.m., which meant a good three hours of uninterrupted work before the window opposite could start presenting problems.

She crossed over and studied it, glad to see that both blinds were pulled fully down.

Her gaze drifted below to the street.

Not too many souls yet; just a straggle of workers entering the Ulster Bank, next door.

Her eyes settled on the entrance to the Kevin Barry Arms. Someone was standing in the doorway.

God, he must be desperate for the booze! He's going to have a long wait till eleven.

She was about to move away when the figure shifted out of the shadows, the bright green sports-top as unmistakable as the gaunt face staring up at her.

Vivienne froze, her worst fears confirmed.

The purloiner of her business card.

The nuisance from the bus had *followed her.*

TWENTY-THREE

"Now, what's yer name, luv?"

"Josie."

"Now, Josie, you can call me Ma*dame* or Ma Bryn. It's all the same tae me."

Tilda Bryn, in her latest incarnation as "Psychic Medium to the Needy"—as her ad in the post-office window boasted—was sitting across from her first customer.

The reading was being conducted in a box-room off her bedroom. It was just about big enough to accommodate a small table holding the trappings of her trade—crystal ball, pack of tarot cards, a Spirits of Destiny horoscope chart—and two armchairs.

On the wall behind her she'd affixed two posters: one of the Virgin Mary making a pastel-hued ascension into heaven, the other of a smiling angel holding a crystal ball under the heading YOU ARE MAGIC. Ma Bryn believed in covering all bases when it came to matters spiritual.

"And what'll it be, daughter; the palm, the ball or the cards?"

"Erm... what's the price then?" Josie asked nervously.

"The ball's £2, the palm is £1.50 and the cards is a pound. But you can have the ball-an'-the-palm for £2.00, the cards-an'-the-ball £2.50, or the-ball-the-cards-the-palm-an'-the-scope—which I'll throw in for nothin'—for a fiver."

Josie looked confused.

"Which would give the best readin'?"

"Oh, well now, daughter dear, the ball gives the best readin'. That's why it's the dearest."

"Right, I'll go with the ball," Josie said, dipping into her purse and handing over two pound coins.

"You won't tell me anything bad, will you, Ma? Canna call yeh 'Ma'?"

"Ma doz me all right, daughter. Now us fortune tellers are not in the bissness of telling a body anything bad. Sure we wouldn't be long in bissness if we did. No, daughter dear, any time I see a wee bitta darkness round a body—not that I'm sayin' I'm gonna see a bitta darkness round yeh, mind—I ask the angels to lift it and they always do. So, there's nothing for you to be worried about a-tall."

"That's good," Josie said, feeling more confident.

With the deal done, Tilda spread her hands above the crystal ball, as if warming them over a hot stove, and launched in.

"Mmm ... now I see here, Josie, you weren't a happy child, but then none of us wuz too happy as children, on account of being children—if you get me drift. Not that I'm sayin' yer mammy and daddy didn't do their best. They maybe tried their best, but I'm gettin' here that you've no brothers or sisters, so that's maybe where the wee bitta unhappiness would of come from ... the ball's showin' me that there's times when you like going out, then other times when you just wanna be alone. That's on account of being an only child. Would that be right?"

"God, how did you know that?" Josie asked, amazed.

"Oh, the ball never lies, daughter. Now, I'm getting here a boy in the background."

"Er ... but ... but I don't have a boy."

Ma Bryn didn't think she had, 'cos she was a plain wee slip of a thing with mousy hair and a hoopy nose on her, but if she believed there was a boy for her she'd maybe make more of an effort with her appearance.

"But that's why he's in the background, daughter ... waitin' in the wings ... as I say. So yeh won't be a flowerpot for ever, even if yeh *are* a bit hard to please when it comes tae boys. But you'll know this boy when yeh see him, like."

"Hope it's not Johnny Woodpecker from school. He got Woodpecker on account of his beaky nose. Can't stand that oul' slabber. Always pesterin' me."

"No, it's not him. This boy's far from being an oul' slabber... he'd be a bit more cultured ... the type that would wear a suit and tie but enjoy a joke and a bit-of-a laff, like the rest of us. And he'll be coming into yer life very soon and yer gonna meet him at a gathering of some sort."

"So I don't know him now, do I?"

"No, yeh don't know him now, but that's not to say he's not about, if yeh get me drift? He could be looking at yeh from afar... biding his time for the right moment, like."

"Would he be one of the men what come in the hotel? I meet all sorts at the tables. Some durty oul' friggers that can't keep their hands to theirselves, but there's some nice ones with clean hands and nice shoes. Me ma sez you can always tell a man by his hands and feet, so she does."

Josie was a chambermaid by day and waitress by night in the Belfry Hotel and Guesthouse, a flophouse of ill repute in the larger town of Killoran.

"Could be, Josie," Tilda concurred, "but you'll know him when yeh see him, as I say... now let me see what else's here." Her bracelets jingled melodically as she rearranged her sequinned scarf and gazed more intently at the ball.

"Now, I'm gettin' here an older man with a bad hip—"

"God, I wouldn't want no oul' boy with a dodgy hip!"

"No, this older man's coming across as a relative. Close to you he is. Sigh-attica I'm gettin' and maybe a wee touch of the dropsy too. But there's nothing to worry about, 'cos the sigh-attica will clear up of its own accord if he keeps off the leg. Neither doctor or pill needed. He just needs tae take things aisey."

"God, that'll be me da, but he doesn't touch a dropsy of anything."

"No, I'm not talkin' about the drink, daughter. This man had a fall of recent."

"God, that's amazing! Da slipped in the graveyard last week, prayin' over Granny Lizzie-Mae Peter's stone. I'll tell him when I get home. He'll be so glad to hear that."

"There yeh are now!" Ma Bryn was pleased she was scoring so many bullseyes so early in the spiel. "Just tell him tae take things aisey and keep off the hip for now, and in no time he'll have no hip a-tall till bother him, as I say. Rub a bitta liniment on it. Rest's the best med'cine in these situations, as any doctor will tell a body."

She eyed the ball once more.

"Now, there's a bitta money coming yer way. I see a cheque in an envelope dropping on a mat."

"Och, that'll be Da's sick money, 'cos he's outta work, he's gettin' the welfare now for the hip, like."

Cheeky monkey, thought Ma. "Don't think so," she shot back, "'cos the cheque's made out to *you*. So maybe you're gonna win a bitta money. Do you do the football pools a-tall or comp'titions or the like?"

Josie shook her head.

"Maybe you should start doin' them, 'cos if yer not in then yeh can't win, as they say. There's money comin' tae yeh anyway."

"And how soon is it comin'," Josie asked, eyes wide with wonder, "the money, like?"

"In the space of three. So that could be three days or three weeks or three months, but the sooner yeh do them comp'titions the sooner it'll come to you, daughter."

Tilda stole a quick glance at the clock behind Josie. Time was going on. Maybe start rounding things off, 'cos she knew there were likely to be questions. Josie seemed the questioning sort, alas.

She cast her eyes downward once more.

"Now, I'm seeing here that you'd be a picky eater.... "

Josie was a waif, weighing no more than a bag of Bangor Blues by the look of her.

" . . . and you'd be hard on yerself . . . worrisome betimes about what might happen in the future, and that puts you off yer food."

"But I've always been a small eater. Are you sayin' it's 'cos I worry too much that I'm a small eater? Or I'm a small eater 'cos I worry too much?"

Now even Ma Bryn was confused, but she rallied quickly.

"Aye, a wee bitta both. Yes, indeed, but that's not a bad way for a body tae be, 'cos it means you don't rush into things in a hurry . . . . Betimes you're undecided and other times you wouldn't be so sure."

Josie was nodding avidly as Ma Bryn continued her ramble through a list of Barnum Statements—a series of personality traits to flatter and please that could apply to anyone—taken from every psychic's instruction manual of faux fillers, to round things off on a high note.

"Maybe don't be so critical of yerself when things isn't going yer way," she continued, "'cos I can see you've a lot of talent you're not using . . . and you're a bit of a daydreamer, and that keeps you back from getting things done. But big changes is on the way and the future's lookin' bright for yeh,"

Josie was elated. "That's great! D'you see anything else, Ma?"

"No, that's all the ball's showing me now. But yer palm would show me a bit more."

Josie bit her lip. "Oh . . . how much more would that be?"

"The palm's £1.50, but I can throw it in for the pound."

Josie dithered. "Maybe I'll come back another day . . . money's a bit tight this week, like."

"No bother a-tall, luv. You come back anytime you like. I do me readings between six and eight, weekdays and weekends."

Josie got up, smiling broadly.

"Thank you, Ma . . . will I send in me friend now?"

"Yes, indeed, Josie. Just don't shut the door completely, luv. It's terrible hot in here."

"Right yeh be."

Josie left the room to join her friend, who was sitting in the hallway.

Tilda cocked an ear to the pair's conversation.

Friend: "God, Josie, is she any good?"

"She's brilliant, Maise! Knew about Da's hip and everything... and I'm gonna meet a fancy man and come into money."

Maise: "She could see all that? God, I hope she's as good with *me*."

Ma Bryn smiled to herself.

No, she hadn't lost her touch. Starting up her readings again might be the best decision she'd ever made. The money was coming in again. What with it and whatever Cousin Ted could put their way, Manny losing the job could turn out tae be the best thing that could-a happened to the pair of them.

TWENTY-FOUR

Early morning. Rain battering a raucous refrain on the Bryn roof, and Manny—looking like twenty miles of bad road—came awake anxious and bothered: bothered by the soldiers and how they'd treated him, bothered by his ma and the way she was behaving, what with her fortune telling and moving-statue talk; bothered by the run-in with Bumper Magee in the dole office and where it might lead. Where would it all end?

All these occurrences would, he decided, have consequences.

He sat on the edge of his bed, staring down at his toes, directing a movie of worst-case scenarios in a vain attempt to control the uncontrollable.

What if the soldiers pull me over again, and arrest me on some trumped-up charge? It wouldn't be the first time they'd collared someone from the Nationalist community for as much as looking at them sideways. I might end up in prison and what would Ma do then? She'd have nobody to drive her about no more and she'd be stuck in the house getting crazier than a bag of roosters. As for Bumper Magee, even though I haven't seen him since, there's always the chance he might flag down the taxi for a lift. Then I'd really be in for it.

With hindsight, the job at the bakery hadn't been so bad; kneading dough and firing cake mix into tins was a cosy enough wee number compared to driving Fred's taxi. You met the same people every day at Baked-4-You and knew where you stood. Oul' Cooney was easy enough to work for, so long as you kept on his good side.

Now, you never knew who you were gonna meet. Weekends were the worst—as Fred had predicted. Listening to the rambling talk of drunks, repeating themselves like parrots, and not knowing when they were gonna lash out. Jonah Mulgrew had dragged him to the ground in an unholy embrace the previous night when he was trying to wrestle him from the vehicle. They'd ended up rolling about in the mud outside his farmhouse, with Mulgrew swearing at the moon like a lunatic.

When Manny tried to get the fare from him he'd raised his fists and told him to go to blazes or he'd set the dogs on him, before breaking into song.

It was no idle threat either. The pair of German shepherds were growling ominously from behind a locked gate, their glassy eyes savage in the headlights' beam.

"I'll get it in the mornin'!" Manny shouted as the old-timer stumbled through his half-door and fell a clatter, promptly ending his "Foggy Dew" rendition mid-verse.

"Serves yeh right, y'oul' frigger!" he hurled as an afterthought, knowing Mulgrew wouldn't hear.

Christ! Maybe he hit his head and is lying out cold, not having made it as far as the bed—and I'll get blamed.

He saw the heading in the local paper:

TAXI-DRIVER ACCUSED OF MANSLAUGHTER
OF FRAIL PENSIONER.

His ma might be a bit crazy but she was right about seeing that big dark cloud over his head. As he pulled on his clothes he was already reading the report.

Manus Bryn, 37 years, was the last to see 78-year-old Jonah Mulgrew alive. "He was all right when I left him," Bryn told the court.

"I put it to you, he was far from all right," stated the prosecuting barrister. "Furthermore you knew he was far from all right. His door was open and he was collapsed on the floor.

You drove away knowing the old man had fallen, knowing he could have hurt himself badly and was perhaps bleeding to death. That makes you a heartless fellow and an accessory after the fact."

Manny sighed. He'd call in on Mulgrew first thing, just to make sure.

He looked at the clock. It was 7.15. He had a fare to pick up at 8 and needed to get a move on. The set of meandering directions Fred had given him late the previous night down the telephone line weren't the most accurate, and he shrank at the thought of what lay ahead.

"It's about four mile from the Doody sisters' place. That would be about three-and-a-bit fields over in a northerly route as the crow flies. You'll not see it from the road 'cos it's halfway up the mountain in the Muddymacreek Forest, behind Dumb Annie's Gorge. I believe the brother, Long John, used tae live up there afore he was shot dead by the IRA for being mistooken for a tout."

The mention of "IRA" and "tout" in one breath had turned Manny's innards to jelly.

"*What?! They shot Dumb Annie's brother?*"

"Nah, yer not listenin'.... They shot the Doody sisters' brother. ... In the back af the head, aye, and him ridin' his bike home of an evenin'. They nicknamed it the Psycho Path ... that wee road they kilt him on, 'cos a couple more bodies turned up out there after him. Well, only the bones wuz found, 'cos it's so outta the way nobody thought-a looking, 'cept the ferrets and burds, if yeh get me meaning. Anyway, yeh can't miss it 'cos it's the only way through the forest."

"Er ... I-I dunno if I wanna go there, Fred. Sounds a bit dangerous, and what if the car broke down and I was stuck, like?"

"Not-a-bit-of-it. Them things happened a while ago now and that wee car's as sound as Father Mulcahy's sleep."

"I dunno why anybody would wanna rent a house in an outta-the-way place like that."

"Nan and Biddy said he wuz a bissnessman . . . wanted somewhere quiet to get away from it all."

"Well, he's gettin' that all right."

"Aye, offered them big rent money too, so they could hardly refuse. They're gettin' new dentures and glasses out of it, the pair of them. So they'll be able tae see more and ate more, but it won't stop them pissin' in my car. I hope yeh minded to put that plastic sheet down."

"I did, aye," Manny lied. "But they were all right. Nothin' happened, like. Aye, and before I forget, Fred . . . the soldiers pulled me over and were gonna book me 'cos you had a baldy spare yeh didn't know about."

"Baldy spare, me arse! They were comin' the dog 'cos you're a Fenian. Wouldn't treat a Prod like that. Now the man you're collectin' is called Tommy Fitzwell."

"What kinda name's that?"

"Don't know. Yer to take him to Killoran post office to collect something, then back tae Long John's house again."

"Yeh mean I've to drive out to that place *twice?*"

"Aye, well, he's hardly gonna walk from Killoran back tae Long John's, is he now?"

"Suppose not," Manny conceded wearily, hoping the car wouldn't start in the morning and he'd be spared all the anxiety of having to go at all.

"But what if—"

"Right-yeh-be, Manny. Keep her lit!" Fred chirped, before hanging up.

Finally dressed, fed, watered and on the road, Manny was driving into the nightmare he'd been imagining in full Technicolor all night.

First off: Jonah Mulgrew.

He slowed as he approached the cottage, praying he wouldn't see the old-timer lying dead in the doorway. But a thread of smoke curling meanly from Jonah's chimney and the front door firmly shut told him the pensioner was still alive and well.

He breathed a sigh of relief. Celebrated by opening a bag of Funsize Mars bars and drove on.

Tommy Fitzwell was expecting him at nine and he couldn't afford to get lost.

It was coming 8 a.m. so he turned on the radio to catch the news.

The introductory jingle ended and the serious tones of a Radio Ulster newscaster filled the car.

> *The Prime Minister, Margaret Thatcher, in a speech to the American Bar Association in London, referred to the role of the media reporting the conflict in Northern Ireland. She stated that it would be necessary to starve paramilitary organizations of the oxygen of publicity.*

The announcer then went on to detail the latest series of shootings and bombings across the Province, which kind of flew in the face of Mrs Thatcher's declaration. Daily violence had become so commonplace it was no longer shocking to hear about.

Manny reached to switch off the radio—but stayed his hand.

> "*... an IRA prisoner, who escaped from the Maze prison last week, is still on the run. Forty-five-year-old Martin Connor was convicted earlier this year of directing acts of terrorism and orchestrating a bombing campaign in mainland Britain during the early 80s. Judge Robert Dundas, in his summing up, called him 'a man capable of some of the most heinous and barbarous acts I've ever had the misfortune to pronounce upon.' Connor is five feet eleven, of medium build with short dark hair. When last seen he was wearing blue jeans, white*

trainers and a black hooded top. Members of the public are advised not to approach him, as he is a highly dangerous individual. Any sighting of him should be reported immediately to the police.... Now for the weather—"

He'd switched off the radio, wishing he hadn't heard that last bit. Now, on top of all his troubles, there was an escaped convict on the loose. Another mini Mars bar was needed to steady his nerves.

At the approach to the Doody sisters' lane he slowed. The next small road that ran parallel to their house would take him up the mountain.

Gingerly he steered into it, seeing a series of waterlogged potholes, which gave every forewarning of a bone-rattling ride.

The sky didn't look too promising and he cursed as the rain started up again, making visibility even more difficult. He switched on the wipers, pressed his face against the windscreen Mr Magoo style, and proceeded at a snail's pace up the long, narrow road.

There was barely room for an oncoming vehicle and he hoped he wouldn't meet one. At this rate, would he ever see Long John's house?

A whole twenty minutes and four chocolate bars later, the road ended and the forest loomed up before him, dense and impenetrable. There was a small road on the left, the only one as far as he could see.

He looked forlornly at the empty chocolate bag and recalled Fred's doom-laden words:

"They nicknamed it the Psycho Path ... that wee road they kilt him on ... anyway, yeh can't miss it 'cos it's the only way through the forest."

Manny gripped the steering wheel more tightly, sweat breaking out on his fevered brow. There were *more* potholes to circumvent! The car jounced and capered, protesting the further torture Manny was putting it through.

He crawled along, getting deeper and deeper into the forest.

The road seemed endless.

He was giving up hope of ever finding Long John Doody's place when suddenly, about ten yards up ahead, he saw a dark figure step into his path.

His hands froze on the steering wheel. Leg shaking wildly as he eased off the accelerator. He thought of the escaped prisoner. He thought of Long John lying dead on this very road.

"Good God! Who the hell is *he* and why is he standing right in the middle of the road?"

Through the rain-washed windscreen, as he inched closer, the sinister figure assumed the shape of man wearing a black jacket, a beanie pulled down over his ears.

He was just standing there.

Maybe I should reverse away right now!

He was about to shift gear when he saw the man raise his right hand in the manner of a traffic cop and move towards the car.

Manny's heart sank.

He shut his eyes, fearing the worst. Heard the passenger door being pulled open. Thought of his ma and how she'd miss him. Smelled the pong of damp wool and cigarette smoke as the stranger got in. Waited for the touch of cold steel on his left temple.

Then:

"Tommy Fitzwell at yer service."

He heard the thick Belfast accent—Holy God—and forced his gaze upon the man. Saw a pair of chilling eyes flashing like flints, and a smile as wide as a lunatic's set in a ravaged face.

"Er ... em, right, right yeh be," he said. But, when he went to put the car in gear he glimpsed white trainers peeping from beneath a pair of blue jeans. The news announcer's voice boomed loud in his head.

When last seen he was wearing blue jeans, white trainers and ... Judge Robert Dundas described him as "a man capable of some of the most heinous and barbarous acts...."

"Till... till Killoran, is it?"

"Nah, till the house."

"Whadaya mean... the house? Fred said—"

"Never you mind what Fred said," Fitzwell cut across him, tone gruff and threatening, eyes drilling into him. "He's outta the pitcher now. This is 'tween you and me. Told yeh you'd be hearin' from us in that wee phone call, didn't we? Me name's Connor, but Fitzwell's what yer gonna call me from now on."

Manny could feel the blood draining from his face, icy fingers squeezing at his heart.

"Ugh-ah... I-I don't know... wh-wh-what yeh... what yeh mean, like."

"Yer gonna run some wee messages for me and the boys, under the radar, so tae speak."

"But I-I—"

Fitzwell grabbed him by the collar, forcing his face so close that their noses were almost touching. "I don't take no for an answer, Manny, me oul' son. Is that understood?"

Manny, me oul' son.

"I spent too much time in a fuckin' slammer till take any lip from *you*. D'yeh hear me?"

Manny, dumb with fright, could only nod.

"Good... now, I'm gonna direct you to the house, so yeh know exactly where tae find me. Then you'll wait further instructions from me and the boys in the comin' days. Right?"

"R-r-right."

"Good... I think you know what I'm capable of, so no funny business. If yeh grass on me tae anybody yer a dead bastard walkin'. D'yeh understand me?"

Manny nodded.

Fitzwell released him.

"Good... just so long as we're on the same page. Now, drive on.

You and me's a team now."

Trembling, Manny put the car in gear, realizing with a terrible certainty that his life would never be the same again. A trap had been set, starting that day in the dole office, and he, like a hapless wee mouse, had blundered right into it.

TWENTY-FIVE

The first evening of Jay Lavelle's installation at Cedarwood Manor, Ellen retired to her bedroom, feeling a little conflicted.

On the one hand: something had been accomplished by his having moved in. But on the other: things had developed much faster than she'd anticipated.

She placed her cup of camomile tea on the bedside locker and got into bed, lost in recollection of the evening's events.

Jay had arrived precisely at 6 p.m., as promised.

His luggage consisted of a glossy portmanteau in burgundy leather and two suit bags. She saw the insignia of the fashion house Givenchy on one of them. Expensive tastes indeed!

"How many more trips do you need to make?"

"This is it!" he grinned, swinging the suit bags over one shoulder and coming towards her, fizzing with the energy of a child. "I believe in travelling light at all times. Now, which door shall I use?"

"Oh, do come in this way. It's easier. But it'll be the outside one, naturally, from now on." She hesitated. "But yesterday, however, I forgot and gave you both keys."

"Oh, really? I hadn't noticed."

"Remiss of me I know," she said, feeling awkward. "I'll-I'll need the one back of course."

"Well, of course you will, Mrs P. We all need our privacy."

He dug into a pocket and produced the keys. Held them out.

"Now, the Chubb's yours for the outer door and I'll retain this one."

She attempted to release the key from the ring but, to her

embarrassment, became flustered and dropped both.

"I'm so sorry, I—"

Quick as a flash, Jay had retrieved them. He had the key levered off in seconds. Handed it to her.

"Think nothing of it, Mrs P.... Key rings can be quite challenging at times."

"You're so kind!"

He patted her arm in a gentlemanly fashion. "Well, I'm glad that's all settled."

And before she knew it, he was plunging down the hallway and opening the door to the studio. Such confidence, she mused. But perhaps I'm out of touch with young people. Perhaps these days such self-assurance is the norm.

She waited while he deposited his stuff, still feeling a little awkward about the key incident.

"That's us," he said, coming out, briefcase in hand and shutting the door behind him. "I'll be off again."

"Er... I'm sorry, but there's just one more thing I need to cover before you go."

She saw him discreetly check his watch.

"Every Monday, you see... I do the cleaning."

"Wow, in a house this size! I'm impressed. I thought someone like you would engage a maid."

"Yes, well you're not the first one to say that. But I actually enjoy cleaning. Perhaps I'm the only woman in the world who does."

"I'd say! Believe it or not, I'm a bit like you in that respect."

Ellen raised an eyebrow.

"Really?"

"I like tidy surroundings. Can't stand clutter. That's why I tend not to accumulate much. Makes things easier when it comes to cleaning."

She smiled. "I'm glad you feel the same way. It's refreshing to hear such an idea coming from a young man like yourself. Anyway

... on that subject—if it's all right with you, that is—would Monday afternoon suit?"

Jay looked puzzled by the question. "Sorry ... suit what?"

"Erm ... for me to clean your quarters."

"Oh, heavens, no! I wouldn't hear of it. I prefer to do my own, you see. Always have. It comes from my Aunt Edith's training."

Now it was Ellen's turn to look puzzled.

"Gosh, you wouldn't *believe* how strict she was with me." He rolled his eyes dramatically. "Sergeant Major wouldn't even begin to describe her. So you see, there's no need for you to bother yourself on that score." He tapped his nose cheekily and lowered his voice. "The bedsit will be very well looked after. I've had the training."

"Are you sure? I don't mind really. It's no trouble."

"Not at all, Mrs P. You have quite enough to do in a house this size. I wouldn't dream of imposing. Besides, we modern men don't mind doing a bit of women's work these days."

Yes, I'm obviously out of touch, thought Ellen. It was probably impertinent of me to think I could encroach on his space anyway. That was another thing she hadn't thought through properly.

"Do forgive me. I'm new to all this landlady business you see. It'll take time for me to find my feet."

"You're grand, Mrs P. I can tell that you're going to be a splendid landlady. We're going to get along like a house on fire, you and me."

"Oh, thank you," Ellen said, her tension easing with the compliment. "I *do* hope so."

What effortless charm this young man possessed! She imagined he sailed through life on a wave of simpering approval from the fairer sex. His Aunt Edith had certainly done a good job raising him.

She wanted to ask about his parents, but felt it was not her business to pry.

He glanced at his watch again. "Now, I really must dash. Can't keep the old clients waiting."

"Why, of course."

On the doorstep he turned. "Just another thing: I might be late this evening. I do hope the sound of my car doesn't disturb you."

"Oh, I'm a light sleeper anyway. Don't worry about me."

How gracious of him to be concerned, she thought. How fortunate to have such a considerate young man as my first tenant!

"Bye, now." He smiled his winning smile and was off.

Ellen looked at the clock. It was nearly 11 p.m. and he still hadn't returned.

She studied the bottle of sleeping pills. Dr Flynn had given her stronger ones. Perhaps she'd just take half of one. Yes. She swallowed it with the last of the tea, lay down and soon drifted off.

Some time later she was jerked from slumber by a clunking sound.

She sat upright in the bed, hand pressed to her heart.

Was that a door opening?

Had Jay returned? But the security light would have come on, surely. There has to be another explanation.

She slipped out of bed.

Checked that her bedroom door was locked. Went to the window and peered out.

As she expected, there was no sign of his car. But, since her bedroom was at the front and the bedsit was at the rear, there was no way of knowing for certain.

She got back under the covers. Perhaps I imagined it.

Creak-creak-creak.

The faintest of sounds—as though someone was on the stairs.

She strained to listen.

Creak-creak, creak-creak, creak-creak.

There it was again. But more distant this time, as though retreating back down.

A hovering unease filled the room.

Oh, George, if it's you, please stop doing this! Please!

She sat rigid, ears alert, keeping vigil for the tiniest sound that might confirm her fears. But all was silent, save for the usual sighs and creaks, the familiar language of ancient houses only Cedarwood could speak.

Then a thought occurred to her.

Maybe Jay *is back* and moving about in the studio. What I thought was someone on the stairs are simply the echoes of his movements reverberating through the house. After all, I'm not used to anyone else being here. How silly of me! That has to be the logical explanation of course.

She relaxed a little and lay down again.

But not for long.

Presently, the low hum of a car engine was filling the room. She sat up, as a knife of light sliced through the drapes.

The clock showed 11.45.

Her lodger was back.

Ellen listened, throat tightening, panic rising, as the car drew to a halt and the engine was switched off.

She tracked his movements as he locked the vehicle, crunched over the gravel to the door of the bedsit and let himself in.

At which point the security light died, throwing the bedroom back into darkness.

Ellen sat hugging her knees, trying not to weep as her mind pursued two paths that could not be reconciled. On the one hand: Jay's return had confirmed that it wasn't him making those noises earlier. On the other hand: that fact only added to her terror.

If it wasn't him then *who—or what—was it?*

TWENTY-SIX

Ma Bryn knew that all a body needed to muddle through life was a wishbone, a backbone and a funny-bone—she had all three in full supply. She also understood that all good things come in threes. Now, on this, her third twilight visit to the shrine at St Timothy's church, she *knew* that, third time lucky, the Virgin would *definitely* be making a move.

On all of these trips, however, she had to be careful not to be seen. Manny would drop her off well away from the main gates and she'd sneak in via a side entrance.

The parochial house was situated within the grounds, facing onto the area where the shrine was located. If Father Mulcahy were to look out of his front window he'd have a clear, unimpeded view of her. Fortunately, at that time of evening, with the affairs of the day behind him and the curtains drawn, Tilda felt safe enough—God and Redwing Maeve would see to it that she could pursue her meditation undisturbed.

In the sitting-room of the parochial house Father Mulcahy and curate Father Hill, mugs of cocoa in hand, were seated on either side of a crackling fire, each lost in his own private world.

Patrick Mulcahy, 76, sporting a cloud of white hair, a paunch he made no effort to hide, and a face of puckered weariness, would much prefer a glass of whisky at that hour, but did not want to set a bad example so soon in front of his newly arrived acolyte. He needed to keep up appearances for a wee while longer until the new man found his feet.

But for now only the sound of the lisping flames and the ticking clock broke the quiet, which the older man found soothing. Age and all those years behind the confessional grill had bestowed upon him the gift of being able to sit in meditative mood without feeling the need to converse. It was a quality Hill would develop over time too, he mused, noting the mild tension emanating from the younger man; hands clasped tightly around the mug, frown deepening as he tried to think of something to say.

The fire spat out a coal.

Hill immediately seized the tongs.

"Didn't have time to do any damage," he said, examining the rug before placing the ember back carefully in the grate. "I suppose we should put the guard on now."

"Aye … wouldn't do no harm."

Father Mulcahy took out his pocket-watch and checked it, then settled back into his armchair and had another sip of cocoa.

Hill cast a glance at the newspaper. "The statues are still moving, by the looks of things."

"What?"

"Ballinspittle … in County Cork … the moving statues. I hear they're moving in quite a number of counties now: Wexford, Waterford, Limerick, Laois and a couple more. Just wondered what you thought of it all … now that there've been more sightings."

"Who's to say? One crazy person thinks they see something and before you know it the whole country thinks they might be seeing the same."

"You think there's nothing in it then?"

"No, I wouldn't think so. A load of superstitious *piseoga* if you ask me."

"But if it deepens the faith it can only be a good thing," argued Hill. "Not only for them, but for the Church too I mean."

"Aye … but how do we know where it's comin' from? 'Now the Scripture says that in later times some will depart from the faith by devoting themselves to deceitful spirits and teachings of demons.' Timothy 4:1. So long as that shrine of ours out there doesn't become a focus for every deluded woman in the parish, you and me's got nothing to worry about. Let's hope it stays that way."

"Well, just when you say that, Father, I did see a woman kneeling out there the other night."

"Yeh did? Why didn't yeh hunt her home then?"

Hill didn't know what to say. "Er ... well, I didn't want to disturb her meditation."

"Meditation me eye! Who was she anyway? A parishioner?"

"I couldn't say ... it was dark and she had her back to me."

"Let's hope it's just a passing fancy then. Now, tell me: just when we're on the subject of the supernatural or whatever yeh want to call it, how did you get on with that blessing ... at the Purboy house?"

"Uh ... um ... all right. Yes, all right ... I suppose."

"But you're not sure."

Hill set his mug to one side.

"Well, Mrs Purboy didn't think it was necessary ... said her sister exaggerates and she was having lucid dreams about her dead husband ... that's all."

"Aye ... she maybe would say that ... doesn't have a great history, that house."

"No?"

"Blackbourne, who built it, was a Freemason. The Reverend Purboy, her father-in-law, was a Protestant minister, and his son—her husband—was a heathen. So there couldn't be much luck about the place."

"I see ... and Mrs Purboy, is she a believer?"

"She's a lapsed Catholic. That husband of hers turned her against the Church. But maybe now he's gone she'll come back to the faith. I've seen her at Mass a couple of times, so maybe there's hope."

"God willing," Father Hill said.

"They used to have some sort-a ceremonies in that place ... back in the day. I suppose you noticed the symbolism."

"Symbolism?"

"Aye, two-headed eagles and the like."

The younger priest looked askance. "But I don't understand. What am I not seeing?"

"Chequerboard tiling in the hallway, like the square and compass, a nod to their like. I used to visit Mrs Purboy's mother in her final days."

Father Mulcahy studied the dying fire. "Heaven knows what other tomfoolery they got up to in that house back in the day. The Reverend Purboy got it for a song. Never a good sign. There were stories about old Blackbourne haunting the place. Died in mysterious circumstances, as they say. You know how people talk. But it wouldn't surprise me in the least. Where you have that kinda wealth you have skulduggery of one form or another."

Outside at the shrine, Ma Bryn, eyes closed, hands joined, was summoning the angels and saints, the spirits and ethereal guides, to reveal to her what she most wanted to see: the Virgin Mary acknowledging her humble presence with a tangible sign.

Indications were good. Already she was feeling tingling sensations in her arms and knees. The light behind her eyes was getting brighter. The moon was full. The breeze was soft. Redwing Maeve was in her left ear, trilling a sweet lullaby. The moment she stopped singing, Tilda understood that it was the signal that her meditation was complete and she could then open her eyes to witness the great revelation.

"Well, tomorrow's another day," Father Hill said, not wanting to hear any more about the Purboy residence and its unsavoury past. He hadn't got a good feeling on entering the house and, now that the parish priest had filled him in on its history, knew why.

Father Mulcahy checked his pocket watch once more. "Late

enough, aye."

"I'll go up, so ... goodnight now, Patrick."

"Good enough, Frank. Sleep well."

After he left, Mulcahy hauled himself from the depths of his chair, went to the sideboard and rewarded himself with a generous Scotch.

He took a grateful gulp. Maybe he'd have another wee one, now the coast was finally clear.

Ma Bryn gave a gasp of delight on opening her eyes. She blinked several times, so coruscating was the vision. For no longer was the statue garbed in modest blue and white, its eyes raised heavenward, hands joined meekly in prayer. Now the Virgin's robes were glittering like the sun; her smiling gaze was trained on Tilda, and instead of rosary beads she was holding a golden sceptre, the other hand raised in a beckoning gesture.

"Oh, Jesus, Mary and Joseph!" Tilda cried out, falling on all fours. "I knew it'd happen. I just knew it. Oh, dearie me! What a sight!"

Father Mulcahy, whisky finished and dozing off, was promptly brought back to full mental alertness by a woman's cry.

"What in God's name's that?"

He put the glass down and went to the window to investigate, hoping it might be nothing more than a stray tomcat marking his terrain.

To his horror he saw someone prostrating themselves before the shrine. He recalled Father Hill mentioning seeing a woman. This must be the lunatic he was referring to.

He grabbed a flashlight, peeved at the inconvenience, but glad that he'd caught the intruder red-handed and could put a stop to it.

Meanwhile, Tilda was in ecstasy. She'd clambered over the small railing and was nearing the Virgin, arms outstretched, transfixed by her smiling gaze and beckoning fingers.

A sudden gleam from the golden sceptre was so blinding she had to put a hand up to shade her eyes.

She stumbled, lost her footing and fell on her back.

Then, from above, came a male voice, deep and thunderous.

"What in the name of God are you doing down there, woman?"

Oh Jesus, Mary and Joseph, could it be the Lord himself?

She lay panting, not daring to open her eyes. *What would He say next?*

A dark shape was looming over her. Another shaft of bright light pierced her closed lids.

"Ah, Mrs Bryn. I *thought* it was you."

The light was shut off. It was safe to open her eyes.

To her shock, Father Mulcahy was standing over her, flashlight in hand, wearing a frown worthy of the Divil himself.

"Get up this minute! What in God's name are you doing down there!"

"But she *moved*, Father!" Tilda protested, heaving herself into a sitting position, hot with embarrassment. Her head ached and her knee stung.

"Moved, me eye!"

"I'm sorry, Father. I . . . I was only tryin' tae make contact with the Virgin, like."

"Contact? The only contact you made tonight was with that wet ground. Heavens above, woman, you could'a broke something with this tomfoolery."

He helped her to her feet.

"Now yer comin' inside to recover yourself. And thank your lucky stars I'm not reportin' you to the RUC for trespassin' on church property at ungodly hours. My shrine is off limits after eight."

Tilda was near to tears.

"But-but, Father, I saw her move!"

"We're going inside," the priest said gruffly, ushering her away from the statue. "And let that be the end of it. *Moved* indeed!"

VIVIENNE

Friday evening and Vivienne was happy. She was en route to the town of Fairmoy on the outskirts of Londonderry, to spend the weekend with Tricia, her friend and fellow-student.

Tricia would be exhibiting some of her work in the city's Fountain Gallery and the opening was the following day.

Vivienne was so excited about this adventure. Relishing another new experience, which, like the acquisition of the studio, was hard won.

"Londonderry, of all places!" her father declared, slipping swiftly into Lord Justice mode at the supper table. "You'll be going into enemy territory. You *do* know that, don't you?"

"A predominantly Nationalist area does not mean everybody's an IRA terrorist, Father. And anyway, Tricia doesn't live in Londonderry. Her home is in a little village *outside* it. I'll only be in the actual city for the opening."

"We'll drive you, dear," her mother chimed in, as always trying to keep the peace.

"No, I've already bought my bus ticket, and Tricia's dad is collecting me at the bus-stop. So you see, it's all planned and there's absolutely nothing for you to worry about."

"I'm still not happy about this," her father grumbled on the doorstep, trying once more to dissuade her. "You're out of your depth, Vivienne. The studio was one thing. Going off on your own is quite another. Promise me you'll call us the minute you arrive at your friend's house."

"Of course, Dad. Scout's honour! There's no need to worry. Truly."

She'd hugged them warmly.

"See you Sunday then."

Now, seated on the speeding bus, she saw their worried faces flash before her and felt guilty that she was deserting them for a whole weekend. She imagined them moving about the "empty" house, saying little, holding all their concerns within, lest they upset one another. They would not rest easy until they saw her again, but there was nothing Vivienne could do about that.

She'd return safely. She knew this with the foolhardy certainty of youth. Another victory won; another notch on the bedpost of her journey into selfhood.

The Glenshane Pass unfolded majestically as the bus sliced through the Sperrin mountain range. The undulating hills rose and fell, stretched and sprawled as far as the eye could see. Rock chips gleamed in the lemony sunlight. Swathes of heather abounded, shifting from mauves to pinks as if being woven on some heavenly loom across the thick boggy peat that blanketed the landscape. Vivienne was already viewing the expanse as so many acres of beautifully crafted fabric to be draped and swathed, shrouded and hung in so many domestic settings.

The thought took her back to her studio, and she smiled at her ingenuity in finding the beautiful Japanese screen. Its installation promptly solved the problem of Declan, the spy.

When she'd spotted it in a Cornmarket thrift shop she knew immediately she'd buy it—no matter the price—and knew exactly how she'd utilize it.

The screen—comprising four panels of lacquered wood—when strategically placed against a certain section of window, blocked his view completely.

It was an exquisitely rendered piece of coloured etching displaying the most enchanting array of waterfowl: flamingos and herons standing on islands of pearly golden light.

It only cost a tenner. But its value she reckoned much higher. The shopkeeper was eager to be rid of it, even arranged to deliver it to her, which was just as well because it was quite a weighty piece.

Since its installation the previous week, she could come and go as she pleased and apply herself to her work without feeling intimidated.

The weirdo from the bus journey hadn't appeared either. She'd consigned him and the Kevin Barry Arms to history—where they belonged.

Perhaps I *was* over-reacting, she thought; too sensitive for my own good.

But such is life.

The bus rounded a sharp bend, the momentum pitching her against the window-frame. She righted herself, checked her watch, surprised to see that nearly an hour had elapsed. In no time she'd have to change buses in a town called Killoran. Tricia had advised her not to get out in the centre proper but at the next stop, farther along on the outskirts. This connection was the quickest route to Fairmoy.

She was getting nervous now, hoping everything would go to plan; that she wouldn't miss her stop, that she wouldn't be late and that Mr Kane would be waiting when she arrived. The Kanes lived five miles outside the town and it would be dusk by the time she got there.

All too soon the splendid scenery was giving way to more mundane terrain as they entered the fringes of a town and the sign for Killoran came into view.

The bus slowed for a roundabout then continued past several housing estates before entering the town proper.

The main street was wide and busy. She glimpsed the usual outlets: a Spar supermarket, a greengrocer's, a hotel named Derby's.

Just beyond the hotel the bus came to a halt.

She watched from the window as her fellow-passengers drifted off in several directions, each one looking happy that the working week was done.

An elderly couple embarked: the man wearing a hat, the old lady with a head of perfect grey curls. She looked as if she'd just come from the hair salon. They took a seat near the front.

The driver pulled out again, slowly negotiating his way back into the steady flow of traffic. Before he picked up more speed she decided it might be a good time to retrieve her holdall from the luggage rack.

She stood up. Gathered up her things. As she did so, the old couple turned as one and looked her way.

They obviously thought they were the only passengers, she thought, giving them a smile.

So far, so good. Judge Dundas's dire deliberation of my situation is proving unfounded.

Gratified, and with a lightness of heart, she prepared to disembark.

TWENTY-EIGHT

Mrs Purboy awoke at 9 a.m.

She paused for a moment, squinting at the clock. Could it be that time already? But I'm so tired.

She lay very still, listening to the faint bustle of morning; heard a car pass by on the road. Slowly, her mind steadied. Realization dawned.

She jumped up quickly.

The solicitor. Her appointment was at ten-thirty.

I never oversleep! How could I be so careless?

SLAM. BANG.

The sound of a door shutting downstairs pulled her up short.

Jay?

Suddenly the happenings of the night before came rushing back: the noises on the stairs that had awoken her. Maybe Jay could throw some light on things. Maybe he'd seen someone on the avenue as he drove up. But she'd have to get ready in double-quick time or he'd be gone.

After thirty minutes in lieu of her usual hour, scented and groomed, she descended the stairs, nerves on edge; the courage that had fired her up initially slowly dissipating as she moved towards the inner door of his quarters.

Am I going crazy?

He'll think I'm foolish but I *need* to know.

She knocked gently and waited.

Nothing stirred within.

She tried again. "Jay ... are you in?"

Still nothing.

Vroom! Vroom! Vroom!

The sound of a car starting up had her rushing down the hallway.

He was leaving. She remembered him saying he had a busy day ahead.

By the time she made it to the front door and unfastened the three locks he was gone, a plume of dust billowing in his wake.

Disheartened, she sighed and turned back inside.

All that effort for nothing! Never mind. I'll have a chat with him later.

It was going on for ten. She'd have time for a cup of tea before her taxi arrived.

She opened the kitchen door—and was pulled up short.

Placed on the table was a box of Black Magic chocolates with a small envelope on top.

With trembling hands she tore open the envelope.

> Dear Mrs P,
>
> I'm sorry for getting back so late last night. I hope the sound of the car didn't disturb you. The chocs are to say thank you for accepting me as your first tenant at such short notice. You won't be disappointed, I assure you.
>
> I took the liberty of entering your kitchen because I discovered that you'd forgotten to lock the inner door. I do hope you don't think it presumptuous of me but I wanted you to have the gift before I left for work.
>
> See you later,
>
> Jay

Ellen stood staring at the note. How come I forgot to lock the door? I really thought I had. She went directly into the hallway and tried the handle. It clicked open immediately. Jay was right. She *had* forgotten. Oh, dear!

Not daring to look in, she found the key and locked it immediately.

Back in the kitchen she sat down at the table and tried to calm herself by finding rational explanations for all that had occurred.

I was nervous about Jay moving in yesterday and fearful that I might have overlooked something. I was too eager to have everything just right for him. All that wanting to make a good first impression meant that I wasn't concentrating. That was the reason I forgot to lock the door. And if I forgot to do that then it's not beyond the realms of possibility that, in my agitated state, I imagined hearing those footsteps on the stairs.

She felt a little more relaxed—having unpicked those knots of angst—lifted the note once more and studied his handwriting. How elegant it was! Neat, precise and highly readable.

How thoughtful of him to give me a gift! Perhaps it's me who should have been giving him something as a welcoming gesture. But I just didn't think.

Again Ellen Purboy thanked her lucky stars that her very first tenant had turned out to be such a paragon.

She ran a finger over the glossy box of Black Magic. He's not to know I'm not a chocolate lover. But never mind; they won't go to waste. I can always gift them to someone else.

"Oh, all shall be well," she sighed. "All manner of things shall be well." It was a dictum oft quoted by her mother in times of trial, and somehow seemed appropriate in the circumstances.

She glanced at the clock. Time was going on. The tea would have to wait; she couldn't be late for Fintan Kavanagh. Finally hearing George's will was another obstacle to be overcome.

She went through to the sitting-room to collect the letter and the box of strange objects. The solicitor would perhaps be able to throw some light on the meaning of both. Clear up yet another mystery or two.

The letter was where she'd left it.

But, to her consternation, the mysterious casket was nowhere to be seen.

TWENTY-NINE

Manny was in a quandary. Late last night he'd received an anonymous phone call with a set of detailed instructions. He was to collect a package from a certain address and take it to Fitzwell's hideout.

"It's a sensitive package," the voice intoned gravely. "We wouldn't want it fallin' into the wrong hands. For that reason yer tae hide it well outta sight in yer car. 'Cos if the Brits were tae stap yeh and discover it, you'd be lookin' at the inside of a cage for a quare bit."

"But I-I—"

"The marra evenin' before six. *Don't be late.*"

With that, the line went dead.

Now, the following morning, Manny was sitting in the living-room, eyes shut, head in hands. He was drinking beer to calm his nerves—something he'd never done at such an early hour in his whole life—and was waiting for his ma to wake up.

He'd collected her from the parochial house after a terse call from Father Mulcahy in the wee small hours. The priest had administered first aid and warned him to keep her away from the shrine, because if she trespassed again after dark he'd be having her committed or arrested—one of the two.

"And warn her also not to be spreading rumours about that statue of the Virgin Mother out there moving. Because *it didn't move*. Your mother's delusional and needs her eyes tested as far as I'm concerned. The last thing I need is hordes of demented people flocking in here and tramping through my church grounds at all hours of the day and night because *your mother* lives in fairyland

and believes in hobgoblins and the Divil knows what else."

"Aye, Father. Sorry, Father."

Manny got up and went over to his ma now, who was sprawled on the sofa with a plaster on her eyebrow and a bandage on her knee, snoring like a buffalo after breakfast.

"Ma, wake up, wake up!" he implored, leaning over her.

Having managed to get her home after enduring Father Mulcahy's scalding tirade, Manny found that he couldn't manoeuvre her up the stairs—what with the hurt knee, the sore head and her rambling on about something she called the "extizzy" at the shrine—the sofa seemed the better alternative.

She'd fallen into a deep slumber almost immediately after the drama of the evening, and he'd put a blanket over her and retired himself, hoping she'd be all right, and that by morning would've forgotten all about the moving-statue business she'd sworn she'd been a witness to.

He shook her shoulder again, this time more vigorously.

"Wha'-wha'-wha'?" Tilda moaned, her eyes shooting open.

She stared up at the ceiling.

"God, am-a … am-a in heaven?"

"Och, Ma, don't be talkin' silly. Yer in the house, on the sofa."

He helped her upright.

"D'yeh not mind last night?"

In a way he was hoping she wouldn't mind last night, but some straight talking was needed if he were to keep his promise to the parish priest.

"God, son, it was powerful. Get us a cuppa tea and I'll tell yeh all about it."

"Look, Ma, I've tae collect a fare soon, so I'll make yeh the tea, but I don't have time tae hear no more … you tolt me all about it last night anyway."

Tilda grabbed Manny's hands.

"But son, I didn't tell yeh the best bit."

Manny, fearful now, could see his ma was in earnest. He'd have to humour her. An argument was the last thing he wanted, given what he'd be facing with Fitzwell later in the day.

"Aye, I'll get the tea."

"God, son, she tolt me I had the gift of healing. She sez I must heal the minds and souls of the affected and bring them back to the Lord. 'The people of Ireland need tae come back to the faith, my child....' That's what she called me: 'my child'. God, son, I wuz in extizzy the whole time, like the angels and saints when the Holy Spirit come upon them in the upper room."

Manny handed her the tea.

"Aye, right ... and that word yer using's wrong. It's ecstasy not extizzy."

"Aye, whatever, but better than that: she blinked at me three times, Manny."

"Who?"

"Och, who d'yeh think? The Virgin Mary, and she nodded her head at least three more times ... three's always a good sign ... and after telling me that, she sez that me hands could cure the people. And when she tolt me that, if her face didn't change into the face of the Lord himself—a brown face with the bluest eyes yeh ever seen and a wee bitt-of a beard. Not as long as you see in the pitchers of him, mind you ... it then went back to her own face...."

Tilda took a grateful gulp of tea, all the better to oil the wheels of her scintillating tale.

"But, Ma, yeh only *thought*—"

"Then she changed into St Theresa of Leesucks, or it might-a been Theresa of A-vile-a. I always get them two mixed up, so I do. Anyway it was one-a them French ones but it was hard tae say which."

"Look, Ma, I have to go. I'm picking up a Mrs Purboy—"

"Mrs *Purboy?!* God son, yer not, are yeh?"

"Aye, what's it to you?"

"That's the very grand lady that lost her husband of recent that I wuz tellin' yeh about . . . lives out in that big house they say is haunted."

"Aye, maybe anyway, I don't wanna be late, 'cos Fred sez she's very well off and will give me a big tip if I play me cards right. So I wanna be on time."

Ma Bryn saw an unmissable opportunity.

"God, canna come with yeh, son? 'Cos I'd love tae meet her."

"*What?*"

"I wanna help her, son."

"Aye, and how d'you know Mrs Purboy wants *your* help? How d'you know she believes in all that malarkey?"

"When you lose a loved one you'll try anything, son. I could do a séance . . . show her the husband's happy on the Other Side. That would put her mind at ease and stop her worrying, so it would."

"Ma, that's crazy. Sit there and drink up yer tea. I'll be back in an hour's time. Now, I gotta go."

Manny was pulling on his coat and making for the door.

"Son, I promise I won't go back to the shrine, if you'll just let me come with you. I need-a see the doctor about me head and knee anyway."

Manny couldn't believe his ears.

He turned.

"D'yeh mean that, Ma? You'll never go back tae that shrine ever again?"

"On me mammy's grave, son."

"Promise?"

"Promise. I'll not let yeh down 'cos I've give you me word, haven't I? I only needed to see the Virgin Mother once anyway, tae know the moving was real."

"All right," Manny said with reluctance.

At this stage he'd agree to anything to keep her from making an exhibition of herself at St Timothy's.

"And another thing: you'll have to take the bus home. I'm tied up the rest of the day."

"That's no bother, Manny. No bother a-tall."

Half an hour later mother and son were turning into the magnificent grounds of Cedarwood Manor and cruising up the winding driveway.

Tilda was flabbergasted.

"God-savus, son, I've never seen anything like it! She's a very grand lady, this Mrs Purboy… must be powerful wealthy. But then I knew by the look of her when I seen her in the Shearlock Combs that she was grand."

"Aye, don't you be saying anything silly till her, Ma, and affronting me."

"God, look at her floribundas and Bristol Fairies! I could never grow them meself. She's got good green hands on her too, 'cos—"

"*Ma!*"

"I'll not say a word in front of you, son."

Tilda meant it too, since she had a plan.…

They drew to a halt.

"Now, I'm warning you," Manny said again. "Don't let me down!"

"No, I won't, son. I'll just ask her can I use her toilet, like."

"*What?*"

"Not be long."

Tilda had needed to act fast. The call of nature was the only ready excuse she could think of.

Before Manny knew it, she was out of the car.

"Ma, for Chrissakes!"

He whipped off his seatbelt. But by the time he'd gotten out of the car, she was already labouring up the steps of Cedarwood.

"Ma, come back here!"

Should he run after her and contain the damage or would that make a bad situation even more embarrassing?

He saw her push the bell.

Too late already. With a resigned sigh he got back in the car.

Moments later the door opened.

"Hello ... I mean good morning, Mrs ... Mrs Purboy," Tilda began breathlessly, putting out a hand. "Me name's Mrs Bryn ... Tilda Bryn."

Ellen was taken aback to see a dishevelled-looking woman smiling back at her, garbed in a multi-coloured kaftan with what looked like soil stains down the front. Somehow she looked familiar.

"Oh ... er ... erm ... nice to meet you. Are you all right? It's just that I was expecting my taxi."

"Well, we're the taxi, Mrs Purboy, but I'm not the driver. It's me son Manny over there. I came with him 'cos I had a wee bit-of a fall last night and need tae see the doctor. Thought I would take the lift with him tae save time. I hope yeh don't mind."

"Why, of course not. That's no problem. I'm sorry about your fall, Mrs ... er ... ?"

"Bryn.... Thank you, Mrs Purboy, but you can call me Tilda if yeh like.... Now, me clients they call me Ma*dame*, on account of me psychic gifts."

"Oh ... how interesting!" Ellen said, thinking about her own spooky experiences and the priest's blessing of her house. "I'm Ellen by the way. Haven't I seen you somewhere before?"

"Yes, in the Shearlock Combs saloon a wee while back."

"That's the place ... of course."

"Yes, indeed. Ellen ... that's a nice name." Not one for standing on ceremony, Ma Bryn went in for the kill. "I'm a clairvoyant yeh see, Ellen ... do readings and séances for them that's lost loved ones and the like. I knew when I saw you that time in the saloon that you'd lost a loved one."

"You did?" Ellen was amazed.

"Yes, indeed."

Tilda had come prepared. She drew a note from her handbag.

"Now, there's me name and phone number. If you ever want to make contact with your husband you just call me."

"My husband? But... but how did you know he was... he was..."

"Passed? Oh, I sense these things, Ellen. But don't you worry, 'cos things is gonna work out for you... even if there's a wee bitt-a darkness tae be got through first, like. He'll always be with you in spirit, so he will."

Ellen was near to tears. She'd never heard anything like it.

"Well... thank you. I-I—"

Honk! Honk! Honk!

"We'd better go, Ellen. Me son's a bit impatient, so he is. And yeh don't wanna be late for your appointment. Now, you call me any time yeh wanna chat about things."

Ellen nodded solemnly and locked the door.

"Here, let me help you," she said, noting Tilda's limp.

They descended the steps arm in arm.

The casual onlooker could have been forgiven for thinking that the two ladies had known each other all their lives.

VIVIENNE

The bus-stop for Fairmoy turned out to be on a deserted stretch of road quite a distance from Killoran.

There were very few houses and Vivienne felt a bit nervous having to wait there.

The elderly couple—who got out in front of her—went off in the opposite direction. They must live round about, she thought, and made for the bus-shelter.

Her connection would arrive in twenty minutes. She comforted herself that it wouldn't be too long a wait.

A couple of cars passed, their drivers slowing to take a good look at her. Feeling uncomfortable, she pulled out her magazine and feigned interest. As she leafed through the pages the sky clouded over. She looked up, heart sinking. She hadn't come prepared for rain and chided herself for not having checked the forecast. With no umbrella she'd get soaked—the bus-shelter was open-fronted. She huddled in a corner as a curtain of rain bemisted the landscape.

In the field across the road a few cows were cropping the grass. Sheep dotted the hills beyond. They were a pretty sight. She rarely saw farm animals and wondered how they could cope with being outside in all weathers. The cattle were the colour of desert sand, their pelts gleaming darker as the rain intensified. One of them lumbered to the gate and studied her intently. She wanted to go over and stroke its cute velvety nose, but the sound of another car approaching deterred her.

She squeezed herself further into the shelter so she wouldn't be noticed.

The vehicle was drawing closer. She registered the gears shifting down. Buried her head deeper in the magazine.

The car drew to a halt, engine idling.

She felt a flutter of fear but kept her eyes rooted to the page.

Then:

"Are you all right, dear?"

Vivienne forced herself to look up. The kindly face of an old lady was smiling back at her from the passenger seat of a small blue car. It was the elderly couple who'd shared her bus journey. She was sure of it. Immediately her nervousness lessened.

She got up and went over, relieved.

"Er ... erm, yes ... I'm just waiting for the bus, thanks."

The driver, whom she assumed was the husband, was staring straight ahead. The woman consulted him. He mumbled something Vivienne couldn't catch.

"Is it Derry you'll be goin' to, dear?" the lady asked.

"Erm ... no. Fairmoy. But it's all right; the bus will be here soon."

"Oh, but that's on our way! We'll give you a lift."

Vivienne hesitated.

At which point the man leaned over and looked up at her. He had a thin, worn face and was wearing bottle glasses, which made his eyes look disconcertingly owlish.

"That bus tae Fairmoy's nivver on time," he said. "So you could be waitin' here a good wee while ... maybe the hour. Better if we give you the lift, since we're goin' yer way anyway."

Vivienne couldn't imagine standing *a whole hour* on that isolated stretch of road. God knows who or what might come along. She'd be safe with this kindly couple.

"If you're sure it's no trouble," she said, picking up her holdall and stuffing the magazine into it.

"No trouble at all," the lady smiled.

Once in the back seat, she placed the holdall beside her and settled down. The driver turned and nodded.

"Is that us?" he said, putting the car in gear.

"Yes. Thank you . . . thank you so much!"

He smiled. Turned his attention back to the road. Moved off.

She was glad to be out of the rain. *Very glad!* It was drumming steadily on the roof now and she'd be soaked to the bone had these kindly people not come along.

"It's my first time in this part of the country," she said, attempting conversation. "It's really beautiful!"

"Aye, it is that," the lady said.

Vivienne got the feeling they were shy and didn't wish to talk.

She relaxed a bit and studied them. The lady was wearing a beige Aran cardigan, which looked hand-knit. Her silvery hair was perfectly set in rows of flawless little pin curls. The whiff of lacquer holding it stiffly in place told Vivienne her earlier assumption about a hair salon visit was probably correct.

The husband had a tartan scarf tucked into the collar of his thick jacket. The trilby hat sat slightly askew.

Why, she wondered, wear such heavy clothes in summer? Old people obviously feel the cold more.

She shrugged the thought away and gazed out of the window, taking in the view of the pretty countryside and marvelling at the fresh greenness of it all. Such a change from the city! I should take more trips like this, she thought.

It was stuffy in the car. Maybe she'd roll down the window just a crack. They'd hardly notice.

She reached for the window winder.

What?!

There was *no winder.* She couldn't open the window.

The other side-door was the same.

And there were no door-handles either.

There was no way to get air.

She sat there, captive, trying to allay a rising fear: *I'm trapped here.*

Stop it, Vivienne! she upbraided herself.

Stop it this very minute! That imagination of yours is working overtime.

With the reprimand firmly given and received, she took a deep breath, tried to relax, and sank back in the seat once more.

THIRTY-ONE

Fintan Kavanagh was a little apprehensive about finally seeing Ellen Purboy in his office. Getting George's will out of his in-tray was something he was not exactly looking forward to. He'd been speculating that the meeting wouldn't be an easy one. Wills were often difficult territory to navigate. Dangers lurked like landmines liable to be stepped on, most especially when things weren't exactly straightforward.

For the fact was that George Purboy had secrets; secrets that required carefully nuanced disclosure if he were to spare Ellen further upset. He knew that such a situation would present difficulties.

A balance had to be struck between what served the interests of both parties best, without transgressing the rule of law too much. He'd been a friend of George's since schooldays, and in death—just as in life—had a duty to protect him.

"So good to see you, Ellen," Fintan said now as she entered his office, relieved that crunch time had come.

They hugged briefly.

"And you too, Fintan." Ellen felt the weight of the meeting like a heavy cloak the solicitor would relieve her of very soon.

She sat down opposite him, taking in his framed accreditations on the oatmeal walls, the desk teeming with papers. A pretty, owl-shaped paperweight was perched on a stack of letters. It made her think briefly of the golden owl in the trinket box. The whole scene avowed to make her nervous. Officialdom in all its forms made her feel all at sea; but the daunting world of bureaucracy was hers to deal with now, whether she wanted to or not.

"And may I say," Fintan continued, "you're looking rather well in the circumstances. How are you coping?"

"Oh, good days and bad days, Fintan. You know how it is."

"Yes, it must be very difficult being without him. He was such a force of nature: George. But time heals ... a worn cliché I know, but it holds a lot of truth. You must come to dinner one evening. Marjorie would love to see you."

He said this knowing that Ellen would not be accepting the invitation. Not after this momentous meeting at any rate.

"Thank you, Fintan... maybe... maybe I will... when I'm feeling more myself."

"Of course. Whenever you feel ready just call us. It goes without saying. Now ... "

He shuffled some papers to indicate that it was time for business. The last thing he wanted was Ellen breaking down. He was not much good with tearful relatives, no matter how many times he had to face them.

He handed over the will, which amounted to a single page.

"We'll get this over as quickly as possible, shall we? Strictly speaking, as you can see, everything is yours naturally: Cedarwood Manor as well as the Edgewater summerhouse in Portaluce and their respective contents, his portfolio of shares totalling £20,000. Plus the balance on the current account, which amounted to £4,833 at the time of George's demise.... "

Kavanagh waited a beat, giving Ellen time to absorb the fallout from what she was reading.

Then came the question he was dreading.

"Is that it?" She was staring at him.

"Yes ... I'm afraid so, Ellen."

"But I-I don't understand ... what about his savings ... the life-insurance he took out when we married? There should be over a hundred thousand at least. Why aren't they included?"

Kavanagh leaned back in his chair. Now came the hard part.

"I'm afraid George had many debts."

"Debts? But to whom? He was always careful with money."

"Er . . . erm, I know, but . . . but the truth of the matter is . . . in recent years he'd developed a habit."

"Habit?! What sort of habit?"

Kavanagh had difficulty maintaining eye contact. He lifted the owl-shaped paperweight. Set it down again. "Gambling. A gambling habit."

Ellen was stunned. "*Gambling? George?* That's preposterous! He always had contempt for those who frittered away their pay packets at the bookies. This is shocking! I-I can't believe what you're telling me!"

"I know, Ellen; it's hard to take in. I'm so sorry you have to find this out now... but he... uh, he... well, he made me swear not to tell you... was so ashamed you see, and he, well, he loved you so much. The last thing he wanted to do was upset you."

Ellen felt faint. How could she not have known? How could he have been *so* deceitful? How could Fintan *not* have warned her? It took real effort to hold herself together.

"When... when did this start . . . ?"

"About two years ago—"

"*Two years?*"

"Well, as I say, Ellen, as with all addictions it started out small ... a wager here and there... then alas before you know it, you're in the grip of it and it's impossible to stop."

"I-I... I just can't believe this. *You should have told me!* I could have . . . could have *helped* him. We could have *worked things through.*"

The sense of betrayal was enormous. Her head began to throb. She took the letter from her handbag, hands shaking violently, and let it fall on the desk.

"I suppose it would explain *this*. I found it unopened among his papers. Who or what is MH Ltd?"

Kavanagh opened the letter and studied it. It's a pity George didn't shred this one, he thought. But ...

"A finance company he borrowed from. One of several I'm afraid. He was paying them off bit by bit. Then, with his terminal diagnosis, he knew they'd come after you. So he used his savings to settle things. As for the life-insurance ... well, he just couldn't keep up the payments. But look, Ellen, it's not as bad as you think—"

"Oh, isn't it? It's so easy to say, Fintan."

She got up and began pacing the room. Somehow sitting there taking it all in was just too much. "Over one hundred thousand pounds of life-savings frittered away on horses and the two of you colluding behind my back."

Fintan spread his hands. "Look, Ellen, it's not all bad."

"What? Next thing you'll be telling me to find a job. At my age ... with minimal typing skills and ... and ... "

She broke down.

"No, I'm not saying that. Ellen, please sit down. We'll ... we'll work this through together. I'm so very sorry and you have every right to be angry with me. I *pleaded* with George to come clean with you but he wouldn't hear of it. How could I break the confidence of a friend who was dying? I was put in a very difficult position. Truly."

Reluctantly, Ellen resumed her seat. Mopped her tears. She needed all the help she could get right now. Fintan Kavanagh might be the only one in a position to offer it. No one else would be hearing of this, least of all Nettie. She could just hear her scathing tone. "Atheist George—well, I told you so, didn't I? No morals whatsoever. He was never a good one."

" ... and there *are* alternatives," Fintan was saying. "It's not as bleak as it looks. Just hear me out, Ellen, please. Firstly: Cedarwood at today's prices is well over half a million."

"That's out of the question. I'm *not* selling my home."

"I know, I know you have no intention of selling, but you could move to Edgewater permanently. Make Portaluce your home. Secondly: if you didn't want to sell, you could auction off some of the antiques. Those alone could bring you in at least thirty or forty grand. Thirdly: the shares could be cashed in now. The markets are healthy and you could see a very good return on them. So, all in all, you're not facing destitution, if you understand me."

"If you say so," she said wearily, thinking suddenly of Jay Lavelle. "It's just as well I decided to rent out his office, given what I now know."

Kavanagh stared at her.

"You did what?"

"Yes. Perhaps I should turn the whole place into a guest house."

"And do you . . . do you have a tenant?"

"Yes, as a matter of fact I have. A lovely young man by the name of Lavelle."

Kavanagh's expression changed. She could see the news discomfited him.

He paused.

"What of it?"

"A young *man?*"

"Yes, a young man."

He shook his head; fumbled with some papers.

"Er, no. I'm just . . . well, I'm just a little surprised. . . ."

"Surprised?"

"That you'd let a strange man under your roof . . . I mean, someone you know little about . . . with so many valuables. That's all."

"Well, there you are. I turned George's office into a bedsit. He doesn't have access to the rest of the house, obviously. Besides which, Fintan, you're hardly in a position to criticize my decisions—in the circumstances."

She got up. "Now, if you'll excuse. I'll see myself out."

Kavanagh hastened to open the door.

"Look, Ellen, I'm sorry. I've only your best interests at heart. You know that, don't you?"

"Do you, Fintan ... really? If you had my best interests at heart, as you put it, I wouldn't be in this mess now. Good day."

After Ellen left, Kavanagh sighed deeply. The worst was over—for now at least. But he feared what the future might hold. Ellen was fragile but she was clearly determined. That last was a side of her he hadn't seen before. It could turn out to be her saving grace or her undoing. He desperately hoped it wouldn't be the latter.

VIVIENNE

Vivienne sat grimly in the moving car, panic rising.

She'd just seen a sign for Killoran and wondered why. The bus left her on the far side of that town not so long ago, so the old couple seemed to be travelling in the opposite direction. They must have taken a wrong turn.

She leaned forward.

"Is this the right way?"

"Aye, why wouldn't it be?" the man said gruffly.

"It's just that I saw a sign for Killoran and—"

"It's a quicker way we're goin'," the old lady piped up, turning to her, smiling. "Ronnie knows these wee roads better than anybody. Don't worry, dear, we'll be in Fairmoy in no time. You didn't tell us yer name. This here's Ronnie and I'm Alice."

"Vivienne."

"Vivi-*enne* ... that's a nice name."

They came to another junction and stopped to let a tractor pass. The farmer saluted them and turned into a field, spritzing mud across the windscreen. Ronnie harrumphed and depressed the window-washers. Turned down a narrow road—barely wide enough for two cars abreast—and trundled on at a reduced speed.

Will we, Vivienne thought, ever arrive at this rate? She sat back again, tried to calm herself by concentrating on the scenery.

The rain was easing, the sky a vault of grape-tinted clouds softening into the pinkish grey of a pigeon's breast. Pools glittered in waterlogged fields. Corn stood sodden and bunched, defying the reaper's blade. Farmers needed bone-dry corn to make their hay; that much she knew. The harvest would be a poor one.

Her eyes searched the landscape, hoping for a purchase on something that might tell her where she was. But it was a featureless region of mist-blurred boundaries. Dry-stone walls marked the perimeters of nearby fields. She wondered idly about the skill and patience required in building such walls. When were they erected? Long, long ago, she thought. If I had my camera I'd photograph them. Superimpose the image on coasters and place-mats; make that long-dead artistry live again at the dinner table.

The car bounced over yet another potholed road. She was thrown from side to side and her head began to throb.

"Aye, it's a rough stretch, this bit," Ronnie commented.

"Yes, but sure we'll be there soon enough," Alice assured her.

"If-if you say so," Vivienne said, trying to quell her fears.

They passed a small white cottage with a red roof and matching door; Venetian red she thought. She saw a rooster standing proud on an old tractor; two cats asleep on a sill. What a quaint scene! A Van Gogh quote came to her: "I see drawings and pictures in the poorest of huts and the dirtiest of corners." She wondered idly about the occupants of the little house and the lonely life they must lead, stuck out there in the middle of nowhere.

A dense wall of trees in the distance gave the impression of a forest. Her thoughts began to spin. Tricia never mentioned that she lived near a forest. Woodland of any kind scared Vivienne witless. She once got lost in a forest as a child. A kindly lady found her and returned her to her parents. She'd never forget the terror that shot through her six-year-old body at the thought of never seeing them again, the brooding darkness of the trees closing in.

Oh, the desolation, the abandonment!

Now that same feeling was rising, reaching up from the darkest depths to clutch and squeeze at her heart. Her stomach was folding in on itself.

This is the wrong way.

They're not taking me to Fairmoy.

They're heading into the forest.

Oh, dear God! I must get out!

She felt faint. Tapped Alice on the shoulder.

"Please," she said. "*Please* stop! I want out!"

The old lady looked back at her.

"Why's that, dear?"

She'd play it safe for the time being. Be nice. Feign illness.

"I-I feel sick. It's travelling in the back and . . . and I can't wind down the window to get air . . . would you mind?"

"That's no bother, dear . . . sure I'll put down *my* windee a wee bit."

"But you . . . you . . . don't understand. I feel like throwing up. Please let me out. I-I don't want to ruin your car."

The couple exchanged looks.

"Do we stop, dear?"

Ronnie let out a laugh. "What d'you think?" he said mockingly. "Sure didn't we come prepared for the like-a that. There's a beg on the floor beside you. You can throw up in that."

Vivienne saw a squished-up plastic bag at her feet. Oh, dear God! Did they plan this? She thought about the white cottage moments ago. If she could get out of the car she'd make a run for it.

"Let me out now, *please!* Just for a couple of minutes. I need air. I'm sick and I need air."

But they ignored her. Pretended not to hear.

"I said, *let me out of here!*" Louder now. "*Do you hear me? Let me out, let me out! Let me out!*"

She shook the woman's shoulder.

Alice turned.

Vivienne stared in shock.

The kindly face of the sweet old lady was gone, replaced by eyes of glaring hatred, the wizened mouth twisted in scorn.

"You're goin' nowhere," she snarled. "So just shut your mouth, young lady."

Vivienne's worst fears were confirmed.

"*Oh, dear God! N-o-o-o-o-o-o-o-o-o!*"

She bawled. She screamed. "*Let me out now! Please, let me o-u-u-t! Someone help me, p-l-e-e-e-a—s-s-s-e!*"

She hammered on the windows.

Kicked at the doors with all her might.

But they just kept on driving, getting deeper and deeper into the forest, the screams of their terrified hostage resounding through the air unheeded.

THIRTY-THREE

Ellen opened the door to Cedarwood, close to tears. The visit to Fintan Kavanagh had changed everything.

George the gambler! George the deceiver! George the traitor! How could she *not* have known? How could she have been so blind? How could she have allowed the last years to elapse without an inkling?

Now she understood all those business trips to Dublin. They were likely opportunities to indulge his addiction. There was a time when she would accompany him but in recent years such invitations had dried up; explained away by "cutbacks", "the recession", "downsizing". He had a raft of words to explain why she couldn't come along.

She went into the kitchen to put the kettle on.

Jay Lavelle's chocolates sat on the counter.

She gazed at them.

I must check later if he saw someone last night.

She glanced out of the window and was surprised to see his car parked at the side entrance. He was back early.

No time like the present.

At the door she paused, feeling a little guilty at eavesdropping.

Jay was talking. He had company.

"Now, *come on*," he called out. "We really *must* get going."

The sound of a door opening and shutting had Ellen darting back to the kitchen, just in time to see him help a little boy into the passenger seat of his car.

She dashed out.

"Hello there!"

He turned swiftly, a little surprised to see her.

"Oh, Ellen ... didn't think you were at home."

She simply had to know who the child was.

"I just got in. Who's this lovely boy? Your son?"

He faltered.

"Ah ... no, no. Goodness, no. I'm not married. He's my nephew."

The child didn't look up. Sat with his head bowed, as if playing with something.

"He's a little shy of strangers I'm afraid." He came round to the passenger door and opened it.

"Aw, that's all right. We were all the same at his age."

"Toby, say hello to Mrs P, won't you?"

"Hello, Mrs P," Toby said obediently, gazing up at her.

"Pleased to meet *you*, Toby." Ellen hunkered down beside him. Up close he was a beautiful child: olive skin, glossy chestnut hair falling in a fringe over soulful, brown eyes. He was dressed neatly in blue shorts and a matching T-shirt. Even his socks were the same shade.

"And how old are you, Toby?"

"Five and a bit."

"My goodness! That's a grand age to be. You're a lovely boy, Toby. I hope we meet again."

"Thank you, Miss," he said, his attention turning once more to the Rubik cube in his lap.

"I have him for this afternoon," Jay said, shutting the door. "The mum had an appointment. You know how it is. Was there something else, Mrs P?"

"Oh, no. I won't keep you. Goodness, where are my manners? I just wanted to say thank you for the chocolates ... such a thoughtful gesture. There was really no need."

He smiled. "You're most welcome. It's another little thing my

Aunt Edith taught me: never visit a new home without bringing a gift."

"Oh, she was very courteous: your aunt. She taught you well. I *do* apologize for forgetting to lock the door. It won't happen again; I promise. Well, what am I saying? It won't happen again because I locked it immediately when I read your note of course."

Jay waved a hand. "A mere trifle. Right, Mrs P, I'll—"

"Oh, just one more thing, Jay. When you were coming in last night, you didn't … erm … meet or … see anyone, did you?"

He shook his head. Dug his hands in his pockets. "See anyone …? Can't say I did." Then: "Only your visitor of course."

Ellen was shocked. "Visitor? But I didn't have a visitor last night."

"Didn't you?"

"But where … where did you see—"

"Look, I *thought* I saw someone at the drawing-room window as I drove up. But it was obviously a trick of the light."

Ellen was beside herself. "But that's impossible … I-I was in bed when you got in."

Sensing her distress, he came forward and laid a consoling hand on her arm. "Look, I'm sorry I mentioned it. I was obviously mistaken. I didn't mean to upset you, Mrs P. … Truly. Only my old imagination playing tricks."

She thought of the missing casket. The noises she'd heard on the stairs. Should she mention it? No. He'll only think me a foolish old woman afraid of her own shadow.

"Yes … yes," she said. "Probably."

"As I say, the reflection of a tree or something in the glass. I hope I haven't upset you unduly."

"No … no … It's just that one can't be too careful these days."

"I quite agree." He smiled and went round to the driver's door again.

"Mind how you go," Ellen said.

"I will."

She was standing watching them depart when little Toby looked her way and waved.

The gesture had Ellen's heart melting.

She stood in the courtyard until the car disappeared, treasuring that rare moment, a moment she knew she'd replay again and again in the future: the boy raising his little hand to connect with her in such an innocent and beautiful way.

She turned back to the house, but before long Jay's troubling words, "only your visitor", were uppermost again.

Tears filled her eyes as she shut the door behind her, gazed up at the portrait of Sir Wilfred Blackbourne. Perhaps Nettie was right about *you*. Cedarwood *is* an alien place.

An alien place that no longer feels safe to me.

THIRTY-FOUR

Manny Bryn drove into the Rossmara council estate with a grave sense of foreboding. Rossmara—a housing development on the fringes of Killoran—was the address Fitzwell had given him. There he would take delivery of a package from number 28 The Crescent, and ferry it directly to Fitzwell's hideout in the Muddymacreek Forest.

No stopping on the way. No talking to anyone. Those were the instructions.

Conscious of his vice-like grip on the steering wheel, he wondered for the umpteenth time how in God's name he'd got himself into such a predicament so soon into his new job. Never in his wildest nightmares did he think he'd be on the radar of an escaped IRA terrorist.

Life had taken a bizarre and most unwelcome turn.

Maybe I'll only have to do the one run, he decided, trying to console himself as he wound his way through the warren of streets that comprised the housing estate. The grim development was a jungle of semi-detached houses, each looking as soulless as the next. He passed Rossmara Drive, Rossmara Heights, Rossmara Avenue but no sign of The Crescent.

It was not the kind of place you'd want to delay in. Gaudy murals loomed large on gable ends, hoardings hosted anti-British slogans, kerbstones were intermittently plastered in the green, white and orange of the Irish tricolour.

This was Republican territory and he was an interloper, even if he was a "Fenian".

A bother of young boys lolling against a low wall stared at him as he passed by. Manny hoped they wouldn't ask him for a lift. He knew he wouldn't be able to handle their sort. He stepped on the gas. Made a mental note to take an alternative route out.

Cresting an incline, he continued on his way, head roving from side to side like a dashboard dog in panic mode.

"Where the bloody hell is The Crescent?"

Bong!

A tennis ball had bounced off his windscreen. He screeched to a halt. The ball came to rest in the middle of the road.

A young boy, aged about ten, racket in hand, ran out to retrieve it.

Annoyed, Manny wound down the window.

"Hey, you!"

The boy, clutching the ball, approached him warily, the tennis racket trailing the ground. He had a grubby face and ginger hair in much need of a good combing.

"Did you not see me comin' there? I could-a knocked yeh down. And you threw that ball at me on purpose, so yeh did."

"Och, *I didn't,* mister! It just slipped outta me hands."

"Aye, a likely story.... I've a good mind to tell yer mother."

"Don't have a ma, mister. Only me da."

"Well, yer da then."

"You wouldn't, 'cos ... 'cos if yeh did, Da would bate the crap outta you. He's a boxer, so he is."

"R-right." Manny was sorry he'd said anything. A swift change of subject was required.

"Aye, anyway, maybe you could tell me where the Crescent is. I need number twenty-eight?"

"That's *our* house!" He pointed farther along. "The last one there. Whaddaya want me da for anyway?"

Manny groaned inwardly. Dearly regretted having upbraided the boy. "Oh, I just need to collect something from him."

He reached into the glove compartment and found a Milky Way. With a father like that he needed to show his good side.

"There's some choclit for showin' me the house."

The boy grabbed the bar with delight. "Gee, thanks, mister! I'll tell me da you wanna see him."

He took off like a hare and disappeared into number 28.

Manny steeled himself.

To buy some time and muster his courage, he decided to get out of the car and walk the short distance to the house. Walking anywhere was anathema to him, but on this occasion it was necessary.

On his approach he noticed that the dwelling beside number 28 was all boarded up. Not a good sign. Maybe the neighbours had been driven out by the boy's father?

He reached the door and knocked a couple of times, bringing himself up to his full height in an attempt at bravado.

In seconds the door flew open.

Manny gaped in shock.

Bumper Magee, the thug who'd roughed him up in the dole office, stood before him, bloodshot eyes searing into him, arms akimbo.

"Well, if it isn't Superman himself," he snarled. "Told yeh you'd be hearin' from us."

He turned and reached behind him, spider tattoos on show. Produced a package and pushed it flat into Manny's chest. "Now, you know what tae do with that, don't yeh?"

Manny nodded, dumbstruck.

"Didn't hear yeh. What was that?"

"Aye ... aye."

Magee thrust his face into his. "If yeh go to the cops you're a dead man. You know that, don't yeh?"

"Eh, aye ... aye, I do."

"Just so you know. Good to have yeh workin' for us."

He jabbed him in the chest once more. Manny stumbled but

managed to keep upright.

"Yeh better not drop that or it just might go off."

"*What!*"

He sniggered. "Hide it in the door-panel."

"What? But it's . . . it's not my car."

"I know that, yeh eejit! But that's not *my* problem! *Door-panel*, yeh hear me? Just in case the Brits stop yeh . . . wouldn't wanna be caught. 'Cos if they find it and you grass on Fitz and me, you'll be as dead as the pig cheeks I ate for breakfast."

He produced a screwdriver. "A wee gift for yeh. Free of charge. Help yeh get the panel off. Now fuck off outta here and give that tae Fitzy. The sooner the bloody better!"

With that, Magee returned inside and banged the door shut, leaving a stunned Manny frozen stiff as a statue on the doorstep.

THIRTY-FIVE

Dr Flynn sighed discreetly at the sight of Ma Bryn in his surgery. He hadn't seen her in a while, and quickly steeled himself for a feeder stream of blather before she got to the point of what exactly had brought her to his door. Dear me, but the woman could talk!

"Mrs Bryn … what can I do for you?" he asked cautiously as she flounced down in the chair, dress collapsing about her like a landing parachute.

"Gosh, doctor, it's good till see you . . . well, in a way it is and in another way it isn't. 'Cos it's been a while, hasn't it . . . which is probably a good thing for me anyway, 'cos nobody wants tae see a doctor unless it's very necessary. And me, I've been keepin' terrible well … even more well than ever these past couple-a days—"

"I'm glad to hear it! If you're well then what brings you to my clinic on this fine morning?"

"Oh, Manny brung me here . . . got hisself a new wee job as a taxi-driver, don't yeh know … doin' well at it too. Fred Bain broke the leg, but I s'ppose you knew that already, you being the doctor and—"

Dr Flynn raised a hand. "Sorry. What I meant was what *problem* brings you here, Mrs Bryn?"

"Oh, I'm with you now, doctor. Well, more or less three things."

He was afraid of that. "And they are … ?"

"Well, first: I've a wee cut on me brow, as you can see, and a bigger one on me knee that you can't see on account of me dress … but that's the one needs looking at, in case it might be enffected. Now, having said that, I don't think it would be enffected 'cos of the circumstances that brung it about, like. I need-a tell yeh about that first. 'Cos yeh wouldn't believe, doctor, how I came by them … the couple-a cuts I mean."

"Try me," Dr Flynn said curtly but forcing a smile to remain civil. He had a busy morning ahead. Could already hear the squalls and shrieks of infants in the waiting-room. At midday his baby clinic would commence and he needed to get on.

"Well, it's like this, doctor," Tilda began, her face lighting up like a harvest moon. "I was in the shrine at St Timmy's last night and if I didn't see the statue of the Virgin Mary *move.* I'm the first in the parish—if not the very first in the north of Ireland—to see the merickle, and God I can't believe that she picked *me.* Now, having said that, it isn't really a wonder that she picked me, given me psychic abilities.… "

The doctor was afraid she'd say that. What Mrs Bryn believed to be "psychic abilities" were, in his considered opinion, grandiose delusions brought on by sporadic episodes of mania, exacerbated by the early onset of menopause, which she didn't believe she had, since her mother had never gone through what she termed "the change". She was on medication for the condition, so she'd either stopped taking it or was in need of a dosage increase.

"Hmm … " he said vaguely, realizing it would be best to let her roam loose like a goat in a bramble patch, free to do as much damage to his ears and precious time as possible, if he were to fully determine the extent of her paranoia.

He slouched in his chair, twirling his pen.

" … 'cos I'm more tuned in than the usual body would be to these things, so that's why I got the vision, like … knew it was comin' too, 'cos I saw three crows on me cherry bush the morning afore last when fryin' a couple-a soda farls and timin' me boiled egg. But sure that's neither here nor there, doctor, as they say, and my goodness me, if I wasn't in extizzy the whole time—"

"You were in *what?*"

"Extizzy, doctor."

"Ah, ecstasy—as in rapture, you mean ... that's why you fell over, I suppose?"

"Yes, indeed. The light nearly blinded me ... never seen the like of it afore. Well, it nearly would-a blinded many a body, it being a heavenly light. She was shining like the sun and beaming like the crown jewels ... oh, it was powerful, doctor! She give me the power tae heal the sick too.... "

That'll ease things for me, Flynn thought wearily.

". . . and said that I should get a medal struck in her honour. Now, the medal she showed me wasn't oval like the merackless medal that French nun seen, but more of a roundie shape. And she wasn't standing on a globe crushing a snake, but on a kinda pinky bush ... when I thought about it, didn't it look like me cherry bush, the one I'd seen the three crows lighting on that morning ... so it all came together in the vision, like. Well, these things usually do. Everything's a sign leadin' up to something bigger."

"I see," said the doctor. "I don't suppose you were wearing your glasses during all this?"

"Oh no, doctor. Me third eye doesn't need no glasses."

"Quite so." As he feared, the delusions were at an advanced stage. He leaned forward in earnest. Some straight talking was required.

"But you see, Mrs Bryn, that's all very well. However, from where I'm sitting I sense that you've gone off your medication. Would I be right?"

"Oh no, I'm still taking me tablets, doctor. Have no fear of that. I know it's hard for you tae believe ... hard for many a body to believe, come to that—my Manny included—but it's the God's honest truth, so it is. I swear, doctor!"

"In that case, it's high time I increased your dosage, Mrs Bryn."

He got up quickly, fearful she might start up again.

"Now, let's have a look at that wounded knee of yours. We wouldn't want an infection to set in, now would we?"

. . .

Manny Bryn was berating himself. If I hadn't defended Iris Rainey that day in the dole office none of this would-a happened. That bastard Magee had it in for me from that day on. But she's a nice girl, Iris, and I didn't like her being treated like that, and she appreciated what I did. If she only knew what it had got me into. I'd like to meet her again, but… I wouldn't know how to go about that at all. No woman would look at me anyway.

After a very fraught drive through a maze of unapproved roads, to avoid being stopped by the army, he was nearing destination's end—Fitzwell's hideout: Long John Doody's cottage.

His nerves were in shreds and there was a litter of sweet wrappers on the car floor to prove it.

He'd made it without being caught, though, and that was the main thing.

But as he was turning into the lane that led to the house, he saw, to his consternation, that Fitzwell had visitors. A blue car was parked out front.

He had to think fast.

I could play it safe and wait until they left. But then I could be waiting a good wee while and I'm desperate to be rid of this damned thing. Maybe I'll chance it and leave it on the doorstep.

Something told him it was best to keep the taxi out of sight. Whoever was in there didn't need to see him. The fewer witnesses the better.

He reversed into an area shielded by a stand of bushes and cut the engine. Found the screwdriver and proceeded to ease off the door-panel once more. It wasn't as difficult to remove the second time around and he was able to retrieve the package without delay. He looked at the gaping panel in dismay, imagining the scowl on Fred Bain's face if he could actually see what he was up to. But there was no time to think about that now. He'd make sure to fix it properly when he was safely out of harm's way.

Job done, he got out of the car and trudged up the lane, side-stepping a series of potholes. The last thing he wanted was to fall a clatter, even if it was more likely that the parcel contained a gun rather than a bomb. But even so, if the gun was loaded maybe it could discharge and blow his head off.

Manny's mind was manufacturing whole tapestries of lurid possibilities, which would only cease on delivery of the damned package.

As he gained the yard the smell of smouldering turf hit him. Smoke was rising from the chimney. Fitzwell had a fire going.

He could see that, when new, the old three-roomed cottage would have been pretty: ledges and door painted green, a lattice of vine creepers trained over the lintel, the once-gleaming windows blinded now with yellowing newspaper.

He was too afraid to inspect the blue car. But just as he was about to set the package down on the step he heard the sound of raised voices.

"Tie the bitch's feet!" Fitzwell shouted. This was followed by a scuffling noise and the strangled cries of a woman.

"Get off me! Let me go! Let me go!"

Panicking, he hoofed it back to the car, heart beating like a Lambeg drum.

From a safe distance, through the bushes he had a good view of the house.

Luckily, he'd got offside in the nick of time.

A few minutes later, the door opened and an elderly couple emerged: a grey-haired woman and a man in a hat.

Manny's knees went weak.

For he *knew* in his heart of hearts it was *not* the screams of that old lady he'd just heard.

This evil pair had brought *a young woman* to Fitzwell's lair.

For whatever reason, the unfortunate woman was now being held prisoner by him.

THIRTY-SIX

Ellen Purboy was beginning to doubt her sanity.

Jay Lavelle's words were haunting her, night and day. He claimed he'd seen someone "visiting" that night. He'd witnessed something, even though he'd made light of it to save her distress. Whoever it was, had *they* stolen the casket of gold objects?

She'd looked everywhere for it, but it seemed to have vanished into thin air.

George's deception gnawed at her constantly. The more she dwelt upon it, the more fractured her mind was becoming. She couldn't eat. She couldn't sleep.

Every night, she went to bed ill at ease and on two occasions she thought she heard movement on the stairs again. She'd be jolted awake, but hear nothing further. Were these just "dreams within dreams", as Dr Flynn had explained, brought on by the stress of it all, or was there something more sinister at play?

An endless reel of her mother's final months kept looping in her head. She'd moved into Cedarwood to recover from a fall and ended up losing her mind. Had the house done that to her?

In her final days she'd said some crazy things.

"You were moving furniture round in the middle of the night *again*. Why do you keep opening and shutting doors?"

And, most disturbing of all, about a week before she died: "Someone was on those stairs last night and they knocked on that door. That was Death knocking. This is a bad house."

Ellen hadn't paid much heed to those ramblings back then. Her mother was senile; thought everyone was out to get her. But now in retrospect here was the daughter taking on the mother's mantle:

she too thinking the house was haunted; she too thinking someone was out to get her.

On her knees in the garden, she was trying to distract herself by weeding the flowerbeds. She needed to be outdoors; needed to put order to things, wrest back some kind of control. Gardening had always served as a stress-reliever.

It was a beautiful sunny afternoon. Even though she was exhausted from lack of sleep, she'd forced herself out—anything to be free of the stifling aura in the house. It carried too many memories of a past she'd sooner forget. She needed distance from it. The history of Cedarwood had never bothered her until now. All those stories of Sir Wilfred belonging to a cult; the mystery surrounding his untimely death. Maybe there *was* truth in the rumours? George had discounted it all as poppycock. But she could no longer see George as the man of integrity she'd once thought him to be.

She sat back on her heels. Removed her gloves to wipe the tears away. Word of so much betrayal foisted upon her so suddenly was hard to take.

A beautiful butterfly landed on one of the gloves, its dark brown wings and creamy pattern vibrant in the light: a Speckled Wood. She loved butterflies. Had studied them as part of a horticultural course many years before. This little exemplar she knew to be the most territorial of them all: fighting off intruders and other insects to stake its claim. She wished she could have some of those qualities: strength of purpose, determination, more like her dear father, really: a man who could stay focused in an earthquake.

The butterfly flew off, and with its departure came the realization that she really needed to get to grips with the happenings in the house. Talk to someone who knew about such matters. Share her concerns. That would be a start. But whom could she confide in?

Not the priest. Father Hill's blessing had achieved next to nothing. Not Dr Flynn, who would only tell her she was stressed and prescribe *more* drugs. Not her sister Nettie, who would tell her to pull herself together—and order a full-blown exorcism, God forbid.

All at once, the vision of a woman came unbidden. A woman who'd called at her door not so very long ago.

"The psychic ... why, of course!" she cried aloud. "Tilda!"

"Mrs P, are you all right?"

She flinched at the sound of the voice. Turned, and to her astonishment, saw Jay Lavelle standing over her, looking concerned.

Where had he come from? How come she hadn't *heard* him?

"Oh, y-you gave me a fright ... I-I'm okay ... yes, I ..."

She made to get up.

"Here, let me help you," he said, placing a supportive hand under her elbow. "I'm sorry if I startled you."

"Th-thank you ... it's ... it's not a problem." But his little act of gallantry made her voice crack. She searched her sleeve for a hankie, knowing she didn't have one, and broke down.

Like a stage magician, the lodger at once produced a pristine white one. Handed it to her.

"Thanks ... I'm so sorry. Things haven't been easy of late."

"Oh, please don't apologize, Mrs P. We all go through trying times. Tell you what: why don't I get rid of that bucket of weeds for you? We can have some tea and a chat. It's time we got a little better acquainted."

Ellen nodded through her tears.

"Yes ... that-that would be nice."

"Great!"

He lifted the bucket and carried it off.

Ellen returned indoors, on edge, but thinking that perhaps having a chat with Jay would weaken the blizzard of misgivings and uncertainties assailing her.

She decided to serve tea in the palatial drawing-room. It was by far the most elegant chamber in the house; neoclassical in design, the colours muted, the furniture beautifully grained with glowing patinas.

In light of Jay's interest in antiques, she hoped the room would serve as a diversion. The last thing she wanted was to burden the young man with *her* problems.

When George was alive the drawing-room was used only at weekends or on special occasions. He was so protective of its many rare and precious pieces it could have been a museum. Now, opening it up to receive a new visitor seemed like the right thing to do. It was also an act of rebellion against George's proclivities, because of which she'd most likely have to sell off most of its ancient artefacts anyway.

She tried pushing all thoughts of her errant husband aside as she poured the tea. Jay was sitting across from her, an impressive marble coffee table between them. She saw that a fine film of dust was marring its surface, but no matter. There were more important things to think about now. The cleaning could wait.

"My, what a wonderful room!" he exclaimed, his glance sharpening on its many treasures. "This house has so many hidden gems."

"Thank you."

She handed him the cup and saucer, wondering what note to strike with him, this charming young man who'd appeared so suddenly in her life.

"Well, they're just *things* really. Given your appreciation of antiques, I thought you'd like to see this room."

Sunlight, sudden at the window, gilded a cufflink, burnished his perfect blond hair.

"Sugar?"

He shook his head.

"I'm rarely in here. It was my husband's favourite room, but since he passed away, I—"

"Oh, I *am* sorry to hear that. I had no idea.... Has it been long?"

"Nearly five months now."

"So recent?" He put his cup down gently, a look of sorrow briefly distorting his handsome face. "Please accept my sincere condolences."

Such empathy in a man his age was touching. Ellen wanted to weep again but held herself in check. "Thank you. That's kind of you, Jay. But life must go on."

"Alas, yes. You know, Ellen ... uh, may I call you Ellen?"

"Of course."

"I ... um ... I think I owe you an apology."

"An apology?"

"Well, here I am breezing into your life without a care in the world, not giving a thought about anything. And here you are living alone in this big house, trying to come to terms with your great loss. It must be so hard for you." He leaned forward in earnest. "Because when I really think about it, renting to a stranger ... I mean: starting out on a totally new venture like that ... well, that takes courage, *real* courage, Ellen."

She was moved by his insight. "Well ... we all have our ways of coping, I suppose."

He nodded, and lifted the teapot before she had the opportunity.

Now it was *her* chance to sound *him* out. "Thank you! Now tell me about your little nephew. Such a lovely child!"

For a moment she felt the air sag, as if a dark bird of prey had swooped through the room.

"Toby ... well he's ... he's a good child." He set the teapot aside. "I'm afraid I wasn't really straight with you ... the other day, I mean ... when you saw us."

"Sorry I ... I really don't mean to pry."

He shook his head resignedly. "No, it's all right. You took me by surprise you see. Toby ... well, Toby isn't really my nephew."

"Oh ... "

"He's ... he's my son."

His son! But hadn't he told her that day he wasn't married?

"I see.... But you said—"

"I wasn't married. Yes, well, I'm not—in a manner of speaking."

She saw his fingers tighten on the cup. Offered him a tea-cake to mitigate the awkwardness of the moment.

"No, thanks. That day you saw him ... Toby ... the day you took me unawares. Well, I didn't expect to see you.... That's why I-I ... "

"Think nothing of it," Ellen said, seeing his discomfort. "And Toby's mother, is she in Dublin?"

He stared at the floor for a moment or two. Lifted his eyes to meet hers. She could see that the question upset him.

"Alas, no. You and I have much in common, believe it or not."

"Oh ... ?"

"I'm grieving a loss too. My wife, Hannah, she ... she died nearly a year ago."

VIVIENNE

Vivienne awakened, lying on her back on a mattress; hands and feet bound, mouth gagged with duct tape.

Slowly she let her eyes adjust to the gloom as a sludge of dark notions began stirring.

Where am I?!

Rafters above her: old, broken, with just enough light filtering through to give shape to things; a light bulb suspended from a beam, the faint outline of a window on the far wall.

An odour of mildew prevailed.

Somewhere a bird was singing. Bright bursts of song.

Is it morning?

She tried to lift her head, but it felt as heavy as a boulder. Her throat constricted. A snake of nausea, coiled tight in her stomach, stirred.

Motion was dangerous. If she sat up, the snake would move again.

All she could do was roll onto her side. Carefully she did so, stiffening every muscle.

The movement threw the room into focus.

The mattress was positioned along the rear wall. She saw splintered floorboards, dingy walls of flaking plaster, a green door. *Terre Verte,* she thought—seeing a blob of paint on a palette in another life far, far away from this.

There was a bucket near the bed. A steel folding-chair sat inside the door. A small window on the left was papered over, gaps of light spilling through.

Questions scrabble, topple, seeking purchase.

How did I get here? Why am I here? Who brought me here?

Focus. *Focus.*

Remember.

Think. Think. Think.

Fragments of fact spun in her head. Shot back and forth, trying to accommodate the horror of recall.

Bus-stop ... old couple ... lift ... blue car ... *doors no handles* ... trapped ... forest ... house ... old house ... man ... MAN.

Kidnapped!

Oh, dear God!

They kidnapped me! The old couple kidnapped me and took me to the man ... the man in the forest!

This is the nightmare my father feared! I am in the nightmare my father feared, the nightmare I would not allow myself to contemplate. All that went before. All that I ignored—the barman in the pub, the weirdo on the bus, the strange elderly couple—dropping crumbs on the trail that would end here. I ignored the signs. I did not tell my father because my studio and my freedom meant more to me than ...

She tried to scream against the duct tape.

"*Hmmmmm! Hmmmmm!*"

Tears wet her cheeks. It was useless.

I should have listened to him.

Suddenly, beyond the door, the sound of a chair scraping back.

Footsteps were approaching. She lay very still.

He was coming. *Her captor was coming.*

She shut her eyes. Heard the rattle of a key in the lock. A bolt being drawn back.

The door, keening on its hinges, admitted a waft of cool air.

He entered and stood over her. She smelt cigarettes and after-shave as he leaned close.

A hand was placed on her shoulder. Gently.

"Vivienne, now... would yeh be awake?"

Against her better judgement she opened her eyes.

Stared into a face swimming above hers: into eyes that held the predatory gleam of a wild dog. He had a beanie pulled down over the ears. She *knew* that face: a photo from a newspaper Miss Mills dropped.

Words, random and quick, flooded back: *prisoner-escaped-convict-judge-barbarous!*

"*Hmmmmm! Hmmmmm!*"

"Now, *now*."

He hauled her into a sitting position, crouched down beside her.

"I go by the name-a Fitzwell, Viv, but yeh can call me Fitz."

The snake of nausea twisted violently.

"That's what we'll call yeh from now on: Viv. Three syllables too much of a mouthful for the like-a me."

She tried to shift away from him.

"*Hmmmmm! Hmmmmm!*"

She convulsed.

He ripped off the duct tape and thrust the bucket under her chin just in time. She puked into it.

The relief she felt was extraordinary. She spluttered. Gulped. Let out a scream, wretched and unending, while trying desperately to free her hands.

From nowhere a knife appeared. The sight of it striking her dumb in an instant.

"No point in tryin' that out here, Viv. Nobody tae hear you but the wee birds and me. If yeh do it again there's no tellin' what I might do with this. D'yeh understand me?"

She nodded wildly. Her breathing filled the room.

"Good! Yer here for the foreseeable ... so it's best you and me get on, see?"

He stuck the knife in a back pocket; got up and trailed the chair over to the mattress.

Sat down before her. Legs spread wide, elbows resting on knees, fingers laced together. She saw a wedding ring. Wondered about the woman who married this monster.

"W-why ... why am I here?" she stammered. "If it's money you want ... I-I can get you some. Just let me go ... *please.* I won't go to the police. I-I promise I won't."

He emitted a derisory snort, leaned back in the chair, produced a pack of cigarettes and lit up.

"Yeh think it's that aisey, Viv? Money, eh? Sure where would a wee student like you get money? That's sayin' I *wanted* money."

"Not me ... my-my father. He'd—"

"Ah ... yer da, the judge. Daddy good for everything, is he?"

"I-I know he ... I know he convicted you. Your name's Connor, not Fitzwell ... that's why you're doing this, because he—"

"Listen, Viv," he said quietly, "I don't want yer da's fuckin' money! Not yet anyway ... just want him to sweat ... 'cos of what he did to *me.*" He drew deeply on the cigarette, squinting at her through the smoke. "Taking you away is the best way I can think of at the present moment in time."

She wanted to yell out long and hard but something told her it would be a dangerous move. He'd likely gag her again and that was the last thing she wanted.

"I-I'm sorry," she said, trying to pacify him. "B-But, he ... my father ... he was only doing his job."

He guffawed loudly. "Jayzis, the cheek of it!"

Next thing she knew, her hair was bunched in his fist and the knife was pressed to her throat.

"Only doing his fuckin' job, eh?"

"I-I-I'm sorry. *Please, I-I didn't mean it.*"

"Good ... yer sayin' sorry a lot, Viv, so yeh are. Now if you yell again, or give me any bother, that duct tape is goin' back on yer gob ... and maybe ... maybe y'know ... "

He bunched her hair more tightly, left the knife aside, pushed his face into hers as a hand moved up her thigh.

Vivienne's body turns to stone.

"Or maybe ... just maybe," he leered, "I might be inclined to try something else with you. Gets lonely for a man out here all on his own. So don't give me any more bother, if yeh know what's good for you, Viv."

She nodded several times, speechless with terror.

Promptly, he released her, pushed her down on the mattress, trailed the chair back into position.

Opened the door. Turned to her.

"Food's on its way ... wouldn't want yeh to starve on me, Viv. Need-a keep yeh alive ... *for now anyway*."

THIRTY-EIGHT

Manny might have delivered the package, but he certainly wasn't out of the woods—or indeed the Muddymacreek Forest—just yet.

When, if ever, would he be able to extricate himself?

As he pushed a trolley self-consciously into Barney's supermarket, "Things Can Only Get Better" blasting out over the shop's speakers—a fitting soundtrack, given his predicament—he was barely aware of his surroundings, for the forest and Fitzwell were uppermost.

After the elderly couple had taken off in the blue car, he'd left his hidey-hole and braved it up to the cottage door.

He was sure it was a young woman's voice he'd heard and hoped he might hear something else before knocking.

He stood very still, listening.

If someone else was in there they were likely to be in the far room on the right. He'd edge his way down and have a listen.

But, just as he was about to do so, the door opened.

"So, yeh got here finally!" Fitzwell barked, snatching the packet from him. "'Bout bloody time too! Next time I send you to do something yeh'd better be quicker."

Manny thanked his lucky stars he hadn't moved.

"Uhh… I had to take all them wee roads so I wouldn't get caught by the army," he tried to explain.

"Aye, right… d'yeh think the dunderhead Brits would have the brains tae look in the door-panel, yeh eejit? Wait a minute."

He disappeared inside.

Manny seized his chance. He began soft-shoeing it back to the car, relief gushing through him like water from a holy well.

But Fitzwell was way ahead of him.

"*Where the fuck d'yeh think you're goin'?*"

He had no option but to stop.

"Yeh wouldn't like tae end up like Long John bloody Doody, *would* yeh? Didn't I tell you tae friggin' wait?"

"Uh, I-I . . . didn't hear yeh right."

"Fuckin' try that again and you'll not only not be *hearin'* right, you'll not be *walkin'* ayther, 'cos I'll get Bumper tae put a couple of holes in yer knees the size of saucers when yeh least expect it. D'yeh hear me?"

Manny nodded dumbly.

"Good, just so yeh know where we stand. Where the fuck's the car anyway?"

"It's . . . it's out on the road. I-I didn't wanna get a flat in them potholes."

"Aye, right!" He pulled a note from his pocket and thrust it at him.

"Get them fuckin' groceries and bring them back tae me sooner than a Brit outta a Fenian pub on Paddy's Day."

Now in the canned-food aisle, Manny sighed, looked down at the scrawled list once more:

5 BAKKED BEANS
5 CORN BEEF
LOAF
BUTTER
MILK
SPUDS A BEG OF BIG BOYS.
NOT WEE SKITTERS
TAY BEGS BIG BOX
6 PECK SMITEEKS BEER 2

. . .

He found the cans of beans and the corned beef, dumped them into the trolley and steered it towards the tea aisle.

There weren't too many shoppers, which was good, and there was no fear of his ma disturbing him, 'cos he'd left her off at Mrs Purboy's house for a couple of hours. That gave him plenty of time to take the stuff to Fitzwell and be back again to collect her.

He checked the list once more, glad to see that he'd got everything apart from the beer, but he'd buy it in the off-licence next door.

He pushed the trolley quickly towards the checkout.

In his haste he collided with another cart exiting one of the aisles.

"What on earth!?"

Of all the people to smack into! Nettie Buckley's reproachful eyes were staring at him.

"I-I'm s-sorry," he stammered. "Didn't see you there, Mrs Buckley."

"Obviously not! Strange sight: to see you doing the shopping, Manny Bryn. Has the world ended or what?"

"Aye ... well ... "

"That's your mother's job surely."

"Uh ... aye, oh ... aye, me mother's not well, Mrs Buckley ... bad with her leg, so she is."

"Is that so ... and how did she come by the bad leg?"

He was reduced to a schoolboy in front of a tyrant headmistress.

"She-she fell somewhere."

"Oh, I know she fell but it wasn't just *somewhere.* It was in the shrine of St Timothy's in the dark of night, chasing that moving statue nonsense ... nearly give Father Mulcahy a heart attack. Could-a kilt the priest, she could of, with the shock she give him."

"I know ... but she's not goin' back there again. She promised me, like."

"I sincerely hope not."

She scanned the contents of his trolley disdainfully. "Beans and corned beef are hardly the proper sustenance to help her back on her feet, are they?"

"She ... she likes the beans—"

"Next, please!" the shop assistant called out. He was thankful for small mercies.

"You keep an eye on your mother, d'you hear me?"

"Aye," he said, off-loading the goods from the cart.

"Any more talk of moving statues and Dr Flynn will have her committed, and you wouldn't want that, Manny ... to be left *on your own*."

"Nah ... aye, right. I know that, Mrs Buckley."

She marched off.

"Pay no attention till that oul' divel," the checkout girl said. "She's like that with everybody; bitter oul' bag. Got tongue enough for ten gobs."

Manny grinned shyly. Looked idly through the window as the shop assistant bagged the groceries.

To his alarm he saw Minnie Bain, Fred's wife, chinwagging with another woman. If she saw him she'd want to know why he was shopping during *her Fred's taxi hours*.

"A penny for them," the assistant said.

"What?"

"Eight pounds ninety-five all in."

"Sorry ... thank *you*."

After paying, he took another glance out of the window, hoping Minnie Bain had disappeared.

Alas she was still there, back turned, continuing her parley.

It was too risky to leave. He'd wait another wee while and pretend to look at the newspaper stand.

He unfolded a copy of the *Irish News*.

Stared in disbelief.

In seconds was right back there in the forest on the doorstep of the cottage.

A scuffle.

A scream.

The voice of Fitzwell raised in anger: "Tie the bitch's feet!"

There was a photograph of a young, dark-haired woman on the front page and above it a screaming headline:

DAUGHTER OF JUDGE DUNDAS GOES MISSING

Manny stared in disbelief, hearing a news bulletin on his car radio not so very long ago.

"*Judge Robert Dundas, in his summing up, referred to Connor as a man capable of some of the most heinous and barbarous acts....*"

With a feeling of absolute dread, he knew that the girl in the screaming headline and the girl he'd heard screaming in the old cottage were, without doubt, *one and the same.*

THIRTY-NINE

At Cedarwood Manor, Ma Bryn, after much ooh-ing and ahh-ing over the splendour of her surroundings, was preparing Ellen for her first reading.

Ellen was nervous. Never in her wildest dreams had she contemplated engaging the services of a clairvoyant!

Tilda, on the other hand, was thrilled to have the wealthy widow as a client and was eager to impress her with knowledge of all things spiritual.

They were in the drawing-room: Tilda seated grandly on the scroll-armed sofa Jay Lavelle had occupied a few days earlier, Ellen on the opposite one. Assembled on the coffee table were the tools of Tilda's trade: cards, crystal ball, bunch of white sage—for tae keep the Divil away—and a smoky quartz crystal.

"I've never done anything like this before," Ellen said nervously.

"Well, there's a first time for ever'thing, Ellen ... if I can throw any light on things for yeh, sure all the better. We'll start with the ball 'cos it gives me a general impression of where things stand at present in yer life, and take it from there."

Ellen nodded apprehensively. "It's just so hard for me to know what's going on. I think I hear things in the night. I've had strange dreams about George... then things get moved and I have no memory of doing it. There were stories about this house being haunted but I never believed them ... I suppose because I'd never experienced anything out of the ordinary. Until now, that is."

"I know it's hard for people tae believe in the spirit world," Tilda said soothingly. "But yeh see, Ellen, I've lived with it all me life. I've been practissin' me craft for many a year ... like me mother afore me, and her mother afore that. The gift was passed down the maternal line, yeh see ... and when God gives you a gift, it's a body's duty to use it to help them that's in need of some guidance."

"That's very noble," Ellen said. "So you've been doing it for some time then?"

"From the cradle, to be honest ... saw angels when I was a wee one and thought everybody else did."

"Really!"

"Yes, they used tae comb me hair and tickle me toes when I was lyin' in me wee cot. God, I thought it was the most normal thing in the world, till me mother tolt me—God-love-her-cotton-socks—it wuz me gift to see them, and nobody else could. They tolt me I was a light bearer, like a torch for till light up the dark ... only here in bodily form for a while on this earthly plane, tae spread their message afore I'd be took back to paradise."

Ellen was fascinated. She'd never met anyone like Tilda before; had never *heard* anything like it before.

"That's amazing!" she said, feeling a little more comfortable about the soon-to-be reading. "George didn't believe in God, you see, and when I married him I lost touch with spiritual things. It's so refreshing to hear that it's all real."

"Oh, it's real all right, Ellen. The angels is calling yeh back to the faith. That's why they sent me to you ... there's a path laid out for you, and yeh just need a little help tae get back on it, so we'll get this reading started, Ellen, and I'll tell you what they show me."

Tilda felt confident that the session would go extra well because she'd already picked up some key pieces of information on the way into Cedarwood.

Without further ado, she went through her elaborate summoning ritual—three deep breaths, hands extended over the crystal ball, eyes directed heavenward, face holding an expression of rapt attention—while Ellen looked on in nervous expectation, wondering what was to come.

Presently, Tilda broke out of her trance and focused on the ball. "Now . . . I see that there's a bit of darkness round you but it'll soon lift. All that's needed tae lift it is a bit of trust in yer higher power and a bit of faith that things'll work out the way God intended."

"Is-is the darkness my grieving, d'you think?"

"Yes, that would be a big part of it indeed, Ellen."

Ma Bryn paused and shut her eyes. "Now, there's a man coming through. They don't usually come through so quick, but I see him here all right."

Ellen was fearful. "Here . . . d-do you mean, in the room? You mean George is here . . . in the room?"

She clasped her hands to her face.

"You could say that . . . dark-haired he is."

Tilda was recalling the wedding photograph she'd glimpsed on the way into the house—funny it didn't have no glass. She saw orbs of light rather than people—there was one hovering over Ellen's left shoulder—but, unfortunately, the bereaved always wanted details and sure there was nothing wrong telling a body what they wanted to hear.

"Would be a good head taller than yerself . . . thin . . . but he's got the loveliest smile, he—"

"That's him!" Ellen cried. "That's George. But where is he?"

"On the Other Side, Ellen."

"No, I-I mean, is he . . . is he . . . ?"

"In paradise," Tilda added helpfully. "Well, of course he is, Ellen dear."

"But . . . but that's just it. He . . . he didn't believe in God and I was so . . . so afraid he'd be lost for evermore in . . . in . . . " She couldn't bring herself to say the word.

"Hell? There's no such place, Ellen," Tilda assured her. "Y'see, for them that don't believe, what you and me thinks is a bad place on the Other Side is just a bitta confusion . . . like a limbo where they try tae figure things out. It's like a pack of people waiting at a bus station for the bus tae come. Them that believe in God know the bus is gonna come . . . but them that don't believe have no idea they're even *in* a bus station, if yeh get me drift. It's only when the bus comes they understand where they were all along, like, and get on the bus no bother."

Ellen was confused.

"Aye, I know it's hard for a body not versed in the spiritual like yerself tae get a hang of these things . . . but what I can tell yeh, Ellen, is George *did* get the bus . . . even if he waited that wee bit longer tae figure out where he was. . . . He saw the bus. He got on it no bother. He went till the light, and he's now happy in paradise."

Ellen broke down.

"Oh, I'm-I'm . . . so relieved to hear that! I-I was so afraid, you see, that . . . that he was lost . . . and that was why he . . . he was coming to me for help in the dreams."

"I know, luv. . . . George just wants to reassure you. . . . He's telling me that all he wants for you, Ellen, is tae be happy. He sez he'll always be around you and he'll always love you, so there's no need for you till be afeard of anything."

Ellen dried her eyes. "That's so good to know. Can you ask him something?"

"Anything a-tall, luv."

She didn't know how to phrase the question without giving too much away, but . . .

"Can you ask him why . . . why he deceived me?"

Tilda paused. Saw the orb of light disappear immediately. That meant there'd be nothing more from George. She'd just have to make the best of a bad situation by talking up the positive.

"Erm, he's . . . he's saying he wasn't always straight with yeh betimes, and he's very sorry about that. But things is different now and he's sayin' what's done is done and yeh need to move on."

Ma Bryn observed Ellen's rigid posture, jaw set, arms folded.

She could see Ellen was in a lot of emotional pain. Whatever the husband had done would not be easy to forgive.

"Will we see what else is here for yeh, now?"

She saw Ellen blink. Detach herself from the memory of George's wrongdoing.

"Sorry.... I was miles away there."

"No matter a-tall. These things is hard for most people. But where there's light there's hope, as they say... and George is in the light and that's the most important thing, so it is."

Ma Bryn studied the ball once more, brows knitted in a fair imitation of intense scrutiny. As with all clairvoyants, the paraphernalia on the table was more for show. She was a reader of *people*. Saw images around a sitter and tuned into their feelings, rather than seeing anything of significance in the crystal.

"Well now, it's odd what I'm seeing... but I can only tell yeh what the ball's giving me. I see you in another house in the space of three."

"Oh... another house? I don't understand."

"Well, this is strange but I can only tell you what the ball is giving me and what I see is you looking out the windee of a house by the sea... and it's gonna happen in the space of three."

"My goodness!" Ellen thought back to what Fintan Kavanagh had said about relocating to the summerhouse in Portaluce.

"And there's a younger man here. Fair hair. Fond of you he is. Would he be a relative? Can't say right. I'm getting a J... maybe a James or a John. D'you know anybody of that description, do yeh?"

When Manny left her off, Tilda had glimpsed the young fair-haired man she'd seen in the library disappear around the side of the house. It had to be him, because the white sports car was parked nearby and nobody else in these parts had a car like that.

Ellen couldn't believe her ears. Mrs Bryn had hit on two things that were absolutely true.

"That's amazing," she said. "We have a house by the sea. And...

and the young man ... he's my new lodger."

"There yeh are then," Tilda beamed, pleased that her little bit of creative assumption had hit the target, memory keen on the details of her last library visit, when she'd seen the stranger getting a book on antiques from Miss Curl and the librarian calling him James.

"He likes collecting things, this young man ... antiques would it be?" she added, just for good measure.

"My goodness me! You're amazing, Tilda!" Ellen was awestruck. "He told me he had an interest in antiques."

"There yeh are then. Oh, the ball's rarely wrong. Now, there's something else. He'll be good for you, this young man, but I'm gettin' a bitta darkness round him. Would that make sense till you?"

Ellen thought of Jay's dead wife, but didn't think it appropriate to disclose that to Tilda.

"Perhaps," she said, nodding carefully.

The gods and guides were certainly on Tilda's side during this reading. Together with the beneficent effect of having witnessed the Virgin Mary move not so many nights ago, her psychic powers were sparkling and quivering like a shivery hedgehog on a frosty night.

But wiser to stop while ahead, and end things on a high note before Ellen started asking any probing questions.

She reached for her carpetbag and placed it on the sofa.

"Now, Ellen, that's all I can see at this present moment in time. But all in all there's great t'ings ahead of you. There's no need to mourn George no more. He came through today to tell you that. All yeh have to do is forgive him ... trust the Lord that created us and the angels that guide us, to follow the path that's laid out for a body."

"Thank you *so* much," Ellen gushed, getting up and fetching her purse. "I can't tell you how much I appreciate your help. It's been most revealing! How much do I owe you?"

"Well, it's usually a tenner, for contacting the spirit world, like.

Takes a lot outta a body. But a fiver will do . . . sure what's money between friends?"

Ellen extracted a twenty-pound note and pressed it into Tilda's palm. "Now, you deserve every penny of that, Tilda. I'm so glad I met you."

Ma Bryn couldn't believe her eyes. She saw her catalogue debts paid off in one fell swoop. "Och, you're a very good woman, Ellen . . . and nothing but good is coming your way."

"And there's something else you must have," Ellen said, a thought coming to her.

She went to a sideboard drawer and drew out Jay's chocolates. Ma Bryn's eyes lit up.

"My goodness me, Ellen! Black Magic's me favourite. How did you know?"

Ellen smiled in a non-committal fashion. "Well, you can't go wrong with chocolates," she said, glad that Jay's gift was finding a grateful recipient.

"Y'know, it's me birthday in a couple 'a weeks, so I'll keep them for that."

"Perfect!"

In the hallway, Ellen helped Tilda into her coat.

"You must come again . . . for tea and a chat. We'll sit in the garden next time."

"I'd luv to, Ellen . . . that garden of yours is a credit to you. Give me a ring anytime. My Manny's always on hand."

"I certainly will."

Tilda headed down the hallway—but halted suddenly, her attention on a spot just below the staircase. Having heard the rumours about old Sir Wilfred having died from a fall down the stairs, there'd be no harm in putting another ball in the net.

"What is it?" Ellen asked, concerned.

"Did anything happen there? I'm . . . I'm getting a cold spot."

"Oh, I-I don't understand. What … erm … what d'you mean, a cold spot?"

"Och, it's maybe nothin'," she said, waving a hand. "Don't mind me. I get these odd feelin's betimes."

Ellen smiled nervously back at Tilda. "Well, thanks again."

"That's no bother a-tall, Ellen. May your pockets be heavy and your heart be light, and may good luck folly you mornin', noon and night. But looking round this grand place, Ellen, there's no fear yer pockets would ever be light."

Ellen smiled as she waved goodbye to Tilda.

She turned back indoors, slightly conflicted, but feeling better for having been in Mrs Bryn's presence.

Things could only get better. Tilda certainly had given her much to think about. Maybe it was time to make a fresh start. Just leave the past behind and move to Edgewater by the sea.

She collected the tea-tray from the drawing-room. Carried it into the corridor.

She didn't make it to the kitchen.

The last thing she remembered was the noise of the tray crashing down, as her legs buckled under her.

The world turned black as Ellen collapsed.

FORTY

"You can't treat him like that!" Iris Rainey cried. "He's a good man and he's done nothing wrong."

Manny stood in the dole office, terror-stricken. The two soldiers who'd accused him of having a baldy tyre were sneering gleefully as they handcuffed him.

"Your Prince ruddy Charmin's involved in IRA activity, luv. Kidnapped a judge's daughter. He'll get life for that."

"I'm not involved in anything," Manny pleaded, turning on the lanky soldier. "Magee and Fitzwell set me up. And you-you shouldn't talk to her like that. She's ... she's only tellin' the truth."

"I'll talk whatever soddin' way I want, sonny! You wouldn't know truth if it bit you on the arse."

With that, he was abruptly trailed outside and bundled into a waiting Land Rover. A group of locals had gathered; familiar faces looming out at him, hardened and accusatory.

"I'm glad yer takin' that boy away," Nan Doody spat. "He's got a durty mind ... toilet, indeed!"

"Aye, sure he could-a kilt me!" Jonah Mulgrew shouted, emerging from his bubble car. "Left me lyin' at the door of me house ... could-a died on the spot ... and dhriv away like the Divil, leavin' me there.... Didn't give a tinker's damn about a body."

"You're all liars!" Iris cried. "Don't listen to them, Manny. I know you're a good man."

"A wee lassie like you knows nathin' about that boy."

Now it was Fred Bain's turn. He raised his crutch at Iris. She backed away, tears streaming down her cheeks.

"He smashed me single rear fog-light, so he did, and the inside door of me taxi's in bits 'cos of him. Good man, me arse! He's a bloody nuisance."

The back doors of the army jeep were slammed shut in Manny's face.

Darkness fell.

He cried out in desperation....

. . . and awoke in a sweat, to find himself not in the army Land Rover but sitting in his armchair by the fire.

It was only a nightmare—or a *day*mare! The relief was immense.

He sat upright, heart banging, and rubbed the sleep from his eyes.

On the floor lay the *Irish News* with its shocking headline, the face of Vivienne Dundas smiling up at him. The dream could be discounted, but not this new horror he was now privy to. He nearly wept at the thought of what lay ahead.

Fitzwell was holding the judge's daughter prisoner. It *had* to be her. He'd heard a young woman's cries that day. Judge Dundas had sentenced Fitzwell to life without parole. Manny could call the Confidential Helpline anonymously, but Magee would know it was him and he'd be as good as dead.

He'd have to find another way—a way to rescue her.

A distinctive puttering noise broke into his troubled pondering. He went to the window and was met with an odd sight: a green bubble car was making its slow and bumpy way down the lane.

"Christ, Jonah Mulgrew. What's *he* want?"

He thought about locking the door and hiding, but the taxi sitting out there was a dead giveaway. And he wouldn't want Mulgrew to think he was asleep in the middle of the day—even though he *had* been.

It was an awkward situation. The last time he'd seen the old soak he was collapsed drunk in his doorway the night he'd driven off.

But, given his present troubles, Manny wasn't too bothered about getting a telling-off.

He watched as the odd-looking three-wheeler came to an abrupt halt in the yard.

Jonah, cap askew, opened up the bulbous glass door and began the complicated process of unloading himself.

The clock struck three.

Then it dawned on Manny: he was supposed to collect his ma from Cedarwood Manor half an hour ago.

Brilliant! Now he had the perfect excuse to get rid of him.

He was rooting around for his car-keys when Jonah pushed open the door.

"Hullo, Jonah."

Mulgrew stood in the doorway, long black coat skimming his wellies, cap in hand, an odour drifting off him that would flatten a bullock.

"Aye . . . a bit of a breezy boy it is."

The wind smacked at a cherry tree over his shoulder, proving his point.

"Aye, Jonah . . . erm . . . it isn't such a . . . such a good time, 'cos . . . 'cos I have tae collect me ma, like."

"She's in me bubble."

"*What?*"

"Aye, saw her outside Mrs Purboy's and give her a lift 'cos *you* forgot. Would-a got soaked to the skin had I not came along. You'll need tae come and help, 'cos it wuz a job getting her *in* the bubble, but it'll be a bigger job getting her *out*, 'cos as I say I—'"

The phone rang, cutting Mulgrew's spiel. Manny heard its clanging like so many electric drills wielded by the psycho Fitzwell.

"Aren't yeh gonna answer that then? Might be a fare."

"Aye, maybe," Manny said. "But it'll wait. . . . We need-a see to Ma first."

VIVIENNE

Vivienne lost track of time.

The light sank into darkness then rose again. Birdsong soared like an anthem, pure as a mountain stream seeping through the roof cracks: some solace amid the horror. The birds trilled to another day dawning and then fell mute when the monster rose and unlatched the front door, scattering them from the trees, the shrubbery, the habitat that was theirs, *not his.*

Oh, the beauty of that morning chorus: those precious moments in the placid hours before reality dawned!

She seldom heard them in the city: the birds. She never paid attention, but now she took account.

I was nineteen when first I heard the birds sing.

She practised the sentence over and over; wanted to be able to utter it aloud in the future. The idea brought images of her seated at the dinner table, dropping it into the silence like a pearl into the stillest pond.

She imagined her father looking up from his plate. Her mother putting down her fork, resting her hand on the linen cloth, eyes fearful.

"Are you all right, dear?"

"More right than I've ever been."

"You can tell us about it . . . when you're ready," she heard her father say.

But I will never tell them anything about this. They will never be privy to the darkness I'm enduring. Why would I share such horrors? It is *my* responsibility and mine alone to be accountable for the events that *I* put in train.

She pulled herself upright on the mattress, blinking tears away.

Never.

The room was warm and stuffy, even at that hour.

It was 7.30. Her watch was teaching her the long, hard business of waiting.

She did not know how many days had passed. Fear had sucked time into a dimension without frontiers. The hours dissolved, floating in a limbo; weightless, useless.

He brought food twice a day. At nine o'clock and six.

At first she refused it, but then hunger overpowered her. The need to live overpowered her, giving her clarity about what mattered: to see her parents again, to hold a paintbrush again, to feel the sun on her face and breathe the summer-perfumed air outside this prison.

There was a picture on the far wall, time-faded and warped: *Jesus in the Garden of Gethsemane*. It showed Him praying in a shaft of light under a leaden sky, his crimson cloak spilling like blood upon the dark earth. She wondered whom it belonged to. Who lived there in the long ago. Imagined an old couple nodding by the hearth in the other room, where Fitzwell was now stretched out.

This room was likely their bedroom; the holy picture above the bed to remind them what Christ suffered to give them life.

It was a fitting metaphor for her situation.

Every morning she contemplated it. The same illustration was in one of her Sunday-school books. The inscription beneath it read:

My Father, if it is possible, let this cup pass me by.

She mouthed the words to herself over and over and over.

Father, if it is possible, let me live.

Father, if it is possible, let me escape.

Father, if it is possible, let my dad find me.

Father, if it is possible . . .

Freedom *will come*. I will not allow myself to imagine the alternative. If I can't imagine it, I *cannot bring it into being.*

Her hands and legs were no longer bound.

He'd freed her of the restraints, on condition she remained quiet and gave him no trouble.

"No point in yellin' out here anyway, Viv, 'cos nobody will hear yeh. But give me any bother and I'll shoot you dead. Not before havin' me way with yeh of course."

That was the day he pulled a gun from his belt and put it to her forehead.

"The longer I keep yeh here, the more your da suffers. But I could maybe decide tae make him suffer the rest of his days . . . if you get me drift. Just so yeh know, Viv. I don't make idle threats."

She didn't doubt him for a second.

Sudden in the lane: the sound of a car approaching.

She went to the window and peered through the tiny crack in the board.

A black car.

As she watched, it disappeared from view then reversed right within her eyeline.

A horn blared.

She heard Fitzwell rouse himself and go out.

The car engine was shut off. The driver's door opened and a young man stepped out. Vivienne froze at the sight of him: that gaunt face, those jutting cheekbones. It was the weirdo from the Belfast bus. The one who'd nicked her business card.

He'd been following me that day.

"Did yeh bring the shovels?" she heard Fitzwell call out.

"Aye. All present and correct."

Did yeh bring the shovels?

Terror sank its teeth deep into Vivienne's heart.

They plan to kill me. In her mind's eye she saw a grave being dug. Those shovels would dig her grave.

She saw the boot being opened.

The shovels were handed over.

Strained to hear their conversation, but could not.

The weirdo got back in the car.

Fitzwell moved out of frame.

He started the engine. "What time the morra?" she heard him call out.

"Better wait till after dark!" Fitzwell shouted back.

Vivienne fell to her knees, imploring the picture on the far wall.

My Father, if it is possible, let this cup pass me by.

Let me *live.* Oh, God, *please let me live!*

FORTY-TWO

Nettie Buckley was monumentally annoyed.

Ellen was behaving foolishly. The last time she'd visited Cedarwood they'd parted on a sour note. Normally her older sister would telephone and apologize for her imprudence, but no call had been forthcoming.

Any hope that George's death might draw them closer was fading fast.

Now there was a young man installed under her roof. Nettie had indisputable evidence: a certain James Lavelle had come into the pharmacy and introduced himself as the new tenant at Cedarwood. He wanted something to help him sleep. "A new place disrupts the old shut-eye in the beginning," he'd said. Well, was that not evidence enough that there was something shady about him? Those who couldn't sleep at night were usually wrestling with a guilty conscience, especially someone as young as he.

He also wanted hand cream—of all things. What sort of man uses hand cream?

Oh, the sheer brashness of him! And the sheer rashness of Ellen, not listening to her when she'd warned against renting out rooms to strangers.

God knows what sort of designs he had on her or where it would all lead. She knew immediately he was the devil-may-care sort, with his good looks and silky manners. Just the type to home in on lonely women—vulnerable women of means, like her sister—and charm his way into their bank accounts.

Nettie strode along the road leading to Cedarwood, carrying

her indignation like a flaming torch raised high. She needed to have it out with her silly sibling once and for all. Tell her exactly what she thought of *Mister* Lavelle. She prided herself on being a good judge of character. It came of having studied the antics of the Castlebrook community for so long.

Ellen felt her body go limp, as if weighted down by something solid and immovable. She tried to open her eyes, but her lids were so heavy she could not. It was best to stay put, tipping and turning into darkness; wait for the world to refocus itself. Someone would take care of her. She was certain of that because she could sense a kindly presence hovering just above her and knew that this being would protect her.

Then, of a sudden, arms were lifting her: strong arms, one cradling her shoulders, the other supporting her knees. It was a strange feeling, giddy-making, scary, like when her father used to give her piggyback rides as a child. The fear that he might let her fall at any moment suffused with the near-certainty of knowing he never would.

Her head swam and her stomach heaved but these arms, whomsoever they belonged to, kept a steady hold.

"George," she murmured, "Is that you?"

But no answer came and she allowed herself to be carried, knowing that she was safe, completely safe in the arms of this beneficent presence.

On the doorstep Nettie pressed the bell and waited.

No answer.

Lifted the heavy brass knocker and rapped three times.

Still nothing.

Deliberately not answering because she knows it's me.

Now that I think about it, she'd forgotten to lock it the last time.

Maybe ... just maybe ...

She turned the handle and, to her dismay but relief, the door opened.

"Ellen, are you in? It's—"

The sight confronting her took the words away.

Farther down the hallway, bits of crockery and a tea-tray were strewn about the floor.

What on earth . . . ?

Tentatively she stepped inside. Had the house been burgled? Ever resourceful, she decided to be as quiet as possible and surprise the intruder in the act.

The drawing-room door stood ajar. She glanced at the Eiffel Tower doorstop. I could use that thing to defend myself, if needs be.

She peeped inside.

To her shock she saw Ellen lying flat on the sofa, pale and still.

"*Oh, my God, Ellen!*"

She rushed over in a panic.

"Ellen, Ellen, are you all right?"

The front of her dress and legs were damp. Nettie did a quick summation. She'd dropped the tea-tray then decided to have a lie-down. But why not change first? Ellen was very particular about tidiness. It just didn't make sense.

"Ellen . . . it's me! Nettie."

She shouted in her ear. Shook her shoulder.

Ellen's lips moved briefly; her eyelids fluttered.

"Thank heavens you're all right! Ellen, can you hear me? What happened? I'll call the doctor."

On hearing the word "doctor" Ellen caught her hand. Opened her eyes. Her vision was blurred.

"Nettie . . . I'm . . . I'm . . . is that you?"

"Yes, yes, it's me, Ellen. It's me . . . you're all right now."

With Nettie's help she managed to sit up. Her back ached with the effort and she felt nauseous.

"I'm-I'm all damp! What happened?"

"I was hoping you could tell *me*, Ellen. I came in just now, and found you. You fell with the tea-tray in the hallway. Are you sure I can't get the doctor? You look very pale and you might have broken something."

Ellen sank back on the sofa and waved a hand. The last thing she wanted was a fuss, or a visit from Dr Flynn.

She shook her head.

"It's … it's nothing, Nettie. I slept badly … that's all." But even as she uttered the words she knew something altogether more concerning had happened.

Nettie surveyed the scene. There were sugar grains on the coffee table. One of the chairs had been tipped over. Cushions lay on the floor. Some framed photos on the grand piano were lying face-down. Why were things in disarray and why was she serving tea in *this* room? It was off limits to the likes of her and her husband John on the rare occasions they got an invite. She understood George had treated it like a museum, due to his precious collection of Blackbourne memorabilia.

"Er … who were you having tea with, Ellen?"

"I-I … I can't remember."

"You *can't remember!*"

Ellen's troubled expression told her this was not the time to press the issue. She seemed disorientated and put out. Nettie knew that look all too well. Their mother's face often bore that same haunted look as the dementia took hold. She feared for her sister. Best to leave all queries until she'd recovered from the episode.

"I think it's best you change out of those wet things," she said cautiously. ". . . and have a lie-down."

"Yes … that's perhaps the best thing."

"I'll help you upstairs then tidy up down here."

But when Ellen stood up the nausea worsened. Nettie managed to get her to the bathroom just in time. Whatever she'd had for tea certainly hadn't agreed with her.

Returning downstairs, having settled her sister, Nettie proceeded to clear up. She was unnerved by what she'd witnessed. There was the real possibility that Ellen might be losing her mind. George's death was affecting her more profoundly than she'd imagined. It was the second time she'd found the front door unlocked. In a house with such treasures it was a foolish thing to forget.

Perhaps I should stay the night. Monitor things.

As she swept up the broken china, a wave of sadness engulfed her. The beautiful set, now reduced to remnants in the dustpan, had belonged to their mother. It had been passed on to Ellen as a wedding gift.

What a waste, she thought, tipping the pieces into a bin-liner.

She went through to the kitchen, unlocked the backdoor—noting that at least Ellen hadn't forgotten to lock that one—and carried the clinking cargo out to the wheelie bin in the yard.

The rain had cleared and the sun was coming out: a little blessing in an otherwise bleak afternoon. All was quiet, save for the rustling of the morning-glory that braided the garden hedges. Birdsong floated on the windless air. It was good to be out of the house and she stood awhile, breathing in the heady scents of the lobelias and roses.

She'd never liked Cedarwood. Had never felt comfortable within its walls. Now that sense of unease was gathering apace. Ellen should sell it. That would be the best solution all round. She didn't belong there any more. There were too many memories of George. Besides which, it had a past; an evil past, if she was any judge. God knows what unsavoury rituals had been enacted during the Blackbourne era!

A car horn blared out on the roadway, pulling her back to the present. She turned, her gaze falling on the door to the rented bedsit.

I wonder if Mr Lavelle is at home. She skirted round the rear of the house, but his car was nowhere to be seen. I can't blame him for anything then, even if I wanted to....

Back in the house she decided she'd tidy up in the drawing-room then relax with a rewarding cup of tea.

She locked the backdoor and went into the hallway. Mindful that Ellen was sleeping, she moved as quietly as possible. The large chandelier creaked ominously and she stopped to study it, imagining what catastrophic damage it might do were it to fall. Her eyes travelled over the gloomy portraits of the Blackbourne family. Sir Wilfred stared balefully down upon her and she thought: If I had my way, you'd be in the bin.

On the wall opposite, Ellen had hung her own paintings and framed photographs, and Nettie studied them by way of distraction. But she noticed something rather odd.

One of the pictures was turned back to front.

She reached up to right it. It was a photo of George and Ellen on their wedding day. Odd. There was no glass in it.

When did *that* happen? How come I didn't notice it until now?

Nettie pressed a hand to her mouth, heart thudding with fright. She was remembering something Father Mulcahy had told her a couple of years back. It concerned a particularly "difficult case" he'd had to deal with in a former parish.

"Things thrown about and pictures turned to face the wall. Poltergeist activity they call it. Always a bad sign."

She saw again the overturned chair in the drawing-room, cushions scattered on the floor, the upset photos on the piano, and backed down the hallway.

Was that what Ellen had seen? The disturbance. Was that why she fainted?

Nettie knew now for sure what she must do. She must act immediately! She needed to leave the house, and fast. The drawing-room could wait. No way was she going to tidy it.

She locked the front door and hastened away. She'd telephone Ellen later and advise her to go to Edgewater to rest. Time away from the benighted place was crucial.

The evidence was *indisputable.*

Cedarwood *was haunted.*

FORTY-THREE

"Manny, I'm gonna spend a few days in the Dormouse," Tilda Bryn burbled.

"It came timme when I was doing Mrs Purboy's readin'—heaven's above, she's such a grand lady and it went so well—and the forecast sez the weather's picking up so there'll be plenty of them 'uns about the Port that'll be wanting their fortunes told ... it being the school hol'days an' all. Son, are you list'ning to me?"

Manny, sitting at the table staring at a ham sandwich—curled up at one end like a Turkish slipper, tongue of dried meat lolling—could not have been further away from the Hillside kitchen. The face of Vivienne Dundas kept pushing into his mind. He imagined her tied up in the dilapidated cottage, terrified and alone, at the mercy of the maniac. He'd have to act, but since seeing the story in the newspaper he felt trapped in an attitude of agonizing torment. The only person he could share his predicament with was his ma, but she was the last person he could trust with it. She would likely make a bad situation worse and he couldn't risk that. God knows what Magee was capable of....

No, he had two options: to be courageous and try and free her; or do the cowardly thing and run away, and pretend none of the horrors of recent weeks had ever occurred.

"And yeh haven't touched yer sambiches," he heard his ma say. "Is there something wrong with them, son?"

"Nah ... aye, the Dormouse," he repeated, since that was the only word he could recall from his ma's rigmarole. "Why do yeh wanna go there?"

"Och, son, I knew you weren't listenin' proper. It's the time of year. Me mammy always did the August run. Now that I'm back reading it's as if I never left it. I could clean up, son. Mind you, I'd have to clean up that caravan too, 'cos I know that you and that friend of yours wouldn't-a done much cleaning the last time the pair of yeh were in it."

Manny thought back to the previous summer, when he and Mickey Mullan had stayed in the Hemley Dormouse. What a great time they'd had! Living on fast food and six-packs, partying on the beach till all hours, with not a care in the world. He was in full-time employment at Baked-4-You and his ma was "on an even keel", as the doctor would say, not reading fortunes and talking crap about moving statues. Compared to his present situation it seemed like paradise.

"But you'd have to drive me," Tilda was saying.

She got up to reclaim the teapot, which was bubbling up a storm on the hot stove, steam billowing upwards as if a genie might appear at any moment.

"God, I hope I haven't burnt it!" she said, topping up her mug, an acrid stench of stewed tea filling the kitchen like mustard gas.

"That's if Fred would give yeh the time out, son. His leg should be near mended now, but come to think of it, them legs can take a while tae set when you're a sartain age, so they can."

I could go with her, thought Manny. Hide out in Portaluce in the caravan with Ma. Pretend none of this ever happened. Fitzwell and Magee would never find me 'cos they'd have no way of knowing where I was.

The idea brightened him momentarily and he reached for the sandwich.

"Maybe I'll come with you, Ma. Get away from here for a bit."

"Yeh would?" Tilda was surprised. The last time Manny joined her in the caravan he was fourteen if a day. It was a strange offer. She knew something was wrong. "But what about yer job? Did you fall out with Fred or what?"

"Nah ... you're right.... I couldn't let Fred down," he sighed, letting the shiny thought slip away like a trout in a stream.

The phone rang. Manny had an idea who it might be. He didn't want to answer it.

"I'll get it." Tilda headed into the hallway. "God, it might be Mrs Purboy." Ellen was on her mind because she was the first grand client she'd read. Grand people didn't usually need the services of a fortune teller, but Mrs Purboy was different.

Manny cocked an ear, nerves in bits.

"A fare from where? Aye, right, Boyle's you say ... in ten minutes? Right yeh be. I'll tell him."

"Who was that?"

"A man needs liftin' from Boyle's. Didn't give a name and hung up afore I had time tae ask, son."

When Manny pulled up at Boyle & Sons, the bookmakers, there was no one waiting outside. It was the kind of place Magee would frequent and he was dreading seeing that ugly face again, not to mention his fearsome fists.

He got out of the car, trepidation rising.

"Manny, is that you?"

He swung round, astonished to see Iris Rainey, the clerk from the dole office, standing in the doorway.

"Uh ... I-Iris ... isn't it?"

"Aye, the taxi's for me," she said, going to the passenger door. "Mr Boyle rang for me."

Manny was perplexed. He didn't have her down as the gambling sort. Women rarely went into betting shops in these parts.

He opened the rear door.

"D'yeh mind ... d'yeh mind if I sit in the front?" she asked shyly. "I get car-sick in the back, so I do."

That was something else women never did. He recalled what

Fred had said: no passengers in the front. But he'd make an exception for Iris.

"No, that's ... that's all right."

Iris settled in, fastened her seatbelt. Manny put the car in gear and took off.

"Where to then?"

"I'm going home. It's about three miles ... outside the town on the ... on the Ligananny Road. Do you know it?"

"I think so."

Manny noted that she seemed just about as nervous as he was. She kept her head turned away from him, gazing out of the window. He checked the rear-view and saw a blue car.

"I-I missed the bus yeh see."

"R-right, that's no bother. You're ... you're finished up for the day then?"

"Aye."

"Still workin' in the dole office?"

"Aye." A pause. "Is your nose all right?"

"What? Oh, aye ... it's grand, aye. Grand."

"That's good."

Little does she know, thought Manny. Little does she know.

He reached the edge of town and continued along the main road, all thoughts of Vivienne Dundas temporarily put on hold as he tried to figure out what a nice girl like Iris was doing in a betting shop after work.

"You take a left turn here," she said.

Manny slowed and put on his indicator.

In his wing mirror he saw that the blue car was making the same turn.

"Do you like the horses then?"

"Horses?" Iris peered at him briefly as if he'd blasphemed. "God, no. Daddy wanted me to put a bet on for him ... for the race tomorrow."

Manny blushed. "I was just wonderin'. 'Cos it's not something wimmen do, like . . . go into betting shops."

"No . . . I-I hate having to go in there . . . but I do it for Daddy 'cos . . . well, he's in a wheelchair and can't get about."

"Sorry to hear that."

"Aye, he fell off scaffolding six months ago and was laid off. So he's on the sick now. It's only me and him, so he depends on me a lot. You make a right turn here. And what about you . . . do you live on your own?"

"Nah . . . with me ma," Manny admitted, sensing that Iris would immediately have him down as a mammy's boy. "There's just . . . just the two of us as well," he added, fumbling for some common ground between them.

"That's nice," Iris said, smiling. "You're lucky you still have your ma. Mine died when I was a wee one."

She pointed. "That's our house now, comin' up on the right."

He shifted down a gear and soon was pulling up in front of a smart bungalow with a rather overgrown garden. He found himself regretting that the journey was at an end so soon. Being in Iris's company had postponed his anxiety about Vivienne for a wee while at least.

"That's you now," he said nervously, wondering how he was going to see her again without sounding too desperate. "It's two-fifty but the two will do."

Iris opened her handbag and rooted for the money. "That's very good of you," she said, handing him the coins.

She reached for the door handle. "Right yeh be then, Manus. Thank you."

At that moment Manny had a brainwave.

"I do a bitta gardening in me spare time, if yeh want me to mow that lawn for you."

Iris turned back to him, her hazel eyes lighting up. Her skin also seemed clearer than that first time he'd seen her in the dole office.

"Would you?" she said, biting her lip. "But the mower's broke. Daddy used to do it before his fall.... "

"That's no bother. I'll bring me own mower. Could come next Saturday... that's if you're free, like."

Iris smiled. "Would you? That would be great! I'd pay you of course."

"Och, it's no bother."

"See you then," she said, getting out of the car.

Manny waited until she reached her front door.

Was thrilled when she turned and waved.

He waved back and reversed the car into the driveway, feeling like he'd just won the lottery.

There was a car coming from the left and he waited. It slowed down, and for a moment he thought the owner wanted to turn into the Rainey driveway.

But no....

He gripped the steering wheel more tightly, fear flaring.

The old lady in the passenger seat stared out at him, face set in a grim mask. The man beside her wearing a dark hat was unmistakable.

It was the same oul' pair he'd seen coming out of Fitzwell's cottage *that* day.

That fateful day he'd heard a young woman's screams.

Were they following him? How the hell did they know him? He'd kept well out of sight that day. No way could they have seen him.

Infuriated, Manny stepped on the gas, overtook them swiftly and roared away so fast their old jalopy wouldn't have a hope in hell of catching him up.

FORTY-FOUR

Edgewater House in Portaluce was a world away from the stately interiors and sombre atmosphere of Cedarwood.

Perched atop a rock face overlooking the ocean, it gifted the resident panoramic views of sea and sky that few houses could compete with.

Ellen sat in the light-filled conservatory, contemplating a glittering stretch of the Atlantic beneath an opaline sky. She was sleeping better since coming here, lulled into slumber by the lilting waves and waking to the peal of church bells, the cries of herring gulls.

She'd relocated to the summerhouse at the insistence of Nettie. Her sister had been very accommodating, going so far as to drive her there, even if the journey had turned out to be quite a trying one.

I could sit here for ever, she thought. Being alone in this house is so much easier than being alone in Cedarwood. Perhaps I should move here for good. If Jay wasn't renting I probably could.

He was not around when she was leaving so she'd pushed a note under his door, giving her telephone number if he needed anything.

Nettie had informed her that she'd met him in the pharmacy and wasn't impressed. But since Nettie was against the idea of her renting in the first place she doubted *anyone* would have met with her approval.

She recalled their conversation on the journey to Portaluce: a conversation that had started out on a conciliatory note, only to end on a sour one.

"He was in the pharmacy asking for something to help him sleep.

Which in someone his age can only mean a guilty conscience, if I'm any judge . . . and buying *hand cream* of all things! Why on earth would a man need such a thing?"

"Well, I expect he likes to take care of himself, Nettie."

Nettie threw her a scathing look.

"Oh, stop making excuses! Taking care of himself indeed! You know very well what I'm talking about. He's one of those . . . those homo . . . homosexual types. . . . It's obvious. A blind man could see it."

Nettie's observation was hardly revelatory. She wasn't used to meeting urbane and cultured young men, the likes of Jay Lavelle, in her daily doings. Being cynical was the safest way to deal with them.

"Nettie, you have a vivid imagination," Ellen said calmly. "Jay is certainly not what you think he is. He couldn't be, since he's grieving just like me. Lost his wife a year ago, which is why he's having difficulty sleeping. He's also bringing up his little son on his own."

Nettie took her eyes off the road for a second time.

"Well, I'd no idea he was *married*, let alone a father. How was I to know?"

You shouldn't be so judgemental, Ellen thought, but didn't dare say. It was important to keep the atmosphere light when her sister was around.

Nettie's next comment, however, changed all that.

"I don't think you should go back Cedarwood. It's not safe."

"Not safe . . . what on earth do you mean?"

"There are evil forces at work in that house, believe me. I know the signs."

"Oh, Nettie dear, I do wish you'd stop exaggerating."

"I *saw* the signs. Your wedding picture was turned to face the wall when I found you collapsed. No glass in it either. How d'you explain that? It was hardly you. The chair overturned in the drawing-room . . . things disturbed. *You* didn't do that. Poltergeist activity

Father Mulcahy calls it... mischievous spirits."

Ellen was unsettled. There was a lot of truth in what Nettie was saying. The series of questionable events which had unfolded in recent weeks *did* merit further scrutiny; footsteps on the stairs in the dead of night, her bedroom door left ajar when she was certain she'd shut it, the misplaced jewellery case, Jay saying he'd seen a mysterious someone on his first evening. Not to speak of the box of trinkets, the one found in her mother's old divan, inexplicably disappearing.

"Well, aren't you going to *say* something?"

For now, Ellen would keep her misgivings to herself. "Well the glass... the glass in the wedding photo broke when the string came loose and it fell. I haven't had time to replace it.... So a gust of wind could have blown the picture back to front since it's lighter and the frame is quite flimsy. There's quite a draught when the hall-door is left open you know."

Nettie let out an exasperated sigh.

"I'll get Father Mulcahy in to say a special Mass. That Father Hill wasn't very effective... too young and inexperienced for my liking... and I think that lodger of yours should leave. It's not safe for him either. I'll tell him on your behalf, if you like. You'd be doing him a favour."

Ellen had heard enough. Nettie was attempting to run her life again, like she had in their younger days, as if her marriage to George had never taken place. It was time to take a stand.

"You'll do nothing of the sort!" she snapped back. "It's *my* house and I'll decide if Jay stays or goes, thank you very much. How would it look you telling him such crazy things?"

"How would it look if something happened to *him* then?"

"Nothing *will* happen to him," Ellen flung back, exasperated. "Now, can we *please change the subject?* It's pointless trying to draw me into your questionable theories."

There was a tense little pause.

"You still haven't told me who you had tea with that day. Was it him . . . the lodger?"

"Jay, you mean? He does have a name. And no, it wasn't him, if you must know. He was at work. What does it matter anyhow?"

"You collapsed after they left; that's why it matters."

Ellen sighed. "A lovely lady . . . Tilda Bryn, if you must know."

"*What?!*"

Nettie had veered into the middle of the road. An oncoming truck blared its horn loudly.

"Watch where you're going, Nettie, or you'll get the both of us killed."

She brought the car to an abrupt halt on the hard shoulder. Stared at Ellen, speechless.

"What is it? Tilda came to do a reading, if you must know . . . and very good she is too. Told me things about George she couldn't possibly have known."

"Oh, my dear God!" Nettie crossed herself. Put a hand to her heart. "It's *her*, don't you see? She's a lunatic! As if that house wasn't bad enough. She's brought something in . . . made a bad situation even worse."

"I haven't the faintest idea what you're talking about. Tilda's the first person who's given me any hope since George's death, which—"

"Reading fortunes is the Devil's work. She's also deluded . . . has been on medication for years. Is it any wonder you fainted after she left? The next time I see that woman I'll be having a stern word."

"You'll do nothing of the sort, Nettie. I'm not a child and you're not my mother. Stop this now, please."

They'd driven the rest of the way in silence.

Ellen sighed. Well, her sister would always be her sister. There was nothing she could do to change her opinion.

Sitting there in George's favourite spot—the wicker chair across from her vacant, his reading glasses folded on the armrest—was, strangely enough, not the trial she'd imagined it would be. The knowledge of his betrayal was dissipating her grief and replacing it with a newfound strength. She could think of George now in a more forgiving light. See him as a flawed man simply too proud to admit his frailties to her.

That tumble in the hallway of Cedarwood was giving her pause, however. And she would not rest until she got answers.

She could not figure out how it happened, no matter how many times she replayed the events leading up to it. It was important she recall those events in the right order, because doing so helped her keep a grip on reality, negating any ideas that she might be going crazy.

So she went over them again.

She remembered saying goodbye to Tilda Bryn on the doorstep and feeling fine. She remembered retracing her steps back to the drawing-room, lifting the tray and leaving again, but after that all was a blank.

She'd awoken on the sofa to Nettie's voice and her concerned face hovering above hers. There was a feeling of lightness in her head, followed by that dash to the bathroom to throw up. Sleep had overcome her the moment Nettie helped her into bed.

She'd slept the entire night, which was unusual. Her sleep had always been fitful, and more so since George's death.

Dr Flynn had visited the next morning, taking a blood sample and recommending bed-rest. The results would be back soon.

"Mental exhaustion," he declared. "The best place for you is the seaside . . . away from it all. You don't have to be around for that young lodger of yours. Put yourself first, Ellen . . . look after yourself. Nettie can take care of things here."

She'd followed his advice.

She got up and stood by the window.

Perhaps she'd have a stroll along the beach. It was a beautiful evening, the streams of holidaymakers thinning out as the sun withdrew.

Feeling a better degree of control, having thought things through, she drew on her cardigan, lifted her handbag and left the house.

FORTY-FIVE

Nettie was afraid. Very afraid.

She'd promised Ellen she'd keep an eye on Cedarwood, but her sister could have had no idea how much of a trial that would be.

Ellen didn't believe in the supernatural—that was her failing. Nor was she religious. How could she know anything about the realms beyond the physical plane if she refused to listen and acquaint herself with the facts?

"I tried talking to her," Nettie said suddenly without looking up, knitting needles clacking furiously, the sleeve of a green sweater growing on her lap. "But d'you think for one minute she listens to me . . . oh no, always the stubborn one. Always knows better. It's a godless house: Cedarwood. Always has been and always will be. Had I not come across her when she fell that day I shudder to think what might have happened. Doesn't bear thinking about."

She finished a row. Held up the sleeve for inspection, looped more yarn through her fingers and started again.

"Let's just say God was good on that occasion, but I can hardly be with her all the time. I just don't trust that house. Old Blackbourne was pushed to his death by an unseen hand . . . he used his dying breath to tell the groundsman that he felt a presence . . . a *hostile presence* . . . and he was pointing at the top of those stairs. How d'you explain that?"

Husband John, sitting in the opposite armchair, head buried in the *Irish News*, lowered the paper a fraction and peered at his wife.

"Hmm . . ." he murmured in placatory mode.

He'd had a long day at the post office. Now, sated after supper, all he wished for was a bit of peace and quiet while he read the newspaper, with Jasper the terrier dozing happily at his feet. Signs were that such peace might not be so easily won on this occasion.

At the dinner table his wife had fulminated at length about Ellen and Cedarwood. Apparently Tilda Bryn had conducted a séance at Ellen's request and "brought something in". He'd listened in nodding agreement because experience had taught him that being compliant when Nettie was agitated was the best way. But...

"I have to go over there soon," she was saying, eye on the clock, "before it gets dark. The last place I want to be in the dark is Cedarwood. But I promised Ellen I'd check on things and I'm not one to break a promise."

He saw her throw down the knitting. Lean back in the chair, and shut her eyes, as if appealing to the gods for protection.

"You don't have to, you know... go over there. Sure *I'll* go... save you the bother." John said this, knowing that the last thing he wanted was to leave his easy chair and go out. But it might be worth it, to keep the peace.

Nettie opened her eyes and leaned forward.

"You'll do nothing of the sort. It's *my* job and mine alone. What if something happened to *you?*"

"Nettie, don't you think you're taking this ghost thing a bit too far? I've never heard of a ghost killing anybody in me life."

"Stop makin' fun of something so serious!"

"*You're* blowin' things out of proportion, dear. It's all in your head. You've no proof of anything."

At that moment there was a loud *thwack* at the window.

Nettie, startled, put a hand to her heart. "Oh, my God!" She sank back in the chair again.

John cast his paper aside. Got up. Crossed to the window and looked out.

He saw a small starling lying stunned on the ground.

"Och, it's only a wee bird. I'll see to it."

Nettie caught his sleeve. "I *knew* it!"

"Knew what?" he asked, exasperated.

"The bird... it's... it's a sign!"

Jasper stood up on his hind legs and barked.

"Calm down, Nettie! Now you've set Jasper off. It's not a sign of anything. Birds sometimes get confused when they see their reflection. There's nothing supernatural about it. You're beginning to sound like that woman Bryn you so disapprove of."

But Nettie hung onto his sleeve.

"The same thing happened before Mother died. Don't you remember? I said at the time it was a bad sign and I was right."

The dog padded over and looked up at Nettie, head tilted, eyes soulful.

John took her hand and placed it back gently on her lap.

"Now, dear," he said kindly, "you go look in on Cedarwood and take Jasper with you. Looks like he wants to go. Don't you, boy?"

He caressed the dog's ears and Jasper gave a series of grateful little *woofs*. "Be good for him to get out."

"Ellen never liked having dogs about."

"Well, Ellen's not about and *I* won't tell her if *you* won't." He glanced at the clock. "Go now and you'll be back before eight. Just in time for a sherry and *Coronation Street*."

Nettie smiled nervously.

"If I'm not back within the hour you'll come looking for me, won't you?"

"Of course, dear. But nothing *will* happen. Now on you go and I'll see to this unfortunate starling."

Nearing Cedarwood, Nettie slowed the car, willing herself not to be so cowardly. On the seat beside her was Jasper, who was sure to protect her from any burglars that might be lurking. In her pocket she carried a medal of St Michael the Archangel, for protection of another kind entirely.

She was eager to get the visit over with and hoped the lodger would not be around. He'd likely ask after Ellen and she'd no desire to disclose anything about the nature of her sudden departure.

To that end she decided to park the car, out of sight, on the road. That way he wouldn't hear her approach and hopefully not even be aware of her visit.

"C'mon, boy," she said, attaching the lead to Jasper's collar. "Let's get this over with."

The dog sprang down from the seat excitedly and they set off.

It was a calm evening, the cedars throwing eerie shadows across their path. Crows squawked in the trees. Leaves murmured quietly in the gentle breeze.

Nettie held tight to Jasper's leash as he scampered ahead, sniffing the ground excitedly. It was new territory for him and he was making sure he inspected it properly. She was glad he'd come along. He was a distraction of sorts, making her feel a little less anxious.

Caw-caw-caw-caw-caw!

Of a sudden, a large raven had crashed out of a tree, glossy wings thrashing fiercely. It swooped in front of them, setting Jasper off in a frenzy of barking.

Nettie gasped—the raven was *another* bearer of ill tidings. She patted her beating heart, bent down to the dog.

"Sh-shush, Jasper! It's only a *bird*. . . . Oh, dear me!"

They continued on, the rough gravel amplifying their footfalls.

I really don't know how Ellen lives out here all on her own. It was bad enough when George was alive, but now? Maybe that's why she decided to get a lodger. I can see how having a man about the place would make her feel safer. But still . . .

The day was losing its heat and she pulled her cardigan about her as Jasper tugged on her arm. She allowed him to sniff out something of interest on the grassy verge for a second or two.

"C'mon now."

He left off his inspection immediately and trotted on faithfully, tongue lolling, tail raised, revelling in this unexpected outing.

"That's a good boy. Nearly there."

She quickened her step past a stand of doomy cypresses—more suited to a graveyard surely. She knew the Blackbourne clan were buried on the estate. Was that their final resting place?

The thought had her almost breaking into a speedy retreat.

Soon the house was in view and they were making their way across the courtyard.

"Let's check if the lodger's here first, shall we?"

Jasper cocked an ear, whimpering softly.

"Now, you be a good boy. I'm just as nervous as you, you know."

To her relief, his car was nowhere to be seen.

She doubled back to the front again, mounted the steps and unlocked the door.

"C'mon, boy."

But Jasper growled again, this time more ominously, and hung back on the step, ears flattened, forepaws stiffening.

Nettie grew more nervous. She knew dogs were sensitive to the unseen, their sense of hearing and sight being much sharper than a human's. She tugged hard on the leash but Jasper wouldn't budge.

She'd have to go it alone.

"I know how you feel," she said, tying his leash to a low railing. "Have it your way. I won't be a minute."

First: the downstairs.

In the hallway she was careful to avoid the grim portraits, searching out the wedding picture, fearful of what she might see.

It was as it should be: facing the right way round.

Feeling reassured, she checked the kitchen, pantry, living-room, bathroom, opening each door and shutting it again quietly.

Everything seemed in order.

Now: the dreaded drawing-room.

The heavy oak door cried out on its ancient hinges as she pushed it open. Gingerly, she stepped inside. Nothing was amiss. She was glad to see the chairs upright, the cushions on both sofas neatly arranged. Framed photos on the piano in their proper place.

It was time to do a quick check upstairs; with that, she'd have done her duty and could leave.

But, as she made to go, the door slammed shut in her face.

Fear gripped her.

She moved quickly to open it, but it was stuck.

She rattled the doorknob several times, telling herself it was ancient and needed a drop of oil, but it wouldn't budge.

A rush of cool air had her pivoting round.

One of the top bay-windows was open.

Was that why the door banged?

Relieved, she crossed the room, reached up and shut it. But even as she did so she was recalling that she and Ellen had secured all doors and windows before setting off for Portaluce that day.

On the doorstep Jasper began snarling more loudly.

"I'm coming! I'm coming!"

She tried the door a second time, turning the doorknob anticlockwise, but to her astonishment she felt it being forced hard against her grip, *as if someone was on the other side.*

"Oh, my God!"

Petrified, she backed away, gaping in disbelief.

Then:

"Hello.... Ellen, is that you?" a man's voice called out.

Abruptly, the door was pushed open.

Of a sudden, Nettie's terrified eyes were staring into those of the lodger, Mr Lavelle.

"Oh . . . I was expecting Ellen," he said. "I saw the front door open just now. Is that your dog?"

Nettie strained to get her voice back.

"Er ... erm, I'm ... I'm Ellen's sister."

"Ah ... the sister. Mystery solved."

He treated her to a disarming smile. At close quarters he looked much more handsome than she remembered from the pharmacy that day.

"Nettie, isn't it?"

She nodded dumbly, still trembling from the shock.

"Well, Nettie ... I hope you don't mind me saying so, but you look as though you've just seen a ghost."

FORTY-SIX

"Now, you just rest yourself," Mr Lavelle said, handing Nettie a glass of water. "Take some deep breaths and you'll be fine."

He led her over to one of the sofas and sat her down.

Nettie was beside herself. She always liked to be in control of things, but here she was losing the run of herself in the presence of this stranger.

"Er... I thought. I really thought it... it... "

"Was a ghost?" he supplied, raising an eyebrow.

She gave a feeble little nod and took the glass from him, conscious of her trembling hand. The shock of having been locked in the room when there was clearly no one else in the house had truly shaken her.

"There are no such things as ghosts," Mr Lavelle was saying, "only the old imagination playing tricks, I fear."

She didn't know what to say, but found his manner reassuring. The soft cadence of his voice was lulling her back to normality. He had the most mesmeric eyes—the colour of cornflowers in a summer meadow—and Nettie couldn't help feeling privileged to be the focus of his attention.

That said, she couldn't quite agree with his views on ghosts.

"Maybe," she conceded, just to humour him.

Mr Lavelle seated himself at the opposite end of the sofa and gazed up at the ceiling. "Cedarwood has quite the history I hear. That fact alone would play on the mind. Nonetheless, you shouldn't let such tall tales cloud your judgement, Nettie. Doors in a house this age can stick from time to time."

She noted his casual use of her first name but didn't mind at all. He obviously had very good breeding; that lovely, polite accent, the beautifully cut suit and easy manner belonged only to the well-to-do. Ellen was fortunate to have him as a tenant. She found herself swiftly adjusting her previous—rather cynical—opinion of him.

"People in the old days dined out on such stories as a form of entertainment," he continued in confident tone. "There was no TV or radio back then, so they made their own amusement. We live in more enlightened times, I'm glad to say."

Put like that he *did* have a point. His words were thawing her reserve a little and she felt slightly embarrassed for overreacting.

Thank heavens I didn't faint like Ellen. Imagine if Mr Lavelle had found me just lying there, my clothes in disarray. She shut her eyes briefly to dispel the distasteful image.

"I know. You're probably right. It's just that . . . well, I fear for Ellen being on her own here you see. It hasn't been easy for her these last few months since ... since George passed away."

"I dare say," he said, staring at the floor. "Losing a loved one is never easy."

Should I sympathize about his wife? Perhaps not. It would mean Ellen and I were discussing him and that would hardly be proper.

She saw him release the dark memory. Shut the thought down. He looked back brightly at her.

"How is she by the way—Ellen?"

"Much better, thanks.... The change of scene is doing her good."

"Excellent! She didn't say where she was going. Somewhere nice I trust?"

"To the seaside ... Portaluce. Do you know it?"

He shook his head. "Can't say I do. So long as she finds the place agreeable, that's the important thing."

She saw him glance discreetly at his watch.

"I'm keeping you from your work. I'm sorry."

He held up a hand and smiled.

"Not in the least, Nettie. But if there's anything I can do around here… in Ellen's absence that is, just say the word. I'd be more than happy to help out."

"Kind of you to offer, Mr Lavelle—"

"Jay, please."

"Jay… yes, well, I-I wouldn't think to impose. I'll drop by in the evenings just to check on things, like I promised Ellen. I'm sure you're a busy man with far more important matters to think about than—"

Woof! Woof!

"Daddy! Daddy!"

Woof! Woof! Woof!

My goodness, she'd totally forgotten about poor old Jasper tethered on the doorstep; and where had that child suddenly sprung from?

"My son," Jay explained, clapping a hand on each knee and pushing to his feet. "I told him to remain indoors, but your dog would be too much of a curiosity I'm afraid. He's the inquisitive sort, alas. Please excuse me."

He went into the hallway.

Nettie followed in the slipstream of his expensive scent.

She saw a little boy with a head of shiny brown hair standing near the steps, holding a balloon. He looked terrified.

The father went to him and took him by the hand.

Nettie bent down to Jasper. "Now, shush!" she scolded, patting his head. "It's only a little boy."

Jasper calmed down immediately.

"Toby, don't be a feardy-cat," she heard the father say. "Jasper belongs to this nice lady. He won't touch you. Come and say hello."

Nettie's heart went out to the little one. She knew what it was like to be a child who feared dogs.

"Nettie, meet Toby."

"Aren't you the lovely boy, Toby! Jasper won't bite you. He's just a little afraid of someone new at first. You can stroke him if you like. He likes being stroked."

Toby hesitated, staring up at her, the tracks of his tears visible on his little pink cheeks. He obviously took after his mother, she thought with a tinge of sadness: those dark looks and lovely brown eyes. Such a terrible thing to lose a mother at such a young age! She wanted to take him inside and give him ice-cream, but doubted Ellen would have such a thing in the freezer.

Jasper, tail going like a windscreen wiper, offered up his paw.

"See . . . that means he likes you," she said. "He wants to shake hands."

"Go on, Toby," the father urged. "He's only a little doggie, not a monster."

Gingerly, Toby came forward and touched Jasper's paw. It took a lot of courage she could tell.

"See, Toby, you're both friends now," she whispered, seeing the briefest smile light up his sad little face.

Jay squeezed his shoulder. "Run along now."

At the prompt, Toby swiftly disappeared.

"Well, we'd best be getting on. Are you sure you're okay, Nettie?"

"Quite sure, Jay. Thank you again. Erm . . . does . . . does Toby stay here with you?"

"At the moment, yes. His grandparents are on holiday for a few weeks . . . a cruise of some sort."

"Must be lonely for him . . . I mean being indoors all on his own."

"Oh, so long as he's got TV, puzzles and his toys, Toby's happy. Anyway, we'll leave you to it."

"Thank you again," Nettie said, feeling somewhat deflated they were leaving her. "You've been so kind."

"Any time. Perhaps I'll see you tomorrow if I'm around. What time did you say you were coming?"

"Oh . . . after six, I expect."

"Ah, I'll be tied up. Well, another time then."

"Yes, indeed."

Nettie stooped to release Jasper's leash.

"Oh, and Nettie … "

She turned.

"Don't forget: anything you need doing round the place, just ask."

"I will," she said, the episode in the drawing-room all but forgotten. "Bye now."

He walked off towards his own quarters.

Nettie locked the door, cheered that all had ended well and she could finally leave. I'll bring ice-cream tomorrow, she thought, and look in on that little boy. It can't be much fun being stuck inside all day long, *especially in such a daunting place as Cedarwood.*

The sky darkened and Jasper snarled again, straining at the leash to be gone. She'd never seen him so jumpy.

"All right, Jasper! All right! Let's go."

He bounded across the courtyard towards the avenue, yanking her arm so forcibly she had to run to keep up.

"Slow down, boy, *slow down!*"

Caw! Caw! Caw!

The crashing shrieks of a raven sudden in the swaying trees. The same one, Nettie guessed, that had crossed their path on the way in. A territorial old madam by the sounds of her.

Jasper spun round and started barking up at the house.

"No, boy, *no!* We really have to go *now!*"

She glanced back at Cedarwood, strange and impenetrable in the failing light. Jay Lavelle's calming words came back to her: *"There are no such things as ghosts, only the old imagination playing tricks."*

He's right, she thought. I'm so glad I met him. I have to stop being a silly old woman with all this ghost stuff.

A low rumble of thunder signalled a heavy downpour in the offing. They'd have to be quick.

She forced Jasper back onto the path and they practically ran all the way back to the car.

"Now, Jasper," she said as he settled himself in the passenger seat, "I won't be bringing you again. You're more trouble than you're worth. D'you know that?"

He whimpered softly, gazing at her with sad eyes.

"I know, Jasper, but that's just how it's going to be from now on."

She started the engine and eased the car back onto the road, happy to be under cover as the first raindrops fell.

VIVIENNE

Desperate situations demand solutions of the most ingenious kind. The will to survive at all costs calls forth a fervency as fierce and focused as a laser beam.

"Did you bring the shovels?"

Fitzwell's words had sent lightning rods of terror through Vivienne. All night long she burned in a hell, the like of which only a Bosch or a Blake could imagine.

They'd dig it together: her grave; the sick monster assisted by the villain from the bus. She'd be gagged and hauled before its gaping maw. Feel the gun's steel barrel pressed hard. Fall lifeless into nothingness and be gone.

Vivienne Dundas would be no more.

She'd be remembered bleakly in the national psyche as "the judge's missing daughter," the memory of her soon fading, along with her newsprint photo.

The monster would have won.

He'd take her parents too. They'd die from the pain and grief of having lost her.

I can't let that happen. There has to be a way out.

In the early hours, the condemned prisoner in the condemned cell of her musty room rose to face another day.

But this day would be different.

This day demanded an act of wilful daring never before engaged. She felt a prompting—base and primal—stirring deep within her. Realized she must fight to win, even *kill* if she had to.

Wildly she scoped the room. The answer to her plight lay somewhere within those walls.

Straightaway, her eyes fastened on the folding chair.

It was if she was seeing it for the very first time, her acuity of vision freakish in the jaws of impending death.

It was the *only* heavy object, the *only movable item* in the place.

In her hands that chair could become a weapon.

A *weapon!*

The word blasted in her head like a siren call.

Her heart lifted. Her throat constricted.

One chance—*her only chance*—of freedom lay in the blunt trauma that that humble piece of furniture could inflict.

The next time he stepped over the threshold she'd be ready.

And that would be very soon.

Soon he'd be coming with her breakfast tray.

She felt giddy. The light of freedom glittered.

She must not fail. She could not *afford* to fail.

Quietly she stole across the floor and hefted the chair. Folded, it was heavy enough to do injury. Not enough to kill, perhaps, but enough certainly to floor him and buy some precious minutes so she could flee.

She'd bide her time.

Wait, as alert and silent as a cat, behind the door.

Strike as soon as he pushed through to start the day.

An hour or so later she heard him.

By then she knew well the language of his movements. He wore boots with metal heels. Those boots gave her access to his routine, and that would be his undoing.

She tracked him as he went outside, conscious of her heart's thumping refrain. *Thump-thump! Thump-thump!*

He came back indoors.

Turned the water tap on.

Thump-thump! Thump-thump!

Filled the kettle.

Struck a match.

Ignited the gas-ring.

Thump-thump! Thump-thump!

She followed him as he opened the cupboard doors.

Set the crockery down.

Wet the tea.

Buttered bread.

The time approached.

She braced herself, every nerve and sinew tightening.

Feet planted firmly.

Chair raised high.

Thump-thump! Thump-thump! Thump-thump!

He put her food on the tray.

His metal heels cracked across the floor.

She counted his steps coming down the hallway.

Thump-thump! Thump-thump! Thump-thump! Thump-thump!

Heard the key turn in the lock.

The door swung open.

"*Where the fuck … ?!*"

He didn't have time to turn.

She lunged.

With all her might she wielded the chair, bringing it down upon his head with great force.

Thud! Thud! He yelled out. The tray clattered to the floor.

Thud! His legs folded.

He went down.

Lying prone, he tried to get up. She stood over him and brought the weapon down hard again.

He moaned loudly, and collapsed, arms spread wide.

His legs twitched; those legs that could give chase. She smashed the chair down hard on his ankles.

He groaned again.

But another blow to the head and all movement ceased.

Silence.

The deed was done.

Frantically she cast the chair aside.

Dashed out. Turned the key in the door. Locked him in. Raced down the hallway. Flung the keys aside.

She'd knocked him cold. She had time to get away. A half-hour head start—that's if she hadn't killed him.

But she did not care.

Outside, she gulped the pure, clean air so long denied. Stood a moment dazed, blood pounding in her ears, whole body throbbing, not quite believing what she'd done.

The shovels were leaning against the wall. The villain from the bus would arrive at nightfall to dig her grave. She must be gone.

She couldn't risk the road.

The forest—that evocation of childhood nightmares—loomed up to meet her. Another battle to be won.

She charged towards its dark embrace, shaking, weeping, frantic—scared to death, but buoyant that she was free.

Alive and free!

For now, at least, *she was free.*

FORTY-EIGHT

Ma Bryn was in her element.

Having sat for years in the wings—resisting her psychic urges to save Manny's embarrassment—she was now front of stage, picking up where Madame Silver Crown left off.

It hadn't taken long to get the Dormouse caravan knocked back into shape. A tad rusty it might be on the outside, but sure didn't it just add to the charm, and give the impression she'd been in business a goodly wee while?

She'd freshened up the interior with some touches of fuchsia paint, suspended tinfoil stars from the ceiling, covered the seating with purple satin and hung a curtain of dewdrop beading over the door. A couple of sandalwood burners staved off the mildew smells. A lump of black tourmaline kept negative energies at bay.

Her reading table was positioned just inside the door, with a collapsible chair for the sitter. It was a bit cramped but did the job grand. Behind her own chair she'd suspended a net curtain to screen off her sleeping quarters; 'cos a body needed a bitt-a privacy when dealing with the public, like.

Outside on the pathway sat her mother's old sign: a sandwich-board showing a pair of bejewelled hands clasping a crystal ball. With a touch of sadness for the old days, Tilda had blocked out her mother's title MADAME SILVER CROWN, replacing it with her very own new title, which read, albeit with wonky spelling:

MADAME MATILDA, CLAREVOYANT, SEER,
PALMIST, CRYSTAL-GAZZER AND SO MUCH MORE

Several days into her new business venture and she was doing a brisk trade. A spell of fine weather had brought the day-trippers out in force.

Women of a certain age were her stock-in-trade—them that had "missed their markets" in the marriage stakes—and there was no shortage of them about. Tilda, in her prime location on the main path leading from promenade to beach, was able to cast her net and haul them in as they strolled along.

Another practical aid in her psychic toolkit was her ability to observe and take in the goings-on. Between sessions she'd sit by her window, vigilant. You could glean a lot of information from a body's way of going when they weren't looking. To this end she could predict with some accuracy who would push through her beaded curtain for a reading, and have the patter ready from the get-go.

Now, on this lazy afternoon, from behind the covert screen of her net curtain, cup of tea in hand, a plate of Yo-Yo biscuits in her lap, Tilda was observing the normally steady stream of usual seaside fare: old ladies in floral frocks leaning on grumpy husbands in blazers, happy parents with giddy children, the odd lone farmer-type with Brylcreemed hair, awkward in his Sunday best. All at once she glimpsed a strange-looking couple approach. Pushing her harlequin glasses up on her nose, she peered more closely through the nets.

They might be husband and wife, but more likely mother and son. The woman, short and stumpy. Tight dress of scarlet splashed with big daisies—white patent belt with a buckle the size of a cake tin clinching a waist long disappeared. She carried a walking stick and was leaning on the arm of the man. He was wearing a blue raincoat and matching beret, wide beige trousers flapping in the breeze. Odd attire for a sunny day indeed.

She saw them sidle up to inspect her sign.

It was time to make a move.

"Hullo there!" the Madame trilled, poking her head through the beaded curtain. "You'll be wanting a reading done, so."

"Only... only if it's not too dear," the woman said warily, studying the sign. Hair blacker than a raven's wing piled high. Powdered face with more creases than Shrub Mountain on a wet day. She looked like she'd pulled herself through a troubled life with many a dip and dive: a survivor still clinging to the rock-face of hope.

Tilda thought she'd seen her somewhere before—she was wearing sunglasses, so couldn't be sure—but then when wimmen got to a sartain age, with wains, weight, wrinkles and worries, they all looked the same anyway.

"Och, sure you'd spend more on a pair-a tights," Ma Bryn chirped, "and it all depends on what I see. And I see great t'ings for the pair of yeh."

She saw the woman pucker her brows, mentally counting the dosh in her purse no doubt. Moments later, the face unfrowned itself and she nudged the man.

"Whadda ya think, Derek? Should-a give it a go?"

"Aye, Ma, go on surely. She's not too dear."

"Right yeh be. Now, when I'm gettin' me fortune done by this lady, you wait over there on that sun-seat like a good boy. I won't be long so—"

"Canna go and buy a 99, Ma?" Tilda heard him whisper in a low, croaky voice.

Odd question for a man of his age she thought. And could that be make-up on his face? He looked very smooth about the gills.

"Aye... have yeh got the money for it?"

Derek dived into a string bag and drew out a fat red purse.

"Aye... got plenty, Ma. Canna-canna get a cuppa tea and a bun as well?"

"A cuppa tea and a bun as well," the mother repeated, consulting her open-toed sandals as she considered the request. "Aye, why not? But mind the sugar now and what the doctor said about yer diabeeties."

"Aye, Ma. How long will you be? 'Cos, I—"

"Twenty minutes at the most," Tilda cut in, feeling that if she didn't intervene, the parley between the pair-a-them could well run on 'til the tides came in and darkness fell.

"Right, on yeh go, darling. You heard what the lady said ... and don't you be talkin' tae any-a-them-strange men that do be going about, d'yeh hear me?"

"Nah, Ma. Aye, Ma." Derek raised a gloved hand and toddled off, grinning like a circus clown, string bag swinging merrily.

Tilda beckoned the mother inside.

"Now, I'll need yer first name, daughter," she began, assuming the mantle and mannerisms of the seasoned fortune teller; bracelets jangling, eyes keen on the subject.

She watched the woman settle herself—noting her rough skin, crooked lipstick, cheap jewellery, ringless wedding finger—and made a quick appraisal. Cash-strapped single mother with bad eyesight, still hopin' for the right man to come along. From the look of that son, she was disappointed she didn't give birth to a girl. Fond of the booze too if that high colour and bad leg were anything to go by.

"Always better tae know a body's name," Tilda continued, "'cos there's a lot in a name ... and your date of birth too, for tae place you on the scope."

"Bella," came the reply.

The client peeled off her cardigan—bust wobbling—and slung it on the back of the chair. "Christ, this long-line bra's killin' me in this bloody heat. What's a scrope when it's at home?"

"What scrope? Nah ... a *scope*. Hory-scope, Bella."

"Och, aye, like the stars in the meggazines."

"That's right. I knew a Bella once. Och, it was a long time ago.

You look a bit like her. Yeh wouldn't be from Derry, would yeh?"

"Aye, Derry city born and bred." She dipped her head suddenly so that her chin skimmed the tabletop. What, in heaven's name, was she taking off now? Her tights? At this rate she wouldn't be getting much reading done.

"Feet's killin' me too. Need-a take off these bloody sling-backs. It's Derek, yeh see. Wants to walk everywhere and I canna keep up." She sat up again and removed her sunglasses.

"There! That's better."

Tilda stared in disbelief. She'd recognize them brown eyes anywhere. It couldn't be, could it? A memory stirred and suddenly she was seeing the sagging features of the woman sitting across from her transform themselves into the youthful, attractive girl's face she'd known once. Saw her standing outside the Astoria ballroom smoking a cigarette, cursing the fact she'd missed the bus, the evening breeze lifting her long black hair, dress whirling about her legs like Marilyn Monroe's in *The Seven Year Itch.*

"God, it's not Bella Prunty, is it?"

"Aye . . . why?"

"Och, Bella, I *knew* it was you! D'yeh not mind me? Tilly Bryn . . . from the Astoria dances!"

"*What?!*" Bella's mouth fell open, red lips forming a lopsided "o" of astonishment.

"Tilly . . . you mean . . . you mean Tilly *Bryn* . . . Witchy Wilma's daughter?"

"The very same."

"Ah, for Chrissakes! So you're . . . you're—"

"Follying in me ma's footsteps, aye. Well, I'm not long started up, mind you . . . the gift's passed on, yeh see. So, I thought it was time."

"God, I canna believe it!"

Bella dipped beneath the table again and hauled a voluminous handbag onto her lap.

She began rummaging.

"Now, Tilly, this calls for a celebration," she said gleefully.

"Oh, heaven's above, I'll put the kettle on." Tilda got up and parted the curtains to her private quarters.

"Not a-tall, Tilly. Sit yerself down there."

When Tilda turned back, Bella had offloaded the entire contents of her handbag. She saw a packet of sausages, a make-up bag, a pot of jam, a pair of tights and a corkscrew, amongst other things.

"I mean a *real celebration*. Now, where the frig is it? Ah, here we are!"

Without ceremony, a half-bottle of malt whiskey appeared and her effects were swept back into the bag again with the swiftness of a gamer at the tables.

Tilda couldn't remember the last time she'd drunk whiskey, or alcohol of any kind for that matter. Bella had introduced her to Babycham in the early days. Her mother had introduced her to gin then put herself in an early grave because of it. With Manny to raise and money tight, the grog ceased to feature in the Bryn household.

"A wee drop of the cretur for oul' time's sake," Bella trilled as they clinked mugs.

"God help us," Tilda sighed, taking a sip. "Never thought we'd meet again after all this time. What about that!"

"Thought you could see into the future," Bella teased.

"Och, away with yeh! You were always a one, Bella Prunty. But, I'll tell you this. I had a dream about the Astoria the other night so I knew something was comin'."

"Get away! Whaddya call that, a ... perm'tation?"

"Nah, that's what yeh get at the hairdressers."

They both fell about laughing.

"A premminition it's called. When I dream, it's me spirit guides and angels comin' through, to show me what I'm gonna see ... but I'll tell you something, Bella Prunty: I nivver saw meself drinking whiskey with you again. You were always a bad influence on me, yeh divil."

"Would yeh listen to her? Yeh didn't need much help in them days. But sure what did we know? Them GIs could smooth-talk their way with any girl. What was that joke they had about utility knickers?"

Tilda's face dimmed a little but she was determined to focus on the fun they'd both had before ... before ...

"One Yank—"

"One Yank and they're off!"

They dissolved in giggles once more as the memories flooded back.

Bella grew pensive. "But what were we back then, Tilly, but ... but a pair of greenhorns who knew nothin' about the wily ways of them Yanks? Out for a good time and divil the consawquences."

Tilda's old friend was drifting into territory she thought she'd never have to visit again. Part of her didn't want to go back there, but now, seated across from Bella with the whiskey doing its work, she was back on the dance floor of the Astoria ballroom, a tall, handsome man in a pristine uniform coming towards her.

"Would ya like ta dance?" he drawled as the band struck up "Chattanooga Choo Choo".

And Tilda, against her better judgement, allowed herself to be led out onto the dance floor by the tall Texan named Ted Romero—a handsome prince for sure, but he wore a tarnished crown.

Over several heady weeks during the summer of 1947 he'd romance her, enchant her, get her pregnant and then take off, leaving her heartbroken and alone to give birth to Manus Edward Patrick in a mother-and-baby home.

"Did you marry, Tilly, did yeh?" Bella's voice cut in on the memories.

"No, never did, Bella ... never met the right one."

"Me neither ... never got the three rings of marriage."

"*Three* rings?"

"Aye, three rings: the engagement ring, the waddin' ring—and the *suff*ering."

They collapsed in giggles once more. When they'd recovered themselves, each sat in silence for a while, reflecting on what might have been. The two unmarried mothers, jilted by the wily GIs who'd taken away their virtue, girlish dreams and so much more.

"God, Tilly, them were the days," Bella said finally, raising another toast. "Them were the days all right."

Tilda looked back at her, misty-eyed. "Aye, I s'ppose they were, Bella. I s'ppose in many a way they were."

FORTY-NINE

"What school did yeh go tae?" Mervyn Rainey asked, sitting wheelchair-bound, big ten-to-two feet splayed out on the footplates, twenty-past-eight moustache drooping lushly to draw the eye away from his baldy head.

Manny's heart sank as Iris hovered, silent and flush-faced, in the background.

"Uh … erm … er … S-Sai-Saint Malachy's," he stammered, knowing that with the disclosure he might as well have sprouted horns and danced an Irish jig right there in front of Rainey senior. Any man of Manny's age who went to a school with a saint's name was obviously Catholic, most likely in the IRA and therefore a sworn enemy, if Mr Rainey's kitchen was anything to go by.

The place left little doubt about his religious and political affiliations. Protestant with a P taller than the Tullamore radio mast. Holy Bible on the table and insignia of the Loyal Orange Order in the hall. Several framed photos of him marching proudly on the Twelfth were lined up in an orderly fashion on a far wall.

"Aye, thought it might be wan o' them Taig schools," Rainey said, emitting a heavy sigh of disapproval at the lowly papist specimen his only daughter had the temerity to drag into his home.

Iris led Manny outside, in a bid to placate.

"Don't mind Da," she said. "He's very set in his ways . . . and … and since the accident he's got worse. Too much time to think about things … listening to Radio Ulster all day long has turned his head. But he's glad that yeh came to do the garden … just can't show it, like."

"Aye, no worries,"

Manny fetched the mower from the boot of the car, illusions about any dalliance he might have had with the lovely Iris disappearing faster than snow on a hotplate.

He fired up the mower and got on with it, fully conscious that Mervyn Rainey was watching his every move through the kitchen window, and knowing it would likely be the first and only time he'd be in their garden, never mind their home.

Now, sitting in the kitchen of Hillside Cottage by himself—Ma away in Portaluce—he was feeling despondent for what might have been; a nice girl like Iris gone before anything could begin. He'd been working up a fantasy of taking her out of an evening to the pictures or maybe for an ice-cream—alcohol would be the Devil's buttermilk to Rainey senior he reckoned—and introducing her to his ma. But with a da like that there was little hope of such fantasies becoming reality.

He reclined on the sofa with his second beer, wondering whether to turn on the television. It was nice though, just to sit in the silence, not hearing his ma's voice ringing out through the place, the creaking of the upstairs floorboards as she waded about the bedroom.

That day at the Rainey house had been a distraction of sorts, even if short-lived. He'd given Iris his telephone number but she hadn't rung. He was too afraid to make that call, for he was certain old Rainey would pick up, and no way did he want to get poor Iris into trouble.

He was grateful, however, that the short-lived distraction of Iris had, albeit temporarily, pushed the ugly Fitzwell, Bumper and poor Vivienne Dundas to the back of his mind. They were still there in the shadows, though, poised like bats in the rafters of his mind, ready to swoop at any minute to do him harm.

He took another sip of beer.

The phone hadn't rung for a while and he'd gone about his business with the taxiing. Those soldiers at the gates to Castlebrook had left him alone, waving him through every time. Maybe Fred had had a word with the local cops, or maybe that pair of Brits had found somebody else to pester.

He downed the remainder of the beer, trying to steer his thoughts away from Iris Rainey and the obstacle that was her oul' fella. Checked his watch. It was nearly time for his favourite programme: *Only Fools and Horses.* Another beer was needed.

The phone rang as he was heading towards the fridge.

Since his run-in with Magee the phone had become a monster of the deep, no longer the benign carrier of mutual communication it once had been.

Should he answer it?

He went out into the hallway and stood staring at it: a shiny black toad vibrating wickedly on the half-moon table, its repetitive, eerie cadence filling his mind and ears with dread.

Could be Magee. But could also be Ma. *Even Iris*, at a stretch.

Steeling himself, he snatched it up.

"Och, son, were yeh on the toilet or what? I was about to hang up, so I was."

"Aye, Ma. Nah ... aye, aye, Ma," he said with a mixture of relief and disappointment. "Was outside, so I was. Didn't hear. How's it going anyway?"

"Makin' a fortune, son. God, the place is hivin' with wimmin wanting readin's done. And you'll never guess, but I met an old friend from me young days in Derry. Bella Prunty no less."

Manny heard the sound of tinkling glasses and the strains of classical music playing in the background. His ma was definitely not in the Dormouse.

"Aye, so. Where are yeh callin' from then?"

"The Ocean Spray guest house, no less."

"What?! But that woman ... what's-her-name, that Mrs Millman put granny out one time, yeh told me."

"Och, that was a long time ago and that oul' snob of a Mrs Milkman wouldn't remember me . . . gettin' on a bit, like the rest of us. Not that she *could* put me out, even if she wanted to . . . 'cos my friend Bella and her son are booked in for a week no less, so she's making a fortune outta the pair-a them."

"R-right . . . they must be loaded to be able to afford the Ocean Spray."

"Well, it's like this. A man that was friendly with Derek . . . that's Bella's son . . . 'bout your age too . . . 'tween you, me and the kettle, a wee bit of an odd creatur, but that story'll keep till I get home—"

Tilda's spiel had come to a halt and Manny heard a deep swallow of something.

"Aye, and what?" he prompted. "Are yeh at a cuppa tea, or what?"

"Er . . . aye, son. God, where wuz I?"

"You were sayin' Derek was a bit of an odd creatur—"

"Och, now I mind. Well, if this man he knew . . . that's Derek I'm talking about . . . well, if he didn't die and leave him a heap-a money."

"Did-he . . . right?"

"Did indeed. Died of a sudden, this oul' boy . . . wasn't a relative as far as I know . . . and don't ask me what he died of . . . maybe gout or the palsy or whatevir, but if he didn't go and leave Derek two farms-a land, a car, a house and a sowin' pig."

"God, he was lucky!" Manny said enviously, mourning the fact that he didn't know any such oul' boys in the locale that might offload their assets onto him.

"Was a widda man with no wains or relatives from all accounts, so Derek got everything. And if he didn't decide to treat his ma to a wee hol'day, and no better spot than Portaluce and no grander hotel than the Spray no less. Any word from Cousin Ted yet, son?"

"Nah, nothin'."

"Well, y'know when he comes through with a bitta dosh for the pair of us we'll come here for a celebration, like."

"Aye, maybe," Manny conceded, admiring his ma's optimism. More than a month had passed since he'd written that letter to wealthy Cousin Ted in Texas, telling him he'd lost his job and hoping he'd put some funds their way. So far, no reply had come. It was likely he'd kicked the bucket already and left everything to the cat's home after all.

"You getting enough tae eat, son? 'Cos I left sausages and a bitt-a bacon in the fridge for yeh."

"Oh, I'm all right, Ma. Don't you be worryin' about me. When'll yeh be back?"

"Monday… it's slack at the beginning of the week, but I'll get the bus, so. God, maybe Derek and Bella'll run me home in their new motor car, you know. That way you could meet them over a cuppa tea and a bun. Maybe get some buns in, son, on Monday mornin'. Them nice coconut fancies from Barneys, just in case."

"Hey-hoo-hoo-Tilly, yeh whiskey's gettin' caul'!" Manny heard a woman's slurred shouts in the background.

"Who's that?"

"Och, that's Bella. She's very fond of it, you know."

Manny grew concerned.

"Ma, you can't be drinking with your tablets y'know."

"Only had a couple of wee ones, son … and Derek's paying for all, so it'd be a pity tae waste it, like—"

"Excuse me, Madam!"

A woman's voice, brisk and sharp, cut in.

"There are other guests waiting to use this phone. You are not in a public kiosk now you know."

"Yes, Mrs Milkman, just finishin' up now," he heard his ma say.

"Sorry, Manny, 'ave to go now."

"Right. See yeh Monday then."

"Aye, son. Cheery-bye now."

He put the phone down, not a little concerned. He'd never seen his ma drink alcohol before; not in the house anyway. Hopefully it would just be a one-off with her old friend and she'd be back to normal on her return.

It was 8.05 p.m. *Only Fools and Horses* had already started. He grabbed another beer and went to switch it on.

Thump! Thump! Thump!

The sudden hammering on the door had him wanting to drop everything and run out the back.

"Yeh better open this fuckin' door!" came the roar. It was Magee. *"Or I'll kick the fuckin' thing in!"*

He'd have to open it. How would he explain a broken door to his ma when she got home? And if them friends were leaving her off he'd never hear the end of it.

"Aye, I'm-I'm comin', I'm comin'."

No sooner had he opened the door than Manny found himself being lifted off his feet and pitched to the floor.

Magee stood over him, panting like a bulldog.

"Whaddaya think you're playin' at?"

"Wha-what—"

"She fuckin' better not be here!"

"Who? Me-me... ma? She's-she's—"

He grabbed Manny's collar in both hands, bringing his big, angry face close.

"Not yer friggin' ma. Now: *is she here?*"

"I-I-I don't know who y-you're talkin' a-a-about. Honest."

Magee hesitated.

Manny thought immediately of Vivienne, but Magee wasn't to know that he knew anything about the kidnapping.

"Aye, right," he spat, promptly throwing him aside.

He ran upstairs and thundered about like a bullock, checking all the rooms.

Manny tried to recover himself. Had just got to his feet when he heard the thug pounding down the stairs again. To his alarm he saw he'd swiped his ma's birthday gift from Mrs Purboy: the box of Black Magic chocolates.

"Yeh can't take *them,*" Manny pleaded. "They're for me ma's birthday."

"Fuck you and yer ma! I'll take whatever *I* want!"

He came at him again, grabbing him by the collar and crushing him into a corner between the fridge and the stove. "We'll be watchin' you, Manny Bryn," he growled. "'Member when you were tolt that in the long ago? Well, I've got me spies keepin' a tight eye on *you* and we don't like the fact you're consortin' with that Prod bitch and her Orangeman da."

My God, he was referring to Iris!

He thought of the oul' pair in the blue car, that day he was followed to the Rainey house.

"I wuz . . . wuz only mowing the lawn for them, so I wuz."

"If we see yeh anywhere near her again you'll be sorry. D'yeh hear me?"

Manny nodded dumbly.

"Yer workin' for *us* . . . for *the cause.* Not for the fuckin' enemy. Just so yeh know."

With that, he threw Manny aside again and left, banging the door so hard a statue of the Virgin Mary teetered on the sideboard, and a picture of his Granny Wilma bounced off the mantelshelf and fell to pieces on the floor.

FIFTY

She was running for her life.

The forest floor was wounding, flimsy slip-ons no match for the pummelling terrain.

She felt the slash and burn of spurge and stone, but gritted her teeth and dashed on, crashing towards freedom like a winged creature, driven.

Away, away, away she went!

Frail, enfeebled Vivienne, fleeing for her life, flying forward fast.

The birds above her scattered.

Branches smacked and swayed.

Bracken broke before her, making way.

The monster could awaken at any moment.

He had a gun.

The swifter she ran the weaker *his* chances. She could smell the smoke of his rage. Saw him coming to on the fetid floor; foggy gaze clearing to behold the mattress.

Empty!

Gone!

His captive gone.

The thought emboldened her.

Victory!

Her victory.

She halted to catch her breath. Scoped wildly about. The old cottage—her prison—was far enough behind her to let her buy a chunk of time.

There was a narrow path to her right. She moved towards it, fighting her way through an agony of nettles, hopeful. Heard the tinkling of a stream. Her heart lifted. Water runs downhill. If she followed its course she'd reach the road.

She careered towards it.

The path was long and steep.

Down, down, down it plunged.

Halfway along, she slipped.

Fell on her back, feeling the dampness of the earth seeping through her thin, ragged clothes.

She lay there as the trees above her spun.

Shut her eyes.

Took four deep breaths.

Waited.

When she opened her eyes again the trees once more were still, leaning over her like concerned visitors at a hospital bed.

She dragged herself back up. Sat awhile; head in hands, elbows propped on knees, looking down.

Waited.

Her jeans were filthy. White T-shirt no longer white. Blue slip-ons scuffed and muddied. She couldn't remember the last time she washed. Couldn't remember much at all. Time had melted like Dali's clocks, sliding over rocks, lost in a wilderness of desperate, aching pain.

Her breathing steadied.

She crawled over to the edge of the stream.

Knelt beside it. Cupped water in her hands; splashed her face. The cold water was an elixir. She took one mouthful. Then another.

Quenched. Revived. She rose.

She could do this.

Nearing the end of her downhill track, she saw a gate. Beyond the gate, the most cheering sight: an open field, spreading out like velvet in the morning light.

She halted, breathless, ears alert.

Heard the low distant peal of church bells, the throbbing hum of traffic on a faraway road.

She'd made it through.

Elated, she raced towards the gate—forest slumping behind her like a demon felled—and clambered over.

In the distance, two tumbledown farm-sheds were taking shape. She could hide in one of them, rest a while.

She dashed through the fields, ducking and diving so as not to be seen. Scaled a dry-stone wall; climbed over two more sets of gates. A flock of sheep turned their black faces towards her, curious.

Cows stood still and stared.

Finally she reached the perimeter of the farmyard.

Skirted a huddle of old barns leaning askew, and saw the rear of a neat little cottage—white-washed, pristine—its roof painted a bright, Venetian red.

Red!

She remembered that roof.

Her kidnappers drove past this very house. The colour of the roof so vibrant it drew her attention immediately.

The backdoor was painted in the same coruscating shade. She wanted to dash over and hammer it in.

But, suddenly, a terrible thought assailed her.

What if this was *their* home? The evil old pair who snatched her.

She couldn't take the chance.

There was a hayloft in one of the barns. Better to hide out first and observe things.

A rickety ladder creaked under her weight as she climbed up.

She hunkered down near a small window.

Eyes rooted on the door, she'd wait.

For as long as it took *she'd wait.*

FIFTY-ONE

Ellen Purboy was settling in nicely to the relaxed way of life in Portaluce. She'd initiated a routine that kept her on safe terrain.

Every morning at nine she'd have a brisk stroll along the promenade, buy the newspaper, pick up something in the supermarket if needed, and return home to engage herself with whatever household chores demanded attention.

Always a stickler for cleanliness and never trusting a cleaner to do things properly, she prided herself on keeping a neat, tidy house at all times. Cleaning was therapeutic in Ellen's opinion and she applied herself to the task with the vigour and enthusiasm of an artist pursuing her craft.

It was nearing eleven on another bright, sunny morning. Today's routine would be different, however. She intended to take a break from her chores at one o'clock, to do something courageous. Something that she'd been putting off but knew she had to face: have lunch in the Ocean Spray.

The food there was by far the best around and she and George had enjoyed many a fine meal in its elegant dining-room. Now, she'd have to be brave and dine there for the first time without him. She wasn't looking forward to it, but felt that she needed to accomplish this feat, a test that would finally prove to her she was over the worst of her grieving.

She poured more Windolene on a cloth and was wiping it across one of the larger panes in the conservatory when the phone rang.

"Hello. Edgewater House."

"It's only me, Ellen," Nettie said brightly. "I was going to call you last night but it was late and I thought you might be in bed. How are you?"

"Feeling much better, Nettie. And I have to thank *you*: you were right about me coming here for a while. It's so beautiful and relaxing."

"That's good to hear!"

Ellen noted her sister's upbeat mood, which was unusual, given her normally contrary nature.

"Everything okay with you?"

"Never better. I couldn't wait to tell you but I called in on Cedarwood yesterday evening, and who should I meet but your lovely lodger, Jay."

"Really!" She'd never thought to hear the word "lovely" ascribed to anyone in Nettie's world. Most especially not with regard to the lodger whom she'd previously so singularly disapproved of.

"Yes, I feel so silly, thinking about ghosts and such like. I got locked in the drawing-room you see, and only for Jay I might still be in there."

"Really!"

"The door stuck and I panicked, thinking it was old Sir Wilfred haunting the place again ... daft I know."

"Well, don't say I didn't tell you, Nettie. It's all in the mind, really!"

Ellen was wondering how the door got stuck. She'd never had such a problem in the past, but she'd keep that to herself. Nettie was in a better frame of mind about the house and that was a real plus.

"Yes, I know you were right. Jay said the same thing. He was so polite, getting me a glass of water and reassuring me. I feel so foolish."

"Never mind. Thanks for keeping an eye on things. I appreciate it. Truly!"

"That's all right. He asked after you of course, and I met his sweet little boy Toby too. Poor little mite, losing his mother so young. Did you know he stays in the bedsit when his father's out working?"

"Erm ... yes. He did mention it would happen from time to time. But that's his business, Nettie. The bedsit is his for now."

"Yes, well ... but it can't be pleasant for a child of his age. So I thought ... well, with your approval of course, that I might bring him some ice-cream when I go over this evening. Jay is working, you see, and it'll be nice to give Toby a wee treat ... that's if you think it'll be all right?"

Ellen was again surprised. "I don't see why not. But, you can't enter their quarters. Just knock the door."

"Oh yes, I know that."

"Fine ... good ... yes, why not."

"Well, I'll get on. John's about to do his rounds ... just thought I'd check with you first."

"Oh, Nettie, before you go. I forgot my iron tonic ... the one Dr Flynn gave me. It's on the drainer in the kitchen. Also my jewellery box ... top drawer of the dressing-table. You wouldn't mind bringing them up at the weekend, would you? You and John are still coming on Saturday I hope?"

"Of course we are ... looking forward to it."

"Righty-o! See you then."

"Bye now!"

Ellen put the phone down, pleased that Nettie was happy. She could relax easy, knowing that Cedarwood was being well looked after. Nettie did nothing by halves and the fact she'd given up all those silly notions about the place being haunted was a real bonus. She could thank Jay Lavelle for that. It would seem he'd made quite the impression.

A couple of hours later Ellen was entering through the doors of the Ocean Spray. She'd rung ahead and Gladys Millman, the proprietress, had reserved a table for her by the window.

Now, feeling nervous and on edge, she halted briefly on the

threshold and surveyed the dining-room, conscious of the weight of this seminal moment.

Mrs Millman, as audacious and dramatic as a pantomime dame, was moving among the tables, making small-talk. Stylishly attired as usual, Ellen saw: a fitted dress in chartreuse green, auburn hair beautifully coiffured, diamond earrings glinting. She'd always felt intimidated by Gladys Millman, a lady whose elegance had the power to throw most women into a quandary about their own looks.

Gladys pivoted round and caught her eye.

"My dear Ellen!" she gushed, coming forward, air-kissing her in a cloud of scent and clacking bracelets. "So good to see you! I know it's difficult, but we'll get through."

Without further ado Ellen found herself being steered towards her appointed table. It was set beautifully with linen and silverware, but the sight of the single placing made her sad and she felt the tears rise.

"I'll join you if it will make things easier," Gladys said, seeing her distress. She drew out a chair.

"Erm, no... no, thank you, Gladys. I-I have to start somewhere."

"Well, I'll hover then. George was such a dear gentleman!" She pressed a hand to her heart. "So cruel that he should be taken so soon. But I guess that's all the more reason to treasure the life we have and enjoy it while we can."

"Th-thank you, Gladys. He always liked you." Ellen mopped her eyes. "This is difficult, but I'll manage."

"Of course *we* will!" Gladys gave her arm an encouraging little squeeze. "You *do* look very well you know, which, given the circumstances, is quite a feat!" She lowered her voice. Leaned in. "And you're still in the market, so to speak."

Ellen didn't know how to respond to that but knew something conciliatory was required.

"Kind of you to say... and may I say you look as glamorous as ever, Gladys. How do you do it with such a busy schedule?"

Mrs Millman simpered, hands circling the air. "Well, thank you, Ellen dear. One does one's best. Now, I'm going to get you a glass of my finest champagne."

She snapped her fingers at a passing waitress, who halted in mid-stride to absorb the command.

"But, I—"

"It's on the house, my dear. Think of it as a recognition of your courage in coming here again."

She patted Ellen's shoulder.

"You'll be fine. When Freddie passed on, I thought the world had ended also. Little did I know that my life was just beginning. Things work out; trust me. Now: the soup is sweet potato and courgette. The chef's special: Dover sole in a white-wine sauce on a bed of celeriac with potato dauphinoise. I highly recommend both."

"Sounds lovely," Ellen said, too afraid to disagree. Mrs Millman was a formidable force. The lightning-fast switch from sympathy to trotting out the menu list was a cue to let Ellen know she was a busy woman with work to do.

"I'm sorry; I'm keeping you back."

"Not *at all*, Ellen! You're a much-prized guest. Always have been and always will be I hope."

She spun round suddenly.

"And here is your champagne … Veuve Clicquot. Just what the doctor ordered!"

A timid waitress set the glass down carefully as a raucous burst of laughter erupted from one of the tables. Gladys turned and threw a look at the offenders, so withering that she could have been seeing a skid mark on one of her luxury, monogrammed towels.

"Maureen, how many drinks have those Prunty people had so far?"

Ellen followed the proprietress's gaze. She saw a couple seated at the opposite end of the room: the woman in a garish dress of cerise pink, which looked far too small for her burgeoning figure, and the man in a Hawaiian shirt and wide, green flares. They seemed in merry mood, clinking glasses and tittering playfully.

"Just the two whiskies," Maureen said. "But they ordered glasses of champagne when they saw me opening the bottle."

"Did they now? Serve them Prosecco. Their sort would hardly know the difference."

"Yes, Miss," Maureen chirped and scuttled off to perform the deceit.

"I hope everything's all right," Ellen said, taking a sip of champagne and feeling rather guilty that she was being favoured over the poor Pruntys.

"Well," said Gladys, lowering her voice, "between you and me, Ellen, that mother and son are staying for a whole week. Goodness knows how they can afford it but they've been nothing but trouble since getting here. Last night they brought the resident fortune teller to dine with them and I had to intervene or the carousing would still be going on."

"A fortune teller?" Ellen's interest was suddenly piqued. After the revelatory reading from Tilda Bryn it might be interesting to pay a visit to another one and compare notes. "You mean there's one here ... in Portaluce?"

"Alas, yes . . . has a caravan down there on the seafront. A Madame something or other—well aren't they all *madams?* Talk about lowering the tone. Disreputable isn't the word. Enjoy your lunch, my dear. And anything you need just let me know."

"Thank you, Gladys. You're so kind."

More loud chuckling was heard emanating from the Prunty table. Mrs Millman rolled her magnificent kohl-lined eyes and sped off.

Ellen cast a glance at the "disreputable" pair, feeling a little sorry for them. Who would want to get on the wrong side of the redoubtable Gladys Millman?

The man caught her eye and raised his glass of Lambrusco.

Ellen smiled and discreetly returned the gesture, fearful that Gladys might catch her. The merest hint she could be consorting with the reprobates in the corner would never do.

She took another sip of champagne. It was certainly lovely! The chat with Gladys had really helped her morale; so much so that having lunch on her own suddenly didn't seem so onerous after all.

VIVIENNE

"H-e-r-e, chucky-chucky-chuck! H-e-r-e, chucky-chucky-chuck!"

Vivienne was jerked awake by the lilting cadence of a woman's voice drifting up from below.

She lay still—very still—as her heart erupted into a frantic, throbbing beat.

Where am I?

She braced herself, stricken.

Willed herself to open her eyes.

Before her a ceiling rose into a high-raftered emptiness. She gripped the mattress supporting her body and felt the stinging itch of straw. Smelt dust and grass and wood.

No longer captive in the decrepit cottage.

Free.

Her eyes burned with the knowledge.

Tears ran down her cheeks.

A moment of triumph, relished.

But just a moment....

I was not supposed to fall asleep.

How long was I out for?

She pushed herself up with such force that pain shot through her legs. The legs that propelled her out of the nightmare cottage, through the nightmare forest, over walls, across fields, up a rickety ladder and into the hayloft of this barn, could not now rebel.

She thought of her parents, closer than ever.

She thought of the grave's dark maw that would not now receive her.

She thought of the monster she left spread-eagled on the grimy floor.

Felled by her mighty blows.

She would not give up.

She'd push on.

The finish-line tape, strung out in the distance, was there for her to break.

"H-e-r-e, chucky-chucky-chuck! H-e-r-e, chucky-chucky-chuck!"

Through a chink in the wall she observed an old lady in a floral pinny moving about the yard.

She was feeding chickens.

Vivienne stared intently. She had to make sure that the woman was not her captor: Alice, wife of the man in the hat.

This lady was taller, only slightly stooped, with grey hair pulled into a tight knot. There was an energy about her. She stepped about at a brisk pace, in her little laced-up bootees. The chickens circled her, clucking softly as they hunted and pecked at the falling grain.

Can I trust her to help me?

What if she's a sister of old Alice?

What if going into her house is akin to getting back into that blue car with the locked doors and the demon pair?

I have to be sure.

The old lady left off her feeding chore.

Set the bucket down.

Went back inside.

Vivienne trained her eyes on the rear windows of the dwelling. Two of them had curtains neatly drawn: bedrooms. The one to the right of the backdoor had none. Kitchen most likely.

As if on cue the lady appeared in the window-frame.

Vivienne saw her washing her hands. She made a decision: when the woman disappeared she'd sneak across the yard. Peek in. Check if anyone else was there before making her approach.

But she needed a weapon. Just in case.

Carefully she creaked down the ladder.

Saw an old bench at the back of the shed.

Her heart lifted. There were tools strewn upon it.

She grabbed a small hammer. Jammed it into the back pocket of her jeans.

The failing light would give her cover.

She made a crouching run to the kitchen window.

Peered in.

There were two of them, sitting either side of an open fire. Sisters most likely.

They looked harmless.

Satisfied that she was on safe ground, she skirted around to the front.

A cat bounded out of nowhere.

She gasped.

Its green eyes inspected her. She'd never been that close to a cat before.

All at once it leaped onto a window-ledge, settled down, training its luminous gaze upon her; a mute and watchful witness to her trespass.

She put a finger to her lips and tiptoed over to the crimson front door.

Rapped softly.

Waited.

Nothing stirred within.

Perhaps they were hard of hearing.

She took the hammer and thumped more loudly.

Returned it to her back pocket.

Moments later she heard a bolt being drawn back.

The door opened a crack, security chain in place.

An old lady, clad in black, stared at her in alarm.

"Hello, can you help me, please? I'm-I'm lost."

"Gettaway tae blazes or I'll call the polis!"

The door was banged shut.

Vivienne, shaken but determined, stood her ground. She knew she must have looked a fright to the woman; soiled and unkempt, like a tramp.

"Please, I won't harm you!" she shouted through the letterbox. "I got lost in the forest. I really, really need your help."

Voices rose.

"Don't let her in. She's one of them bloody gypsies."

"Well, maybe not, Nan. Let me see."

The sound of footsteps.

Vivienne straightened.

To her delight the door opened, to reveal the woman with the floral pinny.

She gave Vivienne the once-over. "God-save-us, daughter dear! What happened yeh anyway?"

"I-I ... *p-please,* I need your help!"

The old lady removed the chain. Stood back and beckoned her forward.

"Come on in outta the cold."

Vivienne broke down as she was led to an armchair in the cosy room, lit up by the glow of a dwindling hearth fire.

"There, there, daughter dear. You'll be all right now. Sit yerself down there and tell us all about it."

FIFTY-THREE

Ma Bryn woke up with the sun poking at her eyelids, head heavier than a bag of spuds, and a thirst on her like a desert camel with no humps. It took her a wee minute to realize she wasn't actually at home—but in the Dormouse caravan in the guise of Madame Matilda—and that last night she'd drunk enough whiskey in the company of the Pruntys to sink the Titanic all over again.

Heaven's above, it was after one o'clock and there'd be punters to be got through in late afternoon, her busiest time. But not to worry; a cuppa tea, a bitta toast and an aspirin or two would see to the head and leave her as right as rain in no time.

It was Bella who'd introduced her to the Devil's buttermilk in the first place. Now here she was again, her old friend, turning up like a bad penny in a crammed trunk, making her do things and look at things buried in the long ago.

"Dearie, dearie me!"

Tilda sighed and put a match to the Primus stove. Filled the speckled kettle, thoughts of Ted Romero coming and going like the sounds of the lapping waves beyond the window.

It was the drink too that had led to Manny's conception. That night, after the dance, Ted had taken the young Tilda to the Boozy Cow pub and filled her with so much alcohol and stories of Amerikay that she lost the run of herself, and...

Tilda pushed away the regrettable memory, poured the tea with a trembling hand. Sat down on the sofa-bed, deep in thought.

Present times were all that mattered and she'd done the right thing. Manny was a gift from God. In light of that, inventing a wee story about his beginnings was the best way, even if lying a bit was a sin. The truth that he was the illegitimate child of a womanizing GI, who'd flown back to Texas in 1947, oblivious to the fact he'd fathered him, would have hurt too much. For that reason, inventing a father called Andy who'd taken off in the early days seemed the lesser of two evils.

Ted had written his address on the back of a cigarette pack. A godsend in a way. Had he not done so he might never have known of Manny's existence. Of course, in the beginning he denied the boy was his, but Tilda, at her mother's insistence, had sent photographs every birthday until the resemblance between father and son could not be denied.

Those photographs, along with the threat of an imminent visit to his hometown of Galveston, were enough to keep Ted sending money. The last thing he wanted was Tilda turning up, bastard child in tow, to muddy the waters of his cushy life.

Ma Bryn finished the tea and remained seated by the open window, pensive. The sea air was clearing her head and the tea was reviving her spirits. Funny how things work out, she thought. Me mother never told me who *my* real father was neither. Said he was a ne'er-do-well not worth mentioning, who took off when I was a wee one. Men like that were ten a penny.

Then:

"Hello ... *any-bod-dee* at home?"

She jumped up at the sound of a strange male voice.

Dearie me, it was rare for a man to want a reading. But sure wonders will never cease in this world.

She pulled back the curtain and saw a little man wearing a fedora peering up at her.

"Would *ye* be the ma-*dam?*" he enquired.

She couldn't place his accent; a wee touch of the for'n country about it. Maybe India or Amerikay or a bitta both.

"Yes ... yes, indeed, that'll be me all right ... Madame Matilda. Is it a readin' you'll be wanting, sir?"

"Yes ... maybe so, ma'lady," he said, rubbing his chin, eyes glinting like a couple of coins in a wishing well. "Maybe that's indeed what I might be requiring on this fine summer's day."

"Er, aye ... c'mon in then, sir, and take a seat."

Tilda suddenly felt out of her depth, the needle on her psychic gauge wavering wildly. How was she gonna figure out this cockalorum?

She watched as he placed a shiny toecap on her shoe-worn step and hauled himself up with nary a gasp or sigh; as spry as a young boy, however that could be, and him maybe seventy if a day.

A well-dressed gentleman, she noted: chequered jacket, paisley scarf tucked neatly, the fern of a peony corsage waving, graceful, on his breast. Maybe coming from a wedding. Particular in his habits by the look of him. Not a loose thread, bitta fluff or a stain anywhere to be seen. The divil of a man tae live with but likely a widda-man—for why else would he be wanting his fortune told?

The gent sat down and removed his hat, revealing a swarthy, lined complexion stretched tight over the cheekbones like an Indian chief. White hair swept back sleek and neat as a badger's. Handsome in his day and still able to turn a head or two no doubt.

His dark eyes flashed about the interior like a cop hunting clues. She saw him squint up at her tinfoil stars, comb the walls, bedazzled; frown briefly at the ball and Tarot, before returning to her face.

"Interesting place you've got here, Ma*dam*—or would you prefer Ma Lady?"

"Whatever yeh like, sir," Tilda said. "I don't mind a-tall."

He gave a respectful little nod.

"Been practisin' this peculiar craft for long, Ma Lady?"

"Aye ... the gift's been passed down, y'see. Been in me family many a year."

"You don't say?"

"Er . . . aye . . . now, what'll it be, Mr . . . uh . . . ?"

"Samuel Monroe-Johnson."

The name was delivered in the singsong manner of a preacher-man at the pulpit. Tilda felt on edge. She sensed things wouldn't go so well between her and the odd wee brown-faced man sitting across from her, but she wouldn't be one to turn a body away.

"But you can call me Mr Samuel or just plain ol' Sam—whichever sits more comfortable on your tongue, Ma Lady."

"R-right yeh be . . . Mister . . . erm . . . Samuel did yeh say?"

"Yes-sir-ee."

"Well now, Samuel, will it be the Tarot, the ball or the palms, for I can see great—"

"Don't want none of them," Samuel interjected, messianic eyes fixing on her. "'Cos the *Lord-Gawd Hisself* sent me a-fishin' today. He sez this morning: 'Reverend Samuel, go thou to the woman that dwells below in that car'van of *in-nick-quid-tee* and lead her back to *Jez-sos* . . . that she may *recover* herself from her *wicked, blaspheemeous* ways, and with the help of the *Good Gawd Hisself* be cleansed—nay, *renewed*—in the healin' waters of the *H-o-l-y Spirit*, amen.'"

"Is that so?" Tilda said, thinking: I had a feeling yeh were one of them oul' Bible-thumpin' types, coming in here to waste my time. "Well, if yer not here for a reading what is it I can do for yeh?"

"It's not what *you* can do for *me*, lady, but what *I* can do for *you*."

He waved a knotty forefinger. "Are you willing to turn away from your *ungodly* ways and come onto the *Lord-Gawd* and *sayviour?* Praise be to *Jez-sos*."

"Och now, Sam, I'm only trying tae make a living. There's no harm in it. I'm only using the gift God give me, like me mother afore me."

Samuel smacked the rickety table lightly, making the crystal ball jump and the tarot cards shiver.

"Your gift is *not* from *Gawd.* Stop *lyin'* to yourself. And stop tellin' other people *lies,* for them lies come straight from the *Devil's tongue . . .* Bee-el-see-bub, the demon beast *hisself.* Anyone who practises *dee-vin-er-ation* or tells for*tunes* or interprets omens, or is a saucer-er—"

"I'm no saucer," Tilda cut across him, peeved.

". . . *meedee-um* or a *neck-crow-mancer*—"

"*What?* Dunno what any a them big words mean, to be honest."

". . . or she who makes contact with the dead, for whoever doth do these things is an *abomination* onto the Lord. *Juter-ronamee* chapter *eighteen*, verse eleven. *Praise be to Jez-sos!*"

"Well, I don't s'ppose you want a readin' done then," Tilda ventured, wondering how in God's name she was going to get rid of him.

Samuel Monroe-Johnson sat back in the chair, making a lattice of his bony fingers, and fixed her with his stoat-like eyes once more.

"Only *Gawd* knows the future, Ma Lady. How much you charge for these readings anyway?"

"A fiver for all three . . . or one pound and fifty apiece." It's about time I give this wee man a bitta-me own mind, man-o'-the-cloth or no.

"Now, you don't know nothin' about me or me circumstances. I needa earn a bitta money, 'cos me son lost his job. Aisey for other people to make judgements . . . didn't Jeesis Hisself say to not look at the blob in a body's eye without takin' the bigger blob outta yer own first?"

"He did indeed. I'm glad you know a little of the Scriptures. But I got no blobs in *ma* eyes, 'cos I follow the teachings of the *Bible.* And as a man of *Gawd* it's ma job—nay, duty—to show people the *error* of their *wicked* ways and try ta *save* their *souls.* And your soul's in need of saving, Ma Lady."

He shifted in the chair. "Not unless you wanna end up like your mother."

Tilda was affronted.

"You know nothin' about me mammy, God rest her soul. What are you incineratin'?"

"I saw how your mother used you as a little girl on this very promenade . . . you—a little innocent child with your yellow curls and frills—standin' out there, drawing the gull'ble people in. She *used* you. And she went crazy and died of *al-co-hol* poisoning, 'cos she never repented. You don't wanna end up like her, lady . . . that's all I's a-saying."

Tilda's mouth fell open. She tried to speak but the words just wouldn't come. How could this wee preacher-man know about her poor mammy's past life?

Samuel Monroe-Johnson got to his feet. Took a card from his wallet and slid it across the table.

"Call me if you have a change of heart, Ma Lady. My address's on there too. I'm in need of a housekeeper. Need-a woman to cook and clean and look after things and you look like a capable woman worthy of a better life. Would pay you handsome too. It's never too late to repent for you' sins . . . save yourself from the fires-a-hell and ree-cover!"

With that he gave a curt little bow and promptly took his leave.

Tilda sat awhile in the shocked aftermath, trying to compose herself, feeling dizzy; heart beating so fast she thought it might jump out of her chest and chase after him. As if on cue a series of terrible pictures began revealing themselves to her, like stills on a movie reel.

God, what if I was to take a heart attack right now and die alone in this old caravan? What a sorry end that would be, with no Manny beside me, and barely a penny to me name. Nothing of value till leave to me only son.

The thought brought tears to her eyes and she allowed herself to weep, something she's rarely done since girlhood.

"Hello . . . anybody in?"

The sound of a woman's voice made her jump. She dried her tears quickly. The last thing she wanted to do now was a reading. Was in no fit state to talk to anybody. She'd send them away. Say she was closed for the day.

Tilda pulled back the beaded curtain—and nearly had the heart attack she'd just imagined. For who should be standing there but her recent acquaintance and grieving widow, the grand Mrs Ellen Purboy herself.

VIVIENNE

"I'm Brigid and this here's me sister Nan," the lady said, placing a shawl about Vivienne's shoulders. "You're shivering something terrible, but the fire'll warm yeh up.... You could-a caught yer death out there."

I nearly did, thought Vivienne—catch my death—but it had nothing to do with the cold.

Brigid took the armchair opposite, whilst Nan—the one who'd slammed the door in her face—stood like a menacing old crow puffing its wings in pique.

"God, you look in an awful state," Brigid went on. "What happened yeh anyway, daughter dear?"

"I-I..."

A sudden violent shivering took hold of Vivienne, every nerve and sinew in revolt: teeth chattering, heart battering.

"You shouldn't 'ave let her in," Nan snapped. "You donno what trouble she'll get us in."

Vivienne's thoughts tumbled, moving between the two of them: between the friendly and unfriendly, the pleasant and the mean. She couldn't find the words to explain herself. It seemed as though the nightmare had stolen her tongue and buried it somewhere out there in the forest, never to be found again. The carefree young woman who'd had a life before this horror had died out there too. The realization brought gut-wrenching sobs of despair.

"Oh, dear, dear, dear!" she heard Brigid say.

"She's puttin' it on, if you ask me. You're a fool for lettin' her in."

"Oh, for heaven's sake, Nan! No one's asking you anything.... Where's your charity? Go and make us a cuppa tea. Would you like that, dear ... a nice slice of Battenberg? I'm sure you're hungry."

"Humph! Don't say I didn't warn yeh." Grudgingly, the sister left the room.

"Pay no attention to her, daughter ... crabbit as the Divil himself." She lifted the tongs and arranged some coals on the fire. "You'll be all right soon enough, so. You just rest yerself a wee while ... then you can tell me all about it when yer ready."

Sounds were coming from the kitchen: a match being struck, a kettle being filled, cupboards opening and shutting, crockery being banged down. Vivienne heard Fitzwell preparing breakfast, the breakfast that would be his undoing. She knew that in the future those innocent sounds would be for ever freighted with dread, seared into her brain with the burning force of a branding iron.

Gradually her shivering subsided—the warmth of the fire and Brigid's kind-heartedness thawing her a little.

Rest.

Yes, I could just allow myself to rest a little while. But I know that's a foolish thought. The chase is far from over.

He/they will be coming after me.

The realization gave her voice. She forced the words out

"I-I ... I need ... need to use your phone. *Please!*"

Brigid looked askance. "Phone? Oh, but we don't have a phone, yeh see. We're too far out here for the lines, and anyway we couldn't afford—"

"Your ... your car then. Can I borrow it?"

She shook her head slowly. "Oh, no, we don't have a car, daughter dear. Never learnt to drive, yeh see."

Vivienne's heart sank. Somehow she had a feeling Brigid would say that. The sisters seemed to be living in a bygone age, creatures from a fairy tale frozen in time.

"But the taxi comes in the mornin' ... till take us for the pension. He'll give you a lift. Yeh can stay here the night ... get yerself warshed and outta them durty clothes."

"But—"

"You can't go out looking like that, dear."

Why is she so calm? She's no idea how much trouble I'm in.

"But, I-I ... I was *kidnapped.*"

"Kidnapped?"

"You must help me!" *Please!* A man ... IRA man ... Connor.... He ... he held me prisoner in an old cottage in the forest.... I knocked him out ... when he recovers he'll come after me. If there's no phone you'll have to hide me."

"Oh, Jesus, Mary and Joseph!" Brigid put a hand to her throat. Vivienne was sorry she'd frightened her, but there was no other way. She was her only hope. "You're ... you're the judge's daughter?"

"Yes-yes, that's me ... Vivienne ... Vivienne Dundas."

"Oh, God help-us!!! You've been all over the papers. It's only now I see yer face I ... "

Brigid got to her feet, paced the room, anxious. "Nan, come in here!"

Nan appeared in the doorway with the tray, face crumpled with annoyance. "What's it now?"

"Nan, she's the judge's daughter! That scoundrel Connor was keepin' her in *our John's house.*"

"*What?!*"

"Aye. We have to hide her, 'cos he'll be comin' after her."

Nan banged the tray down and shook her fists. Vivienne shrank back but soon understood she was not the object of her fury.

"I *knew* that Magee fella wasn't a good 'un ... comin' round here ... wantin' tae rent our John's place for a bizznessman. *Bizznessman, me eye!* They had a quare laugh at the pair of us ... murderin' our brother and usin' us like we were durt on their shoe, and *you* were the one that agreed to it, *not me.*"

"But we needed the money, Nan!"

"Away tae blazes! If he comes round here I'll fix him with that poker."

She turned to Vivienne. "Don't you worry about him, my girl. Yer poor daddy and mammy sufferin' like that."

"But where do we hide her, Nan?"

"Where d'you think?"

Nan moved to a spot by the backdoor, tipped back a large rug to reveal a trapdoor. "Where Da kept his poteen supplies. It'll be dark but big enough—"

At that moment a car was heard, headlights sliding across the closed curtains like a louring ghoul.

"*Quick!*"

Vivienne packed herself into the cramped space. It was not much bigger than a coffin and stank of black treacle and dead things. She was terrified. Clamped a hand over her mouth as a loud knocking was heard above ground.

"Quick, hide that tray!"

"Why, Nan?"

"There's *three* cups on it—that's why!"

Vivienne heard the door being opened, security chain in place.

"Oh, it's you, Mr Magee. And what would yeh be wantin' at this hour?"

"Yeh didn't see a young lassie about, did yeh? Dark hair, long ... thin of herself ... "

"What kinda question's that? Don't know nothin' 'bout no young 'un."

"She's me sister and she's run away."

"Aye, but what would she be doin' out here? Now away to blazes or I'll get the polis."

"Let me in and I'll check. She could-a got in a windee and be hidin' under yer bed. She's a dangerous bitch. Kill the pair of yeh in a fuckin' blink!"

"Don't use that ungodly language to me, yeh clown!"

Oh, Christ, why is she getting his back up?! Vivienne's body went into spasm. If Magee found her she was as good as dead.

God, please don't let him come in!

Then:

"*Aaaah!*" A sharp scream as the door burst open.

The security chain hit the floor. The trapdoor creaked dangerously with the weight of him. She prayed it wouldn't cave in on her.

"I'll fuckin' decide if she's here, yeh oul' bitch!"

"Come back here!" she heard Nan shout as he thundered down the hallway.

"Don't you dare—"

The house shook.

Voices receded.

"God, Nan," Brigid implored from the safety of the parlour, "don't make him angrier!"

Of a sudden, voices swelling and they were re-entering the parlour.

Vivienne felt a sneeze coming on. She squeezed herself farther down in the hole, stifling it as the squabble continued.

"See, I told you there wasn't nobody here. Now get out of our house, you wastrel!"

"*Damn* the pair of yeh! If we find out she was here we'll do the pair of yeh in, like yer bloody brother."

"*How dare you?! Get out! Get! You murderin' divil!*"

The front door slammed.

An engine started up.

The car roared away.

Vivienne wept with relief.

For the first time in what seemed like an age—imprisoned down there in the poteen hole—she felt the worst of her ordeal was over.

Yes, it was truly, finally over. But more important than that: *she'd survived to tell the tale.*

FIFTY-FIVE

Early morning, a murky blanket of cloud lying low over the land and Manny Bryn, at the wheel of his taxi, was on a mission.

After Magee's visit he'd lain awake for most of the night, livid with the way he was being used and abused by him and Fitzwell. He'd never asked to be part of their evil plans, yet here he was being treated like their bloody lackey. It was no business of theirs that he might have designs on Iris. That was *his* business. The fact that Magee had had the brazen cheek to crash into his house, snatch his ma's chocolates—which meant him having to buy replacements—meant a line had been crossed. What if his ma had been at home? The shock of it could-a kilt her.

Well, it wouldn't be happening again, Manny decided, knuckles whitening on the steering wheel as he jounced through the Muddymacreek Forest towards the hideout.

Vivienne Dundas was being held captive. He was sure of it. Hearing those terrified cries that day haunted his waking hours. He had a duty to try and rescue her. If not, his conscience would eat away at him for the rest of his days and they'd have won.

His ma was due back the next day from Portaluce. There was no time to waste.

He'd figured out a plan of sorts. In the glove compartment he'd stowed the sharpest knife from the kitchen drawer. He'd take Fitzwell by surprise, stab him in the leg to thwart him, rescue Vivienne, drive her back to Hillside and phone for help. That way, his mother wouldn't have an inkling of anything having taken place.

. . .

Nearing the cottage, he pulled the car into a secluded spot behind some bushes and killed the engine. Any sounds would alert Fitzwell and he couldn't risk that. No, he needed to take the psycho by surprise. At that hour of the morning he'd likely be fast asleep.

Anxious but determined, Manny wrapped the knife in a flannel, stuck it in his back pocket and exited the car.

All was quiet as he trudged along, his ears registering the cawing of jackdaws, his nose picking up the odour of wet soil. The smell brought thoughts of the grave, and the possibility he could actually die trying to free this young woman he'd never met. But he didn't care; Magee's audacious trespass had released within him a compulsion to finally settle scores. It was the same urge he'd felt in the dole office that day but magnified to such a degree that rendered consequences redundant. He was tired of being bullied and abused.

He had to take action.

The mist lay heavy as he pushed farther towards the house and he was glad of that. It afforded him a degree of cover and so an element of surprise.

Finally he'd reached journey's end.

Keeping well out of sight, he hunkered down behind an old hayshaker to case the joint.

But what was this?

To his consternation, he saw that the front door was open.

The bastard had barricaded himself in there for obvious reasons. Manny remained perfectly still. If Fitzwell was in he'd certainly hear him moving about.

But the longer he waited the more he became convinced that the place was deserted. Christ, had he moved Vivienne to another location?! He thought of peeping through a window, but since they were all covered it was a dumb idea.

He felt for the knife in his back pocket and removed it from its covering. Steeling himself, he tiptoed up to the front door and peered inside.

The only sign of life was the banked hearth-fire sending thin wisps of smoke up the chimney. Could Fitzwell be out gathering wood? He kept his nerve and moved farther into the room.

The floor was a mess, littered with empty beer cans and food wrappers. By the leg of one of the armchairs he saw something glinting.

Keys.

How did they end up there? Had Fitzwell dropped them? Not likely.

One of those keys might open the door to Vivienne. He needed to be quick.

He went down the corridor, knife held at the ready. The second key unlocked the door. Quietly he pushed it open.

"It's all right, I'm here to—"

"*Jesus!*"

The sight nearly knocked him off his feet.

Fitzwell was lying face-down on the floor.

Back of his head matted with blood.

Face a mask of deathly white.

He was dead!

Horror and relief twisted Manny's insides, wrenching and heaving as he took in the scene: the upturned chair, the old mattress, the scattered crockery on the floor.

Vivienne Dundas had killed him.

He bent over Fitzwell, briefly relishing his downfall. How many innocent lives had he destroyed? The fact that a woman had taken him out was a coup in itself.

Vroom, vroom, vroom!

The sound of a car.

Oh, Holy God!

He dashed back to the living-room, in time to see the dreaded blue motor car belonging to the oul' pair making its slow approach.

There was nowhere to run except out the back.

He dived into the scullery.

Tried the backdoor but it was locked.

There was no escape.

A baseball bat stood by the sink. An extra weapon to brain the pair if needed. He'd wait until they were distracted with Fitzwell then make good his escape.

Moments later the pair were in the living-room. Manny strained to hear.

"Strange bloody thing, that door lyin' open," he heard the woman say, entering first. "He needs tae be more careful or she'll get out."

"Och, he's maybe out gatherin' sticks. You check on the bitch and I'll see tae this fire afore it goes out."

"No son of ours should be livin' in these conditions. How long is it gonna go on for, Ronnie?"

"Look, Alice, the longer we hold on to her, the bigger the ransom we can ask for. It'll not be long now. How much do yeh want that new warshin' machine?"

Manny waited, terrified, but determined.

Through a gap in the door he eyed Ronnie poking at the fire. Heard Alice go down to the bedroom. Waited for the cry to go up.

"Oh, J-e-s-u-s, Ronnie, come here quick!"

Ronnie dropped the poker and ran down the hallway.

Manny opened the door a crack.

Vitriolic exchanges erupted between the pair.

"*Oh J-e-s-u-s, my poor Marty's d-e-a-d-d-d-d-d!*" the old lady wailed.

"*How the fuck did she get out?*"

"*But he's d-e-a-d, R-o-n-n-i-e. She kilt him, R-o-n-n-i-e.*"

Manny shot out of the house, not daring to look sideways.

Crouching down behind their old banger, he had a brainwave.

Took the knife from his pocket and plunged the blade into each of the rear tyres.

He might not have rescued Vivienne, but he'd certainly bought her more time. Now it was *his* mission to find her before Ronnie, the madman, did.

FIFTY-SIX

Nettie was in a hurry. She'd been held up in the pharmacy by a dithering Mrs Peebles, who couldn't quite decide on the proper shade of pantyhose for her daughter's wedding. Would it be the Toasted Almond or the Lightly Toasted Almond or maybe even the Biscuit Beige?

As if it mattered, thought Nettie, driving up the avenue to Cedarwood. Betty Peebles had legs like the stanchions on a grand piano, so who on earth would be looking at her? Black would be best, she felt like saying. Slims and flatters all at the same time. Better still: a long skirt or trousers. But she could hardly tell her that.

She drew up in the courtyard of Cedarwood and checked her watch. She had a parish council meeting in half an hour, so couldn't delay very long.

On the passenger seat sat a small tub of ice-cream for little Toby. Best to deliver it first, in case it melted.

She left the vehicle and made her way round to their quarters. No sign of Jay's car. Well, he did mention he'd be working—so the little boy was likely to be on his own. A pang of pity assailed her. It's not really proper to leave a child alone all day, but I suppose it would be more boring for him spending the day in his father's office.

She knocked on the door.

"Toby, it's me: Nettie. Are you in?"

Nothing.

She tried again, knocking a bit more loudly this time.

"Toby, I've brought some ice-cream for you. Can I give it to you? I won't come in. Promise."

She waited some more, but still no answer.

The curtains on a nearby window were half-drawn. Should I peek in? No, it wouldn't be proper to pry.

Maybe he hears me but is just too shy.

"I'll leave it here on the windowsill for you then. But make sure you eat it soon or it'll melt."

She retraced her steps round to the front again.

At least I've no Jasper this time, to cause a racket.

She mounted the steps, recalling his whimpering cries, and tried not to think about ghostly things or why the dog refused to enter the house. There's nothing to fear, only my silly imagination. I've come here to do a job and I'll jolly well do it.

Boldly, she turned the key in the heavy oak door, ignoring its doomful groans as she stepped inside.

All was quiet in the gloomy interior, save for the ticking of the grandfather clock in the hallway. The place still gave her the shivers, in spite of Jay's assurances, but she had no intention of dallying too long.

She headed down the hallway, carefully avoiding the portraits. Even though I feel braver on this occasion I can't trust myself not to be rattled by that lot.

In the kitchen she looked for Ellen's tonic. It was not where she'd said it would be: on the draining-board. She opened some cupboards but it was nowhere to be seen. Odd. Well, I'm not delaying any longer than necessary. I'll get another done up in the pharmacy.

As she was shutting the door she thought she heard some movement in the studio. She slipped across and had a listen.

"Toby dear, are you in there?"

But, as before, no one answered.

I'm hearing things then. Well, Cedarwood has a habit of doing that to me.

Quickly she checked the remaining rooms and was pleased to see that everything was in order.

She turned to go upstairs but paused a moment. Something was wrong. The Eiffel Tower doorstop that normally sat by the hat-stand was missing. Where on earth could it be? I was sure I saw it yesterday.

Unnerved, she tried not to panic. Gave herself a stiff rebuke.

Now, you came here to get the jewellery box. The sooner you get this visit over the better. So just get on with it!

She mounted the steep, wide staircase. Halfway up she thought she heard the faint strains of a familiar tune.

Oranges and lemons say the bells of St Clement's.
When will you pay me? say the bells of Old Bailey.

She paused a second time.

Oranges and lemons say the bells of St Clement's.
When will you pay me? say the bells of Old Bailey.

There it was again. She recognized the old nursery rhyme set to music. It was very faint, so perhaps it was someone out on the road: a car radio. Someone waiting with the window rolled down, passing the time. Yes, that had to be it.

Feeling a little braver, she set her shoulders and continued her climb.

When she gained the landing she stood for a moment to collect herself. Ellen's room was at the far end of the long corridor. But the strange melody seemed to be getting louder, dispelling her assumption that it was coming *from outside.*

Leave! Nettie, leave, her gut instinct was urging. Forget about the jewellery box and just go. Ellen can do without her rings and necklaces.

She faltered, hand gripping the banister as another voice, her usual pragmatic one, took over.

I can't disappoint my sister. I know how much she likes her jewellery. I promised I'd collect it and it would be very cowardly to back out now, when I've come this far.

Mind made up, she took a deep breath, sped down the corridor, turned the door handle and pushed into the bedroom.

She froze.

"*Oh, my good God!*"

In a few heart-stopping seconds she'd absorbed the extraordinary scene.

The room was a mess. Every drawer in the dressing-table pulled out, the contents strewn on the floor. The jewellery box lay open, the little dancing ballerina pirouetting to the tinkling tune. Most baffling of all, the Eiffel Tower doorstop had somehow transported itself from the hallway and was positioned on Ellen's bed.

Poltergeist activity!

The realization had her backing away.

Oh, dear God, I need to leave this house now!

She banged the door on the travesty. Raced back down the corridor in mortal panic.

At the top of the stairs she paused to find her feet.

But failed to keep her balance.

She flung an arm wide, tried to grasp the banister. But her hand caught thin air and, before she knew it, her legs were giving way.

Nettie toppled, tumbling head over heels, her cries echoing unheard through the empty house.

She slumped down, helpless and moaning, on the same spot where Sir Wilfred Blackbourne had met his end.

She tried to get up, but it was useless. Her whole body convulsed with pain as she drifted in and out of consciousness.

Beaten back by the struggle, minutes later her moaning ceased and Cedarwood was returned, once more, to its eerie silence, broken only by the ticking of the ancient grandfather clock and the tinkling strains of the jewellery box.

FIFTY-SEVEN

Ma Bryn sat on a plush chair behind the sun-thronged glass of Ellen's conservatory, deep in thought. The wee preacher-man's visit had rattled her. But seeing Mrs Purboy in her doorway so soon after he'd left nearly brought on a seizure.

She'd feigned a headache at the sight of Ellen, the very last person she'd expected to see in Portaluce—of all places. But dearie me, hadn't she mentioned a house by the sea in that reading? Just hadn't said it was here in Portaluce. And wasn't her offer of a reviving cuppa tea in her lovely house just too good to turn down?

Tilda contemplated the amazing view as Ellen busied herself in the kitchen. She'd never been in a "glass-room" before and was astonished by the vista of sea and sky stretching away as far as the eye could see. God, it was like paradise! Sitting up so high and looking down on everything; like God himself on his throne.

The neighbouring house, she saw, was just as grand, with a similar glass-room to the front. God, them people that could afford to live in such luxury were very blessed indeed.

She brought her attention back to her immediate surroundings, not knowing what to inspect first.

There was a sofa with plump, creamy cushions embroidered with wee sprigs of heather. A coffee table of woven raffia inlaid with beautiful tile-work. The two pottery floor lamps were as tall as herself and must have cost a small fortune. Tilda felt a pang of regret as she gazed about. It's a pity a body couldn't have had a wee bit of the finer things in life, like Mrs Purboy. If only I'd met a rich man....

But sure that's just how things worked out.

She thought of her humble home with its leaking roof, and windows so loose they rattled every time a car went past. God forbid that Mrs Purboy should ever see it.

Feeling dejected, she reflected again on the words of Mr Monroe-Johnson. Maybe he was right; I *will* end up like me mother if I don't change me ways. 'Cos truth be told, when I think about it, Madame Silver Crown never made a lot of money from the fortune telling. Whatever she did make went on the drink. She'd inherited Hillside Cottage—a calamity of weathered stone with a tin roof and a broken door—from an Uncle Tommy, who drunk hisself to death too. It was in a shambles when they moved in, and was an even bigger shambles now.

Tilda's eyes welled up at the thought of her sorry lot. Meeting Bella Prunty hadn't helped either. Bringing back all that stuff about Ted and what he did. I was never a one to look back at the past and regret things but, for whatever reason, it's coming at me now and it's a sign. Me health's not good and I'm not getting no younger. Maybe it's time I repented for all them years me mother wasted doing the Devil's work, as that wee preacher-man put it.

Footsteps in the hallway pulled Tilda swiftly back to the present. She wiped a hand over her eyes as Ellen entered with a tray.

"Now, here we are! A lovely cuppa's just the remedy for that headache of yours."

It was a tea fit for a queen all right. The tray gleamed with delicate china, silver teaspoons and linen napkins in silver rings. There was a plate of dainty finger sandwiches and another one arranged with thick slices of walnut cake.

"God, Ellen, you shouldn't have went to so much bother on my account. A cup in me hand would of been grand."

"Nonsense. I'm only too happy to have someone to share with. And no better person than you, Tilda."

"Och, yer very good!"

"I had no idea you did readings here in Portaluce," she said, handing her the tea. "How come I haven't seen you here before?"

"Well now, that's easily explained. I only started up me readin' a month or two ago. Used to come here with me mammy, God rest her soul, in me younger days to help her, like."

"You know the territory well then. So what prompted you to start up again?"

Tilda could hardly admit she needed the money. "Och, I thought in the good weather it'd be nice to get outta the house for a bit ... and no better place to be, than at the seaside when the sun's shinin'."

"I couldn't agree more ... such a coincidence us meeting here."

"A great co-instance indeed," Tilda agreed, selecting a sandwich. As she did so, Ellen was suddenly reminded of the last time they'd had tea together.

"That tea we had at Cedarwood before you did my reading ... "

"Yes, and a lovely tea it was too. Just as nice as this one."

"Thanks, but ... you-you weren't unwell afterwards, were you?"

"Who me? No, not a bit of it. Why d'you ask, Ellen?"

"Oh, nothing.... I felt slightly ill afterwards ... that's all. Thought the milk or something might have been off. Anyway, I'm glad it didn't affect *you*."

"No-no, I was fine. But sure I could eat a horse and not get sick. I can see that you'd have a more delicate nature, being so slim and all. Wish I could be your size. Now tell me, how long have you been comin' to this lovely house?"

"Fifteen years or thereabouts.... George bought it a few years after we married."

Tilda saw Ellen's lovely face darken briefly.

"Must be hard to be here without your husband.... But yeh know you've a bright future ahead of you, Ellen, as I saw in the ball that last time. I have a feelin' you're gonna live here permanent, like."

Ellen smiled. Gazed out of the window. "That's good to hear. It isn't easy, to be honest... but time's a great healer." She looked back at Tilda. "Well, you would know, having lost your own husband too."

"It's never easy. But I wonder, Ellen," Tilda said quickly, not wanting to get tangled up in explaining a past she'd sooner forget, "you being used to this part of the world. Would you know a wee preacher-man that lives round here, by the name of Monroe-Johnson, would yeh?"

Ellen put down her cup. Dabbed at her lips with a napkin.

"Oh, you mean Pastor Sam?"

"Aye, that's his name all right. He lives round here, does he?"

"Yes, indeed. He lives next door." Tilda was flabbergasted to see Ellen point to the big house she'd been admiring earlier. "He moved back recently... spent most of his life in Africa... on the missions. That house belonged to his late father, who was also a minister. He passed away a couple of years ago and Sam returned here to retire."

So that's how he knew about me mammy. His father, being a clergyman, would have been very disapproving and when he was a wee one he would of picked up all that oul' fire-an'-brimstone stuff about fortune tellers from him.

"He's a real gentleman," Ellen was saying. "Why do you ask? Do you know him?"

"Aye... well, no... not exactly. Just to bid the time of day to, like."

"He's looking for a live-in housekeeper. Asked me if I knew any dependable ladies in the area. Naturally I had to draw a blank."

"Did he now? So, he never married I suppose."

Ellen shook her head. "No, a confirmed bachelor, as they say."

"That's a pity. So, he wouldn't have nobody to leave that big house to?"

"No. Sad, isn't it? But it will go to the Church no doubt."

The phone rang and Ellen excused herself.

Ma Bryn found Samuel Monroe-Johnson's card in her pocket and studied it, a surge of probable futures opening up before her.

My goodness me! My mother always said I'd meet a rich man. There'd be no romance in it, but he'd take care of all me material needs. Is this wee missionary the one she was talking about? It has to be. Who else could it be?

She quickly tucked the card back into her pocket at the sound of Ellen returning.

"Everything all right?" she asked, because Ellen had turned quite pale.

"It's . . . it's my . . . my sister . . . Nettie. . . . She's-she's had a terrible accident."

"Oh, dearie me! But is she all right?"

"She's in . . . in intensive care," Ellen said, breaking down. "I need to go home immediately."

VIVIENNE

Sleep was broken, fitful. Even though Vivienne was in a real bed for the first time in an age—in kindly Brigid's bedroom—her thoughts roamed wild in a wasteland as endless and daunting as the forest itself.

I need to focus on the good: on what the sisters have done for me. I will not lose faith in humankind, no matter the horrors I've endured.

Tears of joy and sorrow gathered under Vivienne's closed lids as she lay beneath the freshly laundered sheets, the scent of lavender in her nostrils, the warmth of a hot-water bottle at her feet, listening to a faint breeze stirring the trees near the edge of the house, the wind badgering the latch of the loose front door.

Earlier Nan and Brigid had shown her the bathroom, given her towels and a nightdress that was much too big. But oh, the joy of being scrubbed clean of the monster's lair, the mire of the forest floor! To discard the clothes thus defiled, and find herself renewed—reaffirmed—in body, if not yet in soul.

She let her mind dwell on the sisters, to keep the darkness away.

They must have lived here all their lives. She saw their ancient faces morph back into the young girls they once had been. Pictured them confined to the tiny house, wearing their modest clothes and sensible shoes, unable to pursue their dreams, the wings of their desires tied neatly in abeyance. The father, a domineering force most likely. The mother, a kindly soul, powerless to change things.

The thought of parents brought images of her own dear mother and father. She couldn't quite believe she'd be seeing them again.

What cruelties of the imagination they'd been put through! The weeks of suffering they'd had to bear.

But she'd been victorious and was returning to them.

Together and united *they would survive.*

She thought of the gunman on the library steps all those years ago. She thought of the heartache that episode unleashed. Now there was another to eclipse it. She knew she'd have to relive the torments of this chapter, again and again. But perhaps that was what life was all about: overcoming chaos in order to progress, in order to grow.

Quick in her mind she saw Fitzwell lying sprawled on the filthy floor.

I did not surrender. I stood my ground. I fought back and I won.

Did he die?

Her heart pounded frantically at the thought.

Might I go to prison if I killed him?

But he gave *me* no choice. He wanted *me* dead. I wanted to live.

She rolled over in the bed to unseat the dark thoughts and saw, to her surprise, that dawn had already broken, creeping like a blessing through the curtains.

As if on cue the cries of a cockerel rent the silence.

She sat up on her elbows. It seemed as though she hadn't been in this reality at all. It seemed as if something carried her off in the dead of night to a place outside of space and time, then placed her back between the covers and then awakened her.

The clock on the locker read 7.15.

At 10 the taxi would arrive.

Her heart lifted.

She threw back the covers, happy. Lifted a frock that Brigid had left out. It was a shift dress in Air Force blue with a white collar and lace trim. There was a white cardigan as well. Both items looked hand-made. They were too big and too long, but they'd do to take her home.

Home.

The word opened like a flower within her.

If I had wings I'd spread them wide, soar high and free, like a bird.

There was a mirror on the dressing-table and she dared herself to sit before it. Last night she'd avoided her reflection in the bathroom, but now, with the night behind her, she felt more courageous.

The face of a haunted creature stared back: eyes huge and dark, skin like waxen paper, hair so brittle it might turn to ash at the lightest touch.

She wanted to weep.

Then, of a sudden, soft footfalls in the hallway.

The sisters were awake.

A light tapping on the door.

"Are yeh up, dear?" she heard Brigid enquire.

"Uh … yes. Yes, I am."

"That's good. … Breakfast's nearly ready. I'll just wet the tea, so."

She heard Brigid pad back to the kitchen. Squeezed her eyes shut, blinking the tears away.

You made it, Vivienne Dundas.

"Yes, I did," she said, willing herself to smile. "I certainly did."

With that she pushed back the chair, made to rise.

Today I will see my parents.

Today I will begin to reconnect with the life I once knew.

The thought emboldened her.

With that, she reset her focus, rose in one fluid movement and left the little room.

FIFTY-NINE

Ellen Purboy was in despair. Had she not asked Nettie to fetch her blessed jewellery case then the terrible event that had put her in hospital would never have occurred. There'd have been no need for her sister to go upstairs to the bedroom and she'd be carrying on with life as usual, not lying unconscious and broken in Intensive Care, hooked up to machines, suspended between this world and the next.

She'd rushed home from Portaluce the previous evening and was allowed the briefest of visits to her bedside.

Nettie looked as though she'd been in a war zone; the left side of her body had taken the brunt of the fall. Her head was heavily bandaged, face bruised and swollen. Both wrists sprained. She had a dislocated shoulder and a fractured knee.

Nettie's husband John was in the waiting-room when Ellen pushed through the doors. They broke down at the sight of each other, embracing in tearful union. How had it come to this? How could life be so cruel?

"We'll call you as soon as there's a change," the nurse assured them.

But John was adamant he wouldn't be going anywhere.

"You go on, Ellen," he'd said, "and get some rest. There's no point in two of us being here. I'll call you when she comes round."

"Oh, God, it's all my fault! I asked her to—"

"Now, Ellen, don't blame yourself. It was an *accident*."

On returning to Cedarwood she'd examined the stairs and landing. She'd thought perhaps there was a piece of loose carpeting. But no, everything was in place.

Nothing amiss in the bedroom either. The puzzling part was that the jewellery case was still in the top drawer of the dressing-table, where she'd left it. Not in Nettie's bag, as would be expected.

Ellen got up and paced the hallway. Paused at the bottom of the stairs, Tilda Bryn's words coming to her.

"Did anything happen there? I'm getting a cold spot."

Strange that she should say that, and even more peculiar that my sister and I should meet with accidents within a few short weeks—*and* in this very hallway!

She had Nettie to thank for saving her that day. Had she not arrived when she did, God knows what might have happened. The thought brought tears again and she realized with a start that she hadn't received the results of the blood tests from Dr Flynn.

She picked up the phone and dialled the surgery. The receptionist put her through right away.

"I was just about to call you," Dr Flynn said briskly. "I'm so sorry to hear about Nettie. Hopefully she'll be on the mend very soon. Nasty business, a fall."

"Thank you, doctor. Yes, we can only hope and pray."

"Indeed! And how are *you* keeping, Ellen? I trust the sea air helped. No repeats of that fainting spell, I hope? Your blood samples came back clear, by the way, so you've nothing to worry about on that score."

"Oh... I'm glad to hear that. But... but what d'you think caused me to black out like that? It never happened before."

"Well, given that your blood pressure was raised . . . you had visual disturbance and felt nauseous... it could point to poisoning of some sort."

"Poisoning? That's impossible . . . I'd just had tea with a friend that day and when I asked her if she'd had ill-effects she said no."

"Hmmm... not unless... "

Down the line Ellen heard the creaking of the doctor's leather chair. There was a pause, which made her nervous. She wondered if physicians were ever aware of the effect that their words—or lack of words—could communicate to sensitive patients such as herself.

"Er... unless... unless what, doctor?"

"Well, I was thinking... since you're such a keen gardener you perhaps... perhaps—accidentally of course—ingested a poison of some kind. Some of the more innocent plants can be quite toxic you know."

She thought it an odd remark. "Gosh no, doctor. I'm very careful with plants... besides which, I wear gloves when I'm gardening ... always."

"Hmmm... that thought did occur to me... you being such an expert on gardening. Just thought I'd mention it anyway. But all's well that ends well and you've nothing to worry about, Ellen... except for your poor sister of course. She's got a robust constitution: Nettie. I'm certain she'll make a full recovery."

"Thank you, doctor. That's good to hear."

"Bye now."

She put the phone down. Well, that was some positive news at least. Poor Nettie was the one to worry about now. And she wouldn't do much for her, sitting in Cedarwood brooding. She'd go to the hospital and be with John, even though it was only 8 a.m.

She was about to call a taxi when she heard the sound of a car coming up the drive.

Could it be Jay?

There'd been no sign of him the night before. All was quiet on the other side of the bedsit door and she'd been awake most of the night so would have heard him. Perhaps it was just as well he was absent. She wouldn't have wanted him seeing her distress. A pity though that he hadn't been around to hear poor Nettie's cries for help. Lying in the hallway for a whole half-hour before John's arrival hopefully wouldn't have done any lasting damage.

The doorbell rang.

Ellen checked herself in the mirror, mentally preparing a little speech of sorts for Jay.

She drew open the door.

"John!"

He raised a hand and smiled.

"Now, there's nothing to worry about, Ellen. It's all good news. I thought I'd come and collect you. Nettie's gained consciousness. The nurse said to give it a couple of hours, 'cos the doctor needs to run some more tests."

Ellen was overjoyed. "You-you mean she can talk? She recognized you?"

"Aye, knew me all right, but…" He was frowning slightly.

"Oh, come in, come in, won't you. We'll get a cuppa tea."

John stepped inside but halted. She saw him look at the Eiffel Tower doorstop—and do a double-take.

"Ah, so *that's* what she was talkin' about. She isn't going doolally after all."

"Er, I-I don't understand, John. What d'you mean?"

"Well, she mentioned *that*."

He pointed.

"The doorstop? Yes, it always sits there. What about it?"

"Is that what it is? Well, she said something about the Eiffel Tower *on your bed*. I thought she was goin' crazy but now it makes sense."

"But that's ridiculous! How could it have got up there?"

"I know; I thought so too, but she was very certain." John was pensive for a moment. He glanced at the object again. "But why… why would she make up something like that?"

Ellen could think of no reply.

"I-I really have no idea," she said at last. "It's never moved from that spot in all the years I've been here. George's father brought it home from Paris.… They honeymooned there, I believe: his parents. Heaven knows how they carried the thing all that way."

He shrugged. "Odd thing tae buy on yer honeymoon, right enough."

"Let's go through," Ellen said quickly, eager to change the subject. She really didn't want to hear any more. She had to remain in Cedarwood until Nettie recovered and couldn't afford to be thrown off balance by such ludicrous ideas. Nettie had always had a vivid imagination. Ellen thought Jay had talked her out of all that paranormal stuff the day he released her from the drawing-room. But alas, it seemed the tumble had brought her back to her old ways.

"She's bound to be tired," she said, filling the kettle. "Just a little confused and in shock after what she's been through. I wouldn't pay much heed to that."

"Aye, you're probably right. Could be the side-effects of all that medication they're giving her too."

"Indeed," Ellen said, but she was aware that her hands were shaking as she fetched the cups from the cupboard and was glad John was not a witness to her all-too-evident distress.

SIXTY

Manny had endured a bleak few days. What with being attacked in his own home by Magee then finding Fitzwell dead—and discovering the oul' pair were the convict's parents—the pieces of a macabre jigsaw puzzle were falling into place.

He could see now that he'd been set up from the start. That curious phone call all those weeks ago, followed by the run-in at the dole office.

Magee had deliberately come early that day to sign on.

"You're in the twelve o'clock file," he remembered Iris saying. "Come back in an hour."

That was the spark that lit the flame and Manny had walked right into the fire. He'd been waiting for him: Magee. All that blather from him. Sounding him out. Trying to get the measure of him.

If I hadn't defended Iris he'd have got me some other way. Aye, maybe by threatening Ma. That would have been far worse.

The replacement chocolates, for the box Magee had swiped, were on top of the wardrobe, where she'd left them. He'd had to forgo his six-pack of Harp, but worth it as his ma wouldn't suspect a thing.

With Fitzwell dead, and most likely buried now by his comrades, Manny was off the hook. The oul' pair and Magee would have to disappear pretty fast, now that Vivienne had escaped.

He'd checked the newspapers but there was no word that she'd been found. So she must be lying low somewhere. Oh, God, what if she'd been caught and killed by Magee?! He could not afford to contemplate such a horror.

Manny, slouched on the sofa, despondent, with his first cuppa of the day, felt bad he couldn't have done more to help her. God knows what she suffered. By rights he should be going to the police now and telling them what he'd witnessed, but he reckoned that would only make a bad situation worse. No one knew of his involvement except for the perpetrators themselves, and they'd hardly be fessing up to the cops anytime soon.

The letterbox gave out a rattle. The post. Another catalogue bill for Ma no doubt.

Wearily he got up.

To his amazement he saw an airmail letter lying on the mat.

Uncle Ted. *Finally.*

He snatched it up and went back to the kitchen, excitement rising.

I'll get another drop of tea and then open it. God, there might be a fortune in it! Should I wait till Ma gets home? Nah, it's addressed to *me* and I can't wait. I've the Doody sisters to collect at ten, so I'd better get a move on.

Manny tore open the envelope.

There was just a single page and to his delight when he unfolded it a cheque fell onto his lap. Thrilled, he turned it over.

But his elation was short-lived. The cheque, written in Ted's spidery hand, was made out for a miserly $300.

How much was that in real money? A hundred quid? Maybe a couple of hundred at most. But maybe when I read the letter he'll tell me there's more coming.

He set the cheque aside and began reading.

Fofanny Heights, Scutch End
Galveston Texas USA

Howdy Manny,

It was mighty fine to hear from ya ovah there in the ol' country. Tilly always did the writin so it was swell to hear from her little guy for a change.

Thanks for the condolences on the passin of my darlin Pearl. Life just keeps on a-goin. It's the darnest thing but I was fixin to write to Tilly to tell ya'll good news when you letter arrived. Cos I got some real good news. I met myself another fine gal four months previous. We're fixin to marry in the Fall. Don't believe in wastin no time at my age, ya see.

I'm sure sorry to hear ya lost your job. I'm sendin some dosh to tide ya ovah. Would-a been more but the weddins gonna be costly and my gal's got expensive tastes. Smart as a hooty owl Pammy-Mae. Got more snap in her garters than I've got gas in the tank but I knows I's the lucky one. I feel so blessed if I sat on a fence the birds would feed me and then some. Maybe some day ya'll come visit us in our ranch down in the old panhandle.

Sorry this letter's short, but I gotta shoot me a fox and trap me a coon fore sunup.

Say howdy to Tilly for me. Take care of ya-self buddy.

Yours affectately,
Cousin Ted

Yeah, right, thought Manny, not understanding much of what he'd just read. Not caring to either. Ted sounded like a right eejit. Getting married again at his age. His ma wouldn't be too happy to hear that. She was hoping she could stay a couple of days in the Ocean Spray with the windfall she was expecting from him.

Manny put the page and cheque back in the envelope. Well, the $300 was better than nothing. He glanced at the clock. Time to go collect grumpy Nan Doody and her sister.

Aye, nothing came easy in this life, except to people like Ted bloody Romero. Wasn't even his money, if he remembered right. Didn't his ma say he'd married a hotelman's daughter called Pearl, and something about the world being an oyster when he married her. Aye, that was the way of things.

Pity there weren't a few wealthy Pearls hangin' about Castlebrook. Peeved, Manny grabbed his car-keys and left the house.

SIXTY-ONE

The lobby of the Ocean Spray was all but deserted when Ma Bryn stepped inside. A young woman she recognized as the waitress from a few nights before was behind the reception desk, dealing with a guest.

Good, I'm glad that oul' snob of a Gladys Milkman's not about! Now I can say cheerio to Bella and Derek in peace, without that haughty oul' divil lookin' down her nose at me.

She hung back in the lobby, marvelling at the grandeur of the place. That last time she visited was evening time, so she wasn't able to see as much with the curtains pulled and lights low. But now, with the sun beaming through the tall windows, Mrs Milkman's extravagance was entirely on show.

The colour of the carpet was nearly the colour of the sea itself outside the windees! How did she manage that? And the curtains and sofas were in a pinkie-gold shade that was a very match for the sandy beach. Heaven's above, how long did it take her to find all them exact colours?!

Tilda's eyes roamed all over the gilded reception area, awed by the fact that her humble friends the Pruntys could afford to stay in such luxury. God, maybe Ted will have sent us the money by the time I get back, and me and Manny can book in for a day or two!

She caught sight of her reflection in an ornate mirror and adjusted her turban of clam-shell motifs. Well, me turban and orange kaftan look like what Princess Margaret might wear when she's out forren on that island called Mustake she sometimes goes to. If I got meself a pair-a them big clip-on pearl earrings she's famous for, I could pass for her at a distance on a dark night with the light behind me.

The fantasy had her forgetting herself. "Maybe I'll have a wee look in that boutique Glitz-n-Glam on the pommenade afore I go. I've plenty of time. The bus isn't till two and sure it's only turned nine."

"Can I help you, madam?"

She turned to see the receptionist looking queerly at her.

"Er, aye ... I mean yes," Tilda blustered, approaching the desk, embarrassed she'd been caught talking to herself.

The receptionist's name tag read MAUREEN.

"Sorry, Maureen, wuz miles away there. But when yeh get tae my age that's the way of it, so it is ... don't know whether a body's coming or going betimes, but sure a young one like you wouldn't know nothin' like that."

"God, you're the fortune teller, aren't you!" Maureen exclaimed, recognizing her from the previous visit.

"Aye, that's me," Tilda chirped, chuffed that her fame was spreading. "Madame Matilda. But not for much longer 'cos I'm goin' home the day."

"Och, that's a pity! I thought maybe ... "

Maureen looked furtively about her, leaned over the desk.

"I'd love me fortune told but I dare not, 'cos Mrs Millman's sitting-room looks down on your caravan, and if she saw me going in she'd go mad ... eyes in the back of her head and she was very annoyed when she saw you putting that sign out ... said you were lowering the tone. But I think it's great, 'cos you're bringing more people in here. I hear them discussing their readings over a drink in the lounge sometimes and it's all good, so it is."

"Och, is that so? Well, I've been reading many a day, like me mammy afore me. And where would Mrs Milkman be now?"

"She's away for her constitutional."

"Consta-*what?*"

"Morning walk on the promenade. Did you want to see her?"

"Oh no, just wundered where she was, like. How long does it take, this consta … I mean, dander on the prom then?"

Maureen checked her watch. "Oh, she'll not be back for a good half-hour."

"Well, tell you what, Maureen, why don't I do a readin' for you now? Sure when the cat's away the mouse can play, as they say … only take the ten minutes and she'll know nuthin' about it."

Maureen's eyes lit up. "Would you really? But don't yeh need your crystal ball and cards and things, like?"

"Not a-tall. Sure as long as yeh've got a pair-a hands on yeh I can do a readin'. The palms tell just as much as the ball, so they do."

"God, that's amazing! We'll sit over there on that sofa. 'Cos I need-a keep an eye on the desk, like."

"No bother a-tall, daughter."

Ma Bryn took up position on the velvet sofa, feeling like the Queen of Sheba at Solomon's court. She removed one of the gold scatter cushions from behind her and rested Maureen's hands upon it.

"Now, shut yer eyes, make three wishes, luv, and open them when yer ready."

Maureen did as she was told while Tilda used the ruse to rummage around for a hook to hang her spiel on: good skin, no make-up so maybe "saved" … the religious type—gold cross at her throat—a wee bit overweight, too much temptation in the guest-house kitchen—a bit of a mouse if she can put up with a divil like Mrs Milkman without going astray in the head. And them bitten nails sez she's the nervous type—

"Right, I'm ready," Maureen announced, blinking back into the land of the living.

"Right yeh be."

Tilda launched in.

"Now, you've a good, strong head line that's deep and straight and that means you analyse things a bit too much … sensitive like … to what others think, which isn't a bad way to be."

Maureen nodded in agreement.

"But that fleshy Mount of Mercury under yer pinkie there … that would indicate tae me that yeh like working with people, so maybe that's why yer in the hospitality trade in the first place. In the future I can see yeh owning an establishment like this. Runnin' it well and makin' a fortune."

"God, that's amazing! I've always wanted to be like Miss Gladys when I get older, like."

"There yeh go then. The palms is nivver wrong. I see yeh runnin' a boarding-house, guest house or whatevir yeh wanna call it, and you'll be terrible successful at it. God, could even be this very place, for as far as I know that Mrs Milkman's got no wains tae leave it to, so if yeh play yer cards right, Maureen, luv—"

They were alerted to the sound of clacking heels from beyond the open door.

"What on earth is going on here?"

Ma Bryn's jaw hit the floor at the sound of Mrs Millman's voice. She and Maureen turned to see their worst nightmare standing in the doorway.

"I-I didn't … er. I-I didn't think," Maureen stammered, getting up, "didn't think that you'd be back s-so soon, Miss Gladys!"

"*That is perfectly obvious!*" the proprietress spat, hurling the words at Maureen like a knife-thrower at a circus. "I leave you for *five minutes* and you're entertaining this charlatan tinker-woman under my roof!"

"I'm no Charlie-ton and I'm no tinker-woman neither," Tilda piped up, affronted. "It's not wee Maureen's fault, a-tall, a-tall. I ast her if she wanted the reading, like … and there's no harm in it."

Mrs Millman didn't condescend to even look Tilda's way. She kept her regal eyes trained on Maureen, standing arms akimbo, patent courts planted firmly. "Get out of my sight this minute and start on the rooms before I think to sack you."

Maureen dissolved in a puddle of tears and scurried off.

Tilda set the gold cushion back in its rightful place as the air in the lobby plunged to the temperature of Arctic ice. She gathered up her carpetbag, thinking: I'll not be apologizing tae that oul' divil after being called them names. The cheek of her! I'll just ignore her and go, see how she likes being snubbed.

Tilda held her turbaned head high and made for the door.

"And where do you think *you're* going?"

The reprimand, as sharp as one of Mrs Millman's lethal stilettos, had Tilda turning to face the enemy. She felt the onset of a hot flush rising from the depths of her bosom.

"What wuz that?"

"I'd like to know why *you're here*, Mrs ... Mrs-whatever-your-name-is!"

"Bryn... Mrs Bryn, and I came here tae bid goodbye to me good friends the Pruntys, if yeh must know."

At the mention of the Pruntys the proprietress's face hardened into a scowl worthy of the White Witch of Narnia.

She bore down on Tilda.

"Oh, *did you*, indeed?"

But Ma Bryn refused to be intimidated and stood her ground, hugging the carpetbag to her chest like a battle-shield.

"Well, *I might have known*. It may interest you to know, *Mrs Bryn*, that I ordered your friends to *leave* yesterday. They not only dismantled my Corby trouser-press but broke an Edwardian table lamp of cranberry glass. Spilled *alcohol* and *God-knows-what-else* over my Egyptian cotton 300-thread-count bedding, not to speak of leaving scratch marks on an ancestral antique chest of drawers that's been in my family for decades. I have a good mind to report them *to the police*."

"Well, that's their bissness, not mine. I don't care about yer oul' auntie's chester-drawers. They wouldn't be the first people that broke something in a hotel. Now, if yer finished I'll be gettin' on me way. Have more important things to do than stand round here listening to the like-a you screeching like a bat at me."

"How *dare* you speak to me like that?!"

"I'll speak whatever way I like, Mrs Milkman—"

"*Mill*man!"

"Aye, whatevir... it's a free country. I'm sure me friends couldn't wait to leave, 'cos being around you would be enough to put anybody's head astray.... Depress an angel, you would. God help that wee girl Maureen, or anybody for that matter, that has the misfortune to have to work for the like of you."

Gladys flung her arm in the air. "*Leave* my premises *this minute*, you disreputable woman!"

"Don't worry; I'm going!" Tilda shot back, turning on her heel. But as she descended the steps she heard the proprietress hurl another missile she hadn't seen coming.

"You *do not* have a licence to conduct your tawdry business in this town. I'll be reporting you to the council."

Aye, well, she thought... you won't get the chance, 'cos I'm leavin' today anyway. Maybe just as well. For as long as pussy's a cat I'll not be darkening yer door again. There are other nice places a body can stay when Ted's money comes through, and not be treated like a criminal neither.

Outside the gates of the Ocean Spray, Ma Bryn stopped to catch her breath.

"Dearie me, but that oul' targe could start a fight in an empty room. Now I'm gonna treat meself till that pair of earrings like Princess Margaret's, to make up for all the bother she put me through."

Buoyed up by her natural tendency to look on the bright side, Tilda quickened her step towards the Glitz-n-Glam boutique, proud that she'd stood her ground, fought her corner, and could now claim her well-earned, princess prize.

VIVIENNE

Brigid Doody was pacing the yard when Manny drew up. That was very unusual. The sisters normally stayed in until he knocked on the door and shouted through the letterbox.

Something was up.

He switched off the engine and rolled down the window.

"Hullo . . . Brigid. Everything all right, is it?"

She came forward and gripped the window-ledge, nervous but excited.

"God, Manny, we've something shockin' to tell yeh. Thought I'd come out and let you know beforehand, like. 'Cos it was a big shock for us when she turned up."

"R-right. . . . " Manny was perplexed. "She? Who's *she?*"

"The judge's daughter."

"*What!*"

Had he heard right? There could only be one judge's daughter.

"Y-you mean . . . Vivienne . . . Vivienne Dundas?"

Brigid nodded. "We recognized her from the paper."

"But are yeh . . . are you sure?"

"Aye, 'cos she tolt us who she was. So it's her all right."

"Christ! But how . . . how did she end up with *you?*"

"She escaped that lunatic that was holdin' her in our John's house. Knocked him out with a chair she did. . . . "

She did more than *that*, thought Manny.

"Poor cretur; there's not a pick on her . . . she's come through a terrible lot. You need-a take her to the hospital, 'cos she might-a broke something, then she can ring her daddy."

Manny was immediately on edge.

"But aren't youse comin' too? For the pension."

Brigid shook her head. "No, it's better you take her on first. Sure when you've left her at the hospital you can come back for us. The pension can wait for a wee bit."

Manny's legs felt weak as he exited the car. He'd thought he was in the clear when it came to the Fitzwell mess, but it seemed God had other plans. He'd have to be brave and see things through.

Ma Bryn retraced her steps down the promenade, trying to work out some sums in her head. The run-in with Gladys Milkman had given her a bit of a wobble, but not for long. She was determined that the oul' bat wouldn't be spoiling the rest of her day.

She'd been into the Glitz-n-Glam boutique. Had spent a good few minutes perusing, 'cos there was so much to look at besides the jewellery. A couple of lovely frocks had caught her eye and she'd tried both on, at the urging of the owner, a nice lady called Lizzie. Lizzie was around her own age and size so knew what suited a body. But the pearl clip-ons like Princess Margaret's were more expensive than she'd been expecting—a whole £2 over the three she had on her. She'd made her excuses to Lizzie about forgetting her purse and the owner kindly agreed to hold the earrings behind the counter till she got back.

I'll count how much I've saved in me money-box in the caravan first. Maybe I can afford them after all. I haven't counted me takings in a while, so maybe I've a good wee bit put by.

Elated with the prospect of buying the earrings and maybe even one of the frocks, Tilda waited at the crossing. It was taking a while for the light to turn green and she was eager to get going. With no cars in sight she made a beeline across the road, orange kaftan snapping frantically in the sharp breeze.

Well, it's just as well I've got me turban on, or me hair would be like a crow's nest on a stormy night.

. . .

Manny followed Brigid into the house, not knowing what to expect. Part of him wanted to run away but he could hardly do that now. Here was his chance to help Vivienne and make up for the fact that he'd failed her in the past.

He found her sitting hunched over by the fire. Nan was hovering nervously nearby. She managed to crack a smile at the sight of him, the first he'd ever seen.

"Here's Manny now," she said. "Our taxi-driver. He's gonna take you to the hospital. You'll be safe enough with him, so yeh will."

Vivienne rose with difficulty from the armchair and turned to face him.

"H-hello . . . hello, Manny," she said. "Thank you . . . thank you for this. . . . "

Manny shifted from foot to foot, trying hard to mask his shock. "Um, that's . . . that's no bother . . . no bother at all."

Vivienne looked like a survivor from a war zone. Both hands badly grazed. Face and legs covered in cuts and bruises. The dress and cardigan she wore seemed like they were draped on a skeleton. But the smiling face from the newspaper was still discernible behind the sunken cheeks and in the dark, haunted eyes that held him.

"Thank you," she said again. "We need to go now, before . . . "

"Aye . . . aye surely," Manny said, gesturing needlessly at the door. "The car's outside, so it is."

Vivienne came forward and rested a hand on his arm. "I'll-I'll hide down . . . in the back seat, Manny. In case . . . "

"Er . . . aye, that's . . . that's a good idea."

He knew what she was thinking. What if someone is watching this house right now? What if an ambush has been set up farther down the road? What if this is the end of the line for the pair of us? Shot in the head and disappeared. That's why it'd be better if all four of us went. They'd hardly kill us all. Maybe that's why the

Doodys don't want to come. They're as scared as me, but...

He was aware that all three women were looking his way: pinning their hopes on him.

"Aye," he said finally, disengaging from the horrors in his head. "We'd better go then."

Vivienne smiled weakly. Nan and Brigid linked their arms in hers and the four went out to the car.

A couple of hundred yards from the Dormouse, something blew across Ma Bryn's path.

To her consternation she saw it was a tarot card: The Hanged Man. It could only be one of hers.

"Oh, Jesus, Mary and Joseph! I must-a left the windee open and me cards blew out."

She hurried along the path, panting with the effort, and stopped to pick up two more escapees: The Emperor and The Chariot.

The sound of a door flapping to and fro reached her ears before the caravan came into view.

God, I was sure I locked that door afore I left. But it's a blustery day, so maybe it blew itself open. That lock isn't the best. Need-a buy a new one.

Consoling herself that things were all right, Tilda caught a hold of the flapping door and climbed inside.

The place was a mess: her reading table turned upside-down, crystal ball lying on the floor, tarot cards scattered everywhere.

That bloody wind did all this.

She got down on her knees and gathered up the rest of the Major Arcana cards, pleased that all twenty-two were now together again.

Just as well I came back in time. God knows, but me chair and table could-a got blowed away as well.

With the door firmly shut and everything back in its proper place, she could finally get what she came for—the money for the frock and earrings.

She pulled back the curtain to her private quarters.

"Oh, Jesus, Mary and the sweet Child of Prague!"

Tilda's heart fell into her toes.

No, it certainly wasn't the wind that had done all the harm.

The window by her bed was shattered. The money-box that contained all her takings lay open on the bed.

Empty!

Some scoundrel had broken in and stolen every penny she'd saved.

SIXTY-THREE

"Oh, Nettie dear, thank God you're back with us!" cried Ellen, holding back tears and cradling her sister's hand in hers. "Everything's going to be all right now."

Nettie opened her eyes and managed a feeble smile.

She looked so frail and vulnerable, lying there in the starched bed, the ominous bleeps of a heart monitor punctuating the silence, an infusion pump feeding painkillers into her bloodstream.

"Everything's going to be all right now," Ellen said again, trying hard to reassure, but knowing that if she were in Nettie's position such words—no matter how well-meaning—would simply sound hollow and perfunctory. With so many breakages and fractures the road to recovery would be a slow one.

"The doctor . . . the doctor he says your brain scan is clear and that's such *good news,* Nettie, because it was their main concern."

Nettie raised her head from the pillow, gripped Ellen's hand more tightly. She tried to say something but sank back on the pillow, defeated.

"Oh, don't try to talk, dear. You need to rest. John . . . John's out in the corridor. . . . He'll be in next. They only allow one of us in at a time I'm afraid."

Ellen thought back on all the petty arguments they'd had in the past. How silly and childish she'd been! Nettie was only trying to help by getting the priest in to bless the house. Had she not told her about those silly dreams none of this would have happened. What catastrophes we set in train with our frivolous, unthinking remarks!

"It's all my fault," she said, breaking down. "I-I should never have asked you to get that jewellery box. I'm just a vain old woman for wanting it. I'm sorry, Nettie. *Truly* sorry."

Nettie shook her head. There was a look of fear in her eyes. She tried to raise her head again.

Ellen bent over her. "What is it, Nettie dear?"

The grip on Ellen's hand grew tighter.

"Yes, Nettie. I'm here. What is it?"

"L-e-e- . . . "

"Lee?"

Nettie summoned all her strength. Took a deep breath.

"L-ee-aa-vv-e," she managed to say.

"Leave? You-you want me to go . . . now?"

Nettie shook her head, eyes pleading.

"S-e-e . . . See . . . dar . . ."

"Cedarwood?"

She nodded, grateful. Released her grip on Ellen's hand. Sank back on the pillows and shut her eyes.

Manny turned onto the main road and headed in the direction of Killoran, his thoughts awry. Vivienne lay in the foetal position under a blanket on the back seat.

He didn't know how to play this. What to say to her—if anything?

Vivienne Dundas had just come through hell. He couldn't put himself in her position, couldn't imagine the horrors the psycho Fitzwell had visited upon her. But he knew one thing for sure: she'd done the right thing by ridding the world of his like.

"How long. . . . How long to the hospital?"

The voice from the back seat startled him. He hadn't expected her to say anything.

"Erm . . . er . . . about . . . half an hour. . . . Aye, half an hour, at most."

He studied her in the rear-view mirror. The blanket covered

most of her face. Only the eyes were visible. She looked like a frightened animal caught in headlights.

"I'll drive faster if you want. I . . . I just wouldn't wanna . . . wanna cause you more . . . more pain, like. This road's a bit bumpy in places."

"Oh, please . . . please, Manny, as fast as you can."

He floored the accelerator immediately, as eager as *she* was to get the journey over.

"I think that's enough now."

Ellen looked up to see a stern-faced nurse standing by the bedside. Where had *she* come from?

"Yes . . . yes, of course," she conceded, turning back to the patient. She kissed Nettie's forehead. "I'll be back soon again, dear. But John will be in shortly."

"It's best he waits until this afternoon," the nurse said. "We need to run further tests." She came forward and put a reassuring hand on Nettie's shoulder. "Simply routine, Mrs Buckley. Nothing to worry about."

Nettie gazed at Ellen, that same frightened look in her eyes.

"You're in very good hands, Nettie dear," she assured her and, with reluctance, took her leave.

Manny drove through the gates of the General Hospital in Killoran, relieved that they'd made it without being stopped. And hopefully without being seen.

Vivienne sat up and discarded the blanket.

"That's us now," he said, killing the engine, his voice sounding strange to his own ears.

Vivienne started to cry. "I'm-I'm sorry . . . sorry to have involved you in all this."

Little does she know, he thought, that I've been involved in this from the beginning. A wave of pity mixed with admiration washed over him. After all she'd been through she was thinking of *him* instead of herself.

"D'yeh want me to go in with you?" he offered, turning to her. "I'll tell them what happened, like. 'Cos I'm sure yeh ... yeh don't want to go over all that."

She nodded. "If-if you wouldn't mind. I'd-I'd really appreciate that."

SIXTY-FOUR

Tilda sat down on the sofa-bed in her caravan, dejected. Who would have done the like of that, and in the plain light of morning too? Some young boys with too much time on their hands in the school hauldays, no doubt.

She'd had to chase a couple of them away not so very long ago, for firing pebbles at the window when she was doing a reading. But there was nothing she could do about them. She didn't have a licence for conducting business from the Dormouse—as Mrs Milkman had so snidely pointed out—so could hardly report them to the police.

Dearie, dearie me! There'd be no pearl earrings or nice frock. How could the lovely time she was having in Portaluce end so badly?

She gazed sadly about the caravan, knowing in her heart of hearts that her days of telling fortunes for a living were over before they'd even got started proper. But sure, when one door shuts another one opens, as the saying went, and if them three tarot cards that blew into her path were anything to go by, all was not lost.

The Hanged Man meant that sacrifices would have to be made in order to gain bigger things. The Chariot meant a victory of some sort coming soon, and The Emperor pointed to a solid man of authority who'd remind a body of their own power. That man could only be…

Samuel Monroe-Johnson.

"Need-a woman to cook and clean and look after things and you look like a capable woman worthy of a better life."

She'd been cogitating on the Reverend's offer over the past lot of days, and now it seemed events were forcing her to make a decision.

A combination of meeting the Pruntys and seeing them enjoying the high life, visiting Mrs Purboy's grand house with the glass-room, and learning that the pastor had an equally grand house that she could actually be living in if she took him up on his offer, made her realize that scrimping and saving the pennies—which only ever covered the basics anyway—was no way to go on.

Deep down she understood that the visit to Portaluce had been an important one, in that it had shown her that she too could have a share of the finer things in life.

Why shouldn't a body have the carpets and swanky sofas like that oul' Mrs Milkman, with a set of those nice tasselled curtains skimming the floor? And why shouldn't I have a house with hanging lamps and brass knick-knacks and stools and silverware, and china with them nice gold rims that all match, laid out on a polished table I could see me face in?

Tilda wiped away her tears and rose from the sofa-bed. She scanned the dismal interior of the Dormouse caravan with a heavy heart, but with hope rising like the morning sun.

"Well, yeh served me mother well, but that was a long time ago, when people had more manners and didn't think tae rob a body of the little money they had. I can't stay here no more. That's the God's honest truth and that's the end of it, so it is."

No time like the present. She rooted in her handbag and found Mr Johnson's card: The Emperor of the Tarot. She'd go visit him now while she still had time.

As it turned out, Manny didn't have to explain who Vivienne was or what she'd been through. The staff at the County General recognized the judge's daughter immediately.

"You'll be all right now," Manny said, as two nurses rushed to lead Vivienne away.

She hesitated and took his hand. "Thank you . . . thank you so much, Manny . . . for everything."

The older of the two nurses, a middle-aged, brusque woman, with Sister O'Neill on a nameplate, gave him a sharp look.

"The police will be wanting to talk to you, my man."

That was the last thing Manny expected to hear.

"It's all right, nurse," Vivienne said. "This man risked his life for me. He brought me here in his taxi."

Sister O'Neill's face reddened. "Oh, I see. Well, in that case . . . "

"You'll leave your address at the desk, won't you, Manny?" Vivienne said, ignoring her. "My father will want to thank you."

"Aye . . . that's no bother."

Manny made his way back down the corridor, so proud he'd played his part in Vivienne's rescue after all. He left his details at reception and took his leave.

Back for the Doodys now, he thought, walking through the exit doors and going down the steps.

"Manny . . . Manny, is that you?"

He turned at the sound of a woman's voice.

Mrs Purboy was hastening towards him.

"I thought I recognized you," she said. "So glad I caught you, Manny! Can you give me a lift home?"

He was caught off guard.

"Er . . . aye . . . maybe. But it's . . . "

Mrs Purboy didn't wait for him to finish. She was already heading towards the taxi.

Well, the Doody sisters would just have to wait another while. He could tell them he was delayed at the hospital or got a flat tyre or something. The run to Mrs Purboy's house wouldn't take long and wasn't too much of a detour from his route.

"I was talking to your mother yesterday," Ellen said as he started the engine. "I expect she'll be coming home today."

"Aye... be collectin' her soon enough."

Ma Bryn stood breathless outside Monroe-Johnson's house, fanning herself with a parish bulletin to repel another hot flush. She hadn't reckoned on the Calvary-like climb to his door, up a set of steps cut into the rock, which had not only brought on another hot flush but given her such a workout she'd fallen three times, like the Saviour hisself.

Dearie, dearie me!

I'll not knock yet, till I get me breath back. Them oul' hot flushes take a minute or two to go away and Dr Flynn did say I was goin' through "the change", which was news tae me, for me mammy never went through no change as far as I could see. Never even talked about such a thing. But then maybe she didn't even know it was happening, with all the drinkin' she was doing.

She spotted a small sun-seat to the left of the front door and sat down gratefully, panting like a seal on a hot rock. Maybe I'll fix meself up. A bitt-a powder and lipstick would make a body look a bit more presentable. 'Cos this is a kind-a job interview after all. Hopefully he'll not see me out his windee.

Tilda found her tube of Cherry Bomb lipstick and was covertly guiding it round her mouth when the unthinkable happened.

"Hello, there!"

The lipstick had fallen from her grasp at the sound of a male voice.

She turned to see the Reverend Monroe-Johnson in a wide-brimmed sunhat, secateurs in hand, observing her with studied attention over a crooked privet hedge.

SIXTY-FIVE

"I take it you're interested in my job offer," the Reverend Samuel said, exiting the garden and shutting the gate behind him.

His back turned, a flustered Tilda quickly retrieved the lipstick, which had rolled under a planter pot, covertly slipped it into her pocket, and straightened up to face him.

"Erm ... aye, well, yeh give me a bit of a shock there, sir ... 'cos I didn't think you were in at all, at all."

"Fortunate for you I am then."

He squinted at his watch. "It is time for tea. We can discuss things over a nice cuppa rooibos?"

"Ruby-what?"

"Redbush tea ... finest in Africa. I have it shipped over, now I no longer have the privilege to live in that blessed land."

"R-right.... I see, sir," Tilda said, wavering on the brink of what she knew would be a life-changing decision. God might be sending her down a stony path, but she had strong shoes to walk in, and a good heart to guide her.

This opportunity to change life's predictable course might never come again. She'd trust her gut instincts.

"Erm ... I've a bus tae catch at two," she said, because she couldn't think of anything else to say as the Reverend stood there, appraising her.

"A whole couple hours away. You got time aplenty, Ma Lady."

He pushed open the front door and stood back.

Tilda proceeded with a timid assent and stepped inside.

. . .

"I guess we should get the appellations right to start with," he announced as he led the way into an oak-panelled study, replete with books and artefacts from his travels; a shiny brass fan whirring lazily on the ceiling.

Ma Bryn didn't know what the blazes he was talking about, but disguised her ignorance by making a series of polite squeaks as she sank into a leather armchair, thankful for a soft seat at last.

"Your name's Matilda, if I remember correctly?"

"Yes-yes indeed... but me friends call me Tilda for short."

He stood before her with the straw hat pressed to his chest, a gold ring glinting on his pinkie, stoat eyes steady on her.

"In that case I will call you Miss Tilda, and you can address me as Pastor Sam. That all right?"

"That's no bother... no bother a-tall, Pastor Sam."

It was stifling in the room and Tilda felt another hot flush slowly rise. It would be too forward to ask him to open a windee, but she could give him a hint.

"God, it's terrible hot of a sudden."

"In that case I think a glass of lemonade would be more suitable than the tea. Will cool you down."

"That would be the thing. Yes, indeed."

He gave a curt little bow and disappeared.

Tilda, thankful for the interlude, picked up a magazine—*The African Missions Quarterly*—and began fanning herself vigorously.

She looked about the grand room, not a little disquieted.

There were so many queer things she'd never seen before; grinning masks with feathers sticking out of them, figurines with long legs and tiny heads, candlesticks made out of horns, wooden bowls of wooden fruit, fake flowers bursting out of baskets, and strange-looking wee drums with hairy covers stretched over them.

Pinned on one wall, a large poster declared in heavy type:

PREVENT TRUTH DECAY. BRUSH UP ON THE BIBLE.

And on another there hung the portrait of a big African man in a clerical collar, hands joined in prayer.

Wonder who he is? Too dark in the face to be his nosy oul' da, who looked down on me poor mammy when she was only trying tae make a living as Madame Silver Crown. Maybe an ancestor from way back in the oul' days.

She brought her attention to the couch and chairs, which were covered with brown-and-orange fabric in crazy zigzag designs. If a body looked long enough at them they'd get a dizzy head and no mistake.

God, there'll be a lot of cleanin' to be done in here! All them ornaments to be seen to. Hope all the rooms aren't as cluttered as this one.

From a nearby table she picked up a wooden elephant with pink ears and a curly tail, and saw there wasn't a speck of dust on it.

Maybe he had a cleaner and she left sudden 'cos she couldn't put up with him. God, maybe he's been through a clatter of cleaners! Maybe they all collapsed with exhaustion. Maybe he was too hard to work for and they ran away. Maybe I'm the last resort. Maybe...

"One of my students made that."

Tilda, flustered, quickly replaced the elephant. She hadn't heard him come in. And was it any wonder? She noticed he was now in a pair of suede slippers with tassels on the toes. I hope he doesn't make a habit of doing that: creeping up on a body, like.

"Oh... it's-it's a lovely piece," she said, embarrassed. "You've got lots of nice things in here, Pastor Sam."

"Why, thank you!" he said, handing her the lemonade and sitting down in a raffia chair that squeaked quietly as he adjusted his ecru pants and threw one spindly shank over the other. "Most of the things you see in here were made by the Bantu tribe, who live in the Congo Basin. Just one of the tribes I had the priv'lege to convert to the light and love of the Lord *Jez-sos* Christ."

"Aye, I'd say yeh converted a lot of them, right enough.... Now, that man in the painting... who would *he* be?"

"The Reverend Tiyo Soga, 1829 till 1871. The very first black African to be ordained a Presbyterian minister."

"Is that so?"

"Yes indeedy."

Tilda sipped the lemonade self-consciously, hoping he wouldn't start sermonizing again. She'd steer him onto different ground.

"And did yeh have a housekeeper afore, Pastor Sam? 'Cos your place looks right and tidy."

"Yes, as a matter of fact I did. But Miss Greta Gordy had to return last week to her hometown of Creeslough, to tend to her ailing mother. Thought she was coming back but she rang me to say her mother's been diagnosed with a wasting disease and can no longer be left alone. The morning I got her call I looked out the window and ma eyes fell on your car'van, and the Lord sayeth unto me, '*Go thee to that neck-crow-mancer and save her soul. For I have swept away all her offences like a cloud, her sins like that of the morning mist. Return her onto me, for thou hast redeemed her.' Isaiah, Chapter forty-four, verse twenty-two.*"

"God, did he say all that on account of *me?*"

"He did indeed. You up to the challenge, Miss Tilda?"

"Aye... well, it would depend on what the job would involve... me duties and the like."

Pastor Sam set down his lemonade. Leaned back in the chair. Steepled his fingers. Launched in.

"Keeping the house nice and tidy. Cooking three meals a day. Doing the laundry and shopping. You would have a room of your own of course... the one Miss Gordy just vacated, with bathroom attached. You can take your meals with me, or alone if you prefer. Enjoy the comforts of my sunroom and the health benefits of that salt-sea air. Read the scriptures with me morning and evening, as a matter of course.... "

She was afraid he was gonna say that last bit, but he was making an offer she couldn't refuse. Could see herself already fitting her life into the queerly grand house, sunning herself in that glass-room like Mrs Purboy's, being able to afford nice things in the Glitz-n-Glam, walking down the strand with the sand in her toes and the wind in her hair. Sure where else would she get the like?

"I'm prepared to pay you £30 per week, in lieu of the Devil's shilling you'd be forfeiting by leaving your nefarious ways behind."

Tilda didn't know what that big word meant but didn't care. The fact that Pastor Sam was prepared to pay a salary on top of all the perks he'd already listed could not be passed up. Such a chance would never come again.

"How's that sound to you, Miss Tilda?"

"Sounds… sounds good… fair enough," she said.

He clapped his knees. "Excellent! How soon could you start?"

"Well, I'd have to run it past me son first, like. He'll maybe not be too pleased, havin' tae live on his own."

The pastor knitted his brows, confusion tugging his mouth into a tight line of befuddlement. "This son-a yours ain't a kid, is he?"

"Oh, no. Manny's comin' on thirty-eight this September."

"A grown man. Maybe it's time he had some independence. Always lived at home with you, I take it?"

"Yes, indeed."

"A new lease-a life for him then. At his age I was slashing my way through breast-high rabbit bush with a machete blade…. Tracking gorillas with the Ba'Aka people. Sleepin' on a mattress of straw and antelope manure … that's sleeping under the black geometry of Gawd's good heavens with one eye open for bush vipers… gatherin' ma own firewood, fetching ma own water… livin' on a diet of yams and wild honey, while baptizin' pygmy folk in the waters of the Lualaba River. Time that son-a yours fended for hisself."

Tilda had grown exhausted just listening to him. "God, Pastor Sam, you've done a wild lotta things, right enough."

Sam smiled, a gold incisor glinting. "I sure have, Miss Tilda. I sure have. I tell you this 'cos that son-a yours needs perspective. To step outta his shell before it's too late and take on some responsibility."

He shot up suddenly like a jack-in-the-box and plucked his sun-hat from the armrest.

"I'd show you round but I have an appointment. Take a week to consider, 'cos I understand your son might need time to adjust himself to such a diff'rent arrangement. But a week's all I can give."

"Oh, a week... a whole week's grand," Tilda said, following him into the hallway, where sunlight spilled across the floor like water unpenned.

On the doorstep he shook her hand.

"Well, good day to you, Miss Tilda. I'll be hearin' from you soon."

"You will indeed, Pastor Sam. You will indeed."

And she walked away from him, down the stone steps towards the promenade once more; with such joy in her heart she could have been that little girl again, with the Shirley Temple curls and frilly summer frock, standing outside her mother's caravan in the long, long ago.

SIXTY-SIX

"You'll make sure to tell your mother to keep in touch," Ellen said, handing Manny a fiver for the taxi fare.

"Aye, that's no bother, Mrs Purboy. I'll just get yer change."

"No-no, you keep the change. It was very good of you to give me the lift at such short notice."

Such a civil young man, she thought, waving him goodbye.

She paused on the doorstep, hearing once again Nettie's strangled appeals to "*leave Cedarwood*".

With a sense of apprehension, she turned the key in the lock and pushed open the door.

All was quiet in the sombre hallway. She looked up the staircase, trying to dispel the frightful images rushing at her. Those stairs had claimed the life of the original owner and nearly succeeded in ending poor Nettie's as well. Would she ever feel comfortable in Cedarwood again? The place felt distinctly alien now—as if another presence had taken up residence in her absence.

She gazed at the Eiffel Tower doorstop, bracing herself. How could it have ended up in my bedroom? My sister is crazy to believe she'd actually seen the thing there. How on earth could it have gotten all the way up there? Preposterous! She was disorientated by the shock of the fall. There can be no other explanation.

Perhaps if I just got rid of it I could forget it ever happened.

She removed her jacket with a vexed sigh and hung it on the hat-stand. Glanced at the door to the bedsit. There'd been no sign of Jay the previous evening when she'd returned from the hospital. She hadn't heard him anyway.

She went through to the kitchen, unlocked the backdoor and skirted round to the rear of the house.

His car was nowhere to be seen.

A wave of sadness broke over her when she spotted an ice-cream tub on the window-ledge. Poor Nettie had brought it for Toby.

She tipped out the contents and discarded the carton in the bin.

Jay may not be at home, but Toby just might be.

She knocked.

"Toby … it's me: Mrs P. I met you with your father, remember?"

She waited … and waited, but no answer came.

Oh well, when Jay returns I'll break the news about Nettie. Maybe he'll be able to throw some light on things. Was there someone in the house when she made her visit? Perhaps that's why she saw my bedroom in disarray. She surprised a thief and, in her hurry to flee, tripped and fell.

But, at the same time, there was something niggling about the intruder theory.

Why had no valuables been taken?

The question vexed her and, in an effort to distance herself from it all, she stood awhile, eyes shut, appreciating the sun on her face, the heavenly scents drifting in off the gardens, the cooing of some wood-pigeons high in the trees. It was good to be outdoors after the stuffy confines of the hospital.

The last time she'd been in a hospital setting was with George. The fear and despair she'd felt then were attempting to crush her back into that corner of her life, but she would not allow herself to be forced back there.

Things had changed.

Progress *had* been made.

Nettie would recover and life would go on and—

Clank-clank-clank!

The sound of a gate clanking far off startled her.

There was only one set of gates at the rear of the estate. They opened onto a laneway that wound through several acres of woodland, leading back to the main road. In times gone by, workers on the estate used the pathway, but in more recent times all access to Cedarwood had been secured with sets of high wrought-iron gates at either end of the wood.

Perturbed, Ellen proceeded round the back to investigate.

Three old stables lined the rear section. The sight of them gave her pause and she lingered a while, considering their closed doors.

Since George's death she hadn't gone into any of the stables. Even at this juncture, with her grief giving way to a newfound courage, she knew she still couldn't trust herself. There were simply too many memories of him behind those closed doors.

The one on the left housed his car. The middle one contained an assortment of antique furniture he'd been in the process of restoring. The final one was virtually empty. She was about to move on when a thought struck her: You could have a look in that last one. There's nothing in there, so why not? Could be a place to store those boxes of paperwork.

Fortified by the idea, she went directly over and opened the door.

An odour of damp, ancient wood hit her as she stepped inside. She stood a moment, adjusting to the dim interior to get her bearings. The small, high windows admitted just enough light to make visible some bulky objects shouldering out of the gloom.

Ranged along a far wall she saw a broken lawnmower, an old leather sofa and a large glass-fronted bookcase, amongst other things that had outlived their usefulness. Perfect, she thought, studying the bookcase. I can store George's papers in there. They'll be out of sight and no longer a trigger for my sorrow.

She stepped forward to inspect it—but her foot caught on something.

"What on earth ... ?"

In a few heart-stopping moments she took in the scene.

Traced out on the floor in yellow chalk was the image of a five-pointed star, about three feet in diameter. In the middle of this star sat an old shoe.

Perturbed, she backed away. There was something faintly ritualistic about the arrangement. She'd happened upon something she was not supposed to see. She rushed out and slammed the door shut.

Clank-clank-clank!

The sound of the unlocked gates struck. Her mind roared with possibilities. Those gates *were open.*

She dared not look back.

She dared not investigate further.

Cedarwood was being used for something. What that "something" might be was simply too frightening to contemplate.

She dashed back to the house, gripped by fear and foreboding, the implications of her discovery filling her mind with a terrible dread.

SIXTY-SEVEN

Manny Bryn, having left the Doody sisters off to conduct their business, parked in the town square for a well-earned break. He had a good half-hour to kill, which, after all the drama of the morning, was most welcome. He opened a bag of Maltesers to celebrate.

Vivienne Dundas had been delivered safely to the hospital. Fitzwell and his evil parents were out of the picture.

That only left Manny's nemesis: Bumper Magee.

Nan Doody had revealed about him gate-crashing their home in search of Vivienne, which didn't surprise Manny in the least. No doubt the oul' pair would have briefed him of recent events, and now all three were on the run. You don't kidnap someone as important as the judge's daughter and hang around your old haunts when she escapes.

No siree.

He stuffed three Maltesers into his gob, savouring the fact that he was finally free of all past torments visited upon him. The best part was that his ma wouldn't have an inkling about any of it. With everything coming to a head while she was away in Portaluce he'd have no explaining to do.

He gazed across at the dole office, his heart lifting at the thought of Iris sitting in there at her desk, dealing with the unemployed of Castlebrook. How he'd love to go in and say hello. But it wouldn't be the thing to do while she was at work. And anyway, people would see him and tongues would start wagging. It didn't take much to get the gossips going in a small town.

Maybe, if I haven't any fares at five, I could wait outside and offer her a lift. Save her getting the bus. Leave her off near her home, so the father won't see me.

Why didn't I think of that before? But I couldn't, could I? Iris being Protestant meant it was too risky. Magee had warned me.

But Magee is out of the pitcher now, so I can do what I want.

The thought cheered him and, feeling brave, he swung his gaze over to his old workplace: Baked-4-You. Just as he did so, his former employer, JM Cooney, appeared in the doorway, wiping sweat from his big, stove-red face, a stained white coat straining over his mighty paunch.

Manny automatically slid down in his seat. The last person he wanted to see was Cooney; too many reminders of his transgressions; too many memories of what might have been, had he conducted himself and not slept in—no dole queue, no Magee, no IRA involvement, no trouble.

But heavy footsteps were approaching, and when he peeped over the rim of the steering wheel he saw, to his dismay, that Big Jim was heading his way.

He shoved the bag of Maltesers under the seat immediately and sat up straight, like a guilty schoolboy awaiting punishment.

"How do, Manny!" the baker boomed, slapping a meaty hand on the car roof, chins ballooning as he leaned in, a dusting of flour on his eyebrows. "Saw yeh there and thought I'd 'ave a wee word."

He seemed in good form, which was unusual. The pate of his baldy head shimmered. The buttons on his chef's coat gleamed.

"Aye . . . doin' . . . doin' the best, Jim, so I am."

"That's grand . . . and how's the mammy?"

"Doin' all right, aye. Comin' home from Portaluce anytime. Had a wee break in the Dormouse, so."

"That oul' car'van still can be lived in then? Thought it'd be rusted tae blazes by now . . . all that salty air. . . . "

"Nah, alott-a life in her yet . . . good enough nick all right."

"That's good tae hear. Yer mammy's a fine woman, so she is.

Now, I'm glad I caught yeh, like, 'cos I've a wee propissition till run past yeh. Wuz talkin' till Fred this mornin' and he'll be in that seat next week, so you'll be out of a job."

"*What?*" Manny couldn't believe his ears. Best news he'd heard in a while. But he'd pretend to be disappointed.

"He... he didn't say nathin' tae *me*."

"Aye, well, Fred and me go back a long way. Talk on a regular basis . . . he'll be tellin' you today sometime. Saw the doctor this mornin' and got the go-ahead. Leg well-mended . . . which brings me to that wee propissition."

"Aye... what would that be, Jim?"

"How would yeh like yer oul' job back?"

Had he heard him right?

"You mean... you want *me* to come back to the bakery?"

"Aye, not unless . . . " He jerked a thumb in the direction of the dole office. "Not unless yeh'd rather join that pack o' wasters over there. Look what happened the last time yeh stood in there. Fred told me all about that Magee fella."

"Nah," Manny said immediately. "Wouldn't want that. What made yeh change yer mind?"

"Well, it's like this . . . the young boy I got in your place's good for nathin' . . . has burnt the arse outta five of me cake tins already. Aye, if his brains were dynamite he'd be blowing his nose, if yeh unnerstand me? So he's on a week's notice. Whadaya say then? Is it a deal?"

"Aye, surely, Jim!" Manny couldn't quite believe how things were falling into place after all the darkness he'd been through.

"Next Monday at seven then." The car roof got another mighty slap. "Good man!"

He straightened up. "Better get back to me ovens afore that boy sets the bloody place on fire."

"Aye, right enough."

He turned to go. Changed his mind.

"And another thing, Manny: don't you worry about that Magee boyo. He'll get his comeuppance one-a these days. What goes round comes round, as they say."

"I hope you're right, Jim. I hope you're right."

"Keep her lit then. See yeh Monday."

Big Jim took off.

Manny sank back in his seat, smiling to himself. What news he had to tell his ma!

Suddenly, showing her Cousin Ted's cheque didn't seem so bad after all. He had his job back, and that was a bigger prize than any measly donation from that oul' eejit in Texas.

SIXTY-EIGHT

A few hours on from her grim discovery, Ellen Purboy was in the garden, trying to distract herself, when she heard a car coming up the driveway.

Jay at last, she thought. I *do* hope he has little Toby with him. I'd just love to see him again. It would lift my mind out of all this!

She rose from the sun-seat, fully expecting to see the sports car but, to her disquiet, a car she didn't recognize was drawing up out front.

Covertly she watched as the black saloon came to a halt, and two official-looking gentlemen stepped out.

Who on earth can *they* be?

"Hello … may I help you?"

They turned in unison on the doorstep. One was middle-aged with greying hair; the other, a younger man, looked familiar.

"Ah, Mrs Purboy," the younger one said, coming forward. "We met before … the night you called about an intruder. I'm DC Jones."

Police.

"Er … yes … yes, of course I remember. But why … why are you here?"

"I'm Detective Inspector Hassen," the older man said, flashing a warrant card. "May we go inside, Mrs Purboy? We need a word."

She led the two into the living-room, wondering what on earth could have brought them to her door. They seated themselves.

"Would you like tea?"

Hassen shook his head. "No-no; this won't take long. DC Jones tells me that you live alone here."

"Strictly speaking, yes. Is . . . is this about the break-in?" Two sets of eyes fixed upon her. "It's just that I . . . I discovered earlier that someone's been getting onto the property through the back entrance."

Jones broke his gaze and took out a notepad and pen. He thinks I'm deluded like last time, no doubt.

"No, it's not about any break-in," Hassen continued. "Do you know a man by the name of James Leavy, Mrs Purboy?"

"Huh . . . Leavy?"

"Yes, Leavy."

"No . . . Should I?"

"When you say you live alone, you—"

"Well, as I said, not strictly speaking alone. Two months ago I rented out rooms to a young man."

She saw them exchange glances.

"And his name is?"

"Lavelle . . . Jay Lavelle."

"Age?"

"Er . . . late twenties."

"Could you give us a description?"

"Why, has something happened?"

"What does he look like?"

"Erm . . . tallish, slim build . . . fair hair . . . good-looking . . . dresses well."

"And when was the last time you saw this . . . Jay Lavelle?"

Ellen had to think. "Well, I've been away . . . so not in over a week. But he was here the day before yesterday. I can attest to that because my sister spoke to him."

"Could you tell us what kinda car he drives?"

"Erm . . . a sports car. A white sports car . . . a Jaguar I think. I'm not very good with cars I'm afraid."

She saw Jones pause in his note-taking. Both men looked at her steadily. She knew then that something bad had happened.

"Did you know this Mr Lavelle well?"

"No... not well. He... he... well, he kept himself to himself."

Hassen fumbled for something in his inside pocket.

"James Leavy's driving licence," he said, handing it to her. "Do you recognize this man?"

Ellen gaped in disbelief. The man in the photo was unmistakably Jay Lavelle. But the name James Leavy? It simply did not make sense.

She looked at the cops, perplexed. "That's him... that's Jay, yes."

"Are you sure?"

"Yes, absolutely, but I... I really don't understand. Why would he—"

"Call himself Lavelle? Well, perhaps you misheard him. Leavy-Lavelle... easily done. Didn't he write it down when you drew up the contract?"

"Well, er... no. I didn't have time.... To draw up a contract I mean."

Ellen felt immediately abashed. How incompetent I must seem in the eyes of this pair.

"I see. And next of kin... did he mention anyone?"

"Only an aunt... Edith's her name. He... he mentioned her. She's in a nursing home... over the border... in County Cavan I believe."

"Hmm.... "

Hassen sat forward, staring at the floor. Ellen noted the change in tone. This wasn't going to end well.

"Well, Mrs Purboy," he began, "taking into consideration what you've told us so far and, given the fact that you recognize the man in the licence photo to be your lodger, I'm afraid we have some sad news to impart."

Ellen felt the blood drain from her face.

"James Leavy, the man you knew to be Jay Lavelle... his car was found this morning on the north coast... Whitepark Bay. The keys were in the ignition."

"I … I don't understand. What are you saying?"

"His shoes and socks on the floor and a … and a suicide note of sorts on the dashboard."

She felt her every muscle tense against the inevitable.

"But that … that's impossible! He … "

The image of the two cops dimmed as Ellen's eyes filled with tears.

"We found your address in the glove compartment of his car, together with the licence."

"Oh, dear God!" Ellen's heart lurched at the horror of it.

"Your sadness might be misplaced, Mrs Purboy."

Ellen was bewildered. "I-I don't understand. What … what do you mean?"

Jones took over. "There were some irregularities surrounding Mrs Leavy's death. The Garda Síochána wanted to talk to him."

Ellen recalled that afternoon in the drawing-room when he confided to her about his wife's untimely passing. His grief was profound and deeply felt. The best actor could not fake that.

She rallied. "Irregularities, officer? The man I knew was deeply grief-stricken."

"If you say so," Hassen said curtly. "A suave young man, from what you told us, can easily fool many a woman."

She thought him extremely rude. In spite of her sadness, his brazen attitude made her bold. "Well, Inspector Hassen, I'm at an advantage in that I actually *knew* him. He was sincere, polite and respectable. … A model tenant in fact." As she said this a memory unfolded, one she knew, even back then, that she'd treasure always: the image of father and son driving away that day, Toby's little hand raised in farewell. The *last* time she would see them together.

"Toby!"

She broke down again.

"Who's Toby?"

"T-T-o-b-y!" She could hardly get the word out. "His little boy

… was he … ?"

Hassen shook his head. "No, not likely. The note was very much to the point. It simply said '*I* can't go on.'"

"Thank God!"

Ellen wiped her eyes, wishing the two men would just leave. It was as if they'd invaded her home, detonated a bomb and were simply standing there, observing her reaction to the fallout.

"And the boy," Hassen continued. "Where would he be now, d'you think?"

"I-I … don't know. Not … not unless … "

"Not unless what, Mrs Purboy?"

Ellen didn't wait to explain.

She dashed into the hallway to find the keys to the bedsit.

SIXTY-NINE

"Toby, dear ... are you in?"

Ellen rapped softly on the inner door. The last thing she wanted to do was frighten the little boy.

No answer.

"Just unlock it, Mrs Purboy," a brusque Hassen ordered. "This is no time to stand on ceremony."

She felt a sense of betrayal when turning the key, but things had moved beyond her control. Jay's terrible suicide had changed everything.

She tried to compose herself as she showed the officers in. There was no sign of Toby.

"He was a tidy chap, your lodger," Hassen observed, taking in the scene: the place was spotless.

"Yes, indeed," Jones agreed. "Unusual for a man living on his own."

Ellen's lovely studio was just as she remembered it. Jay's words came back to her: "*I do my own cleaning, you see. Always have.*"

Hassen entered the bedroom. It too was spick and span: the bed made and pillows plumped.

But Toby was nowhere to be seen.

"Could he be somewhere else?" Jones asked, opening and shutting the wardrobe. "Like in the house proper?" He moved to a chest of drawers.

"Er, no ... that inner door is always locked. He had no access."

She noticed two stems of oleander wilting in a milk bottle on the drainer.

The sight saddened her and she reached for her handkerchief.

"Are you sure about that?" Hassen asked.

"Well ... yes. I have the only key."

"Hmm.... He could have climbed out the window I suppose."

She saw Jones take something from the bottom drawer of the chest.

"Well, what do we have here?" He placed a small pestle and mortar of greenish stone on the coffee table. "Strange thing to keep in a bedroom drawer."

Both cops looked at Ellen for an explanation, but she was equally nonplussed.

"Er ... I-I haven't seen it before. I mean ... it doesn't belong to *me*. Perhaps it was of some value to him and ... and he didn't want it broken. He ... he was interested in antiques." In spite of everything she felt an allegiance to Jay. Felt she had to defend him against these two inquisitors.

"If you say so," Hassen said glibly. "D'you mind if Constable Jones checks the rest of the house?"

She wasn't expecting that, but could hardly refuse.

"You never know; the boy could be hiding somewhere. Children are curious creatures."

"No ... no. That's okay."

Jones went out.

"Well, James Leavy hasn't given us very much to go on. Drawers empty. A suit bag. A pepper grinder or whatever you want to call it. Is there anything else you can tell us?"

Ellen paused, considering.

"Well, there *is* something ... out in one of the barns at the back. It's best you see it for yourself, as it makes no sense to me."

Ellen drew the stable-door wide and propped it open so Inspector Hassen could see more clearly what she had seen.

He hunkered down to study the shoe.

"Interesting.... Would the shoe be your late husband's then?"

"No ... not that I recall. But it could ... I mean it might've belonged to his father. What can it mean?"

"The shoe is just a shoe, but given that it's been placed inside a star, it's symbolic.... Represents the physical confirmation of some kind of bond ... pact if you like. In ancient times, when you removed your shoes and gave them to someone you were confirming a contract between giver and receiver."

She thought of George and his gambling debts. Had this something to do with a promise of money owed?

Hassen scoped the rest of the interior and went over to the old sofa. Looked behind it. She saw him produce a large black holdall. He brought it over to the light.

"This belong to you?"

"No, but I haven't been in here in a long time ... except for this morning of course. When I ... when I saw *that* on the floor."

Hassen unzipped the bag, drew out a pillow and blanket. The blanket was dark blue with polka dots.

"These from the house?"

Ellen shook her head. "No ... no, not at all."

"You sure?"

"Absolutely. I take care of all the linens in the house. Those certainly don't belong. I never buy patterned bedding. Someone's been sleeping out here, haven't they?"

"Looks like it ... and whoever it was, drew that star and had some connection with your husband."

He rummaged further in the bag.

"What's this little treasure then?"

Ellen's heart did a somersault when she saw the missing casket in his hands.

He opened it. Tipped out the contents.

The scimitar, the owl, the strange eye ornament with the diamond teardrop and the little slipper. They were all there, just as she remembered them.

"Er ... are they pieces of jewellery?"

"Masonic symbols, maybe ... isn't so surprising, given the history of the Blackbourne family."

"Really? But my husband ... he didn't have anything to do with that kind of thing. A lot of heirlooms came with the house. D'you know what they are ... the significance of them I mean?"

He picked up the scimitar with the five-pointed star. "Well, this one's not exactly Masonic ... rather an offshoot.... The Shriners I believe they're called."

"Shriners?"

"Yes. A more fun version of the Masons, apparently. They wear a fez with this emblem on the front as part of their regalia ... something to do with having a liking for all things Arabian."

He inspected the eye ornament. "Now that's definitely Masonic ... an udjat, or Eye of Horus. The optimist would say it's a symbol of protection against dark forces. The pessimist believes it's one of the few symbols that refer to Lucifer himself. That diamond teardrop represents his grief for those outside his influence."

A shiver ran through Ellen.

"The owl ... I'm not so sure of," the cop went on, turning the object this way and that. "Nasty bird the old owl, even though they're nice to look at ... like to torture their prey before killing them."

Ellen thought of the owl-shaped paperweight on Kavanagh's desk. Coincidence?

"You know a great deal about such things, detective. I ... I had no idea what any of it meant."

Hassen stood up. "In our business, Mrs Purboy, we have to be ... cognizant of a lot of stuff. You've seen this little box of tricks before then?"

"Erm ... "

The air tightened. Ellen knew she could hardly lie to a cop as astute as Hassen. He'd already assumed correctly.

"Well, yes. It was in the drawing-room . . . then it just disappeared."

"So someone carried it out here. Interesting. Hmm . . . your lodger, perhaps."

She had a feeling he'd say that. "No-no, that's not possible, officer." Then it dawned on her. "Oh dear, now that I come to think of it . . . on his first night here . . . when he was driving up—Jay I mean—he said he thought he saw someone at the drawing-room window. I told him it was impossible because I was in bed, but now . . . now I see he was probably right. That casket went missing from the drawing-room round about that time."

Hassen gave her an inscrutable look. "Anything's possible. Your intruder was hiding out here it would seem."

He turned his attention to the casket again.

"He forgot to take *this*. Was your husband a Freemason then?"

"No. . . . Not to my knowledge."

Ellen was disturbed by the suggestion. But even as she uttered the words she sensed that the inspector had a point. George had kept his gambling addiction very well concealed from her, so what would she know? Nonetheless, she felt it necessary to defend him against such an accusation.

"George didn't believe in any of that stuff. He told me often enough."

"Maybe he wasn't being honest."

Hassen's directness was verging on rudeness. "With respect, I think I knew my husband better than you, inspector."

He shrugged. Dug his hands in his pockets. "Why would he not tell you he was a Mason? Didn't want to scare you perhaps. People are very suspicious of secret societies—and with good reason. If everything was above board there'd be no need for the secrecy, now would there?"

She had no answer to that.

At that moment, footsteps were heard crunching over the gravel.

They turned as one.

"Look who I found hiding under the stairs, Mrs Purboy."

Constable Jones and a weeping Toby were standing in the doorway.

SEVENTY

Ma Bryn bustled about her kitchen in a frock as colourful as her mood: an eye-watering yellow number raining wedges of honeydew watermelon with patches of cherry-blossom motifs.

She'd happened upon it in the local Discount Diva thrift store some months before and loved it, even though it was a bit "on the wee side". Now, my-oh-my, she'd discovered that, due to all the scrimping recently, she'd dropped a size. What a joy that was, and what with the future looking as bright as a saucepan lid on a sunny day, things could only get better and better!

Manny had ferried her home from the bus station, and on the journey had delivered the great news about getting his old job back. God, it was the best news ever!

And, on top of that, Ted's cheque had arrived. Not as big as hoped for, but what did it matter now with so much good fortune for the pair of them? Sure with all the great things happening, the $300 was a bonus indeed.

I'm not bothered he's marrying again neither, she mused, fetching delft from a cupboard. For as long as a man has money and the charm of the Divil himself, he'll be a magnet for a sartain type of woman. And it wouldn't matter if he wuz a baldy with no teeth, a wooden leg and glass eye, sure they'd still be after him.

Tilda sighed with satisfaction as she spooned tea-leaves into the teapot. How times were a-changing!

She had yet to impart the news about her own new job. But an announcement of such importance could only be made at the kitchen table over a cuppa tea and slice of cream sponge. And

Manny had time for the cuppa tea because his next fare was a good hour away. So "time aplenty", as Pastor Sam might say.

I just hope he doesn't take it too badly! It'll be a big change for him. What if he doesn't want me to do it? Would I go against him and take the job anyway? I've always put him first. All his life. But what if...

Thoughts were pinging in Tilda's head like cue-balls in a tumbrel when she heard the toilet flush and Manny coming down the stairs. I'll just have to leave it tae God and the Fates. Whatever's to be will be.

She cut two generous slices of cake, icing as thick as fur, and transferred them to plates. Opened a biscuit tin containing a selection of Banjos and Bounty bars. This tea called for a celebration, and no better way of celebrating and softening the effect of her new job news than having a blowout of sweet cake and chocolate. With all the making-do over the last month or two at an end, it was long overdue.

"That looks nice," Manny said, coming in.

She pulled out a chair.

"Sit yerself down there, son. God, this is a day of celebration—and about time too."

"So yer not disappointed about Cousin Ted then? Thought yeh would be, with the stingy cheque, like."

"Not as much as I would-a been had you not got yer old job back, son. God, Manny, everything's working out terrible well—as I knew it would."

"Aye... just be like 'oul times."

Even as Manny said it he realized that his ma would never know the full impact of such a statement; a bad chapter had just ended and she hadn't so much as glimpsed a page of what he'd endured. And that's the way it would stay.

"Now, I've another bitt-a news to tell yeh, son," Tilda announced, lips moving carefully round the words as she poured tea into the chipped Friends Forever mugs.

"Oh, aye! What's that then?"

"You're not the only one's got a new job, Manny."

He paused mid-bite, mug halfways to his gob. Had he heard her right?

"Yeh mean ... yeh mean *you've* got a job, Ma?"

"Yes, indeed, son."

That was the last thing he expected to hear.

Tilda put down her tea. Prepared to deliver her sales pitch. She cleared her throat. Paused. Touched the cake plate. Spread a hand on the tablecloth. This was going to be a hard sell, but she'd give it her best shot.

"Now, it's all good, son, and I wouldn't be taking it if I didn't think it was right for me. But I think it is, so all that's left is for you to say it's okay, 'cos I wouldn't want you to disapprove, like."

Nerves overtaking her, Tilda was spitting out words like a scattergun, hoping they'd make their mark in a favourable way.

"But if yeh *did* disapprove I wouldn't be taking it, even though I'd be disappointed, if you unnerstand me, son, and this chance'll nivver come again. God knows, not many chances come for-a wommin up in years like meself—"

"*Ma ...* "

"What, son?"

"Yeh havin' told me what it *is* yet."

"What?"

"The job ... what is it?"

"Aye, well, I was gettin' to that."

"Well, hurry up, Ma. I've not got much time."

"I'd be a housekeeper for a pastor by the name o' Samuel Monroe-Johnson, and it would be in Portaluce, 'cos that's where he lives—in a big fancy house overlooking the sea, with a glass-room tae the front, next door to Mrs Purboy no less. God, he's been all over the world, son, convertin' the people and wee black babies in

Africa. He's a kinda brown himself like."

There! She'd said it.

Manny tore the wrapper off a Bounty bar as he tried coming to terms with what he'd just heard. His ma wanted to leave home and start over *at her age* with a black preacher-man from darkest Africa and live in a glasshouse in Portaluce. Maybe she was off her medication again. Had he heard her right? Maybe she wasn't herself and was making it all up, like that moving-statue nonsense she got involved with not so very long ago. For now, though, he'd play along.

"Yeh mean … yeh mean you'd leave here and move *there?* In with him … a foreign man … permanent, like?"

"Now, it's not what yeh think, Manny. There's no romance in it, if that's what yer thinkin'. No, this is strictly bissness. And he's not forren … was born and brought up here but spent a big part of his life in Africa, which turned him a tanny brown colour, like."

"R-right … and how … er … how did yeh meet him?"

"Well, I was just comin' tae that bit, son. He came into me in the Dormouse and offered me the job, if I'd give up me wicked ways and return to the Lord. That's what he called me fortune-tellin' bissness: 'wicked ways'. And you know, son, the more I thought about it, the more I knew he was right. I don't want to tell fortunes no more. Pastor Sam sez it's the Divil's work, and he's right. Me mammy, God rest her soul, hadn't much luck in her life, what with the dhrink and the making do, and dying afore her time as yellow as a canary in a cornfield, 'cos her liver give out."

Manny couldn't quite believe his ears. "Yeh mean … yeh mean yeh'd give up the oul' fortune tellin' altogether?"

"Cross me heart, son."

"Nivver do it again?"

"Wouldn't go back to readin' again, no. Meetin' Pastor Sam has made me see the light, as they say. I've turned a page … or is it a corner? Nivver mind right. Anyway, all I need is for you, Manny, to give me yer blessing and to be all right with me dissision."

Manny sank his teeth into another chocolate bar, basking in the knowledge that his ma actually *wanted to give up fortune telling.* It was something he'd never thought to hear. From his schooldays he'd been ashamed of what his ma and granny did. Now his ma was packing it all in, at last. If that was the case then living on his own would surely be a small price to pay.

"Well, I s'ppose I could rattle along here on me own, right enough. Maybe it's time I lived on me own. As long as you don't go back till tellin' fortunes, it's all right with me."

Tilda clapped her hands to her cheeks, brimming with joy.

"God, son, I'm so happy you don't mind! Sure I'll have me days off and yeh can come visit and stay in the Dormouse."

"Aye, right enough," he said, a thought coming to him. With Ma away I can invite Iris here for a meal maybe. That way we wouldn't be seen by the gossips and they'd have nothing to talk about.

"Your blessin's the icing on the cake, son," Tilda beamed. "And talking of cake ... "

She got up. Flounced over to the treats cupboard, the fabric of her second-hand frock rustling like wrapping paper on a Christmas morn.

"Sure we might as well finish the rest of this nice sponge ... for the day that's in it, son."

Manny smiled. There was no arguing with that. None whatsoever.

VIVIENNE

When her parents arrived at the hospital Vivienne refused to stay. The euphoria of seeing them again overrode every pain and ache in her near-vanquished body. She'd risen like Lazarus from the crypt. They'd come—not to visit her—but take her home.

She wept.

They wept.

The sister fretted.

The doctor dithered.

But she had her way.

So they patched her up, gave her painkillers, drugs to make her sleep, dressings to help her heal, and she limped to the car, propped between them like some battle-weary soldier leaving a war zone—which in a way was the case.

She'd never known such liberation in her life.

Now here she is, slipping free of her chemical sleep in her own bed, in her own room, to welcome another day. What day it is she does not know. She does not care to know either.

Days and time hold no meaning for her. From the moment she wakes up, unmoored from the depths of dreamless slumber, she celebrates the fact that she's alive; fully alive in the present.

Outside she can hear the world get on with its business: traffic humming like bees; a spill of voices as strangers pass by; the sound of chopper blades high up in the Belfast sky. While in here, in the quiet of her room, she plots and plans her future. When her wounds heal, when her spirits lift, when the life-force she once knew is fully restored to her, she'll join the human race again.

She pictures herself weaving down Royal Avenue, her hair unfurling in the breeze, as weightless and carefree as a bird, her sights trained on another day at her desk in her studio.

Oh, yes, she *will* be returning to her studio, no matter the objections her father might have. That's the strange thing about having stared down the barrel of death. It bestows a strength no one but the survivor of such a horror can lay claim to.

Her ordeal caused a stir in the local press. The hacks, like carrion birds, wait patiently outside the house. She was never expected to come back you see. But she has no intention of engaging with them.

Nor will she be sharing those nightmare days with her parents. Why would she fill their heads with a horror story they'd for ever play, rewind button pressed firmly down, until their dying day? Why should she cause them even more torment on top of what they'd been through?

The monster did not destroy her.

She destroyed *him*.

She does not regret what she did.

The police found the cottage in the forest. Uncovered a shallow grave and found him there. The evil pair who kidnapped her—his benighted parents—are in custody. She admitted that she'd struck him with the chair. It was self-defence. They absolved her of all blame.

Turns out Tricia, her college friend, was the Judas who betrayed her. How was she to know that Fitzwell aka Martin Connor was her cousin? Declan in the Kevin Barry Arms, the weirdo from the bus who'd swiped her business card: ex-prisoners who'd done time with him. All circling like vultures, waiting to pounce on blissfully oblivious Vivienne.

The invitation from Tricia to stay the weekend of the opening was the trap they set. She walked right into it.

Snap!

All of them will face justice and she will see them in court. They will answer for their crimes. How fortunate it would have been for them had she not survived! But from the minute she found herself trapped in that blue car she knew somehow she *would* survive. God was on her side.

Her parents would like her to see a therapist, but she has no need of one. She intends to write down everything she went through in one rapid outpouring. Burn the pages and watch as that part of her life turns to ash.

Then, like that crested phoenix, she will rise.

She will hold onto the kindness she was shown by a trio of complete strangers: Brigid and Nan and Manny.

All three of them gave her hope.

Put themselves in the firing line to save her.

Three points of light in the ugly darkness.

She will not forget their generosity.

Yes, she's come through hell. But she's determined that the experience will not *define* her.

Why would she allow those evildoers so much power?

They stole so many long weeks of her life.

She will not allow them to take the rest of it.

SEVENTY-TWO

Ellen didn't have the heart to tell little Toby that his father would never be coming back. How do you tell a five-year-old such dreadful news? She simply didn't have the courage, let alone the words.

The previous evening she'd put him to bed in the room next to hers. Now she sat in the kitchen, deep in thought, eyes swollen from lack of sleep and the tears she'd shed over all that had been.

The previous day had been momentous. So many revelations, so many unanswered questions: the police visit with the sad news about Jay, leaving a question mark over his past, in the eyes of the police at any rate. That strange business in the stable; someone hiding out there all this time and trying to scare me. But who? And—more importantly—why? Well, they wouldn't be getting the chance anymore. After the police left, a hired handyman had padlocked all the stable doors and secured both gates at the rear with sturdy chains.

Hopefully that would be the end of it.

The police hadn't got very much from the little boy. After a lot of coaxing they learned that each morning before departing his father would leave out food, circle the TV programmes he could watch and instruct him not to answer the door to anyone.

He couldn't say where his father worked and Jay had left behind no personal details.

I blame myself for not drawing up a contract. But everything happened so fast, and as time went on it didn't seem so important.

They decided it would be best for Toby to remain at Cedarwood for the time being. They would try and locate Aunt Edith and see if there was a relative who could care for the child.

Ellen took another sip of tea, staring into space, wondering how things could have taken such a tragic turn.

After all that's happened I must sell this house. I simply cannot live here any longer. There are too many memories. Too many unanswered questions. I could never be at peace. The bedsit a constant reminder of my foolishness.

"A mind stretched by a new idea can't go back to its old dimensions."

She grimaced as she recalled Dr Flynn's words and her willingness to follow his suggestion! Had I ignored it, I wouldn't be in this position now. Would not have met Jay. Would not now be mourning yet another loss.

Something dropped through the letter-box, giving her a jolt. Wearily, she got up and went into the hallway.

The usual fare lay on the mat. She picked up a bill from the electricity board and a couple of flyers from businesses in the town. Nothing much of interest, save for one white envelope. She thought the handwriting looked familiar.

She carried it through to the kitchen and sat down again.

Tore the envelope open. A photo dropped onto the table. She turned it over. The snapshot showed a youthful-looking George sitting on a wall, his arm around a pretty, blonde woman. There was no citation or date. Was she a relative? Ellen had never seen her before.

The letter consisted of a single page.

Perturbed, she began reading.

> Dear Ellen,
>
> By the time you receive this I will be on the Other Side.

She stared at the words, pressed a fist to her mouth, horror-stricken. The letter was from Jay.

I'm sorry it had to end this way. But since my dear wife's death I've found life very, very difficult. I thought I could carry on raising Toby and being a good father, but I'm simply not up to the task. A dark depression overtook me after Hannah's passing which I just couldn't seem able to throw off.

I chose to spend my final days at Cedarwood for a reason. I wanted to be near where my father lived, since I never had the good fortune to know him when I was growing up.

Ellen's hands began to shake. *What?!* What in heaven's name . . . She scanned the room helplessly, as if looking for an escape route. George . . . *his father!*

I know Ellen this will come as a very great shock to you and I'm truly sorry to cause you further suffering. You see the woman in the photo is my mother. She and George were lovers before he married you.

Oh, my God! Ellen got up. More secrets. Did I know George at all?

She felt her head begin to throb, her knees go weak. She grabbed onto the table for support. Sat down again.

Willed herself to continue reading.

To be fair he did not know of my existence and I did not know of his, until recently. I received a letter from beyond the grave, much in the same way you're getting this one. That's something my mother and I had in common. In the face of life's trials we folded. Although, she did not die by her own hand but of cancer, so at least knew her time was limited. Please believe me, Ellen, when I say that from the moment I met you I wanted to tell you the truth, but just couldn't bring myself to do it.

Foolishly I thought things would get easier for me, my depression would lift and that, eventually, I could confide all to you. But you proved to be such a kind and decent lady I could not afford to hurt you further.

Ellen put down the page, buried her face in her hands, weeping uncontrollably. Why could he not bring himself to confide in me? Why did he choose death over upsetting me with the truth? How more torturous can things become? How remiss of me not to pick up on his distress! I should have asked more questions. Cared more. Helped more.

I set myself the challenge, you see. Promised myself I'd give it three months. See if things would improve. But, alas, they did not. It pains me that after twenty-seven years I have failed so spectacularly as a human being – laterally as a father – that the pull of the deep blue ocean holds more appeal for me than the life that lies ahead.

I want to thank you for being so generous to

me. Your kindness helped me enormously through the darkest days and nights. I couldn't have chosen a better person to spend my final days around, than you. My father was truly blessed to have had you in his life.

Please take care of Toby for me. If you can find it in your heart to forgive me, I would like you to become his legal guardian. There is no one else in the world I'd rather have raise him and give him guidance. Under your care I believe his life will blossom and he'll grow up to be a better man than me.

Please don't think badly of me, Ellen. I know what I'm about to do is the right thing. The die is cast and I must be gone.

Adios!

Yours affectionately,

Jay

Ellen set the letter aside as a tsunami of guilt and recrimination swamped her, along with her tears. Oh, how I wish I could go back in time and be a different person! Had I been more attentive, more understanding, he might still be here. Why could George not have told me he'd fathered a son? Was that the real reason he was so anti-children? Was Jay the mistake he could not forgive? I feel so foolish; not only have I been let down by my husband, but worse than that, I failed his son by not being there for him when he needed me most.

But you have Toby, a voice in her head assured her. In dying so soon, Jay's fulfilled your dearest wish: to have a little boy you can call your own.

"But can I even succeed as a mother now?" Her anguish rang out in the empty house, giving her a jolt.

A tear fell onto the envelope and, in an effort to remove it, her name ended up a smudge.

How fitting! I can't even mourn his passing without ruining things.

She thought back to their first meeting on the road. How carefree and buoyant he'd seemed! Their paths crossing a second time, when he turned up out of the blue to rent the bedsit. So he had planned to spend his last days in his father's house and, in the end, to surrender little Toby into my care.

In some strange way, perhaps, it was all meant to be. My grieving for George, not wanting to let him go, brought into play a set of events that would deliver me my dearest wish: a child I could call my own. Were all those strange incidents in the house signals that something as momentous as this would happen? They say God moves in mysterious ways and...

Click-click!

Up above she heard a door opening.

Little Toby was awake.

Quickly she stuffed the letter into the table drawer. Wiped her tears away and went into the hallway.

Toby was coming down the stairs in his blue teddy-bear pyjamas, rubbing the sleep out of his eyes.

"There you are, sweetheart," Ellen said softly. "Did you sleep?" She went to meet him.

He nodded shyly.

"That's a good boy!"

She took him by the hand and guided him down the last few steps. The feel of his little hand gripping hers almost made her weep again, but she had to be strong.

"Now we can have breakfast. Cornflakes with warm milk.... How's that?"

He gazed up at her and nodded again.

She was settling him at the table when the phone rang.

"I'll not be a moment, sweetheart."

She plucked up the receiver, determined to be strong.

"Morning... Cedarwood—"

"Morning, Ellen... Fintan Kavanagh here. How are you?"

"Erm... I've been better, Fintan, thanks."

"I'm so sorry about Nettie! I only heard this morning. How is she doing?"

"She's come round, but it'll take time.... About three months the doctors say, before she's back to herself."

"Well, she's out of danger; that's the main thing. Stairs can be such lethal things when one gets to our age."

"Indeed...."

"Ellen, I won't detain you. Just need your signature on a couple of things, that's all. Say Thursday, two-ish. Would that suit?"

"Yes, that's fine."

"Good-good! Marjorie sends her regards of course. Anything I can do, just—"

"Well, there *is* something, Fintan... now I have your ear."

Nothing like striking while the iron's hot, she thought, eyes on those life-threatening stairs.

"I'm going to take your advice and sell Cedarwood."

"That's an excellent idea! And no better time; the real-estate market is quite healthy these days. I'll see to the conveyancing free of charge, of course. I owe you one."

"That's good of you."

"Thursday at two then."

"Oh, and Fintan..."

"Yes?"

She didn't know how to broach the next subject, but she'd give it her best shot.

"Er, there's something else. I..."

How was she going to frame it? How would Fintan Kavanagh react?

"Yes, Ellen … "

"I'd like to adopt a little boy."

There was a distinct pause at the other end of the line. She heard a sigh and the shuffling of papers. He's busy and I'm taking up his time.

"Fintan, are you there?"

"Yes, yes, indeed. It's a … well, it's a lot to take on … but if you're certain you can handle it … "

"I believe I can. Would you deal with the paperwork for that also? I really wouldn't know where to start I'm afraid."

"Of course.… Now, I really must go. Bye now."

Before she could return same, he'd hung up.

She put the phone down, wondering why he'd chosen to end the call on such an abrupt note.

SEVENTY-THREE

It was Ma Bryn's birthday and she was celebrating. No better time to ditch the old for the new. Dumping all the paraphernalia from her fortune-telling days was now a must. Her new life in Pastor Sam's house was only days away. She had to get a move on.

She stood in her bedroom, a room crammed with a poverty of third-hand gewgaws, wondering where to start.

Pictures of Jesus and Mary, Vishnu and Lakshmi—gods and saviours—were ranged about on the pink-blushed walls, together with a plethora of beads and stones. Buddhas laughed, Madonnas wept, saints gazed heavenward in exalted bliss. Rosaries, crucifixes, hearts and horseshoes abounded; candles crowded the windowsill in blues, yellows and reds. Angels danced on a sideboard and patterned the eiderdown spread.

She gazed longingly at her mother's "inspiration cushion": the makeshift altar, adorned with the tricks of the trade handed down the maternal line. Many's the time I done me meditation there when I needed help from me spirit guide, Redwing Maeve. But all that's over now and I'm making a new start.

She caught sight of some newspaper cuttings lying underneath the altar. They concerned the moving-statue phenomena.

Dearie me, so much has changed since the night I fell a clatter in Father Mulcahy's shrine! No doubt Pastor Sam would say it was all the Divil's work and quote a bitt-a scripture to prove it. And he'd be right too. I'll get rid of them first.

As she stooped down she caught sight of an old cigarette pack peeping out from under the dressing-table. How did *that* get there? She reached in and uncovered the remains of the familiar 20 Player's Navy Cut she hadn't seen in years. On the reverse side, scrawled in a spidery hand were the words:

Ted Romero,
Fofanny Heights,
Scutch End,
Galveston, Texas, USA

Tears filled Tilda's eyes at the sight of the faded lines of ink inscribed there nearly forty years before. How she'd treasured that wee pack in the early days! The only tangible link she'd left of him. Sleeping with it inside her pillowcase and dreaming of the day her handsome prince would return, and spirit herself and baby Manny off to the land of milk and honey that was Amerikay.

It was not to be. Now the old rogue was getting married for the *third* time. Tilda dried her tears. Just as well he never did come back. He was never the dependable sort. Manny and me don't need him no more.

Without a second thought she tore the pack in two and tossed it in the bag. The future was all that mattered now. The past that included Ted Romero was finally over.

Next into the bag went all the cuttings, followed by the accoutrement from the altar. Then she set to work on the walls.

I'll keep all the holy stuff and get rid of the rest. No point in holding onto any of it, even for old time's sake. I promised Pastor Sam I'd give up me wicked ways. The sooner I get it over with the better.

Mind made up, Tilda set to.

An hour later she clanked downstairs with her bagful of psychic tat, bubbling with joy that she'd got everything cleared in such a short space of time. It wasn't as bad as she thought it would be, even though she'd shed a tear or two for the errant Ted, and for her poor mammy and all she'd endured in her chaotic life.

She went outside to dump it in the trash, just as Jonah Mulgrew's bubble car came bumping into the yard.

God-save-us, Jonah's the last person a body wants to see with so much on me plate right now.

"Happy birthday, Tilly!" Jonah called out, unloading himself from the curious vehicle. "I hear yer goin' away."

"God, Jonah, you always mind me birthday, and doesn't news travel fast in these parts."

"Sure didn't Minnie Bain tell me last night. Well, yeh know what they say, Tilly. If yeh wanna bitta news spread, you can telegram, telephone or tell-a-wommin."

"Och, you're a one, Jonah! You'll come in for a cuppa tea? Wuz just about tae put the kettle on."

"Wouldn't say no, a-tall, a-tall."

With that, the two old neighbours went into the house.

SEVENTY-FOUR

Manny's job as a taxi-driver was to end sooner than expected. Not that he was complaining. Fred Bain had called the night before to say he could have the rest of the week off; four days' holiday before starting back at the bakery. He couldn't have been more delighted.

So to say he was as happy as a dog with two tails when he drove into Fred's yard for the last time would be an understatement. He'd be riding home in his own old rust bucket, which had been parked there in the interim. He couldn't wait.

Fred was on a sun-seat at the gable, feet resting on a beer crate, closely observing his three-point turn from beneath the tattered bill of his baseball cap.

Manny grew nervous. What if he notices that inner door where I was made to hide Magee's package? But I put it back perfect. He'd need to be bloody Sherlock Holmes to notice. Anyway, why would he notice? A dent or scratch on the outside maybe—and there's none-a them, 'cos I was very careful. Aye, he caused me many sleepless nights along with Fitzwell and Magee, so if he starts anything I'll just tell him where to go.

Puffed up with the bravado of a heavyweight champ, Manny killed the engine and got out.

"That's her now, Fred. I washed her and give her a good clean out too. So she's all ready tae go."

"Good man, Manny. Minnie didn't have time to see to yours, but she didn't use it much ... should be clean enough all right. She dandered into the town to get the groceries and got the bus home most of the time.... Not too confident at the drivin', Minnie, and didn't wanna smash her."

"No bother, Fred. How's the leg?"

"Well mended and I'm ready to go. Good that yer gettin' your job back, Manny."

"Aye, so."

"Yeh wouldn't wanna be standin' in that dole queue again. Not that Magee could do you much harm these days."

Manny's ears pricked up.

"Why's that?"

"Word's goin' about he's in the hospital."

"Hospital?!"

"In a coma, aye ... ate a feed of choc'lits that didn't agree with him. They say the IRA wanted rid of him so they must of put poison or God-knows-what in them. Odd way tae try and get rid of a body, don't yeh think?"

"Christ! Odd enough all right."

Manny, shocked to the core, saw an image of Magee thundering down the stairs with his ma's box of Black Magic in his paw: the chocolates that were a gift *from Mrs Purboy.* They couldn't be the same chocolates, surely.

"What kinda choc'lits were they?"

"Christ, how would I know that?" Fred said, looking at Manny as if he were a lunatic. "What kinda question's that?"

Manny scuffed the ground to cover his embarrassment. If you only knew what I came through with Magee you wouldn't think it a silly question, Fred.

"S'ppose ... aye."

Fred had another revelation.

"Aye, apparently they wanted him dead 'cos he wuz tied up with the kidnappin' of that lassie ... the judge's daughter. S'pposed to be watchin' her but she escaped. If he comes round he'll be lookin' at a long prison sentence, that's for sure."

"God, that's a good one. I didn't hear nothin' about that. Well, I'll be goin'.... Ma's lookin' tae get her hair done."

That last was a lie, but he was eager to be gone. What with hearing that Mrs Purboy was a possible poisoner and that if Magee hadn't swiped the Black Magic he and his ma might now be lyin' in a coma in hospital instead of Magee was a lot to take in. Today was his ma's birthday after all.

"Right yeh be, Manny. Thanks for takin' good care of me motor. She looks grand, so she doz."

"Goin' like a dream, Fred. Goin' like a dream."

He skedaddled towards his own jalopy, eager to be gone.

"Keep her lit!" Fred shouted out as he drove out of his orbit, fast and free at last.

Now here he was, cruising into Castlebrook.

He slowed for the army checkpoint, singing along to the radio. But to his disappointment the barrier did not lift automatically, as he was expecting.

He hit the brake.

Christ, not again! What the hell have I done now? I knew things were too good to be true.

Out of nowhere, the lanky soldier appeared.

Oh, it would be *him*.

Warily, Manny wound down the window.

"How do, mate," the soldier said cheerily, a blob of chewing gum visible in his smiling gob.

"Aye . . . all right so."

"Can you pull over there, mate?"

Manny was about to say "What for?" but held his tongue and did as he was told.

He got out of the car.

"Sarge wants to see you." He pointed to the Portakabin with the barrel of his rifle. "Just give the door a knock. He's waitin' for you."

What the frig is *this* about?

Manny knocked on the door, nervous.

It was opened promptly by a burly, red-faced cop with quick-to-rage written all over him.

"Come in, Manny," he said in a friendly manner.

Manny felt a tremor of Richter-scale proportions course through him. He's being friendly so he can hit me with some serious charge. He knows I was involved with Fitzwell. How stupid of me to think I could keep it a secret! *An accessory after the fact.* Isn't that what they call it? Now I'm really in for it, and things were going so well. I knew it couldn't last.

"I'm Sergeant Sinclair. Take a seat, won't you."

Manny, frantically sorting through excuses to use in his defence, sat before a desk with a Union Jack mug on it and several clip-files. A youthful Queen Elizabeth observed proceedings from a gilt frame above the sergeant's head.

"Er ... is this ... is this about that baldy tyre?"

The sergeant shook his head. "No-no-no. On the contrary, I brought you in here to congratulate you."

Had he heard him right?

"Er ... erm ... I-I ... "

Sinclair sat forward in his chair, unblinking eyes focused on him.

"You rescued the judge's daughter: Vivienne Dundas. Her father has asked me to inform you that you'll be richly rewarded. Naturally he did not want to give the enemy any heads-up by turning up at your home or calling you. Best to keep these things under the radar. We're all in this together, and you risked a lot by driving her from the Doody house to the hospital. A lesser man would have folded at such a request."

Manny was tongue-tied.

"I-I ... I only did what I ... what I thought was right."

"You did indeed! You didn't allow yourself to be cowed. Later, when things have died down ... when the press pack have lost interest and Vivienne is sufficiently recovered, she and Judge Dundas want to meet you in Belfast, to thank you in person and reward you for your courage."

Manny had never been to the metropolis of Belfast in his life. The prospect scared him.

Sergeant Sinclair read his mind.

"Don't worry. A private car will be laid on for you and your mother—in the event she wants to come of course. Any questions?"

"Er ... when yeh say ... well, when yeh say a reward, d'you mean money?"

"Yes, indeed. Judge Dundas told me to tell you that you'll be richly rewarded. You and the Doody sisters. The judge is a wealthy man and he's indebted to all three of you."

He got up. Manny did likewise.

"You've done well, Manny. Good deeds are always rewarded in this life. A kind act never goes unnoticed. Take care now."

He shook his hand firmly. "We'll be in touch."

"Thank you ... thank you very much!"

Manny made his way back to the car in a daze of delight. Things had turned around so fast he felt dizzy. He couldn't quite believe that he'd be getting a reward. That was the last thing he was expecting to hear from the burly sergeant.

But I can't take me ma. She can't know anything about this. Not with her starting her new job. Maybe later when she's settled in more. But I could take Iris.

Now there's an idea! Her father couldn't disapprove of her getting to meet the famous Judge Dundas.

"Mind how you go, mate," the lanky soldier said, as he got back in the car. "We got you covered."

Manny smiled up at him. "Thanks," he said. "You mind yourself too."

As he drove off he glanced in the rear-view mirror, and saw the soldier give a thumbs up, followed by a cheeky Benny Hill salute.

SEVENTY-FIVE

Ellen sat on Portaluce beach, watching Toby playing in the sand.

The great Atlantic Ocean may have taken his father, but what a beautiful gift was bestowed upon *me*.

It was peaceful now on the near-deserted strand. Just the way she liked it. The sun, weakening above mesmeric waves, was sending bolts of silken reds across a painter's sky as the last of the day-trippers took their leave.

Three weeks had passed since Jay's death and a lot had happened during that time.

Nettie had been released from hospital and was doing well. She would need the use of a wheelchair for a couple of months but the doctors were confident she'd make a full recovery.

Her state of mind would be another challenge, however.

"I was pushed by *an unseen hand*," she insisted to Ellen, when back in the comfort of her own home.

"Oh, dear, Nettie. You must stop believing all the rumours about Cedarwood and old Sir Wilfred's death. It's all hearsay, with no basis in fact."

"That's what *you* think. But you didn't *see* what I saw. Didn't *feel* what I felt when I tumbled down those stairs. I'll never set foot in that house again."

"Nettie dear, you'll never have to enter Cedarwood again. I'm selling the house and all the sorry memories that go with it. I've had enough of the place myself, believe me. It's time for all of us to move on."

"That's good. And not before time, Ellen."

So Cedarwood was now on the market, as promised. Fintan

Kavanagh had been more than helpful with organizing the sale. As well he might. He had some explaining to do.

She thought back to that momentous meeting.

"I'm glad you're selling, Ellen. The market's very healthy, as I mentioned. You'll get a good price I'm sure."

He also agreed to oversee the adoption of Toby, even if he seemed hesitant to begin with.

"Are you sure, Ellen? I mean ... taking on a child at your age."

The comment irked her. "I'll remind you, Fintan, that some women of *my age* are raising young children quite successfully these days. I'm far from the ancient specimen you're implying. Besides which—"

"Sorry, I didn't mean it that way."

"Besides which, Toby is George's grandson. Did you know he had a son?"

"*What?!*" She saw how this news made him uncomfortable.

"Well, you kept his gambling habit to yourself so why not other confidences—"

"Now, Ellen, I had no idea about George's private life, I assure you. He may have been a close friend but there were limits. How did you meet him ... this son?"

"Jay was my lodger. He took his own life a few weeks ago. In his suicide letter he asked me to become Toby's legal guardian."

"Ellen, I'm so dreadfully sorry!" He really did seem sincere. "How very distressing after all you've been through."

She was determined to stay strong. Fintan had let her down before.

"Yes, well ... he wanted to see where his father'd lived before he died. I had no idea who he was or what his intentions were, but that's ... that's the way he wished things to be, alas."

"Look, Ellen, if there's anything else I can do, just—"

"Yes, there is. The money from the sale of Cedarwood. I want it put it in a trust fund for Toby."

"You know, I was about to suggest that myself. It's an excellent idea! It's one way of avoiding unnecessary taxation. The child is fortunate to have you, Ellen, with his father abandoning him just like that."

"Jay had lost his wife very suddenly a year ago. He never got over her death, sadly. For a young man such as he, being left on his own to raise a child ... well, I really can't imagine ... He simply couldn't cope."

Kavanagh shook his head sadly.

"Well, when you put it like that ... a terrible business ... tragic, so very tragic."

"I've something else I need to know, Fintan. Was George in the Freemasons?"

"Erm ... why d'you ask that?" He couldn't meet her eye.

"Just wondered."

"Not that I'm aware of. But even if he was, what difference would it make now?"

"It would explain a box of symbols . . . something to do with Freemasonry he kept hidden from me, and a bizarre drawing on the floor of one of the stables—"

"Really?"

"Yes ... a star with an old slipper placed in the middle of it. The police say someone was enacting a ritual of sorts ... the slipper signifying a contract of some kind."

Kavanagh shook his head. "He never mentioned anything to me. But that's the whole point of Masonry, is it not? The secrecy."

They'd left the subject at that.

Had Fintan Kavanagh been straight with her? Did he know more than he was prepared to say? Perhaps. George had bequeathed a plethora of unanswered questions. But maybe it was best to leave things be. Father and son were united now, in the spiritual realms. At least I knew Jay, even if it was only for a very short time.

The reward of Toby makes up for all the heartache and hurt.

She watched the little one kneeling on the sand next to his bucket, diligently digging with his spade. Four sandcastles already completed.

She got up and went to him.

"Good work," she said, hunkering down beside him. "But tomorrow's another day, sweetheart."

He gazed up at her and smiled but said nothing. He'd said very little in the past weeks and, when he did, it was usually to ask when his father would be coming back. She always gave the same answer.

"Whenever's he's ready. He said he'd let me know."

How could she burden such an innocent child with the truth? He was too young; too untouched by the cruelties of life to absorb the immensity of such a betrayal.

Hopefully, in time such questions would cease, and he'd forget all about his father, as a new life of stability and love opened up.

"Can we come back tomorrow?" Toby asked, reluctant to leave.

Ellen took him tenderly by the shoulders, gazing into his beautiful brown eyes, the eyes that, ever so slightly, reminded her of George. "We can come as often as you like, Toby. We live here now, remember?"

"In the glass house."

"Yes … in the glass house."

"Are you my new mummy?"

"Kind of," she said and hugged him tight, trying hard not to weep.

They walked down the beach together.

Yes, Edgewater House is our home now, the ocean my last connection with you, dear Jay. You will always be Jay to me and you'll always be the father of this wonderful little boy. I will do my very best to instil in him the values I hold dear: love, loyalty and good old common sense.

What a gift you've given me!

Together we'll make you proud.

EPILOGUE

In the heat of Andalusia, Pedro lingers in the doorway of the Santa Rosa Hotel. There are few diners on the patio at that hour and he hopes it stays that way. His shift is coming to an end and he's eager to be gone.

But the hope of escape dies promptly at the sight of a suave young man approaching. He takes him in—linen suit, snakeskin loafers, Panama hat set at a rakish angle—the moneyed gringo type for sure. Perhaps he'll just pass on by.

Uh-oh …

The waiter sighs as he sees him pull out a chair at a far table, sit down, crack open the menu. Smiling through his disappointment, he goes to greet him.

"*Buenas tardes, señor*. I get you som'thing?"

"Yes … a bottle of your finest red," the stranger says with a flourish, squinting at his nametag … "Pedro, my dear man."

"Of course, *señor*. Of course." Pedro notes with envy the glinting cufflinks, the gold wristwatch—a couple of years' salary for a humble server such as he. "The Gran Reserve … I recommend. Is good."

"*¡Perfecto!*"

Moments later a bottle of Rioja is set down with a little tray of tapas, some olives and some bread.

"Enjoy, *señor*. Enjoy!"

"I will," the diner says, flashing him a winning smile.

Pedro withdraws, hoping for a large tip, and leaves the stranger to his thoughts.

The man relaxes back in his chair, hums a little melody, sips a little wine to celebrate the success of his daring little plan.

• • •

As you can see, dear reader, I still move through the land of the living. Invisible, like a ghost, but here nonetheless, ready for my next little performance. That's the wonderful thing about my liminal life. No one knows what's going to happen when I'm around. I've got the wherewithal to go anywhere and exploit the weak in my own inimitable way.

It wasn't always thus.

To give dear old Ellen her dues she never really believed in ghosts till I showed up. Just as dear old George never believed in my existence. But suddenly there I was—all twenty-seven years of me—dropping like a hand-grenade into his life, primed to explode at any moment and ruin the carefully crafted lie he'd lived.

As far as he was concerned I never got to draw breath.

My mother never spoke of him you see. Not until she passed into the realm of ghosts herself. The evidence she left in a letter to moi; the "big reveal" you might call it, along with my birth certificate and a photo.

A fling with George Purboy in the late 50s and the seed of little ol' me was planted. He gave her money to get rid of me and took off, never to be seen again.

I won't bore you with the details of my upbringing. Suffice to say it was as predictably tumultuous as only the loveless childhood can be. But it bestowed upon me an eagerness to survive; to ride the rapids, knowing that one day I'd get the chance to exact my revenge.

By the time I reached twenty-two the scene was set.

Stuck in a mind-numbing job for Dublin County Council. Something had to give. I was destined for better things. That's when I spotted Toby's soon-to-be mother. She was unattractive but rich, with a drink problem. I was handsome and poor, with a plan.

At sight of her, a moment of unwarranted clarity washed over me. I promptly hitched my wagon to her star.

A match made in hell. Love never came into it. A year later Toby was born. I'd never planned on fatherhood. Never entered my head; an inherited streak passed down the paternal line I guess. But women, and that pesky need of theirs to procreate.

So I bided my time. Waited for the day. And that day came with a strange confluence of events: the letter from my mother and Toby's fifth birthday. Poor old Hannah, in a drunken stupor, fell down the stairs that very same night. Sad, I know, but she was an accident waiting to happen I fear. And every cloud has a silver lining, as they say. So naturally I inherited her estate. Got a taste for the high life, then made my move on old George.

He wasn't hard to find. There was only one Castlebrook, and only one bank in the town. He denied it all to begin with of course. But the photo of the two of them arm in arm grinning like loons, and my birth certificate, had him turning as pale as a priest at "cleansing hour".

Ellen had to be spared. He insisted upon that. He put Kavanagh on the case, his Freemason buddy. Thick as thieves those two. Blood brothers you might say. Every communication was to be done through him. It would be written off as a gambling debt. He'd also carry out a ritual with an old "Masonic slipper"—a precious Sir Wilfred heirloom apparently—as a guarantee. As if I believed such rubbish.

But then he got that diagnosis. Perfect timing. I assured him that, on his demise, I could get rid of old Ellen, if I didn't get at least £100k. The blackmail worked a treat. Kavanagh would do as instructed so long as Ellen was left alone.

I promised to leave the stage. A dying man will believe anything because he has to. And Kavanagh would do anything for his dying friend.

I had the pair of them bang to rights.

Oh, promises, promises. We live in a world built upon them, constructed by liars, who expect everyone to play straight but themselves. And you have to be an honest liar in this game.

At the sight of Cedarwood Manor I knew it was simply too good to pass up. My rightful inheritance. How could I bow out? A star turn such as I, with my good looks and impeccable taste, answering to "Lavelle" instead of Leavy, to throw the authorities off the scent; to the manor born, was I not?

I did the decent thing, however. Gave the grieving widow a little space. Let her come to terms with her great loss. Did a little stalking. Met her on the road, quite by accident—*not.* Needed to know whom I was dealing with you see.

Then I moved in—quite literally. First to the old stable. My car out of sight in the wood. And in the dead of night I'd slip in through a rear window like a wraith, to do my ghostly turns. How easy it is to frighten when darkness falls and the spectral veil hangs thin. A creak, a thud, a footfall. And the mistress, terror-stricken, flew awake. Poor Mrs Purboy, the perfect hostess: nervous, vulnerable, alone. Scaring her half to death would be the curtain-raiser to the *main event.*

But oh, how fortuitous when she decided to let out the bedsit! The Devil did a little jig. I took a regal bow.

No more nights in the shed.

Of course I made a copy of that key. But you knew that, didn't you? Now I had full access. Pushing the widow down the stairs would have been the easiest way. But that might have raised suspicions in some quarters.

No, I had to be much more creative than that.

Oleander.

Innocent, but deadly.

Can be fatal in relatively small doses.

Ellen, the gardener.

Accidental ingestion.

Perfect.

In the chocolates first. But she was not for opening them and my impatience grew. One night on my ghostly rambles I spotted her medicinal tonic on the drainer.

One tablespoon daily with meals it read.

Ideal.

I administered the dose then lay in wait the other side of the wall. Toby quiet as a mouse, ignorant of my plans, poor little mite.

When she collapsed with the tea-tray I made my move. Bore her insensate body to the drawing-room and laid it on the couch. Within the hour she'd be gone. But that old meddling sister intervened, and I sprinted back to my lair—pocketing the potion—dismayed but not deterred.

Nettie.

Blunt, brusque old Nettie!

A problem to be solved.

An irritant to be expunged.

Trashing Ellen's bedroom would do the trick. On her previous visit I'd heard her open and shut every door, upstairs and down. And locking her in the drawing-room that day showed me what a feardy-cat she was.

So I lay in wait.

The fright was seismic. What exquisite terror my little scene unleashed! She took that tumble all by herself. No help from me required.

Sweet.

After that I had a change of heart. Toby, a nuisance to me. I wanted—nay, needed—to be free once more. Ellen, the old dear, wanting a child so much; melting like a snowflake at first sight of him in the car that day. A rare spark of compassion flared in me.

I went back to Kavanagh. Promised I'd disappear if he paid me off. I've got a lot on him. Copies of all his deceit in the letters George sent to me as evidence he'd follow through. I could send them to his superiors—anonymously of course. Expose him as the crook he is if the proceeds from the sale of Cedarwood do not accrue to me. The trust-fund for Toby is a mere sham to humour the widow. By the time Toby reaches twenty-one who knows what will have ensued? Will old Ellen even be alive by then? Kavanagh can sort that one himself. But I will be long gone. Out of reach. Playing my starring role in another time and place. We actors have it made. Some might call us con artists but I prefer the thespian tag.

Just one tiny thing I overlooked: that little box of trinkets. Solid gold they were. Would fetch a pretty penny I'm sure. Never mind. One little oversight in a long list of successes.

So you see I'm not such a bad old stick.

I changed the course of Ellen's life.

Gave her the child she so desired.

Gave Toby the doting mum that was his due.

Gave the husband what he deserved.

Got my just rewards.

Happy endings, eh?

The curtain falls.

The lights go out

So ends another show.

"Will you return?" I hear you cry.

Now, *that* you cannot know.

. . .

Jay Lavelle drains the last of the Rioja.

Beckons Pedro over.

He pays the hefty tab.

"Keep the change," he says.

But there's not much change from the 10,000 pesetas note and Pedro's disappointed.

"*Gracias*," he says, crestfallen, and turns to go.

"Oh, and Pedro!"

He looks back, stunned to see the man holding out his wristwatch.

"For you," he says, a little drunkenly.

"No-no.... I could not, *señor*."

"Please.... Consider it a gift... in lieu of the tip. I have no change."

Pedro can't believe his luck as he hefts the precious timepiece in his hand.

"*¡Mil gracias, señor!... ¡Gracias, mil gracias!*"

The stranger tips his hat. "I'll be back," he says.

Without another word, he walks away.

Pedro watches him go, intrigued. A little unsteady on his feet, perhaps, but not so much.

He sees him pause at the traffic lights.

Sends him a little blessing.

Puts on his golden gift.

Goes back inside.

The sound of squealing brakes.

Screech-thump-bang!

The smell of burning rubber.

A truck swerving wildly and Pedro drops the tray. He runs.

Stunned onlookers stare.

A screaming woman faints.

But he knows before he gets there that it's too late.

"*¡Señor! ¡Señor!*" he pleads, kneeling over the broken body and feeling for a pulse as the lifeblood of Jay Lavelle flows into the roadside dust.

A curtain falls.
The world goes black.
Alas, alas . . . alack.
For that mystery man once called Lavelle,
Who played his part so very well,
Is never coming back.

AUTHOR'S NOTES

The Moving Statues in Ireland

In the summer of 1985, Ireland was gripped by a series of extraordinary paranormal events when statues of the Virgin Mary in Marian shrines appeared to move.

The most widely known of these apparitions was observed on 22 July in Ballinspittle, County Cork. Several people described seeing the statue moving in a human manner from the waist up after 10 p.m., while others claimed they saw the face of Christ superimposed on the statue.

Overall the apparition, first witnessed by two local girls, attracted a total of 100,000 people to the site, with some 8,000 turning up every evening in a bid to glimpse the "miracle".

Not all visions were positive, however, and exorcisms had to be performed at certain locations.

The phenomena, which occurred in several other counties, persisted for over a year.

The GIs in Northern Ireland

The first American troops came to Northern Ireland's shores on 26 January 1942. Their numbers peaked at 120,000 in December 1943, which represented one tenth of the total population before the start of WWII.

Troops were stationed all across the province. Londonderry served as naval headquarters and was the main US communications base in Europe.

The arrival of these troops was the stuff of fantasy to the young women of Ulster. It was as if the men, in their well-cut uniforms, had walked right off the big silver screen and straight into their hearts. The consequence of this was that countless GIs left many heartbroken girls and illegitimate children behind, when they finally took their leave in 1947.

Life for these young women would never be quite the same again.

ABOUT THE AUTHOR

Christina McKenna grew up on a farm near the village of Draperstown, County Derry. She attended the Belfast College of Art, where she obtained an honours degree in Fine Art. Having studied English as a postgraduate at the University of Ulster, she taught abroad for several years. She has resided, written books and painted pictures in Spain, Turkey, Italy, Ecuador and Mexico.

Since 2004 she has published eight books. *Mrs Purboy Takes a Chance* is her fifth novel.

Jill Brown

Printed in Great Britain
by Amazon

51790365R00239